PRAISE FOR *BLOOD RELATIONS*

**"SCORCHING . . . FAST-PACED . . . RIVETING . . .
SUMPTUOUS . . . STUNNING . . . FULL OF
SURPRISES . . . PARKER HAS THE GIFT."**
—*Florida Bar Journal*

"Parker takes the legal thriller to a new level in this tale of
greed, grief, politics, and the beautiful people on South
Beach." —*Fort Lauderdale Sun-Sentinel*

"Fascinating . . . sophisticated . . . Parker's eye for local
color lifts her books above the stifling conventions of the
standard legal thriller." —*Green Bay Press-Gazette*

"A strong writer with firm control of her complex plot."
—*Orlando Sentinel*

"An involving novel with compelling characters . . . highly
recommended." —*Sunday Montgomery Adviser*

"Another hit! A fast moving read that brilliantly catches the
southern Florida pace. . . . *Blood Relations* shows her star is
on the rise." —*Romantic Times*

"A winner . . . an enthralling, splendid yarn with vivid
characters." —*Cape Coral Daily Breeze*

"Parker's South Florida setting is well researched and
realistic. Her own expertise in the system has helped create
another attention grabbing, well-plotted page turner."
—*Los Angeles Daily Journal*

"Suspenseful!" —*Richmond Times-Dispatch*

BLOOD RELATIONS

BARBARA PARKER

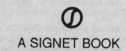

A SIGNET BOOK

SIGNET
Published by the Penguin Group
Penguin Books USA Inc., 375 Hudson Street,
New York, New York 10014, U.S.A.
Penguin Books Ltd, 27 Wrights Lane,
London W8 5TZ, England
Penguin Books Australia Ltd, Ringwood,
Victoria, Australia
Penguin Books Canada Ltd, 10 Alcorn Avenue,
Toronto, Ontario, Canada M4V 3B2
Penguin Books (N.Z.) Ltd, 182–190 Wairau Road,
Auckland 10, New Zealand

Penguin Books Ltd, Registered Offices:
Harmondsworth, Middlesex, England

Published by Signet, an imprint of Dutton Signet,
a division of Penguin Books USA Inc. Previously published in a Dutton edition.

First Signet Printing, January, 1997
10 9 8 7 6 5 4 3 2 1

 REGISTERED TRADEMARK—MARCA REGISTRADA

Printed in the United States of America

PUBLISHER'S NOTE
This is a work of fiction. Names, characters, places, and incidents either are the product of the author's imagination or are used fictitiously, and any resemblance to actual
persons, living or dead, events, or locales is entirely coincidental.

BOOKS ARE AVAILABLE AT QUANTITY DISCOUNTS WHEN USED TO PROMOTE PRODUCTS
OR SERVICES. FOR INFORMATION PLEASE WRITE TO PREMIUM MARKETING DIVISION,
PENGUIN BOOKS, USA INC., 375 HUDSON STREET, NEW YORK, NEW YORK 10014.

With admiration and gratitude
to Lynn Chandler,
a brave and beautiful lady
and a model for us all
(1953–1995)

PRAISE FOR BARBARA PARKER'S
SUSPICION OF GUILT

"Provocative, breathless . . . will surprise you."
—*Cleveland Plain Dealer*

"Excellent! Fully realized characters turned loose in a darkening setting. . . . Barbara Parker has a natural storyteller's gift of grabbing our attention and never letting go." —*Chicago Tribune*

"Sizzling . . . provides plenty of good twists in this story of corporate greed and old-guard pretensions."
—*Orlando Sentinel*

"Marcia Clark, move over! Parker delivers a thriller combining suspected forgery, murder, and legal shenanigans . . . great fun!" —*Indianapolis News*

"Deftly shifts puzzle pieces, building tension to a slam-bang conclusion." —*Booklist*

"Complex and totally involving . . . the action never flags to the unforgettable explosive climax . . . a top-flight read!"
—*Romantic Times*

acknowledgments

A writer never knows if it is a complaint or a compliment when a reader says, "Good heavens, there are so many characters in this book!" The only excuse I can offer is this: So many people told me such good stories that I wanted to include them all.

The best storyteller at the Dade County State Attorney's Office has to be David Waksman of the Major Crimes Division. (Before law school he walked a beat in the Bronx; he'll tell you all about it.)

Again, thanks to Detective Gary Schiaffo of the Miami Beach Police Department (Gary, what will I do for cop stories when you retire?) and to Sergeant Tim O'Regan, who let me ride midnights. I learned more than I wanted to know from Dr. Robert C. Sykes and Dr. Lee Hearn of the Dade County Medical Examiner's Office. Jess Galan, ballistics expert with the Metro-Dade Police Department, filled me in on firearms. Dr. Karen J. Simmons of the Rape Treatment Center at Jackson Memorial Hospital generously shared her time and knowledge.

Modeling agents Allee Newhoff and Deborah Fischer of the Irene Marie Agency took me into the world of fashion, where I met models Klaus Baer and Jeff Gawley, agents Cory Bautista and Judy Lane, and hair/makeup designers Danny Morrow, Scott Barnes, and Rhea White. For Lynn Chandler, her own page.

Photography credit goes to Bobi Dimond, Gonzalo

Miranda, and Scott Foust, who showed me how a fashion photographer sees it.

Angela Lopez was my tour guide to South Beach nightlife, and Louis Canales explained why it's such a terrific place, day or night. Reid Vogelhut is the best storyteller on the Beach. And thank you, as always, Warren Lee.

Merci beaucoup to my panel on foreign languages and culture: Christine Raffini, for the French and Italian; Dolly Yanishevky, who took me from Ukraine to Israel; Sophia Economos, for some lovely words in Greek; Siegfried Grammel, for the bits of German; Trudy Malin, for stories of Jewish life; and Peter Lavery, who made my British character British. The Spanish and any mistakes are mine.

Rolland M. Miller, former infantry first sergeant, U.S. Army, told me what it was like in Vietnam; and Odessa Tevis, Tarpon Springs Historical Society, made that town's past come alive.

Many thanks to my legal experts, attorneys Kelly Luther (wrongful death) and Michael A. Matters (criminal defense). Ray King showed me how to load a Colt .45; Richard C. David shared his knowledge of family psychology; and Elizabeth S. Pittenger supplied horticultural details.

For inspiration and guidance in the early stages, I owe much to Cliff Yudell. For brainstorming me through the tough parts, love to my sister Laura. For insights on the not-quite-final manuscript, who else but writer Judy Cuevas. Thank you, Anne Williams, Headline Publishing, England, for correcting some of my oversights. Credit for final polishing goes, as ever, to all the great folks at Dutton, especially Audrey LaFehr, my champion and editor, and copy editor Juli Barbato.

chapter

ONE

Just after dawn on Saturday morning, as the clouds over the Atlantic brightened from pale blue to white, Ali D., who should have been at a modeling shoot on Miami Beach, was instead in the Rape Treatment Center at the public hospital downtown.

Ali D. was her professional name. Her real name, she told the doctor, was Alice Doris Duncan. Ali made a face, tried to laugh about it. *Alice Doris. You can't be a model with a name like that.* The doctor smiled. She was young, and her clean red hair was held back with a gold barrette. She told Ali to sit up now, please, and she scraped under Ali's fingernails and put the scrapings on slides. Still dizzy from too much champagne, Ali closed her eyes to shut out the fluorescent lights and the horrible pink wallpaper. She wanted to go home. Just go home.

She shared an apartment on Lenox Avenue with two other girls, all of them models at the same agency. Her roommates had the bedrooms, but they let her use the sofa bed for practically nothing because Ali wasn't making much money yet. But someday she would. She planned to establish herself on South Beach, put her book together, then go to New York. But she would have to do it fast, because there wasn't much time. She was almost eighteen. If you don't make it before you're twenty, forget it. Some girls would keep trying, but really, you had to feel sorry for them.

Ali had been thinking about this as she left her apartment just before midnight to walk to the Apocalypse, a nightclub over on Washington Avenue. Her current ex-boyfriend, George, had invited her. Some kind of special party. That's what he did—plan parties for the clubs, or sometimes for people with money, like if it was their birthday.

Red hair bouncing on her shoulders, arms swinging, she made her way through the crowds on the sidewalks. Men followed her with their eyes.

The agency had called this afternoon with a booking for a German catalog company. Here it was, May already, and the models would be wearing boots and wool coats. Everybody had to show up at the Clevelander Hotel at 6:00 A.M. The production van would take them to the site. No problem. Ali had slept most of the day. She would party at the club till maybe three, go home, shower and change, have some breakfast, then go to work. Make about $500.

At the door to the Apocalypse, people were jammed up waiting to get in. Ali pushed her way to the front and told the bouncer that George had invited her. The bouncer sat there on his stool, with his huge arms and fat neck, and told her to get in line. A couple of girls said something to their dates, like, *Who does this bitch think she is?* Just then George came to check on things. Ali held out her arms. "Georgieee!" George was wearing tight jeans and a leather vest, looking totally buff. He had a two-way radio on his belt and a headset looped around his neck. He told the bouncer to unclip the rope, this girl was one of the models, for God's sake.

"Thought you weren't coming." George kissed her cheek and took her through the foyer, which was an aluminum tube with rows of lights leading into the darkness. Music was blasting from the main room. Ali went to clubs three or four nights a week. The owners wanted models to come; then the good people would show up, not just the college kids or the tourists or the causeway crowd from the mainland. It was getting late in the season, but this party looked okay, Ali thought. The heavy bass beat from the speakers pounded on her cheeks and shook the bones in her chest.

George pulled three tickets out of his vest pocket. "Drinks," he yelled.

She put the tickets in her little shoulder purse, then turned around, showing him her dress. "You like it?"

"Nice."

Ali yelled, "I heard Madonna was going to be here."

"What?"

"Madonna. Is she coming?"

"Yeah. I think so. But maybe not, you know?"

Ali had been to one of Madonna's parties. She had a mansion on the water, up the street from Sylvester Stallone's place. Madonna herself had run her fingers through Ali's long red hair, asked if it was natural. Yes, it was. Ali had noticed that Madonna had dark roots.

"I hope she shows up," Ali shouted. "She's really cool."

Moving with the music now, Ali looked around to see if she recognized anybody in the crowd. The Apocalypse had a bar along one side of the long, high-ceilinged room and another on the second floor, with railings and catwalks. The metallic walls were lit by tiny spotlights. A bank of TV screens flashed with MTV videos.

George shouted, "Don't get lost. There are some people coming over. Could be good for you. They're having dinner at Amnesia; then they'll come over. Klaus Ruffini."

"Who?"

He laughed into her ear. "Moda Ruffini, baby."

"Brilliant!" Moda Ruffini was a boutique on Lincoln Road, a few blocks north. Ali had seen Klaus Ruffini around the Beach. Megarich, always with a bunch of models and artists and celebrities. Ali grabbed George's arm. "Dance with me! I love this song!"

George looked down at the beeper on his belt. His mouth moved, something like *Can't. Later.* Frowning, Ali watched him go, then pushed her way to the dance floor. Bodies flashed blue-white in the strobes, stop-action: a girl's hair flying out around her head; a man in a muscle tee and jogging shorts, his body gleaming with sweat. Vents opened in the ceiling and clouds billowed out, settling like blue fog. Ali noticed a funny old leather queen in a biker hat, his round belly showing under an X of studded leather.

She danced with a booker from her agency for a while, then with some frat boys. They had on T-shirts from Boston College. They wanted her to smoke some weed with them in their hotel room. She laughed and said no way, what did they think she was?

An hour or so later, things were cranking. Ali looked around for George, hoping he hadn't forgotten she was there. On the main bar a girl in red thigh boots and a corset laced with chains was zapping everybody with a toy laser gun. Ali had a drink, then danced with an agent who booked TV commercials. They went to the men's room, which looked like the inside of a computer. The floor was tiled with green circuit boards. He closed the door to one of the stalls and laid out a couple of lines on the toilet tank, which was made of shiny metal. There were long smudges where people had run a finger to pick up residue. Ali said she didn't want any. She wanted to know if he needed any girls with red hair, blue eyes, five-nine. He said to come by with a reel or her book and talk to him. Then he French-kissed her. And she'd thought he was gay. She had some coke after all to be polite. When they came out, somebody was barfing into the sink, somebody else wetting a paper towel for his face. The guy who wasn't barfing asked where he could get some downers. Ali said she didn't know. He said she did, that everybody on the Beach knew. He followed her out the door, cursing in German when she gave him the finger.

Ali danced for a while with a couple of guys from Brazil. They bought her a beer, then went off to dance together. A while later she found herself beside a blond girl she'd met at a shoot. The girl was wearing low-cut jeans. There was a ring through her navel. She had just done an assignment in Europe, Ali thought. Or maybe England.

"I heard Madonna might show up," Ali shouted.

"B.F.D. She's over." The girl yelled, "Keanu Reeves is in town shooting. I heard he was going to come, but I doubt it. It's fucking two o'clock already. There's nobody here."

"Klaus Ruffini is coming. He might want to put me in an ad."

"Cool." They danced beside each other for a while.

Then the girl went off to the bathroom with the drummer for a Spanish rock band.

Ali saw someone waving at her, a woman with a camera. Caitlin, who used to model in New York. Ali hugged her. Caitlin said she was taking pictures freelance tonight for the society pages in Latin American *Vogue*. Ali told her that she might be doing some work for Moda Ruffini pretty soon. Then a shriek came from behind them. It was Pussy Katz, wearing a red wig and polka-dot dress with crinolines. She put her arm around Ali.

"Oh, take me, take a picture of me and this cute thing here. Look. All this red hair, both of us. I mean, is this wild? Tonight I'm like Lucy Ricardo. Ricky? Ricky, where are you?" She reached out and pinched the butt of a dark-haired guy walking by. He jumped sideways, and his friends laughed and pointed.

Caitlin took a picture of Ali and Pussy Katz with their cheeks pressed together, eyes wide open, their mouths in big O's. Ali had met Pussy at a gay club on drag night. Ali liked the gay clubs because you could dance without the men hitting on you.

When Pussy Katz left, Caitlin took Ali's arm and asked if she was stoned. "No," Ali said. "I'm having a good time, all right?"

Hands slid around her waist. It was George. She couldn't hear what he was saying, except that he wanted her to come with him. They went toward the stairs leading to the second level, a run of blue lights on the curved wall to show the way. Halfway up, George turned toward the wall so no one could see him and gave her one of the pills out of his vest pocket. On the second level the security guy opened the door to the private room and they went in. The room had black walls, white statues of nudes draped with gold cloth, and blue lights in plaster sconces. Long windows looked down on the main dance floor, and the glass vibrated in time to the music.

There were probably twenty people in the VIP room. Ali recognized an actress from the soaps with her bare feet in someone's lap. A black movie actor. A girl singer for a New York rock band called Phobos, talking about bondage as the ultimate expression of trust. The man next to her nodded, said, *We're all bound in one way or another*. Someone's bodyguard stood by the door. A blond male model was dancing by himself. White shirt hanging open. Incredibly gorgeous. Ali had seen his pictures in men's magazines.

A girl looked up slowly from an armchair, squinted at Ali. "Are you somebody I should know?"

"I model for Moschino."

"Bullshit." The girl hiccupped.

George took Ali over to meet a man in a yellow silk shirt with palm trees and flamingos on it. Klaus Ruffini. He was younger than she'd expected, maybe thirty-five. Ali said hi, and Klaus took a handful of her hair and made a beard for himself. Everyone laughed.

It was late, too late to matter what time it was. The singer left with her people. Then the soap opera actress staggered out, held up by two men. A flash went off. Caitlin had come in to take some society-page photos. Everybody posed and smiled, and finally Caitlin put her camera down and somebody gave her a glass of champagne. Somebody else bumped her and the champagne spilled on the drunk girl asleep on the floor. Klaus was on the sofa drinking Cristal out of the bottle. A Japanese girl sat beside him smoking a joint. Her eyes were closed. Ali held out her champagne glass and he filled it. She said his store was fabulous. She shopped there all the time. "I think I've got the look for Moda Ruffini. Do you want my card? You could call me."

The Japanese girl slid off the sofa.

Klaus pulled Ali onto his lap and kissed her. His tongue slid into her mouth, tasting like tobacco. He rubbed her thigh. She wanted to push him away, but thought it would make him mad. So she laughed and got up to dance with the black movie actor. She tried to remember his name. Klaus was talking to George, looking at Ali, his cigar glowing red between his fingers. Ali dancing, lifting her hair, letting it fall. She stumbled. The heel of her shoe broke, and she kicked them both off. Then George danced with her and moved her toward the back of the room. The floor tilted, and Ali held on to his shoulders.

She asked why he didn't call her anymore. He said something into her ear but she couldn't make it out. His voice sounded like it was coming out of a long pipe. They kissed for a while. Then she was moving backward, bumping against something. A table. George swept the glasses off it and pushed her onto her back. She tried to get up, but he held her down with an arm across her chest. His hand went between her legs, pulling at her underwear. He unzipped his pants. She yelled for him to get off. She tried to twist her hips away but he was too heavy.

When he finished, he kept his hands on her wrists. Someone else was pushing her legs apart. The movie actor leaned into her, eyes squinted shut, while George held her down and told her over and over it was okay, be quiet, baby, it's okay. Ali felt like she was up in the ceiling looking down, and she could see herself, pale in the darkness, and the men around her, and her mouth open, yelling, but there was only the hard beat of the music in her ears.

Klaus Ruffini was laughing silently. He stuck his cigar between his teeth and leaned over to pick up an unopened bottle of champagne off the floor. He shoved the actor aside and motioned for George to turn Ali over on her stomach.

Fingers went inside her, then something heavy and cold. She screamed and twisted when the pain tore through her. Faces floated like moons in the darkness, watching. Finally the thing was gone, and Klaus let her up. He said she was very pretty and tried to kiss her. She hit him in the chest.

George pulled her off Klaus and told her to shut up. Ali was screaming and crying. She grabbed a glass and threw it at him, then a half-full bottle of rum. George ducked and the bottle knocked down one of the sconces. The light glared harsh and white into the room, showing lines of liquid running down the wall. The bodyguard dragged her to the door and pushed her through it. She slid to the floor.

Then Caitlin was there, bending over her. *Bastards! What did they do to you? Ali, please. You have to get up.* The walls tilted and moved. Caitlin gripped her arm and pulled. Half-carried her down the stairs, through the bodies on the dance floor, all heat and sweat and noise.

Outside, people stared. Then somehow Ali was in Caitlin's car. But not going home. Going across the causeway to Miami. Then stumbling barefoot along a corridor with a shiny floor. Caitlin put her into a chair in a waiting room with pink wallpaper.

Ali remembered her booking at six o'clock and tried to get up, hitting at Caitlin and crying when she wouldn't let her go. Caitlin held Ali's head in her lap and cried, too, and stroked her hair. *Oh, Ali, I'm sorry. Damn them all. Oh, God. I'm so sorry.*

chapter
two

The murder of Carlito Ramos brought three television news reporters and a satellite truck to his mother's apartment on Miami Beach to record the scene, but when the case finally came up for trial a year later, none of them covered it. The big trial that week was the robbery-homicide of a Japanese couple who had become lost on their way to Metro Zoo in broad daylight and had stopped to ask directions. The Ramos case, which most people had forgotten about, was a domestic dispute of no real significance for the tourist trade.

Sam Hagen had been a prosecutor in Miami for eighteen years, and by now most first-degree murder trials had become routine—if violent deaths could ever be routine. He could almost accept those cases where the killing was at least explainable, or where the victim was as bad as his killer, but this one had made him burn with rage. Carlito Ramos, four years old. His mother told her live-in boyfriend to get out, she never wanted to see his face again. Luis screamed that he'd give her something to remember him by. He ran into Carlito's room, picked up the sleeping child, and hurled him through the window. Carlito fell sixty-seven feet to a concrete sidewalk. His skull shattered like a melon.

After final arguments the jurors filed out. They would be called back in a while to be given instructions. The judge gaveled a recess. Sam Hagen watched the observers leave the courtroom—the defendant's parents, in tears;

two law school grads here to pick up some pointers; and a
group of retirees who spent their spare time watching
criminal trials. Adela Ramos, the dead boy's mother, went
out leaning on her brother's arm.

At the prosecution table Sam dropped wearily into his
chair. He was forty-six and feeling every year of it. He
reached up to squeeze the younger prosecutor's shoulder.
"Good job, Joe."

He had let Joe McGee make the final argument. Sam or
another of the dozen prosecutors on the Major Crimes
staff would supervise heavy cases to make sure they
weren't lost or reversed on appeal through an inadvertent
screwup by someone with less experience. McGee was a
black Miami ex-cop who had decided he would live
longer in court than on the streets. Smart and aggressive,
he had moved up fast through the felony division, but this
was his first death-penalty murder trial.

Sam saw him glance toward the defense table, nostrils
flaring as if he'd smelled something vile. "I want the son
of a bitch," McGee said between his teeth.

Luis Balmaseda. Good-looking dark-haired guy; twenty-
eight years old, dressed in a neat blue suit. His lawyer
sat on the railing, swinging one foot, talking to an associate
in the firm. The lawyers laughed and Balmaseda smiled.
With the jury out of sight, everybody relaxed. The lawyers
could kid around, and the defendant might laugh at their
jokes. And for a minute you could almost forget what he
had done, just as he could forget he might die for it.

Turning away, McGee pulled a stack of notes and
xeroxed jury instructions out of a box and tossed them
onto the table. He sat down. "You got any inspirations
here, boss?"

"Yeah. A rope."

Before trial the defense had offered a plea to second-
degree murder. Greenbaum denied that his client had
killed the boy, but even if he had killed him, first degree
didn't apply. The act wasn't premeditated. Balmaseda and
his girlfriend were drunk and arguing violently. A plea to
second would mean fifteen or twenty years. Why not take
a sure thing? Sam had said no fucking way.

In a while court would reconvene. The judge would tell
the jury what the law was, reading from instructions

agreed to by both sides. Greenbaum was gambling. He wanted the judge to instruct the jury only on premeditated murder, not on second or manslaughter. The jurors would then have only two choices: first-degree murder or acquittal. If convicted, Luis Balmaseda would face the minimum mandatory of twenty-five years, possibly the electric chair. But if the jury had any doubts, Balmaseda would walk.

Sam looked at McGee. "What do you think, Joe?"

McGee blew out a breath, took another one. "I think Greenbaum wants us to crawl over there and beg him to take a plea to second before the jury gets the case."

"I'd say so." Giving no hint of his own preference, Sam waited for McGee to lay out the alternatives. He'd been told he didn't make it easy for younger lawyers in the office.

McGee said, "We could ask for second degree ourselves. Tell the judge to instruct on lesser-includeds. Give the jury some room to compromise."

"We could do that."

"And Balmaseda could be out in five." McGee stared across the room. "Or we go with instructions on first degree and we pray."

Unfortunately, the case had taken a hit at the outset. When two uniformed officers arrived in response to a neighbor's 911 call, Adela Ramos was incoherent and Balmaseda was on his knees crying. One of the cops put handcuffs on him, dragged him into the living room, and asked what the hell had happened. Balmaseda babbled in Spanish, "I killed them both. I want to die. Shoot me, please." The officers read him his rights. The subject refused to say anything else, either at the scene or later at Miami Beach Police Headquarters. Only that he wanted a lawyer.

On a motion to suppress, the judge ruled that the officers had taken Balmaseda into custody without probable cause; therefore, his statement couldn't be used against him. They should have asked him what had happened, then handcuffed him. The state took an appeal, but the judge's ruling was affirmed.

Alan Greenbaum had leaned hard on Carlito's mother. Through a court translator, Adela answered in a lifeless monotone, unable to meet the lawyer's eyes. A nervous woman with her nails bitten ragged, whose voice shook, whose heart must have been heavy with remorse that somehow she had let this happen to her son. All Sam could do was try to repair the damage on redirect.

Luis Balmaseda turned his soulful brown eyes to the jury and admitted he'd been jealous. He had loved Adela so much. But when he caught her cheating and said he wouldn't stay with her anymore, Adela went crazy. She ran into the boy's room and threw Carlito through the window. *Carlito! He was like my own son!* Sobbing, Balmaseda said Adela started to climb through the window to her own death, but he dragged her back. The police got it all wrong.

Drying his tears, he had faced Sam Hagen's tough questions on cross. Sam had shaken him, but what did the jury believe?

Sam motioned to Balmaseda's lawyer. "Let's talk."

Alan Greenbaum walked over, snapping his fingers in a rhythm, slapping a fist into his palm. He had a high, intelligent forehead, a neat mustache, and a custom-tailored suit. Sam had heard this was his last criminal case; he had taken a job with a civil practice firm.

The three men faced each other in a tight circle.

"What's this shit about instructions only on first degree? Your client could be sent to the chair. Did you explain that to him?"

Greenbaum whispered, "Take it easy, Hagen. He says he's innocent. I can't make him do anything. You want, I'll renew the offer of a plea to second."

"Too late." Sam fixed a look on him. "I told you, we're not pleading this out."

There was a quick grin. "Sure. Then what do you care if we go for instructions on first? You want me to ask for second so the jury can grab it and it won't look like plea-bargaining. I told you, babe, you should've taken a plea last year. He'd be in Raiford as we speak."

The defendant, with an arm extended casually across the railing behind him, turned to speak to his father, who had come back in. The jailer motioned for the man to move back. The father kissed his son, then sat down with Balmaseda's mother, who had a tissue pressed to her nose.

A big man, Sam had a few inches on Greenbaum, and he leaned into his face. "You tell your client, we get a conviction I'll have the press all over this courtroom. This judge will burn him. Give me a plea to first, right here, right now, I'll recommend life."

"Push him in a fucking corner, why don't you?"

"Go complain to the kid he killed."

"Hey. You want an instruction on second degree, go for it." Greenbaum's eyes shifted toward his client, then back to Sam. "Frankly, I don't give a shit. But my client will not permit me to ask for anything but first." With a final lift of his eyebrows to make sure Sam got it, he walked back to his associate, who had drifted closer, listening.

"Oh, boy." Joe McGee's forehead gleamed with sweat.

The court reporter looked over the top of her novel, then turned a page.

A movement at the door caught Sam's attention. A woman was striding down the aisle in a black suit accented with white lapels. Auburn hair curled to her shoulders, and her brown eyes were heavily outlined. Vicky Duran. She pulled Sam aside. "I have to talk to you."

He gave her a look. "We're in trial, Beekie."

Victoria Duran was the state attorney's deputy chief of administration. Born in Cuba, she had a leftover accent, and someone had put a Spanish twist to her name. Beekie. It had stuck.

"The trial is in recess," she corrected. "Come on, Sam. It's important."

"All right. Wait for me outside."

After a glance at her watch, she left. The heavy wooden door swung shut behind her.

"What'd Beekie want?" McGee asked.

"Who the hell knows?" Sam turned back to him. "Okay. Show time. The judge is going to come back in here expecting us and the defense to have agreed on a set of jury instructions."

"You want to give him the lesser-included offenses?"

"I'll let you call it, Joe."

"Oh, shit." McGee breathed heavily in and out. "Okay. If we put in the lesser-includeds, we can't do worse than second degree. God damn. It's as good as walking him." McGee put his hands on his hips. "No. Let's go for it. Fry the bastard."

For a while Sam let himself look at Luis Balmaseda. In his younger days he would have said the same thing: Go for it. A hundred murder trials had taught him not to gamble, but he was sick to death of being careful. Balmaseda must have felt Sam watching him. He looked around and a smile flickered at one corner of his mouth. *Go for it.*

"Is that what you want to do, Joe?"

"Hell, yes."

"All right. Tell Greenbaum he's on. I'll be outside."

In the tiled, echoing corridor, with glass-enclosed entrances to courtrooms along the length of it, and people coming and going, Sam ignored Vicky Duran and spoke for a moment with Adela Ramos. She sat alone on one of the wooden benches along the wall, clutching her purse in her lap.

"Where's your brother?" Sam asked.

"He go . . . for my coffee."

"Are you okay?" He sat down beside her.

She nodded, not looking okay. She was a petite, dark-haired woman who must have been pretty before all this happened to her. Her eyes were fixed on Sam.

"Listen, Ms. Ramos. I think you ought to go home. Rest. Have some lunch. I'll call you when the jury comes back in with a decision."

"When they coming back?"

Sam didn't know. "Maybe this afternoon, but I think tomorrow. *Mañana.* I'll call you," he repeated. "Or you call me. Anytime." He took a card out of his pocket and wrote a number on the back. "I have a beeper. Call me if you need to talk. Do you understand?"

"Yes. Okay."

Still sitting, he shook her hand, thinking how shaking this young woman's hand came nowhere near what she needed. Not for the first time Sam regretted taking this damned case. He should have assigned it to someone else in Major Crimes. The subject matter, losing a child, had slashed too close to the bone. He should have said to

McGee, *Here, finish this. I can't do it.* But he hated to hear excuses, especially his own. Elbows on his knees, he stared blindly at the gray terrazzo floor until he could unclench his jaw.

Adela Ramos said softly, "Thank you. I say to my brother he take me home."

Sam looked around at her, smiled briefly, then went to speak to Beekie.

She was standing near the entrance to the next courtroom. A stack of green-and-white computer pages lay on a wall-mounted desk, the day's business. A girl with a baby slung on one hip came along to thumb through it, and Beekie walked farther along the corridor, Sam alongside. Her arms were crossed, making cleavage at the vee in her jacket.

"What's up?"

Beekie pushed her heavy mane of hair back from her face, and her gold bracelets jingled. In the buzzing fluorescent lights the makeup made her skin look orange. She had a bad complexion, which she managed to hide fairly well. Her full lips were outlined in brown and filled in with bright red. "Eddie left you a message to see him about the sexual battery from the Beach last weekend?"

Eddie Mora was the state attorney, and Victoria Duran, among her other duties, had given herself the role of chief expediter.

Sam said, "And I sent a message back. I don't have time. I don't have time for my own cases, let alone those outside my division."

"It's not just any case, Sam. The people involved are going to draw some media attention. Everything has to be done right. You remember just after Eddie came in, there was a girl who said she'd been raped by that rap singer." Beekie pressed long-nailed fingertips to her forehead. "What was his name?"

"Henry Wells, aka Doctor Deep."

"Yes. We filed the case, and meanwhile she was suing him in civil court. All the time, it was a lie. The case was poorly investigated. The Sexual Battery unit gave it to a prosecutor trying to make a name for herself. We had the black organizations on our neck, and then the women's groups. When we dismissed, the *Herald* wrote that snide editorial, saying we were scared off. That isn't going to happen again."

Good old Beekie. Throwing herself in front of Eddie Mora before the bullets started flying. Victoria Duran had been slogging through the swamps of the juvenile division when Eddie came in. Within two years she'd made it to chief of the felony division, and now she was out of the courtroom with an office down the hall from the state attorney, in charge of the day-to-day operations of the office and its two thousand-plus employees. Despite the inevitable rumors that she was sexually involved with Eddie, Sam had always assumed that Beekie was simply ambitious. She had the brittle, edgy manner of a woman who hears the doors closing.

He said, "Who are we talking about as potential defendants?"

"Three men took part. One of them, supposedly, was Marquis Lamont. You know the name?"

"Sure. Used to play for the Giants, out of Florida State."

"He's acting in movies now."

"No kidding. What was he in?"

"I have no idea," she said impatiently. "The second man is an Italian businessman, Klaus Ruffini, who owns some property on the Beach. The third is a local of no consequence. And the victim is a model. So she says. There are witnesses, but their stories conflict."

"What a surprise. Did the victim show up at the pre-file conference?"

"There hasn't been one," Beekie said. "Nor have there been any arrests. The Miami Beach police want our opinion first."

"You mean, they dump it on us, we say we won't prosecute, and they're off the hook with the press." Sam shook his head, smiling a little. "Uh-uh. Not my thing. Give it to the Sexual Battery unit."

"Eddie wants to talk to you," she said. "You specifically."

"Why?"

"Sam." She squeezed his wrist. "Go talk to him. I think he would appreciate your help."

He gave her a long look. In Vicky Duran's oblique way, she was telling him something.

* * *

It took until past eleven o'clock for the judge to finish reading the instructions to the jury. The two alternate jurors were dismissed, and the other twelve retired to the jury room, where the bailiff would bring them lunch. Balmaseda was handcuffed and taken back to his cell across the street.

Hands braced on smooth black rubber, Sam rode the narrow escalator down from the fourth floor behind a Metro-Dade detective, who asked if a certain strong-arm robbery trial was still set for Monday. Sam said no, the victim had not shown up for her deposition. The state would probably offer probation and a withhold of adjudication rather than see the case dismissed. The detective got off at the police liaison office on three, and a private defense lawyer saw Sam and rode down to second with him. He wanted the state to reduce a burglary to a misdemeanor; otherwise his client, who was completing a drug program, would be kicked out for violation of probation. Sam said forget it, not for a sixth burglary. The attorney shrugged, said he would have to go to trial—both of them knowing the remoteness of that possibility, given Sam's caseload. Something would be worked out.

Pausing on the second floor, Sam took out his memo book to make a note to himself about a home-invasion robbery. In the corridor this morning he had offered the P.D. twenty years, a good deal for perpetrators out on parole when they did the crime. He fumbled for a pen, then wrote slowly in the little book. He knew his handwriting was miserable. The pen went dry. Sam sighed and stuck it into his coat pocket. Coming down to the first floor, where the escalator walls were mirrored, he caught a glimpse of himself—wide face, closely trimmed brown hair, going a little gray. His tie was crooked. He pulled it straight, then leaned heavily on the rubber rails again.

The view of the lobby opened up, making visible a swirl of police, lawyers, criminals, victims, witnesses, people putting briefcases and bags on the X-ray machines just inside the glass doors, and others going out again. A steady flow.

Miami, the Magic City. Number one in crime. Two hundred and fifty prosecutors couldn't keep up. Even with a thousand, there wouldn't be the judges to hear the cases or a place to put the criminals if they were convicted. It had become a plea-bargaining bazaar. There was hardly a case without a deal. A cut-rate discount store of deals, with the public paying in one way or another. More crime, more taxes, residents fleeing over the county line to Fort Lauderdale, which had only the sixth-highest crime rate in the United States.

In the crowded hallway outside the cafeteria, Sam put down fifty cents on the counter for a shot of Cuban coffee, then drank it on the way out the back entrance. He tossed the cup into a can. The pink marble steps were gray with grime. Sam turned right, squinting in the sun. His office was across the next street.

Most of the young assistants signed on for the courtroom experience. They had the energy to handle two or three hundred open cases, with a hundred set for trial at any one time. They learned, they made a name, then they found a job that paid good money and didn't grind them up.

Dina—Sam's wife—used to complain about that. He was never home. He didn't earn enough. How could they send the children to college? Four years ago, after a lot of thought, Sam decided she was right. He took a job at a civil practice firm with a friend of his, a guy he'd served with in the 101st Airborne in Vietnam. They gave him a mahogany-veneer desk in a tenth-floor office on Flagler Street, with clients in clean clothes, most of whom had never been the victims of anything worse than the auto accident or slip-and-fall that had brought them there. Sam filed claims and dictated letters to his secretary. *This firm has been retained by (fill in name) in connection with (describe accident), a result of your negligence, which caused (describe injuries), said injuries resulting in pain, disfigurement, temporary and/or permanent disability, and loss of earnings.*

He did all right in trial, but not many cases went that far. He spent more time at his desk than in a courtroom, signing dozens of letters and pleadings and motions. Then one evening, working late, gazing out his window at the streets of Miami going away in a neat grid, west and north through neighborhoods that didn't seem so bad from that angle, Sam Hagen saw the sodium vapor crime lights come on, and realized that he had turned into a pencil dick.

He got his job back in Major Crimes and moved up to head of the division the following year. Dina understood, or said she did. Sam didn't know what he was accomplishing, if anything. Coming out of law school, ready for action, he had thought he could do some good in the state attorney's office. As a prosecutor he had only seen more crime, more violence. Maybe the criminal justice system was as ultimately doomed as any other product of human invention. But there had to be some system of order, and someone to stand guard.

Sam went through the rear entrance of the curving, glass-and-tan concrete building that housed the state attorney's office. He nodded to the guard, walked past the X rays and metal detectors, and took the elevator to the fourth floor.

"Sam. Come in. Vicky said you were on your way up." Eddie Mora motioned to shut the door, then finished knotting his tie. He looked into a circular mirror propped on a shelf of his bookcase. "Lunch with the Beacon Council." His image in the mirror smiled. "I think that's it. Sit down." He ducked his head to see his hair and smoothed it with his fingers. The hairline was receding. Even so, Eddie seemed younger than forty-one, with his round face and quick movements.

Edward José Mora was a Harvard grad, born in the United States to Cuban parents. His father had run the Hilton hotels in Cuba, pre-Castro, getting his money out before the country went to hell. Eddie Mora had grown up in Manhattan and the family's summer home in Connecticut. He had clerked for Supreme Court justice Scalia, then rocketed upward in the Justice Department. He married the dark-eyed daughter of a former sugar baron, then moved to Miami to reorganize the U.S. Attorney's office, getting some good press in the national media. When the prior Dade state attorney died of a stroke, the governor passed over everyone in the office and asked Eddie Mora to fill in. The Cuban exiles would like it, and the governor wanted to carry Dade County in the election. Sam, considered a safe bet for the job, had clamped down hard on his disappointment.

The office had lurched on pretty much as usual, though last year's dip in the crime rate had put Edward Mora on the cover of *Newsweek*: "Young Hispanics Making a Difference." Sam knew that Eddie respected his work in Major Crimes. On a personal level, he didn't know what Eddie thought, and didn't care.

Mora tossed the mirror into a drawer and stood by his desk, his fingers tapping lightly on its surface. He kept a neat office. Diplomas and certificates marched across one wall. Papers were in order. The furniture was new and modern, with a long leather sofa facing the windows and two chairs at his desk. Sam sat in one of them.

"Vicki gave you the facts on this sexual battery thing."

"Briefly. She didn't seem to think it was much of a case."

"It isn't. Or wouldn't be, except for the people involved." Mora gave a short laugh. "Every time we get a celebrity—especially movie actors—here come the reporters, busily misreporting."

Sam said, "You're referring to Marquis Lamont?"

"Played for the Giants," Mora said, showing he knew football. "Wide receiver."

"That's right."

"Was he any good?"

"Pretty good as a rookie, maybe the first two seasons. I think they would have let him go, but his knee went out and saved them the trouble. He was better at Florida State." Sam added, "I haven't seen his movies."

Mora shook his head. "What passes for celebrity on Miami Beach amazes me."

Sam waited for Eddie Mora to get to the point.

The state attorney sat on the edge of his desk. "First, a summary of what happened over there. Late last Thursday night a young lady by the name of Alice Duncan went to a nightclub called the Apocalypse at the invitation of a George Fonseca, who may have a managerial position there, although that point is somewhat unclear. In any event, he does have—or used to have—a sexual relationship with the alleged victim. According to Miss Duncan, they went to a room in the club where a private party was being held. During the course of the party, Fonseca forcibly raped her, then restrained her while Marquis Lamont did so. She states that Ruffini sodomized her with the neck of a champagne bottle. Most of the people at the scene didn't see it, or say they didn't. Given the general level of intoxication in that room, I wouldn't put much credence in what any of them have to say." A smile slowly formed on Eddie Mora's lips.

"Can you imagine the parade of characters coming before the court? The jury would think they were watching a Fellini film. And the girl—is she credible? The best defense attorneys in Miami will be baying for blood. And assuming we survived a motion to dismiss and went to trial, what would a jury do with a defendant like Lamont?"

Sam said, "I'm surprised the Miami Beach P.D. has gone this far with it."

"They wouldn't have, but the doctor at the Rape Treatment Center called it in, and a detective went over."

"Was the girl injured?"

"Not badly. Some abrasions from the metal wrapping on the neck of the bottle. They have to report a rape when the victim is under eighteen."

"How far under eighteen?"

"I'm not sure."

Sam swiveled the chair, following Mora, who had started to pace around the room. A habit of his. The man couldn't sit still. Sam said, "Vicky alluded to some problem the Beach police have with publicity."

"Correct. In the past they've been accused, as you know, of not filing charges against people with influence. The new chief wants to put an end to that perception. I admire the man. If I can help him, I'll do it." Mora stopped walking. "You want to know why I don't send this case through routine pre-file downstairs and let them mark it 'no action.' "

"It crossed my mind," Sam said.

Mora stuck his hands in his pockets and wandered over to the windows. The vertical blinds were tilted open.

Eddie had the same view Sam did, only two stories higher: trees, white stucco houses and apartments, the expressway arching over them, then the downtown skyscrapers a couple of miles away, silvery against a blue sky. The windows needed cleaning up here, too.

"Yesterday I was in a meeting, and I got an urgent message to call the city manager of Miami Beach. Fine. So I excused myself and called Hal Delucca at his office. Delucca told me that one of his—*his*—most important businessmen was being falsely accused of rape and that a film studio was threatening to pull out of a deal to shoot a movie on South Beach. Delucca said the girl was making an obvious attempt at a shakedown. He said she was coming on to Marquis Lamont when she danced with him. Then she offered to sleep with Klaus Ruffini in exchange for a modeling job, and there are witnesses to say so. Delucca wanted me to tell the police to back off. Well, of course I couldn't do that, and I told him I was insulted at the suggestion." Mora straightened one of the vertical blinds at his window.

He turned around. "This puts me in a touchy position, Sam. Do I file this case to prove Delucca has no influence over me? Or do I let it go and have it appear that he does? That telephone call wasn't only between me and Hal Delucca. Other people in his office must have known what he was doing. He may have made promises to the men involved in this incident."

Even as Sam had grown increasingly impatient, listening to the details of a tawdry case that would never be filed, much less go to trial, he had become fascinated by the spectacle of Edward J. Mora practically hyperventilating because a bozo like Hal Delucca had asked him for a favor.

"What is it you want, Eddie?"

"I want to be able to tell the press—tell anyone who asks—that we looked into it. That we care about this young woman and so forth, but that given the lack of concrete evidence, we decline to prosecute. I can't handle this myself, you understand that. Whenever I become involved with a case, it makes a statement, and I can't make a statement on this. I didn't immediately consider you because, well, I've always felt a distance between us. You wanted this job. The governor gave it to me."

Sam made a little shrug. "I didn't hold it against you."

"I know." Eddie Mora paced back to the window. "You could have caused me some serious grief, but you didn't. That's why you're here now. Why I trust you. You're not flamboyant, but you get the job done. And your integrity is unquestioned. People recognize that. If Hagen says a case is trash, it is." From across the room Eddie said, "I want you to handle this case. Do whatever you think is right."

"I don't want it," Sam said. "Let it go through the system, Eddie. Pre-file can notify the girl to come in, but ten to one, she won't show up. It'll wash out."

"No. I want a senior prosecutor on this. I want you, Sam."

Absently, Sam massaged the joint in his thumb. There was some pain there occasionally. Minor arthritis, his wife would say, dismissing it.

"Eddie—you know, this doesn't seem like that big a deal."

Mora looked at him a few moments, then said, "All right, I'm going to tell you what the deal is, but what I say doesn't leave this office."

"Sure."

"I'm on the short list to run on the Republican ticket this fall."

It took Sam a while to absorb that. "As vice president."

"Correct."

"Jesus."

"That's what I said." Mora smiled. "Who me? The first Hispanic on the ticket. And the youngest man ever. How about that? I'd have to resign from this job, though, to give it my best shot. I can't do both."

Slowly at first, then with a sudden rush of understanding that took his breath, Sam knew where this conversation was going. He gripped the arms of the chair to keep himself steady.

Mora said, "I've been told my name will be on top, but anything could happen." Smiling, he lifted his shoulders in a shrug. "So. There's the situation, Sam. Even small things can be a problem."

"And you want my help."

"I would be grateful, yes."

Three years ago, when Edward Mora, as a political convenience, had been given this position, a man well under forty, with his easy smiles and expensive suits, a man not even from Florida, who had not tried one case in a state court, Sam had kept his mouth shut. He had gone along. He had forced himself not to think about how much he had wanted this job. If he had let himself dwell on the years that stretched out ahead of him—most state attorneys in Miami stayed in office until they retired or dropped dead—he might have come close to despair. Samuel Hagen, the trustworthy plodder, not known for his flamboyance . . .

He kept his expression neutral, but the emotions slammed through his body. He knew then how much he disliked Eddie Mora, had always disliked him.

Mora was smiling slightly, waiting for an answer.

"I'll take care of it," Sam said.

"Good." Mora rose from the chair. "You know, Sam, I feel I ought to apologize, pushing this on you."

Standing up, Sam looked at him curiously. "Why?"

"Well . . . South Beach. The modeling crowd. It's got to be hard for you, so soon after your son's death. Such a loss for you and Dina." The quiet tone was meant to convey sincerity. "Under the circumstances I'm doubly appreciative. I want you to know that." He took a hand out of his pocket long enough to grip Sam's shoulder.

"It's not a problem, Eddie."

"You sure? Tell me." Speaking in nearly a whisper now. The brows knitting.

"I said it's not a problem."

Sam shut the door when he left, then stood there for a moment staring into its slick, painted surface. It had been weeks since anyone outside the family had brought that up. Matthew Hagen. Only nineteen years old. Such a good-looking kid, too. A model. Got drunk at a nightclub and crashed his motorcycle on the causeway at four in the morning. And his father a top prosecutor with the state attorney's office. What a shame. After eight months, Sam was getting damned tired of polite, phony expressions of sympathy.

He wondered how long it would be till someone else said how fucking sorry they were for his loss. And if there would come a time when he could think about his son and not want to smash the nearest thing at hand.

c h a p t e r
three

Fingertips moving quickly over the damp earth, Dina Hagen scraped together the leaves and twigs, then tossed them into a brown paper grocery sack. She nudged the piece of cardboard she'd been kneeling on farther along the walkway. Herringbone bricks bordered the screened terrace, leading across the thick Bermuda grass to the redwood gazebo where she had hung her orchids and staghorn fern. She had planted a low hedge of ixora as a border—a mistake, for the plants were far too uncontrolled. It would take some effort to trim them back.

The clippers fell into a steady rhythm, a counterpoint to the *chk-chk-chk* of a sprinkler over the wooden fence that circled the garden. The smell of wet, rich earth and blooming gardenia floated in the still air.

Of course one did not have a *garden* behind a house in the flat, monotonous suburbs southwest of Miami; one had a *backyard*. But this was a garden, designed with an eye to color and shape and to the dry or rainy seasons as well, so that the yellow tabebuia would flower in one corner while the red bottlebrush stood dormant in another. Just after Dina and Sam and the children had moved in, her brother Nicholas, who owned a plant nursery north of Tampa, had driven three hundred miles with a truckful of soil and fertilizer and pots of flowers, shrubs, and palm trees, all verdant and shining. Nick had installed a sprinkler system and hidden lights on timers, and it was all perfect.

Then two years later the hurricane had blown through, leaving everything smashed and ruined; even the tile roof had been ripped off the house in a great groan and cry, like a limb torn from a body. Nick had returned the next spring with more plants. The garden had been replanted exactly as it had been before—better than before—and the house had been rebuilt.

Sitting back on her heels, Dina caught a glimpse of a face at the kitchen window. Her daughter, watching her. Melanie had shouted from the terrace awhile ago to say she had a phone call, and Dina, feeling invaded, had snapped at her, then apologized. Now the face disappeared, and Dina moved along the walkway. Her knees ached a little, but she paid no mind to that. From behind her she heard the laughter of the teenager next door, a shriek, then a splash as though someone had gone into the pool. The boy's high, clear voice pierced her with a stab of despair so acute it was almost physical.

Taking a few deep breaths, Dina trimmed a scraggly branch down to the proper level. A cluster of blood-red blossoms dropped into her hand. For a while now, she had not taken her pills. They dulled the pain but made her sleep too much, and she couldn't think clearly.

She moved the cardboard and knelt again. She wore loose cotton pants. Her wide-brimmed hat lay across the yard on a step of the gazebo; the sun had gone behind the black olive trees on the neighbors' property. There was time for this today because she'd skipped her doctor's appointment. She had driven by his office in that ugly, square, glass-walled building without even slowing her car. The dread she had felt, thinking of going inside, had changed to giddy exhilaration as the building shrank in her rearview mirror. The last four sessions Dr. Berman had gone probing into her past, as if there he might find some clue to explain why she grieved so. She had wanted to scream at him. *You idiot, this is not in my past. It is here, now. Always with me.* He was poking for faults and weaknesses, as if the fault, once isolated, could be fixed. But is grief a fault? He had given an answer so infuriatingly irrelevant that she had quite forgotten it. She finally understood that he was leading her to his own conclusion: Dina Hagen was weak. Weak and self-indulgent.

Sam had sent her to this doctor hoping it would help. For months Sam had watched her, humored her, treated her like a sick child. Sometimes his patience would fray, then he would go out and run until it was too dark to see, or work out on his weight machine—*clank, clank, clank*— until he could hardly stand up.

His way was to bear it. Be strong. He was such a master, Sam was, at burying things and pouring concrete into the grave, then piling boulders on top and turning his back. But Dina could not do it, and nothing, nothing had dulled her pain. It was too much to bear.

Dragging the bag along, Dina moved slowly toward the gazebo. She tucked a tendril of hair into the knot at the nape of her neck, then blotted her face on her sleeve. The shirt was one of Sam's, tied at her waist, the scent of his body still in the fabric. He didn't wear cologne, so it was only Sam that she smelled. Lie in the same bed with a man for half your life, and you know everything about him: his scent, his voice, the feel of his body, his moods, his thoughts. His infidelity. Three years ago he had been unfaithful. By the time Dina had been sure enough to accuse him, Sam said it was over. He had refused to name this woman, though Dina suspected it must have been one of the lawyers at his office. Dina had seen them at holiday parties. Pretty women, with their white teeth and lustrous hair and narrow waists, doting on Sam Hagen. Young spiders, catching men that age, a trade of youth for power.

After his apology for hurting her, Sam would not speak of it again, as if such things could be forgotten. Then the troubles with Matthew had grown worse. Sam became so angry, so often, that he must have been relieved when Matthew left home, though he would not admit it. Sam had taken his death better than any of them, but he couldn't pretend it had left him unaffected. Sometimes she could see the utter emptiness on his face, and it frightened her because she didn't know what to do.

He had not divorced her, but he had left her in other ways. When he reached out for her in bed, she could have been anyone. Their lovemaking was performed joylessly, in silence. She felt old; betrayed. He was her husband, and he had abandoned her in his heart.

Where had all this begun? Dina was certain that each terrible event had a cause; nothing was random. Dina had once flown at Sam, striking him. It had been his sin that brought this down upon them. His adultery, ripping like a storm through their life, tearing it apart.

"Momma!" Her daughter's thin voice came across the yard from the terrace.

Dina closed her eyes, hoping that Melanie would just go back inside. Instead, the voice came again. "What?" Dina called back.

"Dad's home, and dinner's ready."

She waved a hand. "You two go ahead."

Melanie was fourteen and overly sensitive. Dina often had to force herself to be kind to her, although there was no reason not to be kind. Melanie was sweet; she was compliant. She kept her room clean, and her grades in school were average. She was not pretty, but neither was she plain. From time to time, Dina felt a wave of pity for her daughter. It was as if she had unwittingly poured everything she had into her firstborn, leaving so little for the second. Melanie was a shadow of her brother. Matthew had been . . . beautiful. There was no other word.

Perhaps this was the fault. Dina knew the old warning. If you are proud, if you say your child is beautiful, you make the gods jealous, and they will take him out of spite. Matthew had certainly not been perfect. He had been demanding and hurtful. He had suffered and had caused those around him to suffer, and eventually he had been destroyed. But she did love him. Oh, God. She had loved him more.

Was it her own pride, then? Had she caused this? Dina squeezed her eyes shut. A cry caught in her throat. The pain was like a thorny stem dragged over bleeding wounds, tearing away new bits of flesh. She dropped the clippers and braced a hand on the brick walkway.

When she opened her eyes the sun was a red-orange flame in the trees. She looked down and saw she had clutched the cross around her neck. It was her grandmother Sevasti's Orthodox cross. Dina had seen it in a

drawer two weeks ago. Today she had put it on as a talis-
man, a last resort. For Sevasti's courage.

Her grandmother had come to America in 1921 from a
family of ethnic Greeks with a farm outside Constan-
tinople—now Istanbul. At sixteen, Sevasti had seen her
father shot dead and her mother raped by a Turkish soldier, then bayonetted. She hid in the barn, waiting with
her father's ax. The soldier pushed open the door and
stepped into the darkness . . . then she split his skull. She
ran for three days, starving and hiding, and finally crossed
over to Greece on a fishing boat. She begged money from
relatives for passage to America, not knowing what she
would do when she arrived. On the ship she met a young
man, Stavros Pondakos. By the time the ship docked in
New York they were married. She went south with him to
Tarpon Springs, a Greek sponge-fishing community on
the west coast of Florida, where he had already secured
work on a dive boat. They lived a long time, and had
seven children.

Their first son, Dina's father, was now dying in the
worst way, losing his mind slowly to forgetfulness. His
sister, old herself, took care of him now in the house on
Spring Street. Dina had been reared in that house, two
stories with gingerbread trim and a porch that wrapped
around the side. There were white lawn chairs under oak
trees hung with Spanish moss. Her father had built her a
little boat, which she had mostly kept tied to the dock.
She took it out sometimes along the bayou, which led
through twists and turns to the Gulf of Mexico. Dina
hated herself for leaving: As the eldest daughter she
should care for Costas, but she didn't want to go back to
Tarpon Springs; the town was too provincial and narrow.
Going back would be like exile.

Wincing against a new throb of pain in her breast, Dina
shifted on the walkway.

She had, for a time, considered suicide, seduced by the
idea, flirting with it as she brought the wheels of her car
closer and closer to the shoulder of the road. She had
poured into her hand all the pills that the doctor had given
her. She had unlocked the cabinet where Sam kept his
pistol and stared down at it, gray and cold and final.

Why hadn't she done it, then? It was not fear of damnation for an unholy act. Dina had not believed in damnation for a long time, not since realizing that there was more of it on earth than she thought possible in the hereafter. Dina didn't consider herself Orthodox anymore, or a Christian of any variety. Sam had no answers, either. His mother—long dead—had been Jewish, but he followed no religion.

If she took the pills or pulled the trigger, then what? Nothing. Not even the awareness of nothing. It was much better, she had finally concluded, to remember, and have the pain of it, than to risk having nothing at all.

Dina blotted her forehead again with her sleeve, then picked up the clippers. She would finish trimming the border, then go in to dinner.

In the kitchen, Melanie got up from the table to check the heat under the pot roast. Then she crossed the kitchen to look through the sliding glass door again. Her mother was nearly at the end of the walkway. She would have to come in soon, Melanie thought. The sun was about to set. Her father was upstairs changing his clothes. He would be down in a few minutes.

Melanie had put glasses and plates on the counter, with linen napkins folded like fans, and the good silverware on placemats. She was hoping they could all sit down together. Nobody ate in the dining room anymore, even on holidays. Last year—forget it. Matthew had died in September, and Christmas had been awful. They didn't eat at the kitchen table because it was piled with papers from her dad's office, a TV to be fixed that had been there a month, and a bunch of mail. Plus her mother's briefcase and a stack of tax books. Her mother was a CPA. She used to have a private secretary and her own office, but she'd been sick, and she was just starting back to work full-time.

Melanie had cleared enough space for her homework. She slid back into her chair, nibbling on a carrot stick. That's all she would have, salad. Plus maybe a small piece of roast to keep her dad from asking if she wanted to make herself sick, or what. School would be out in three weeks, and all her friends were buying swimsuits. She'd been working on a tan in the backyard, but her thighs were *gross*. Her mom had mentioned it last night: *Melanie, you're getting chubby*.

A fist under her cheekbone, she read aloud, "Find the values of X where the value of the function of X is zero." She tapped the eraser end of her pencil on a piece of graph paper.

Without even opening the book, Matthew could have figured it out. He was awesome. He made straight As, till he started skipping school. Her mother had said Matthew needed a psychologist. Her dad said he needed a goddamn military school. He never did find out some of the stuff Matthew did, like shoplifting, because their mother handled it herself. Melanie knew only because she'd overheard them talking about it. In tenth grade he got suspended for smoking pot, and he told Melanie he would personally kick her butt if she tried it. Then they thought he was suicidal and put him in the hospital. He told Melanie it was an act, what he did, holding the pistol to his head like that. And he laughed. *Damn! You should have seen the old man's reaction*.

On the graph paper, Melanie ticked off ten spaces above the intersection of the x and y axes, then four to the left. "I hate this. I fucking hate it," she muttered.

Matthew used to come over and help her even after he moved out. He'd never finished high school. He failed his classes his junior year. Their father screamed at him for that and grabbed him by the shirt. Matthew tried to punch him, but he got knocked across the room. Then they both cried and hugged each other. But Matthew started staying away, and finally he moved to an apartment on South Beach. He became a model. Then he died.

Frowning, Melanie brushed aside some bits of rubber her eraser had left on the graph paper. This was useless, she thought. Totally pointless. She'd call somebody in her math class after dinner and ask how to do it.

In the backyard her mother stood up and pushed a piece of cardboard across the walkway with her toe. Melanie thought she would be okay when she came in. Usually she was nice; sometimes she could be a total bitch. At least she didn't cry as much anymore. In fact, she hadn't taken her pills lately either. There was a prescription bottle that Melanie kept an eye on. One of the girls at school, her mother had tried to kill herself that way. But this girl's mother was an alcoholic and totally irresponsible besides.

Footsteps thumped on the stairs, and Melanie looked around. Her dad came into the kitchen in running shoes that looked like he had waded through mud puddles in them. An old towel hung around his neck. She was afraid someone would see him. He wore gray sweatpants cut off at the knees, and a T-shirt with a rip in the pocket. He was starting to get a stomach. He worked out, but it didn't seem to make a difference. There was a fitness machine in the family room and some charts showing the daily reps he was supposed to do, but half the days were blank. When he was in the army he jumped out of helicopters and ran for miles with an eighty-five-pound pack and an M-16, getting shot at by the VC. He used to tell Matthew about it. *That's what it was like in war, son, and that's what it's like in life. You have to be tough.* Blah, blah, blah. And when their dad wasn't watching, Matthew would catch Melanie's eye and mouth the words, and she would nearly crack up laughing.

He walked over to the window, looking out.

She asked, "You're not going running now, are you?"

"I thought so, before it gets dark."

"There's pot roast on the stove. It's leftovers, but I added some more veggies."

He was still staring outside. "How's your mom?"

"All right, I guess."

"You guess?" He looked around.

"She didn't go to her appointment."

"Why not?"

"I don't know. She got home about four-thirty and went right outside."

He sighed, hanging on to the towel.

Melanie said, "She's about done, I think. Then we can eat."

Her dad turned his head toward the stove. "What do I smell?"

"Pot roast."

"I'm sorry, you told me." He came over and kissed her on top of the head and patted her cheek.

She said, "I put plates and silverware out."

"So you did." He left his hand on her shoulder. "It

looks very nice, honey." He let out a breath like he'd been lifting weights.

"Did you have a rotten day or something?"

He didn't answer, then said, "We lost one. Jury acquitted on a first degree."

"Oh. Too bad. What did the guy do?"

"Threw somebody through a sixth-floor window." He turned her math book around so he could see it. "How's school, Mel?"

"Okay." Melanie knew that the murder must have been bloody and gruesome. He never told her about those, even if she asked.

He tapped the book. "Quadratic equations. I remember this."

"It's hard." She looked up at him.

"Study the examples," he said. "That's what I used to do. If you don't try it yourself, you won't learn it."

Lecture number 27, she thought. Which meant that he didn't know how to do it either. She said, "Do you want me to serve the plates?"

He smiled. "Why not? Let me bring your mother in first." He tossed his towel over a chair and went out the sliding glass door.

When Sam called her name, Dina glanced up. There was a streak of dirt across her chin. He wiped it off with his thumb, then bent down to kiss her.

She smiled, tugging the ragged hem of his sweatpants. "Look at us, Sam. We could be street people, the way we're dressed."

The gazebo was a few yards farther along the walk. He moved her straw hat out of the way and sat on the middle step. "How was your day?" He noticed that she wasn't wearing her gardening gloves, and her nails were filthy and cracked. Before, she had been proud of her strong, beautiful hands. Before. Everything was divided into before or after, he had come to realize.

"I had meetings all day and didn't get anything done." She clipped a twig. The hedge was low and green with clumps of red flowers. It ran as straight beside the stones as if she had trimmed it with a laser beam. "And you?"

"All right." Sam propped his forearms on his knees. He

wanted to tell her about the verdict in the Balmaseda case. Not for sympathy, exactly. Just to tell her. But he wasn't sure how she would react.

Sam finally said, "You missed your appointment this afternoon."

"Melanie's tattling on me."

"She wasn't tattling. She's worried about you. Why didn't you go?"

"I didn't feel like it."

"What about next week?"

"Next week we'll see." Dina threw a handful of clippings into a grocery sack. "I went to church this afternoon," she said in a tone that meant he was to ask her about it.

"What church?" They didn't belong to a church in Miami. Dina went several times a year to the cathedral in Tarpon Springs, but never here.

"St. Sophia's," she said, "on my way home. No one was there, except for an old man dusting the sacristy. Then a woman came in to pray. She said the Lord's Prayer in Greek. On the way out, I lit a candle for Matthew. I could feel him with me, Sam."

Studying the pattern in the bricks at his feet, Sam debated whether to suggest they go inside. She had accused him, rightly, of not wanting to talk about their son. For months after he died, all they had done was talk about Matthew. Sam had run out of words.

"It did me more good than Dr. Berman. Look." Dina turned on her knees to face Sam directly. On her breast lay a flat silver cross with the three semicircles on each point that made it look so Eastern Orthodox. Sam hadn't seen it in a long time.

He didn't know what to say.

Dina asked, "Does it bother you?"

He shook his head. "No. If you want to wear it, go ahead."

She smiled. "It wouldn't go with my suits." She went back to trimming leaves, and the cross swung with the movement of her arm, ticking on a button. She was wearing one of his old shirts.

With Dina's head bowed over the clippers, Sam could see how her hair was coming in gray. It was parted in the middle and pinned behind her neck. Dark brown at the ends, more gray at the crown. He could have traced with a finger the line that indicated when Matthew died. She had aged since last summer. Even so, she was still a striking woman, with dark eyes and a mouth so full and red she didn't need lipstick.

He knew he loved her, but in a different way than twenty-some years ago. They'd been through a lot, most of which he didn't like to dwell on. He had considered divorce more than once; had even talked to a divorce attorney. Nothing had come of it for one reason or another. Kids. The job. Money.

Then Matthew died, and she fell apart, and that had made him think about what mattered in the long run. Everything has a time, he had finally realized. There's a point when you can make big changes, and after that you can't. A few years ago he would let himself get worked up over what-ifs. Sit out here in the gazebo by himself and drink, and then he'd feel like hell, as if his heart was going to give out, or any minute he'd start to cry.

Where would they be in twenty more years? Sliding toward seventy, an absurd idea. Wherever they were, it wouldn't be here. The house was too big. When Dina took a leave of absence, too sick to work, Sam had refinanced it. The monthly payments still made him a little light-headed every time he signed the check.

He watched her for a while, then asked, "Dina, doesn't your firm have a fair number of clients over on the Beach?" Jacobs Ross & Rendell, of which she was a partner, was the Miami branch of an accounting practice headquartered on Wall Street.

"Several. Why?"

"What about Klaus Ruffini?"

"Ruffini. No, he isn't one of ours, not directly. I believe someone in the office did a financial forecast for a project he's involved in. A resort. There was an article in the *Herald* a few months ago. Didn't you see it? They want to build a big hotel and several hundred time-share apartments, all very low class, if you ask me. If we're lucky it will all sink under its own weight."

"What do you know about Ruffini?"

"He's from northern Italy. His mother's Swiss, I think.

His father owns a shipping line or a steel mill, something like that. Why are you so interested in Klaus Ruffini?"

"He's been accused of sexual battery. He and two other men, in the VIP room of a nightclub on Washington Avenue. Eddie wants me to check it out."

A cool smiled curved Dina's lips. She brushed some leaves out of the cracks between the bricks. A vacuum cleaner could not have done a more thorough job. She said, "Rape. On South Beach, how shocking. They'll buy her off. Or scare her off."

"Probably so."

She said, "I see people like that all the time. They do what they want and no one touches them."

"Have you met Klaus Ruffini?"

"Someone pointed him out to me in a restaurant downtown. He was with his wife, a fashion designer. They own Moda Ruffini."

"What's that?"

"Sam, you really are out of touch in the Justice Building." Dina tugged on a root. "Moda Ruffini is a clothing store, along the lines of Armani or Versace, but not quite as chic. Matthew tried out for a magazine ad for them, but they didn't use him." Dina dropped the root into the bag. "A little strange, isn't it, that Eddie gave the case to you?"

"Not really. I'm the only one in the office that people know won't kiss his ass. He's trying to dump the case without people thinking he was influenced."

She arched a brow. "Was he?"

Sam shrugged. "The city manager wants the case to go away. Eddie agrees that it should, but he's trying damned hard not to look cozy with Hal Delucca."

"And so he's letting you do the dirty work." Dina laughed. "Eddie's more devious than you are, sweet. Be careful."

He didn't tell her the rest of it, that Eddie Mora might not be the state attorney much longer. That Eddie had hinted at supporting Sam as his successor, in exchange for a little help on this. Sam wasn't sure how much he was reading into it. He wanted to let it sit for a while.

Dina shifted the cardboard under her knees. "Who's the woman? I assume the victim is a female, though one can never be sure over there."

"A model, supposedly. Seventeen years old."

"Seventeen. My God. She's a child. Sam, you have to pursue this."

"You told me a minute ago there's no way I could win."

"What about statutory rape? She's under the age of consent."

"It doesn't apply."

"Why not?" Dina demanded.

"Because statutory rape requires a minor of previously chaste character." Sam said, "This girl isn't. She went to a nightclub, took drugs, got drunk—"

"And got what she deserved."

"I didn't say that. I said it's probably not a case we could win. If the jury won't buy it, we've got nothing." He watched Dina's clippers snap at stray twigs. He said, "The jury in the Balmaseda case came back with a verdict."

She glanced up, waiting.

"An acquittal. It took them four hours."

"They *let him go*, after what he did to that little boy?"

"They had more than a reasonable doubt about who did it, I guess. The judge excluded his confession." Sam flexed his right hand, rotating his thumb. "They might have voted for second degree, if we'd given them the chance. Joe McGee—he's the division chief—wanted to go with jury instructions on first degree, and I let him do it. I feel bad about that. It was a risk. I shouldn't have gambled."

Dina made an exasperated laugh. "It isn't your fault. Balmaseda got away with it. Some people seem to get away with things, don't they?"

"Not all of them, or I'd quit this business," Sam said.

"He murdered a child and got away with it. How many other criminals like Balmaseda get away with it?"

Suddenly weary, Sam said, "Let's go in. I want to hit the sack early. What about you?"

But Dina was still staring intently at him. "Nothing will happen to Klaus Ruffini either. Don't dare tell me the girl was responsible. Three men and a seventeen-year-old girl." Dina's expression darkened further. "Have you spoken to her?"

"Not yet."

"Had you even planned to?" She laughed. "Of course not. She should have known better."

"Yes, I plan to speak to the girl," Sam said, trying not to show his irritation. "If it's a good case, I'll file it. If it isn't, I won't."

A flush of red had risen in Dina's cheeks. "You can't. You're stuck in a system that has no connection to justice, only to expediency, or to whoever has the most money or power. Oh, you'll say it isn't that way, but it is. Men with money can rape a young woman and nothing will be done about it."

Sam leaned heavily against the framed opening of the gazebo. Shadows stretched across the grass. On the other side of the fence the sprinklers slowed, then stopped. When he looked at Dina again, she was twisting the clippers through a handful of stems.

"Is this girl from a good family, Sam? You should find out. Do her parents know what happened to her? I almost want to call them myself. We should have a support group. Parents of Children Ruined by South Beach, what do you think?"

"Dina, for Christ's sake. Matthew died because he got drunk and crashed his damned motorcycle." Sam could feel his neck getting hot. "He did it to himself. There was nothing you could have done to prevent it, and even less you can do about it now. How long do we have to go over and over this?"

She pulled back as if he had struck her.

"Oh, Jesus," he said, "I didn't mean to yell at you. Why don't we go in? Melanie made dinner."

"Sam, do you suppose we're being punished for something?"

"By what?"

"God. Eternity."

"No." Sam rested his forehead on his fists. "I don't believe in that."

"Strange thing for a lawyer to say." The clippers made metallic clicks. "The universe has laws, doesn't it? And laws imply judgment. You know that well enough. If someone suffers, there has to be a reason. A system of laws must be rational. If one is punished, the next question is, *what* is the punishment *for*?"

The breathlessness of her voice made him look at her. She was crying. Tears were spilling down her cheeks.

Sam picked up her straw hat. He said gently, "Come on, honey. Let's go in."

"I'm not finished. I want to finish this before it gets dark."

He stepped down to the walkway, holding Dina's hat out to her. Then he saw her left hand. She was still clipping off the last few branches, and blood ran down her arm in bright streaks, soaking into the rolled cuff of the white shirt.

He knelt and grabbed her wrist. "Dina! What—" The clippers clattered to the bricks.

There was a gash in her left thumb between the first and second joints. "It doesn't hurt," she said wonderingly. "Isn't that funny? It doesn't hurt at all." The blood was dripping onto her slacks now and spattering the walkway. Sam let go long enough to pull his T-shirt over his head. He wrapped the hem of it around her thumb and pressed.

"This is deep. You'll need stitches."

"No." She struggled to pull her hand away. "No, I don't want to go to a doctor. Not for this." Her head sank onto his chest. "You fix it for me, Sam. Please."

With an arm around her back, he lifted Dina to her feet and took her inside.

Sam bound the cut with gauze and tape while Melanie watched, grimacing. He said he would check it in the morning, and if it looked bad, she would go to the doctor, no arguments. Melanie hovered until Dina told her to please stop. She was *all right*, for heaven's sake.

Now Dina lay in bed. She had taken a pill, and her eyes were nearly closed. "I cause so much trouble," she whispered. "Poor Sam. I've worn you out."

"No. Go to sleep." He smoothed her hair, which lay in unruly tangles on the pillow.

"I won't dream tonight," she said. "When I take these pills I don't dream. But this week he's been in my dreams every night."

"Bad dreams?"

She nodded. "Very bad. Do you ever dream of him, Sam?"

"No." He noticed that the silver cross lay upside down on the nightstand, its chain jumbled. "You took it off."

She laughed sleepily. "The pills work better. I think I was having a flashback to my childhood. Put it back in my dresser, will you? Throw it out, I don't care."

He opened the drawer of the nightstand and dropped the cross inside.

"Sam? Lie down with me."

"Sure. Scoot over." He put an arm under her neck, kissed her forehead, then gazed out the window at the darkening sky while her breathing deepened.

They had met when he was twenty-two years old, just out of the army. His father had died the year before in Winter Haven, where he had owned an orange grove. Sam went to settle some matters with the estate, then drove up to the University of Florida in Gainesville to see about enrolling. He didn't know what he wanted to study, but he had some GI benefits and enough pay saved to get through four years if he was careful. He picked up a catalog from admissions, then strolled around the leafy old-brick campus. He was wearing his green T-shirt, and his hair was regulation short.

A pack of hippies began to trail him. Tie-dyed, bell-bottomed freaks. One wore an army jacket with a black armband. They shouted at him. How many babies had he killed in Vietnam? *Hey, soldier-boy, did you bomb any villages? How many women did you rape? Did you get off on it?*

Sam's hands went into fists. He waited for them to make a move, wanted them to. He was ready to break some bones. Then he heard another voice. A dark-haired girl with books in her arms pushed through, shouting for them to stop it, leave him alone. They stared at her long enough for the mood to break.

Sam followed her and asked why she had done that.

She shrugged. "It wasn't fair. They don't know who you are."

"Neither do you. Maybe I did kill people over there. Maybe I liked it."

Then this dark-eyed girl stopped walking. She studied him. "No. I don't think you liked it."

Sam knew he couldn't let her just walk away, vanishing into the crowd of students.

Her name, she told him later, was Constandina Pondakos. And then she laughed. "Dina for short, okay?"

It was still dark outside when Sam woke up. He lay in bed for a while, then swung his feet over the edge, trying not to wake Dina. He went around to the other side and pulled the blanket up around her shoulders. She didn't stir. Sam put on slacks and a T-shirt, then went downstairs to make some coffee. The refrigerator hummed, and a tree frog croaked in the backyard.

Police reports on the Alice Duncan sexual battery case were in his briefcase. He pulled out the folder, lay it on the kitchen table, and flipped it open. He put on his glasses and sat down. The ten pages included a summary by the lead detective, along with supplemental reports by two other men in the Personal Crimes Unit and the four uniformed officers who had secured the premises, gathered evidence, and interviewed witnesses at the scene.

Sipping his coffee, Sam scanned the report. *Victim stated that Fonseca forced her to engage in sexual intercourse with him and then with Lamont. Fonseca and Ruffini then restrained victim while Ruffini sodomized her with the neck of a champagne bottle.*

Sam skipped ahead. *After the premises were secured the following items were taken into evidence.* The sordid list included ladies pantyhose; a used condom; a .22-caliber double-shot pistol; a crack pipe; two hypodermic syringes; several forms and varieties of drugs in vials, plastic bags, pills, rocks, capsules; and rolling paper. Everyone in the room must have tossed their pockets when the police came in.

Victim was transported to the Rape Treatment Center by a friend, W/F Caitlin Dorn, 35 (see attached witness list).

Sam stared down at the name. Took a breath, let it out. Felt the blood squeeze through his chest.

The last time he had seen Caitlin Dorn she was wearing a jade-green silk bathrobe with nothing underneath. He had gone to her apartment, but it was to tell her that he wouldn't be back again. Their affair was over. When he tried to explain, to tell her he was sorry, Caitlin grabbed a lamp off a nightstand and hurled it at him, missing his head by inches.

Sam turned the report over on the kitchen table as if the woman to whom the name belonged might otherwise float up from the page.

c h a p t e r
four

Caitlin Dorn had set up her camera pointing north. It was attached to a fat telephoto lens, and the lens was mounted on a tripod. A beach umbrella shaded Caitlin, the camera, and a cartful of photographic equipment.

Through the viewfinder she could see a backdrop of sparkling ocean, golden sand, and white hotels, all converging at a misty blue point. The sand sloped gently to the shoreline, where the turquoise water broke into frothy waves, a continuous shushing sound. Puffy clouds floated lazily in the perfect blue dome of the sky, and seagulls wheeled and dipped. Slightly to the left, waiting for a signal to begin, stood a family of idealized tourists. Woman in sun hat and flowery dress, sandals dangling from her hand. Man in khaki pants rolled to mid-calf, shirt hanging open. Some chest hair, not too much. And a little boy, five years old, wearing shorts and a T-shirt. All of them with medium-brown hair, an all-purpose ethnicity.

The idea was that they had just escaped to Miami Beach from the frigid blasts of Chicago or New Jersey or Montreal, had taken off their shoes, couldn't wait to feel the tickle of surf on their toes. This shot would go on the cover of a brochure for potential investors in a new resort designed to lure families down from Disney World and Universal Studios to the international playground of the chic and beautiful, safely across the bay from dark, urban, crime-infested Miami.

Caitlin stepped aside to let her assistant take the shot. Tommy Chang was a student at the local community college, working mostly for the experience, which was about all Caitlin could afford to pay him. He had a bandanna for a headband, sunglasses, a collection of silver pendants around his neck on cords, a water bottle at his waist, no shirt, baggy shorts, and Velcro-strapped sandals. She had never seen a photographer's assistant dress much differently.

Tommy pulled out the proof. This camera held instant film so they could check the lighting and composition. She raised her sunglasses to look at it while Tommy changed cameras. They would shoot three or four rolls of 120-millimeter film, 30 exposures per roll.

Caitlin had been a model till a few years ago. She had picked up photography as a hobby in New York, but on South Beach it had become a way to survive. Getting this job had been a stroke of luck: her boyfriend knew the man in charge of the project. Caitlin knew she was good at what she did, but nobody was down at her end of the beach kissing her ass, as they did with most photographers. The two girls in swimsuits she had finished shooting earlier were hanging out on weathered, wood-slatted beach loungers, smoking. They had showered the salt water out of their hair in the production van, which was parked in the metered lot next to the beach. They sipped water out of bright containers with plastic lids and bendable straws. Caitlin could hear bits of chirpy conversation. The van owner sat in a folding chair reading the paper, a fishing hat to keep the sun off his bald spot. It was his kid playing the son in the tourist family.

The art director, a blond woman named Uta, was fussing unnecessarily with the female model's skirt. The model smiled at her. Yes, kiss the art director's fanny, Caitlin thought. Everybody did that.

Tommy took off down the beach to hold a reflector and passed Rafael Soto, the hair and makeup designer, coming the other way. Rafael trudged through the sand in high-top red canvas sneakers.

Stopping under Caitlin's umbrella, he dug a lighter and cigarettes out of his pocket, lit one. The flame reflected in his big round sunglasses. He asked, "How's her hair look? I sprayed the hell out of it."

She told him it looked fine. Caitlin had last seen this model half-dressed in a magazine ad for a South Beach lingerie boutique, but Rafael had made her look like a Girl Scout troop leader from the suburbs.

Holding a meter to the light, Tommy called out the exposure. "Eight-five, eight-two. Wait. There's a cloud. Just a second. Okay, coming out. Eight-eight. Eleven. Blue sky, here we go."

The camera whirred and clicked at two frames per second. The models walked along the same few yards of sand again and again, backing up, going forward, pretending to have a fabulous time. Swinging the little boy by the hands. Laughing. Kicking up the surf.

The art director yelled to the man not to get his trousers wet.

Rafael gossiped with Caitlin while Tommy reloaded the camera, marked the film canister, and sprinted back to the models. Tommy scooped up a reflector and tossed it up and caught it, a giant silver circle. Caitlin took her cap off for a minute to redo her hair into a ponytail.

"Uh-oh. Your roots are starting to show," Rafael scolded, standing on his toes to look. "Want me to fix it for you sometime?"

"Yeah, do me a new head." She looked longingly at his cigarette. "Let me have a drag. One?"

"No! You told me not to." He held it out of reach.

"Selfish. You should quit, too, you know."

"Why? Everyone needs at least one vice in order to remain humble." Rafael smiled, putting the cigarette to his lips. He inhaled greedily.

Sighing, Caitlin peered through the viewfinder again. "What the hell?" She cupped her hands around her mouth. "Tommy!" He looked around. "Tell him to take off his nipple ring! Every time the wind opens his shirt, I can see it."

"He wore that to a shoot?" Rafael laughed.

"Better than the time that girl showed up with a spider tattoo on her butt, and we were doing swimsuits, remember that?"

"God, yes. I had to put on the Dermablend with a putty knife!" His laughter trailed off into a muttered "Oh, shit."

Caitlin turned to see what he was staring at—a man standing by the production van, a tall blond in loose khakis and a white shirt with the cuffs rolled up. Caitlin recognized him: Charlie Sullivan, one of Ford's top male models. British, but living in the States. She wondered what he was doing here. It wasn't for this gig, not playing Mr. Middle America. If Sullivan were on a beach, he'd be lying half-nude in the surf, pulling an equally stunning female slowly up his torso, his mouth pressed to her throat, the sun bouncing off every well-defined muscle in his body. She had seen his model composite, a variety of poses and outfits. A tux. Tweeds. Business attire. A cashmere coat over an Italian suit. Or nothing but low-slung jeans and rippling stomach muscles. He was big time now, double-page editorial shots in *Details* and *GQ*.

Caitlin glanced at Rafael. Under the big sunglasses his mouth was compressed into a tight line. She said, "You want me to tell him to get lost? I could say it's a closed set."

"No, forget it."

She touched his arm. "You all right?"

"Peachy."

Until a few months ago, Rafael had been staying at Sullivan's beachfront condo, keeping the place neat, even paying the mortgage. Sullivan returned from a trip to London and kicked him out. Caitlin had tried to warn Rafael, but he'd been deaf and blind.

She went back to her camera. The man and woman and child filled the viewfinder. The boy had a little Miami Marlins cap on now. Cute kid. Rosy cheeks, round tummy.

Draping an arm over the telephoto she shouted, "Uta! Did you get a release from the Marlins?"

Uta yelled back, "For what?"

"The hat."

Uta put her hands on her hips, then trotted back toward the water. She had long, tanned legs, and her blond braid bounced on her back. She motioned for Tommy to take off the boy's hat. He sailed it toward her in an arc and she ran to catch it one-handed. Coming back up the slope, Uta caught sight of Sullivan and held out her arms. Caitlin heard her voice sliding down the scale. "Hi-i-iiii." They kissed lightly, and Sullivan left his arm around her shoulders.

"Such a whore," Rafael said.

"Which one?"

"Both of them. I saw them at Follia last night with their hands all over each other. Where was her husband, I'd like to know?"

"Sullivan's in his hetero phase," she said. "Next week it will be dogs or something."

Rafael said, "If he comes over here, I'm leaving."

But when Sullivan headed in their direction, Rafael didn't move. The two swimsuit models trailed along behind him, one barefoot, one in thongs. One from a town in Alabama, the other a light-skinned Haitian whose father, according to rumor, had fled to Paris with a big chunk of the island's treasury.

Sullivan sat on a wooden beach lounger a few yards away from the umbrella. The sun gleamed on his dark blond hair. "Hello, everyone." He smiled, showing his perfect white teeth.

One of the models dropped down beside him. "*Comment ça va, mon cher?* When did you get back?"

He gave her a peck on the lips. "Forever ago. Two weeks, at least. I was in Oslo, where I nearly froze my bum off."

The American girl bumped his shoulder with a hip. "I heard something about you."

"Should I ask?"

"You're the runway feature model in Milan for Dolce-Gabbana's winter collection."

"Yes, my agent called last week, and I'm still in shock."

Rafael said coolly, "And here you are, slumming on a shoot for a resort designed for the bowling-alley crowd."

"I came to watch your hair-spray technique."

He glared down at Sullivan through his sunglasses. "By the way. You still have several of my CDs. I would like to come pick them up."

"Whenever you like. I'll leave them downstairs with the doorman." Sullivan smiled.

Rafael spun around and headed up the beach.

Caitlin said, "I don't think it's such a hot idea, your being here. It's upsetting Rafael."

"Everything upsets Rafael. Actually, it's you I came to talk to."

"What about?"

"The thing at the Apocalypse last week, what else?"

The Haitian girl sat cross-legged on the sand and lit a cigarette. Her toenails were painted red, and a thin gold chain glittered on her ankle. "Everybody is talking about it. They say you were there."

Sullivan nodded. "Yes, sorry to say. Having nothing better to do that night, and being in the mood for something trashy, which George Fonseca's parties always are, I went along."

The American girl adjusted the straw in her insulated tumbler. "I can't believe it was rape. I mean, Ali Duncan is such a slut."

Caitlin said, "Excuse me? She's a friend of mine. And not a slut."

The girl raised one slender shoulder.

"I was there, too," Caitlin said, "and I'm not going to talk about it. Sullivan, you shouldn't either."

The Haitian model said, "I read the article in the *New Times*, but they made it to be that everyone was drunk and this happens all the time, every night."

"Oh, doesn't it?" Sullivan drawled. "The tourists will be so disappointed."

The other girl said, "A friend of mine was there with her boyfriend, and she told me that the lights came on and the music went off, and everybody was like, 'What's going on? What's happening?' "

Sullivan said, "Caitlin, after you and Ali left, a policeman barged right into the VIP room. He was screaming, 'Get back, turn on the fucking lights! Nobody move.' Klaus's bodyguard tried to push him out, but he drew his gun and called for some backup. They came in like storm troopers, blocking the exits, taking names. Everyone looked quite dazed. Never, never turn on the lights in a nightclub. The carpet alone will make you ill.

And meanwhile Klaus Ruffini was pouring himself another glass of champagne and smiling as if he'd never had so much fun. They didn't arrest him because, well, look who they'd be arresting, but I personally know that the matter is now under investigation."

The Haitian girl nodded, excited to be in on this. "The police want to raid the Apocalypse for a long time. I heard they have arrest many people that night for drugs. They might close it down because of letting girls in so young, do you think so?"

Caitlin refocused the telephoto, then circled her hand in the air to signal she was ready. Tommy called out the exposure. "Eleven . . . eight-seven . . . eleven . . . Okay, holding at eleven."

In a hushed voice, the American girl said, "Sullivan, tell us. What did they do to her? Like, with a champagne bottle? *Ewww!*"

"Sorry, I've been instructed not to discuss that. But I distinctly heard George tell Klaus that he had arranged a surprise for him. He meant Ali, of course, as if she were an hors d'ouevre. Then Klaus said he wanted to see Marquis Lamont do it to her first."

"He didn't!"

"He offered George five thousand dollars to see the big black guy have sex with her. But he said it in words too crude to repeat."

The American model shrieked. "Oh, God! That is so gross! Five thousand dollars? You lie!"

"It's true, I swear." He broke into laughter. "Oh, stop, that tickles."

"You're a lying sack!"

Caitlin spun around from the camera. "All of you, shut up! I'm trying to work."

The models climbed off Sullivan, and with a sigh he leaned back on the lounge chair, locked his wrists over his forehead, and closed his eyes. There were suffused giggles from the women, then silence.

Caitlin looked through the camera. Little boy digging in the sand with red plastic shovel. Mom looking at a shell. Dad on one knee, hand on mom's shoulder. Everybody smiling. Tommy and Rafael holding the reflectors just right. No harsh shadows. Perfect.

Then the man swung the little boy onto his shoulders. The woman smiled up at them. They laughed silently in the viewfinder, and their feet in the water kicked up froth but made no sound. Again and again.

The camera whirred and clicked. Finally Caitlin signaled the end of the roll.

Someone was whispering midway through a story. "She puked down his back, all over his jacket, which was this really fab green silk, and he was looking the other way and he didn't even notice because he was like totally smashed, and she just walked out of the restaurant—"

Tommy trotted back down the beach to reload. Caitlin could have done it, but he considered it his job. Rafael stayed where he was, arms crossed, kicking idly at a scrap of driftwood. With deft movements, Tommy detached the camera from the lens, attached a loaded camera, then took the film out of the first. He marked the roll, zipped it onto a bag on the cart, reloaded, then jogged back to the models, his black hair flowing out behind him.

Sullivan asked, "Who is that kid? He looks sort of Asian."

Caitlin said, "His father's Chinese, and he's eighteen years old. Leave him alone."

"You're in a funny mood. I was only asking."

Caitlin grabbed some bottled water out of a small ice chest and unscrewed the cap. She had planned to shoot the other roll of film. Just in case. In case what? Maybe Martin Cass, hired by the Grand Caribe Resort—and who happened to be Uta's husband—wouldn't like any of these. Maybe Marty didn't like doing favors. Maybe Caitlin hadn't kissed Uta's fanny sincerely enough. Maybe it would have been better not to have taken this job at all.

Still waiting, the male model cupped his hands and shouted, "Are we about done? I have to take a leak."

Caitlin tossed the bottle back into the cooler. "Yes! That's it! We're done."

Sullivan swung his feet off the beach lounger. "You girls go to the van and fetch me some water, will you?"

"Have some of mine." The Haitian girl held out her insulated tumbler with the straw through the top.

"Don't make me be rude. Go on, I have to talk to Caitlin. And tell that Chinese kid to give us a minute as well." He waited for them to leave, then walked over to where Caitlin was unsnapping the latches on her camera case.

"What is it, Sullivan?"

"Are you going to testify against Klaus Ruffini, if there's a trial?"

"I haven't thought about it." She laid the camera into its fitted niche and closed the lid.

"Have you been to the state attorney's office yet?"

Caitlin stopped with the telephoto half off the tripod. "No. What for?"

"They had me down there for two hours yesterday, asking questions. You mean nobody called you? I went with Mirabelle—you know Mirabelle. She said she didn't see much, but she certainly did. Anyway, we got lost in the criminal courts—God, what a freak show!— and finally stumbled into the right building. Not gray and blocky, as you would expect. The walls are turquoise, and the carpet is deep pink. Sort of Kafka tropicale. They wanted to know exactly what I saw, what I was doing at the club that night, who else was there, who I had come with, whether I was high. As if *I* were on trial. You'll never guess who's in command of the interrogations."

Caitlin lowered the lens into its case. "Who?"

"You remember that boy who died in a motorcycle accident last year? Stavros? Don't look so blank, Caitlin. You know who I mean. You and he worked on a French sportswear catalog."

She stared at him for another second, then said, "Yes, of course."

"Well, the prosecutor is Stavros's father. Can you believe it? His name is Hagen, a hulking, stone-faced man with a government haircut and an atrocious blue suit. I'd never have guessed, because there's not much resemblance to Stavros, but when I told him I was a model, he said his son was a model on South Beach— *was*, as in *deceased*. So I asked who, and he said Matthew

Hagen, who had also called himself Stavros. So I said, yes, of course I had known his son, that we'd been friends, in fact, and that I was terribly shocked when he died, although I had been out of the country at the time."

Caitlin began to fold up her tripod.

Sullivan said, "Hagen asked me if I would testify if it came to a trial, and I said I would. Are you sure he hasn't tried to contact you?"

"Positive."

"He must have done. You were a witness."

"He has you," Caitlin said. "You saw more than I did." She lowered the umbrella.

Sullivan followed her back to the cart. "I'm not keen to be the only one. Not that I'm afraid of George Fonseca or a half-rate movie actor or even Klaus Ruffini. In fact, the publicity couldn't hurt. But if I'm the only strong witness besides Ali—well, I'd feel quite outnumbered."

She loaded the tripod and jammed the umbrella into a corner of the cart. "Sullivan, for a minute there I thought you were developing a conscience. I mean, you didn't do a damn thing when Ali was attacked."

Squinting slightly in the sun, he lowered his face to hers. He smiled. "Neither did you, darling."

"Caitlin?" Tommy Chang was standing a few yards away with the reflectors, which he had twisted into smaller silver circles. "You ready to go?"

She turned. "Sure. Do me a favor? Load up everything and take it to the studio, okay?" She grabbed her Nikon and slung the strap over her shoulder. "And run the film by the lab."

"Where are you going?"

"To get paid for this. See you later."

Sullivan waved his fingers. "Ciao."

Caitlin headed west, crossing Ocean Drive with its slow traffic and packs of tourists, then going farther into the business district of South Beach. Marty Cass lived on Jefferson Avenue. He had said he would be there. Maybe this time she wouldn't have to go to hell and back, looking for her money.

She had brought her camera along because she always

brought her camera, a used Nikon she'd bought in New York years ago. She could hide behind its 70- to 210-millimeter zoom and shoot inconspicuously from a distance. Commercial photography paid the bills, but her heart was elsewhere.

On Washington Avenue she stopped under the shade of an awning outside a market. She looked through the lens at a thin, gray-haired woman across the street bathing herself with water from a garden hose. Caitlin had seen her before, usually on one of the benches near the police station. The woman wore red shorts and canvas slippers, and her breasts hung loosely inside a faded halter top. The hose curled out the side door of a French bistro, and a white-jacketed kitchen helper leaned on his elbows on the railing, smoking, waiting for her to finish so he could mop the steps. The water made rainbows of mist. Caitlin could see everything so clearly through the lens. The white wall, white jacket, blue painted railing, red shorts, the woman's glistening black skin, and a splash of silvery water.

In the instant before her finger pressed the shutter release, she wondered if the finished print would show all this. Too often, between the lens and the developer, the light changed, or the balance shifted, and the result would be no better than an ordinary snapshot. Sometimes, though, her photos were good. More than good. They made her certain that *yes!*, she could do this, put it all on film, more real than life. Caitlin used to work hard at taking photos that would look good in a gallery. Once she had wanted them to *mean* something. She didn't think much about that anymore. They meant what they meant.

The woman was singing now. Caitlin could see her mouth move, see her thin arms swaying above her head. The kitchen helper stuck his cigarette in his mouth and applauded. Caitlin kept her finger on the shutter, and the camera clicked and whirred to the end of the roll.

She had thousands of photographs, color and black-and-white and weird combinations, with no idea what they meant. Less idea now, in fact, than when she had begun.

* * *

She found Marty Cass's apartment on a shady residential block in a fourplex dating from the sixties. Whoever had renovated the place had painted it pink and put a horizontal stripe of purple at the top, trying to get the art deco look, though the architecture was a few decades off.

Caitlin pressed the buzzer outside his door on the first floor. A business card was taped under the peephole: *Martin Cass, Tropic Realty and Investments.*

In the still air, she took off her cap and fanned her face. A muffled salsa tune came from upstairs. The tiled hall ran straight back through the building, opening up to flowering shrubs and a fountain. A plump gray cat in the next doorway got up, stretched, then came to see who she was.

Frank Tolin had persuaded Marty to let Caitlin do the resort brochure. Frank was a lawyer downtown, and the two men had some business dealings together. If Marty didn't pay Caitlin, Frank would handle it. But then she would have to listen to Frank tell her how much he had done for her, and wasn't she lucky?

Rumbling with purrs, the cat wound itself around Caitlin's ankles. She bent over to scratch under its chin. "Hello, kitty-cat."

She and Frank had an off-on relationship. Currently on, she thought. In the middle of the *Miami Vice* craze, she had come down to see what was going on, liked the sunshine, and stayed. No, not entirely true. She had been fired from a *Vogue* shoot for showing up stoned and had no money to get back to New York. Frank had let her stay at his place in Coconut Grove till she found an apartment. They had been together—off and on—ever since. Nobody was talking about marriage. Frank had been married and divorced twice already, and Caitlin liked to come and go as she pleased.

She pressed her ear to the door of Marty's apartment. "Damn." She rang once more, then gave up. He could be anywhere.

At a pay phone a couple of blocks away she left her number at his office and on his beeper. She carried a beeper herself; Marty couldn't say he wasn't able to reach her. She checked a few of the sidewalk restaurants and two real estate offices. No one had seen Marty Cass.

Unwrapping a deli sandwich as she walked, Caitlin headed north toward Lincoln Road. Tommy Chang had an extra key to her studio; he would have taken the cart and equipment up there by now. She owed him a hundred dollars. That and processing the film they had shot would just about clear out her account—unless she put off paying the rent on the studio for another week or so. Or borrowed the money from Frank. At least she didn't have to worry about her apartment. Frank owned the building and wouldn't let her pay.

Stopping at a crosswalk in a crowd of pedestrians, Caitlin waited for the light to change. In the middle of the next block she spotted the Apocalypse, looking pretty tame in broad daylight. Just another white concrete front with an awning over the door, except this building used to be synagogue, which might have amused her under other circumstances. It had curves like Mosaic tablets at the roof—two curves and a dome with silver paint. She supposed the congregation had died off or had moved a few miles north, or off the Beach entirely. A year ago, sure of herself, Caitlin had lain in wait with her camera until a family of Hasidic Jews had wandered by, father in black suit and hat, mother in calico dress and head scarf following behind with the children. Caitlin had clicked happily away, and when she got the photos back, they were one cliché after another.

The traffic light changed. Caitlin didn't move, only gazed through her sunglasses across the intersection.

The prospect of having to talk to Sam Hagen was going through her mind. Having to sit across a desk from him, being interrogated, as Sullivan had been interrogated. That Sam had not already contacted her might mean he wasn't going to. But if he did, what then?

Why had she been at the Apocalypse that night? Well, taking freelance society photographs for a local magazine. And why had she not confronted those men, pulled her friend to safety, screamed for help?

Because in the dark I couldn't see; then it was too late. And because, if you really want to know, at first I was mad at Ali, that she would let this happen, for nothing, for a laugh, for the pure hell of it. Sam knew such things happened, because she had trusted him enough to tell him about that other life.

Sam Hagen, his steady gray eyes on her. As if he had a right to make judgments about her. About anybody, the bastard.

They had met when he started working at Frank's office. She had joked around with him. Nothing serious. But the way he looked at her, she knew what he was thinking. He didn't do anything about it, though. Then later, after he'd gone back to his old job as a prosecutor and she was in one of her off periods with Frank, Sam Hagen showed up one night at her door, and she, like a fool, opened it.

He let her believe he was unhappy, that he would leave his wife. Then after several weeks, and with a suddenness that stunned her, he said he couldn't see her anymore. So sorry. Good-bye. She might have brought herself to forgive him—he had a family, after all—if she hadn't found out that he'd expected to be named as the interim state attorney. Cheating on your wife is one thing; fucking your career is another.

By pure accident, Caitlin spotted Marty Cass coming out of a bank on Lincoln Road. His hair was pulled back into a little ponytail, which he had fastened with a red rubber band, and he carried a small leather bag and a cellular phone.

When she planted herself in front of him, he held out an arm. "Caitlin! How's it going? You look great!" He smiled at her through a pair of Polo sunglasses.

She didn't smile back. "I went by your apartment. You said to come pick up a check."

"Today?" He seemed puzzled and began to walk west on the mall. Years ago auto traffic had been replaced with planters, fountains, and pedestrians. "It's Saturday."

Caitlin fell into step. "I don't care what day it is, Marty. You said you'd be home. You'd pay me when I finished the shoot for the Grand Caribe brochure. It's finished. Where's the check?"

He shrugged. "Where are the photos?"

She said, "The money is for processing costs. You gave me a retainer of a thousand dollars. Now I need five hundred for processing and printing. After that, I'll want the balance."

"Oh, wow, I wish you'd told me that before."

"I did tell you."

Marty Cass seemed perplexed. His brow creased. "The resort development office is closed today, and they have to approve all the checks. Hey, I don't like it either. You know, these guys have put me off, too, Caitlin. They brought me in to do publicity and gave me a share instead of a salary. A share of what, I ask you. The city was supposed to approve a zoning change, but I don't know what's going to happen now. They could get real nervous about what happened at the Apocalypse. I mean, Ruffini's the main player on the project."

"Poor Klaus," Caitlin said. "Pay me for the brochure, Marty, but don't suggest I do anything else for him."

Marty Cass moved closer. "Did he rape that girl? Or is she making it up? What's the story? You were there, right?"

"Yes, but I didn't see anything."

"Right. But what happened? Between you and me."

"I don't know."

"Yeah. If I were there, I wouldn't know either." He stopped walking. "Listen. Was my wife at the shoot this morning?"

"Of course. Uta designed the brochure."

"Who'd she come with?"

"She came in the production van with the models."

Marty gazed through his sunglasses, then slowly smiled. His teeth were small and even. He said, "I drove by, thought I'd see how it was going, and there was that faggot model—excuse me for being incorrect here—you know who I mean."

"He was there to speak to me," Caitlin said.

Marty smiled again. "Are you protecting Uta, Caitlin? Did she ask you not to tell me where she was, what she was doing?"

"Come on, Marty."

"We broke up. I don't know if Uta mentioned it or not."

"No, she didn't."

"Yeah, well. I lay it at the door of our mutual friend. He'll get his one day." Marty unzipped his bag and dropped his tiny telephone inside. "She married me to get her green card. I should have known better."

Caitlin said, "Marty, my check."

"It's as good as done." He glanced at his watch. "Wow, I'm late. Look, call me next week." He was walking backward. "We'll get together for lunch and you can show me the proofs. I can't wait to see them. Call me."

"I will. Monday morning. Early."

Four years ago, Caitlin had exhibited her black-and-white decadence-and-decay prints at a gallery on Lincoln Road owned by a friend who liked such stuff. She sold three prints. There were wine and fruit and a platter of cheese cubes on ruffled toothpicks. People she knew showed up and kissed her on both cheeks and said the exhibit was marvelous. Caitlin wore tight jeans and a denim vest and smoked French cigarettes. She listened to a fashion editor describe the Karl Lagerfeld spring collection he had seen in the company of Paolo di Niscemi. Had Caitlin met Paolo? He had just opened a restaurant at Ocean and Twelfth, which had tiramisu to die for.

Then Caitlin saw Sam Hagen folding his umbrella by the door. The hems of his suit pants were spattered with rain. He saw her, smiled quickly, then went to look at the pictures mounted on the gallery walls. He put his glasses on. The pools of light from the ceiling fell on his shoulders and slid away as he moved through the exhibit. Caitlin was standing there with her elbow on her hip, smoking. She tossed her hair back. Watched him look at her photographs, at each one.

When he came finally to speak to her, she said he didn't have to buy anything. He did anyway, a grainy shot of an empty beach. The gallery closed early, and they went next door for cappuccino. Setting down her empty cup she pointed out that he hadn't said what he thought of her show, be honest.

"I don't know much about photography."

She laughed. "Say it. I don't care. They're pretentious and shallow."

"No, I didn't think that. Why don't you tell me what they're about?" His face was serious; he wanted to know.

With his umbrella over their heads, they walked the

length of Lincoln Road and back again, and she told him
what she saw when she looked through a camera, and how
it made her happier than anything she'd ever done, and,
no, she never wanted to stop.

chapter
five

Sullivan took Tommy Chang to the Seahorse Grill on Ocean Drive. He had offered—rather generously, he thought—both lunch and an insider's look at the top end of the fashion industry.

They sat at a small sidewalk table, one of a dozen, their backs to the polished coral rock wall of the hotel terrace behind them, looking out at palm trees and beach through pedestrians and across two lanes of traffic. Some tables had red Cinzano umbrellas fluttering over them, but Sullivan chose one without. He unbuttoned his shirt and pulled it loose at the waist. The sun felt gloriously warm on his skin.

He told the waiter, "Grilled salmon. A green salad with balsamic vinegar. And cranberry juice. No ice." He looked at Tommy Chang, seated to his left.

The kid was still reading the menu.

"It's on me, Tommy. Whatever you want." When Tommy only nodded, Sullivan said, "Hamburger and fries?"

"Okay. Sure. And a Coke."

"Naturally." Sullivan handed the waiter their menus. The kid sat back in his chair, looking around, one knee bouncing.

Reaching into his pocket, Sullivan pulled out the small plastic vial that contained his vitamins. He counted out four different varieties and took them with water. Tommy Chang watched him. Sullivan asked, "Tell me. How were you hired by Caitlin Dorn?" He tossed back the last capsule.

"My photography teacher at Miami-Dade knows her, and he recommended me when she needed somebody to help out and stuff." Tommy shrugged. "Not like it's any big deal or anything."

"But it is. Everybody starts somewhere. And so you've decided to become a fashion photographer."

"Well, I'm exploring my options. Maybe get on the staff of a magazine someday."

"That's ambitious." Sullivan wondered if he himself had ever been so naive. "Where are you from?" he asked.

"From? Like maybe China?" Tommy smiled broadly. He had clear, long-lashed, almond-shaped eyes. "My dad was born in San Diego."

"You still live at home?"

"For now. They don't make me pay rent." Tommy laughed.

Sullivan settled back into his chair, angling away to make some room for his legs, which he crossed at the knee. "Well, let's see what I can tell you. I've worked with the best fashion photographers in the world. Avedon, von Wangenheim, Arthur Elgort, Helmut Newton, for instance. I could show you my book if you want. I know several local photographers. Caitlin is all right but not very imaginative. Well, can anyone be imaginative with catalog, I ask you? Learn what you can from her; then move on. And for God's sake, get out of Miami if possible. It's full of has-beens, mediocrities, B-list celebrities, and all the fame-fuckers who tag along after them."

The kid grinned. "What are you doing here?"

Such a clever boy. Sullivan smiled. "I come for the sun, not the social life. Genuine social life in Miami Beach is dead. When you see the Gap and Taco Bell, you know it's over. This town after dark has become as phony as Bourbon Street, as tawdry as Daytona Beach during spring break. Tourists come to gawk at the transvestites. Fraternity boys throw up their beer and piss on the pavements. The Beach can't decide between debauchery and commercialism, but either way it's the walking dead."

The kid was staring at him.

Sullivan stared back until Tommy lowered his eyes and worked at unfolding his napkin.

"Have you ever done any modeling?"

"Me?"

"You've got the looks. No, honestly, I'm not kidding you. I've seen, oh, God, hundreds of young models. Thousands. Most of them haven't a chance. You do. I would know, believe me."

Sullivan turned in his chair to study Tommy Chang's face. "The ethnic look is strong right now. You've seen it for years in Benetton ads. Good profile. Great cheekbones. Must be the Chinese blood." He reached out and took off Tommy's bandanna headband and tossed it into his lap.

"Hair's a bit long. You're tall enough, good muscle definition. Asians tend to photograph as rather fragile. I don't think you would, though."

The kid drew back as if Sullivan might go for his underwear next. The edge of his boxers—dear God, a Miami Hurricanes motif—showed over his denim shorts, and a darkish line of hair sprouted between his pecs and vanished below his navel. Sullivan raised his eyes.

Tommy had put on a defiant glare. "I'm straight, man. You'd better know that up front."

"Marvelous, but so what? Most models are straight, in case you wondered about that. But what does it mean? Straight. And don't use labels—it's not polite. Labels don't tell you what a person is, deep within himself. A person is anything he wants to be." *Christ, what drivel.*

Chastened, the kid said, "Sorry."

Sullivan gave him a comradely slap on the back. "Forget it. Listen, you wanted some advice. Stay out of fashion photography. There are too many people in it already. Take Caitlin, for example. She's not without talent, but she couldn't survive if she didn't have a lover who provides some ready cash now and then. He's a lawyer. Am I telling you things you don't know? Oh, take pictures if you have to, but then what do you live on? I'd try modeling if I were you. It isn't hard, and you could fit it around your classes in school."

Tommy took a long swallow of Coke, then put down

his glass. "Nah. I see these guys posing, making faces. I don't think I could do that."

"Of course you could. It's fun. It's like acting. Watch." Sullivan had a repertoire of attitudes. He demonstrated a few of them. The moist-lipped desire of cologne ads; the arrogance they wanted for Italian menswear; the breathless intensity from the jeans ad where he had simulated screwing an anorexic teenage girl against a rusty water tank on a New York rooftop. Then a blue-eyed grin for innocent fun, just the thing for Father's Day, kid-on-the-knee shots.

"Cool." Tommy's eyes made crescent-shaped slits. "That's pretty good."

There was something in his laugh that reminded Sullivan of Stavros's laughter: full, open, nothing fake about it. Whatever else Stavros might have been—sullen, angry, self-destructive—he hadn't been phony.

Sullivan raised his hands, which he knew were graceful and strong, then spread his arms wide, like wings. His white Emporio Armani shirt lifted, then opened, showing everything from neck to belt buckle. He was aware that people on the sidewalk were slowing as they walked by, but he was used to that.

"Look. No tattoos, no rings through various parts of my body. No cosmetic surgery—not yet, anyway." He laughed. "Although I'm thirty-one, and it won't last much longer, will it?"

Tommy shrugged.

"You mustn't get into drugs," Sullivan said.

"I don't."

"Good. Don't drink either."

The waiter brought the food.

Sullivan watched the kid splatter ketchup all over the beef patty. Averting his eyes, Sullivan picked up his own fork and flaked off a wedge of grilled salmon. Fresh and pink. A sprig of basil on top. How much of this damned fish had he consumed on South Beach?

"You're eighteen, aren't you?"

Tommy nodded and chewed.

"It helps, at your age, to know someone who's been around. I've been lucky that way. You remember the TV ad a couple of years ago for Polo cologne, where the man was riding a horse along the beach in slow motion?"

"You did that?"

"Yes. I got the job because I knew someone. I made over a hundred thousand dollars in residuals."

The almond eyes were fixed on him, and Sullivan felt a little electric jolt of connection. He had Tommy's attention now.

At age fifteen in London, Charlie Sullivan had been on one of his customary pilfering expeditions, this time at Harrods, where he'd found a smashing silk shirt. Someone spotted him, a pock-marked man of about forty. A clerk saw him at the same time and grabbed him by the back of the neck, but the man told the clerk he was this boy's uncle, to let him go. The man paid for that shirt and two more besides. He turned out to be a baronet who lived in a townhouse in Kensington with six bedrooms, all of which Sullivan got to know intimately. His benefactor bought him clothes, paid for speech lessons, and taught him which fork to use and other sorts of useful, pretty bits of information. When Sullivan was eighteen he took a gold-inlaid Victorian music box from the baronet's house, pawned it for two thousand pounds, and flew to the Bahamas with some pals. After three months he was broke and starving, pondering whether to crawl home or sell his sweet white ass, when someone saved it for him—a forty-five-year-old woman on vacation from a New York art gallery. She took him to the States and got him a green card. More polishing, more money, more clothes. *Et voilà!* But she liked to be tied up and beaten, and she was a junkie besides. Sullivan began making the rounds of modeling agencies with a few head shots, as one of his girlfriends had suggested. It had taken him five hard years to become established.

Sullivan looked at Tommy Chang and felt a sudden desire to toss his napkin on the table and go home. He took a deep breath. Cold, gray melancholy would descend upon him out of nowhere lately, for no reason at all. Last night he'd gone out with three friends he'd met in Milan last year, even taking one of them to his flat. And then ... nothing. He had preferred falling asleep, and after he'd heard the door slam he'd lain awake for hours, his chest aching as if he might at any moment burst into tears.

The kid was talking about money now. Then a question, and Sullivan had to think of what it was.

"No, men don't make nearly as much as the girls, of course, but we manage well enough." He could see the question in Tommy's mind. "I average about two thousand a day plus expenses, depending on the job. For runway modeling it's less, but you do it for the exposure. I can always find work in Germany or Scandinavia because of my coloring, but it keeps me from a lot of jobs in South America. Oddly enough, the Japanese like blonds. The French are okay to work with. The Italians don't pay as well, but I have a good time. What's really cool—" Oh, God, could he get his mouth around these juvenile speech patterns without gagging? "You get to see places. And meet girls. Lots of them. Do you have a girlfriend?"

The kid shook his head and swallowed, then wiped a finger across his lip to catch a smear of ketchup. "Not at the present time. Me and her broke up about a month ago."

She and I, you moron. Were they all like this? No. Not all of them. Stavros had been more refined, when he wasn't playing at being a delinquent.

How would this turn out? Sullivan wondered. How would he play it? Assuming he wanted to play at all. It was always interesting, never knowing what he himself would do, never mind anyone else.

Men and women had come on to him, some of them incredibly beautiful. He could say yes, or he could tell them to fuck off, depending on his mood. Not that his mood seemed to matter, they would still have that sappy look on their faces. He had slapped a particularly sappy woman again and again, wanting to know how many slaps would knock it off. Six.

With a clank he laid down his fork on the clear glass plate. "Don't expect glamour," he said. "It's just a job. There's no glamour to it. And it's not easy."

"You just said it was."

"It isn't. All right, I'll tell you what it is when you

start out. A phony agent will charge you hundreds of dollars and produce nothing. A photographer will have his hands on your arse. You show up at a go-see, seven A.M., to see if they'll hire you to model cheap sportswear for a discount department store. Everybody and his brother is in line ahead of you. Finally you get into the room, they ask for your card, the art director looks at it, not at you, because you're only what appears on a piece of paper, after all, and he says, 'Sorry, not what we want. Next!' Then you go to another call, and another and—"

"That happened to you?"

"Of course. Do you suppose that someone's going to snatch you off the street for the next Calvin Klein underwear campaign? If you can't stand the word *no*, you don't belong here."

Tommy Chang was nodding, taking a big bite of hamburger, gripping the bun in both hands, wondering if he was up to the challenge. Not looking sappy yet, but give him time.

The screech of brakes drew Sullivan's attention. A shabby red Mustang convertible was making a U-turn down the street, coming back.

"Shit." He didn't know he'd said it aloud until the kid asked him what was the matter.

"It's George Fonseca. He's one of the men who raped that girl in the Apocalypse." The Mustang pulled into a space at the curb, and the driver vaulted over the door. He wore big sneakers and ill-fitting shorts that cupped his genitals.

Sullivan waited, his muscles tensing.

A shadow fell across the table. "I been looking for you."

"What do you want, George?"

"I want to know what the fuck you think you're doing." His black T-shirt had no sleeves. Gold's Gym. Lots of armpit hair.

Sullivan exhaled. "The state attorney's office asked me some questions, and I told them the truth."

"I am not happy, man."

"After what you did, I should think not."

"What I did. You lying fuck."

"Go away, George. You're making people stare."

George glanced around, then grabbed another chair and forced himself down into it, but it appeared he would spring back up at any moment, as if he were a piece of metal that had been bent.

"Look, Sullivan. We gotta talk sooner or later." George's eyes went for a moment to Tommy, whose back was pressed up against the wall. "You're still pissed off about Stavros. Okay. What the fuck do you want me to do, man? That wasn't my fault, I told you."

"This isn't about Stavros. The thing is, George, that Klaus Ruffini is going down the tubes, and you're simply on the same piece of toilet paper."

George spoke through his teeth. "I get it. It's your buddy, that cunt Claudia Otero. She'd give her right tit to put Moda Ruffini out of business. Is she paying you to do this?"

Tommy shifted as if he might have to run for it. Sullivan touched his forearm. "Notice, Tommy, how he froths at the mouth, literally. The spit is bubbling in the corners."

"You're dead meat."

"That's original." Sullivan dropped his voice to a growl. "Leave, George, before I kick your bleeding ass across Ocean Drive."

George's wicker-backed chair clattered to the sidewalk when he stood up. "Do it, motherfucker. I'll bust that pretty mouth of yours. No stomach punches. I'm goin' for the teeth."

A waiter hustled over, followed by the manager, then a cook with a huge neck and a scowl, wiping his hands on his apron. Sullivan knitted his fingers over his belly, relaxing. He could see which way this would go.

The manager took George's arm, spoke close to his ear. "What're you doing, George? Come on, cut it out. I can't have this."

George jerked away and leaned into Sullivan's face. "You're through on the Beach, asshole."

"Gee. I'll never work in this town again."

He watched George stomp back across the street, get into his miserable car, and screech out of the parking space, barely missing a van with an Ohio plate. A horn blared. A cloud of bluish smoke drifted slowly upward. The manager put the chair back.

Sullivan waited until his hands were steady before he reached for his juice. People at the other tables gradually returned to their conversations, and the flow continued on the sidewalk.

The kid's mouth was hanging open. "Aren't you scared he'll do something?"

Sullivan shrugged. "I can deal with George."

Tommy leaned closer, a hand on Sullivan's chair. "What's Stavros?"

"Not *what*. Who." He exhaled. "Stavros was a friend of mine who became involved with George Fonseca. He's now dead."

"No shit. You mean . . . George killed him?"

Sullivan looked steadily at Tommy Chang. "No. Stavros died in a motorcycle accident, but he was working his way up from cocaine and meth to heroin, thanks to George. Ask Caitlin, she knew him." For a while Sullivan sat without speaking.

Tommy Chang's curiosity hadn't run dry. He prodded, "Who's Claudia Otero?" He had scooted his chair closer, and Sullivan could feel the heat radiating off his body.

Sullivan took another swallow of cranberry juice, then set down the glass. In the sunlight, the liquid danced red on the white tablecloth.

"Claudia Otero is a designer from Madrid, born in Havana. She has a boutique on Lincoln Road. She and Tereza Ruffini hate each other's guts. Claudia has talent. Tereza recycles last year's Versace at half the price. Just the thing for South Beach." He added, "Claudia and I spent some time together. I met her on my first trip to Paris, when I was twenty-two."

The kid grinned. "You went out with her?"

Sullivan slid his arm across Tommy's shoulders and said quietly, "I did not 'go out with her,' Tommy. I fucked her for a week solid up and down the Côte d'Azur on a yacht owned by Nino Seruti."

"Bitchin'."

"Believe it. We're still friends. In fact, you should meet her." Just in time, Sullivan stopped himself from mentioning Claudia's party at La Voile Rouge on Friday. He wouldn't mind taking this kid to La Voile Rouge, but not without a haircut and some manners.

"Tell you what. Come over to the Colony Hotel tonight. My agency is throwing a party. Free champagne. Meet the folks."

He could see the emotions flitting across the kid's face. "I don't know these people. I can't, like, just walk in."

"You know *me*." Sullivan spoke softly into his ear. "Listen, Tommy. It doesn't matter who you are if you know the right people. Yes, it's a spurious sort of existence, I grant you, but what other kind is there, when you really think about it?"

"I guess." Tommy was a little dazed. The cream of American youth. At that moment Sullivan wanted to backhand him.

Then he played with the idea of suggesting that Tommy come by his flat first. They could go to the hotel together, wouldn't that be easier? Of course he would say yes. The kid was smiling already, thinking of how to impress all those cool people.

A chill passed over Sullivan's neck as if a blast of air conditioning had rolled out the door of the restaurant onto the sidewalk. He pulled away from Tommy and crossed his arms. The melancholy was settling down like a cold, wet dog on his chest.

Tommy said, "What am I supposed to do? Like, wait for you outside the bar, or what? Hey, are they going to card me? I could get a fake ID."

For several seconds, Sullivan looked at him, unbearably weary. "You know, you really should clean yourself up. It's disgusting. You chew with your mouth open and you have the vocabulary of a twelve-year-old."

Confused, Tommy said, "Hey."

"Yeah. Hey. Like, why don't you shove off? Go play with your Kodak."

After a second, the kid pushed away from the table. "Fuck you, man. You're crazy."

Sullivan watched him through the crowd of pedestrians on the sidewalk, his long, black hair gleaming on his bare shoulders, bouncing with each step. Nice shoulders. Too bad.

He noticed a man at the next table looking at him from behind sunglasses with shiny silver lenses.

Sullivan stared coldly into them for a minute, then turned his chair, closed his eyes, and let the sun pour down on his face.

chapter
SIX

Leaning back with his cowboy boots propped on the edge of the table, Frank Tolin heard the elevator whine to a stop. Then a muffled ding. He went back to the peach yogurt he'd found in Caitlin's refrigerator.

It was quiet here, five floors above the traffic on Collins Avenue. The studio was on the southeast corner of what used to be a stockbroker's office. Light streamed in through the blinds onto an empty expanse of concrete where the carpet had been peeled up. There were lamps on tripods, props and colored backdrops, and a wall of shelves filled with photographic equipment and storage boxes. She had a small darkroom, a kitchenette, and a daybed. Frank's money had paid for it. Caitlin tended to forget that fact.

Taking another spoonful of yogurt, he kept his eyes on the door. A few minutes ago, he'd been gazing out the window to pass the time and had noticed Caitlin talking to Marty Cass down on Lincoln Road. Twenty years as a trial attorney had taught Frank about body language. Now he was wondering whether it had been wise of him to ask Marty to give Caitlin that job. Marty was probably trying to stiff her. He was getting to be a pain in the ass.

Keys jangled at the lock. Frank blotted his mustache on a napkin and set the yogurt aside.

She came in and turned to fasten the deadbolt. A camera swung from her shoulder. She was wearing shorts, and her legs were tanned from the sun. Her streaky blond hair was under a cap, a ponytail sticking out the back.

When she turned around she saw him and jumped.

He smiled at her over the tooled leather toes of his boots. "Boo!"

"Dammit, Frank." She tossed her hat onto an armchair stacked with photography magazines. "I wish you wouldn't just come in here like that."

"Afraid I might catch you at something?"

"Ha-ha." Caitlin set her camera on a workbench by the darkroom door. "I thought you were going to be at my apartment later. Someone wants me to do some head shots at three o'clock, and I really can't stop to talk."

"It's nice to be missed."

"Aww-w-w." She came around the table to kiss him. He didn't respond other than to tilt his face up, wanting to see how much she would put into it.

Not much. It was a friendly peck on the lips.

She patted his shoulder. "Did Tommy Chang come by?"

"He just left. He said to tell you he's taking the film to the lab." Frank watched her go over to the sink to wash her hands and face. Her fanny moved when she worked up the suds. He asked, "How'd the Grand Caribe shoot go?"

"Fine. I think we got some good ones."

"Everything okay with Marty? Did he pay you?"

She dried her hands. "He wasn't there. I'll see him next week for a check."

"You didn't see him today?"

"No." She hung up the towel on a hook. "If I have any problems with Marty, I'll let you know."

Frank smiled. What made her lie like that? It was a challenge, figuring out what she held back, what she would tell him. "Let's go to the Strand tonight," he said. "I've got some clients coming, so wear something nice. The blue dress I bought you. My suit's in my car. I'll change at your place."

She stood with a hand on her hip as if she was going to say something, then shook her head. He knew what that was about. She didn't want him making himself at home in her apartment. They had already had that argument more than once, and he didn't want to start it up again. He decided not to remind her that he owned the building and she didn't pay a dime in rent.

He said, "If you don't mind."

She shook her head, then leaned over to unload the cart her assistant had brought up. Frank noticed the broken vein on the back of her left thigh. And she was getting lines around her eyes. Her body wasn't as firm as it used to be either, but none of that mattered to him. Caitlin Dorn was still a beauty. Eight years ago he had met her at a party for the production staff of *Miami Vice*, and her smile had nearly knocked him out. Some of his friends dated younger women, often in their early twenties. They went through one after another of these girls. Frank didn't want that. What he and Caitlin had was permanent.

But now and then they'd hit a rough spot, and she'd have to be by herself for a few months. He used to tell himself that an occasional separation kept the relationship fresh, but he was getting tired of this game. Maybe he spoiled her. Caitlin didn't realize how few good men there were out there, especially for women her age. Frank knew he was a good catch. He had a successful law practice. He was healthy and trim, appearing younger than his age, which was forty-seven. He got along with just about everyone, provided they weren't total assholes.

Lately Frank had started thinking about marriage, which he'd sworn never to do again, having been through two of them. Last week, in fact, he was about to suggest that Caitlin move her things into his condo in the Grove, but there were those vibes again, like the small tremors that precede a major earthquake.

Something was going on with her, ever since that model had been raped. Possibly that was bothering Caitlin, but Frank didn't think so. He was afraid it was something else.

About three years ago, during one of their longer separations, he had suspected she was running around. He hired a private investigator and got the story. She'd been cheating on him with Sam Hagen. A double betrayal. Frank had brought Sam into his office a year or two before that, paid him a good salary, and spent considerable effort showing him what a civil trial practice was all about. All as a favor for Sam's wife. Dina Hagen had come to him privately, had told him they were having money problems. Then she mentioned that incident in Vietnam, as if Frank owed Sam for something that had happened when they'd been kids. He could see Sam bragging to Dina about saving Frank Tolin's hide. An embarrassment then, more so now.

Sam Hagen lacked the drive for personal injury work, so he'd gone back to the state attorney's office. Then a few months later he started fooling around with Caitlin. Frank had been so torn up he'd had fantasies about getting out his shotgun and blowing them both to hell. He stayed drunk for a week instead, dosing himself on uppers to get to the office. Then Caitlin came back, as she always did.

Now Frank had reason to think she had seen Sam Hagen again. He dropped his feet to the floor and stood up. His boots echoed on the concrete.

Caitlin was dusting off her telephoto lens, putting it back in its case. He went over and lifted her ponytail, and tickled her neck with his mustache. Smiling, she turned around and kissed him. This one was better.

After a while he drew back far enough to see her face clearly. "I heard the state attorney's office is investigating that rape you saw at the Apocalypse."

"Oh?"

"Marty Cass told me." Frank wound a loose strand of her hair around his finger.

"Yes, I heard the same thing," Caitlin said.

"You didn't tell me." He tugged on the strand of hair.

"Ouch." Wincing, she pulled it out of his grasp. "I just found out, Frank. Just this morning."

"Have you talked to Sam Hagen about it?"

"Sam Hagen? No. Why?"

"He's the prosecutor in charge. You didn't know?" Frank locked his hands behind her waist and pulled her up against him.

"I do know that, yes."

"Marty says Hagen is talking to witnesses. You're a witness. You haven't talked to him?"

"No. I said I hadn't." Those big green eyes of hers

could convey such innocence. "There were other witnesses, better than I." She slipped out of his arms to latch the case on her telephoto. "The best witness told me this morning that he has already given a statement. Maybe I won't have to."

He was curious. "What witness?"

She went around a divider that separated kitchen area from studio to put the camera away. He heard her voice. "Sullivan. Charlie Sullivan. I told you he was there that night."

"Oh, yeah. Superstud."

There was silence; then Caitlin said, "If this gets to trial—"

Frank waited, then asked, "If this gets to trial? What, sweetheart?"

She reappeared. "I don't care about Sullivan, believe me, but if he testifies—" Caitlin turned her green eyes on Frank. "You know about trials, how nasty they can get. This one, particularly. Reporters and private investigators rooting around for anything the slightest bit juicy."

"Like what, Catie?" Her affair with Sam Hagen would be a juicy bit for a defense attorney to discover.

She said, "Like the prime witness being involved with the prosecutor's son."

Frank stared at her. "Give me that again?"

"Charlie Sullivan seduced Matthew." Caitlin took his hands. "Please, Frank. Swear you'll never mention this to anyone."

"Matthew?"

"Yes, Matthew. You must have met him."

"Sure, once or twice, when Sam brought him around to the office. I don't remember him very well." Caitlin gripped his hands tighter, and he said, "No, I won't tell anyone."

She let him go. "Sullivan wouldn't deny it, if anyone asked him. It's nothing to him, but Klaus Ruffini's defense attorney would love to use that information."

"How did you find out?"

"Matthew and I worked together. I did the photos for his book. We got to know each other, and I more or less picked up on what was going on with him. He was only nineteen, and he was so trusting. Oh, God,

Frank. You don't know. Sullivan is such a vampire. Poor Matthew."

"Sam Hagen's boy?" Frank smiled, thinking of the irony. Hagen must have gone ballistic.

Caitlin's face flushed. "It's not humorous in the least. It's awful, what happened to him."

"No, Catie, you surprised me, that's all. Look, this is Miami Beach, not rural Alabama. If Sam Hagen's kid had a thing going with another guy, so what?"

"Frank, you don't understand. Matthew was depressed and confused. Sullivan told him he was a loser, he'd never make it as a model. He died in a motorcycle crash only two weeks later, drunk out of his mind. What does that look like?"

"You mean he did it deliberately? Killed himself?"

"People could think so."

"I guess they could." Frank rubbed her back through her T-shirt, feeling the warmth of her skin through the thin cotton. "I wonder if Sam knows about this."

"I doubt it. Matthew told me they had problems talking to each other. He was intensely afraid of anyone in his family finding out."

Frank spoke softly, his lips against her temple. "Are you worried how Sam would take it?"

She laughed. "Not much bothers Sam Hagen." Then her face emptied. "Well, I shouldn't care, but I do. His only son died. You have a son, Frank. What if he killed himself? It would be horrible. Worse than an accident. And not just for Sam. What about Matthew's mother? Think of it. I mean, there was this person you loved, and then suddenly somebody tells you he was queer, and he killed himself because his boyfriend called him a loser. Or maybe he was a drug addict who couldn't stand himself anymore and ran his motorcycle off the road. Whatever twisted image is thrown in your face, the person you loved is not only dead—he's erased. You have nothing. You don't know who he was or even why he died. I'll tell you about Matthew." Caitlin's eyes suddenly glistened. "He was a good person, Frank. He would have been okay."

She went to make herself busy at her workbench.

Frank stared at her, wondering what the tears were

all about. Then he knew: Caitlin was scared. She was afraid he would find out about her affair with Sam Hagen.

Caitlin said firmly, "I don't want to testify. I've seen what lawyers can do, how they can twist the truth and tear people apart." She laughed. "God knows I don't get into much trouble lately, in my old age, but nobody cares about reformed sinners. They only want to hear about the sins."

With his thumbs hooked in the pockets of his jeans, Frank watched Caitlin rewind the film in her camera, pop open the back, and take it out. Finally he went over and turned her around. "Sweetheart, listen to me. You're working yourself up over nothing. The state attorney's office is going to check it out, then do a no-file. The investigation is to satisfy potential critics, that's all."

She looked at him, wanting to believe him. "How do you know this?"

"Marty told me. He says Hal Delucca has a line to the state attorney." Frank kissed one of her eyes, then the other, tasting salt on his lips. "You know Dade County politics. Anything bad for the tourist industry, it's going to disappear. They can't go after Marquis Lamont or Klaus Ruffini. Don't you worry about it, all right?"

She laid her forehead on his shoulder, and her arms went around him. She needed him. He hugged her tightly. Here they were, the two of them, needing each other. He could be a fool sometimes, forgetting that.

"Oh, Catie. If you knew how much you mean to me." He held her face and kissed her, brushing his mustache across her lips, then kissing her again. He moved his hands over her breasts then down to unsnap the waistband of her shorts.

She stirred. "Frank, there isn't time."

"There's time. I want you so much I could even do it on the floor." He dropped to his knees and hugged her. "Nobody else could love you this much. We belong to each other. Do you believe that, Catie?"

Laughing a little, she pushed her hair off her forehead. "I'd better. Who else would have me?"

"Let's go lie down on your daybed."

"Frank!"

"I mean it." He buried his face in her stomach. "I need you, Catie."

She leaned over, put her cheek on top of his head. "All right. Let me go to the bathroom first, okay?"

"Hurry up." He watched her walk across the room, smile at him from the bathroom door, then go inside. Water ran in the sink. Frank stood up slowly. The concrete floor was damned hard. He pulled his shirt out of his pants, started on his belt buckle. Then he heard a knock at the door. He glared at it. The knock came again, louder.

He went over and opened the door far enough to see through the crack. A tall, skinny girl with curly red hair was standing there with her hands twisting at her waist. Long, thin legs sticking out of a little dress.

"What do you want?"

The girl blinked. "Is Caitlin here?"

"Who are you?"

"Ali."

He knew his tone was surly. "Ali what, sweetheart?"

"Duncan. Is she here?"

It came to him. The rape victim. No makeup, skin you could see the veins through, collarbones like coat hangers. He couldn't imagine doing it with a girl like this. She looked fourteen. The men must have been on drugs.

The girl's wide blue eyes shifted to a spot behind him. Caitlin was there, curious, smoothing her hair down.

"Ali!" Nearly shoving Frank aside, she drew the girl into the studio. "I called and called. Where have you been?"

The girl glanced at Frank, then back at Caitlin. "I have to talk to you," she said.

"Sure. This is my friend, Frank Tolin."

"Hi." The girl couldn't seem to get her voice out.

Caitlin mouthed *please* at Frank. He gave her a stern look, then smiled. "I'll just go over there by the windows. You girls chat away. Don't mind me." His boot heels thudded on the concrete. He stood by the row of windows. Waited. There was whispered conversation behind one of the dividers. Then a sob. Beyond the windows, the low roofs and white buildings of South Beach shone in the sun, and light fell in a long rectangle cut by slanting shadows. He looked at his watch.

Finally, Caitlin led Ali to the door and closed it softly behind her. She didn't lock it. She came across the studio to where Frank leaned against a window sill, arms crossed.

She said, "I asked her to wait outside for a minute. They called her yesterday from the state attorney's office. They want to see her."

"Now?"

"Monday. She's so scared. She wants to talk to me about it."

"And who are *they*? Sam Hagen?"

Caitlin hesitated before nodding. "I'll probably go with her."

Frank was outraged. He said calmly, "I told you. The case won't be filed. You don't have to become involved in this. Tell her to go home."

"No. She can't leave in her condition, Frank. Ali is extremely upset."

"What about me? I don't count? I'm upset."

She looked toward the ceiling, exhaling. "Frank. For God's sake."

Frank smiled. "Okay. You go ahead and talk to your friend. I'm out of here."

She said coldly, "I'll be home by six." Not giving a shit if he stuck around or not.

He said, "No. Don't rush. Spend all the time you need with this little whore. You're another one."

"Damn you, don't say that!"

He tucked in his shirt, and his hands were shaking. He had trouble getting his buckle fastened. "What were you doing at the Apocalypse that night?"

She glared at him. "I told you. Freelancing for a magazine. You want me to show you the damned pictures?"

With a forefinger he flipped the end of her nose. She dodged away. "Did you do some lines? Get a little high? Won't do it with Frank anymore."

"Stop it, Frank."

He grabbed her wrist, jerking her toward him. "George

Fonseca gives the stuff away at those parties. You didn't ask for a taste?"

"No!"

"Hell, I don't know what you do." He poked her shoulder with stiff fingers. She bumped into the divider, which rocked on its base. He closed in, poking her again. "I don't know who you go out with. If you're getting laid behind my back."

"Shut up!"

He grabbed her upper arms. "I can't trust you, and that tears me up inside." He shook her. "I'd share everything I have with you, because I'm crazy enough to love you, but what do I get in return? What?"

He shoved her away, got a few paces, then turned around and walked back to where she stood. She flinched, but he didn't touch her. His voice was quiet now, under control. "You know, you really ought to take a good look at yourself, sweetheart. I'm telling you. This is sad. You're thirty-five years old. No college degree. Too old to model anymore. Now you want to be a photographer, like everybody else on South Beach with a camera. You can't keep up with the rent on this studio, and you don't pay a dime for your apartment. Wake up! You're living in a fantasy world, and you want me to subsidize it."

She was crying. Her nose was red, and her face was crumpled. Ugly now, looking old and ugly. He wanted to hit her, feel the release of it. Then suddenly he was relenting, giving in, his feet on quicksand. "Oh, God. Honey, I'm sorry."

She turned away, weeping.

"Come here." He took her in his arms. "Come on, now. I'm sorry if I lost my temper, babe." She struggled a little, then finally went limp on his shoulder.

"I wanted to make love to you, Catie. That's all. You make me want you, then you shut me out. It makes me think you don't love me anymore. You do love me, don't you?" He tilted her head back and looked at her. "Catie? Please. Don't you love me?"

"Oh, Frank. I can't stand this."

"Say it. For me?" He kissed her forehead. "You're tearing me apart." His throat was tight. "Please. Say it, Catie."

Her eyes closed. "I love you, Frank."

"And I love you. More than anyone. Or anything in this world. I'll never leave you, I swear it." He held her tightly, stroking her back. "We're stuck with each other, Catie. Ain't nothing we can do about it."

c h a p t e r

seven

Eugene Ryabin, a homicide detective with the Miami Beach Police Department, sat by the window in Sam Hagen's office smoking. Ryabin was waiting to be called across the street to testify in the strangulation murder of a transvestite prostitute, a young Puerto Rican who called himself Monique when he worked the area around Fifteenth and Collins. "With such a body, even you he would have fooled."

Ryabin was a compact, white-haired man in his midfifties, with sloping shoulders and an expression of weary bemusement. His skin was pale and lined, with pouches around his eyes and the blue sheen of beard under a close, cologne-scented shave. Gold cufflinks twinkled at the cuffs of his starched shirt, and a semiautomatic pistol rested in a holster at his waist. His suit coat, arms neatly aligned, lay across a stack of cardboard boxes containing files for a contract killing Sam was taking to trial in a week.

He had dropped by to see what was happening with the Duncan sexual battery case. Sam told him that the victim was due to show up at two o'clock that afternoon. His latest message on her answering machine, after a week of messages, had threatened to have the police bring her in if she didn't come on her own. It had been Sam's experience that victims who avoided the prosecutor were usually lying.

Considering that for a moment, Ryabin said, "Do you want an opinion?"

"Please."

"My opinion is she's not lying."

Sam asked, "Did she ever get picked up for prostitution? Drunk and disorderly? Possession of drugs?" To each, Ryabin shook his head. Nothing on the Beach, that he knew of. Sam said, "I've ordered her juvenile records."

"This is the victim, may I remind you?"

Sam asked Ryabin what he thought of Alice Duncan.

Ryabin tilted open the window to let out the smoke. A truck ground its gears in the street below. He said, "Ambitious. Smart, but not as smart as she thinks. She left home at sixteen, and earned a high school degree at night. Her parents are divorced. She comes from the suburbs west of Fort Lauderdale. Have you been up there, Sam? So many shopping malls and subdivisions and houses the same as the next, and landscaped walls around them. Miami Beach to a girl like that would be paradise."

Several years ago in the Club Deuce, back when it was seedy instead of tame, Ryabin, sipping a fourth glass of beer, had told Sam how he himself happened to be on Miami Beach. He was not Russian, bite your tongue, but Ukrainian, born Yevgeny Ryabin in the city of Odessa, which, as a seaport with an established criminal class, offered certain opportunities for a clever young man. Yevgeny—Zhenya to his friends—became a *fardzovshik*, a low-level black marketeer. Even so, life was not easy. In 1972, with Jews getting out on special invitations to Israel, he arranged for a Jewish wife. He paid the equivalent of $5,000 for Anna Levitsky, daughter of a poor, intellectual family (such families were nearly always poor). As soon as the system had spit out the paperwork, Zhenya left the Soviet Union with his bride and her sister and their widowed mother. To his surprise, he grew fond of these three women, his new family. They settled near the Golan Heights, where he learned to drive a tractor and shoot at Syrians.

In 1982 his mother-in-law, who with Anna's sister had

gone to live in Miami Beach, was robbed and brutally beaten. She died a week later, her daughters and son-in-law at her side. The suspect was a criminal from a Cuban prison, sent by Castro in the Mariel boatlift, one of dozens of such men who settled on South Beach, which was then in a state of decay. The police sought him until his body turned up in Flamingo Park, neatly garroted. It was assumed, but never proved, that one of the local drug dealers had done it.

Ryabin and his wife stayed in the U.S. with her sister. He changed his name to Eugene, polished his English, and joined the police department. *Better the sands of Miami Beach than the sand of the Negev,* he had told Sam. *It's great here. A piece of cake.*

Now he was looking at Sam over the glowing tip of his cigarette. "What do the witnesses tell you?"

"Depends on whose side they're on," Sam said. "You listed nine of them. Two haven't returned my calls. So far I've spoken to five others. Three now swear they didn't see anything. One is sure she heard Ms. Duncan say she wanted to have sex with Marquis Lamont. A British male model says she was attacked. He's convincing, but I get the feeling he'd like to nail Ruffini. His name's Charlie Sullivan. What did you think when you interviewed him?"

"The same. But a lot of people would like to see Klaus Ruffini go down, if only for amusement. The Beach loves gossip, and what happened at the Apocalypse is on everyone's mind. The best gossip of the season."

"What can you tell me about Ruffini?"

"Besides the gossip?" Ryabin's grin revealed the gap between his front teeth, which were stained with nicotine. "He's a generous man. Last Christmas he sent baskets to the Jewish Home for the Aged. This is true. Swiss chocolates, wine, cheese, paté. He gave the city library a check for a hundred grand. The mayor made a speech, how lucky we are to have Klaus Ruffini in our town. And to the Police Athletic League he gave I believe fifty thousand dollars. For this he can make illegal U-turns and park in handicapped zones."

Ryabin blew a stream of smoke toward the crack in the window. "Last week," he said, "I went to Ruffini's house and had a conversation with the intercom at the gate. He's deeply hurt to be the victim of false accusations. Maybe Alice Duncan wants revenge because he didn't agree to hire her as a model. Then he said I should call his attorney. The same from George Fonseca and Marquis Lamont. Fonseca said to me, 'You're a detective. Go detect.' " Ryabin exhaled a smoky sigh. "It makes me nostalgic for Odessa. People were more cooperative there."

Sam smiled. "All right. They deserve to be prosecuted. So do a lot of people." He gestured toward the files stacked on his desk, laid out across the sofa, and packed in boxes on the floor. "I'm supervising fifty or sixty cases, eight of which are set for jury trial this week. If this one washes out, I'm not going to cry about it."

At the sound of a knock on the door, Sam swiveled around. "Come in."

It was Joe McGee, holding half a guava pastry, flakes of crust dotting his tie. He said, "Got a message for you from Adela Ramos." He lifted a hand toward Ryabin. "*Zdrastye*, comrade."

"*Buenos días,*" said Ryabin.

"You know about Ramos, right?"

Ryabin nodded slowly. "The child whose stepfather threw him from the window."

"Yeah, but Adela Ramos, the kid's mother, never married the guy." Chewing the last of the pastry, McGee wiped his mouth, then said to Sam, "She called this morning, had a neighbor on the line to translate. You were in a meeting, so Gloria put the call through to me. Seems like an acquittal wasn't good enough for Balmaseda. The prick's been following her. He calls her at work, says stuff like, 'You bitch, you think you can talk like that about me.' I told her to get a restraining order and meanwhile stay low till he cools off. Woman's petrified."

Ryabin smiled, cigarette at his lips. "Tell her to buy a gun."

"I'll call her," Sam said. "Make sure I've got her number. Gene, where is she living now, do you know?" It hadn't been Ryabin's case, but the entire department knew about it.

"I think with the brother, who has an apartment on Eighth Street, not far from the station. I'll send someone to check on her."

McGee paused at the door and said to Sam, "You want to grab lunch? We're doing Chinese."

"Can't today," Sam said. "I'm meeting my wife downtown."

After the door closed, Ryabin looked across the office at him. "How is Dina?" he asked gently.

This was more than a polite inquiry. Ryabin had visited her at the hospital a few times. Sam didn't know what to say except, "Better. She's working again. I'll tell her you asked about her."

Ryabin nodded.

When Dina had called an hour ago she hadn't told Sam why she needed to talk to him in the middle of the day, only that it was important. When he said he had no time for lunch, a sigh had come over the line. *Please, Sam. I have to see you.*

Sam pushed himself out of his chair. "Give me a call tomorrow on Duncan. I should know by then what we're going to do."

Ryabin didn't get up. Extending an arm toward the windowsill, he tapped ashes into his Styrofoam coffee cup. "I'm noticing a strange thing, Sam. The physical evidence is still in the property room. Usually by now it would be in the lab for analysis. Blood type, hair samples, semen. But the lieutenant said never mind. I said, 'What do you mean?' He told me never mind sending the evidence to the lab. It would be a waste of time because the case wouldn't be filed."

"Why did he say that?"

Ryabin shrugged. "I asked. He said I could take it up with the captain if I didn't like it. What can I think, Sam? Only that the captain will send me to the chief—unless he first tells me to go to hell. I'm not crazy enough to ask Chief Mazik where he's getting such information." Ryabin took a final drag off his cigarette and dropped it into the cup, where it hissed briefly in the remaining coffee and went out.

"He didn't get it from me," Sam said.

"From who, then?"

"Try the city manager. Hal Delucca called Eddie Mora last week and said he wanted this case to go away. Apparently Delucca likes to take care of his VIPs over there. Eddie told him forget it, then asked me to check it out." Sam spread his arms. "It's my sterling reputation, Gene. Nobody can accuse the state attorney of being pressured not to prosecute. You don't have to repeat that."

"No, of course not." Frowning, Ryabin pulled on his earlobe.

Sam had told Dina that Eddie might leave the office. The only other person he would trust with that information was sitting in this room, but Sam knew how Ryabin might see it: the head of Major Crimes putting his seal of approval on a no-action in exchange for Eddie's job. It wasn't that way, but it bothered Sam enough to make him ask a question.

"Have you heard any talk about Eddie Mora and Hal Delucca?"

Ryabin raised his eyes, pale blue under heavy brows, deep lines at the corners. "Talk about what?"

"Connections."

"No. I don't like either of them. Is that enough in common? Why are you asking this?"

"Just being careful. If I tell your department not to file charges, I don't want to find out later that somebody benefitted."

"Somebody who? Eddie Mora?"

"Anybody. The Tourist Commission. The fashion industry. The Miami Film Bureau. Or any of our three subjects." Sam laughed, leaning back into his chair. "How much do you think they've already paid Alice Duncan to come in here and tell me it was all a misunderstanding? 'No, no, Mr. Hagen, please don't make me testify. I didn't mean it.'"

Dropping his coffee cup into the basket beside Sam's desk, Ryabin said, "What if she says otherwise?"

"Come on, Gene. I had to twist her arm to get her here today."

The street noises faded when Ryabin pushed shut the bottom section of the metal-framed window. He lifted his jacket off the stack of boxes and brushed some dust off a sleeve.

"You know, Sam, if you visit South Beach, and you have money, you expect certain things. Marquis Lamont and his friends, they're in town making a movie. They want to have a good time, so they go out to a club. Klaus Ruffini and his friends go also. The clubs fill up if everyone thinks important people are there. This is how George Fonseca earns his living. He fills the clubs. The owners give him a percentage, and Fonseca gives the VIPs what they want so they'll show up. Drinks, food, music. Girls. The models get in free. And maybe not always girls. You want a boy, okay. Or maybe some cocaine so you can feel good at three o'clock in the morning. PCP, speed, heroin, whatever you want. Enjoy the hospitality. Is this a crime? No, it's a party. All private. Who does it hurt?"

Slipping one arm into his neatly pressed jacket, then the other, Ryabin said, "I know that George Fonseca has friends in organized crime. I know that he distributes drugs in some of the nightclubs. We used to have in the budget money for special undercover units. I myself would see bags of cocaine in plain sight. Not now. We stay out of the clubs. The city wants us to chase the kids from Hialeah and Liberty City who come over to snatch purses, and the thieves who prey on the tourists. Real crime."

"Gene, I can't file a case to make a point."

With a smile, Ryabin said, "Am I preaching? You should tell me to be quiet." He buttoned his jacket over his pistol and adjusted his cuffs.

"All right," Sam said. "Go ahead and send the evidence to the lab. Say I told you to. If you get any heat, call me."

The gap appeared between Ryabin's front teeth. "Maybe we should send it to Metro-Dade."

The Beach police had a crime scene unit, but the county's was more sophisticated—and possibly more secure. Apparently, Ryabin was concerned about it. Sam said, "Whatever. Metro-Dade. Look, even if we get a warrant to take samples from all three guys, and we get DNA matches on swabs from the victim, we've still got consent to worry about. We might prove they had sex with her. It's harder to prove she didn't let them do it."

At the door, Ryabin stood looking into the mauve-carpeted corridor for a moment. Then his eyes shifted back to Sam. "Don't judge her too quickly. You don't like South Beach. The party life, what goes on there. This I can understand. But don't judge her too quickly, Sam."

Eugene Ryabin often spoke in a roundabout way, so that his words, beyond their apparent meaning, carried subtleties that only those who knew the context could discern. The listener would hear the obvious, and then, like the grumble of thunder following a distant flicker of lightning, would come rolling echoes of comprehension.

It was only after Sam was back at his desk with a deposition transcript in another case that he realized that Ryabin had been talking about Matthew.

Close to noon, Sam's secretary stopped him on his way past her cubicle. She had a batch of papers for him to sign. He checked his watch, then felt his pockets for a pen. She gave him one, and he leaned over her desk. The secretarial furniture was modern, sleek, and speckled gray. Gloria's work space was jammed with lopsided craft projects her various grandchildren had made. Their faces smiled from a garden of tiny photo frames.

Sam was supposed to have his own secretary but instead shared Gloria Potter with two other attorneys in Major Crimes, the budget being what it was.

"Joe McGee left Adela Ramos's number for you," Gloria said.

"All right, let me have it." Sam shifted the pen to a better position and scrawled his signature, which consisted of cramped initials ending in straight horizontal lines. His thumb was aching today.

Gloria patted a little yellow note onto his coat sleeve. "Here. And Vicky Duran wants to see you."

"I don't have time. I've got lunch downtown with Dina."

Sam went around an upholstered partition to the next

desk, sat in the empty chair, and punched in the number for Adela Ramos.

Not a damn thing he could do for the woman, he thought, leaning his forehead on extended fingers. The phone purred in his ear. The system had fucked her over. No, not the system. A bad call. The weight of his decision from last week bore down on him. He could make sure the police kept an eye on Luis Balmaseda. Arrest Balmaseda for stalking if it got bad; throw his ass in jail.

"Sam."

He looked up. Beekie.

Victoria Duran came around the partition and stood over him. Bright green suit with black buttons. Auburn hair. Colorful as a parrot. Sam held up a hand, listened through another ring, then replaced the receiver.

Gloria had gone to the copy machine. Her cardigan sweater hung over the back of her chair. Beekie spun the chair around and sat down. She crossed her impressive legs. They shone in sheer hose from thigh to open-toed pumps.

"Do we have a decision on the alleged sexual battery case?"

"The alleged victim is coming in at two o'clock," Sam said.

"Because Eddie is getting phone calls," Beekie said, her eyes going momentarily toward the corridor. "Reporters, the attorney for Klaus Ruffini, Lamont's producer. I told them you're handling the case. They say they called, but you don't call back."

"As soon as I have something to tell them, I will. For now, we're still looking into it." Sam stood up. "Sorry, Vicky, I've got an appointment."

"Wait a minute." She reached up from her chair to stop him. "I asked Dale Finley to help you out. He can do the background checks, collect evidence, whatever you need."

Finley was an investigator for the state attorney's office, hired by Eddie Mora a couple of years ago. The story was Dale Finley had worked for the CIA, got busted in Havana, and spent some hard years in Combinado del Este prison before being exchanged for a Cuban spy grabbed in Panama.

"I don't recall asking for backup," Sam said. "Whose idea was this? Eddie's?"

"Mine."

"Isn't that outside your job description, Beekie?"

Her back stiffened. "I want to help you, okay?"

"Why is that?"

"Are you trying to be rude?"

"No, I'm just curious why you care."

"I care that this matter isn't mishandled."

Sam patted her shoulder, his hand bouncing a little on the jutting shoulder pad. "Thanks for the vote of confidence. Tell Dale Finley I don't need him."

"He would go straight to Eddie. I already told Eddie that Finley is working with you. What would he think? You'll make yourself look bad."

Halfway to the corridor, Sam turned slowly around. "Vicky, pay attention. Stay out of this. If at some point I need Dale Finley, I will talk to him."

Under the already vivid powder on her cheeks, Victoria Duran's color heightened. She uncrossed her legs and stood up next to him. Sam could see the reddish sun blotches on her chest, the skin wrinkling a bit at the cleavage. She spoke in a low voice. "I told Eddie to turn the case over to someone in the sexual battery unit. Treat it more like a routine matter, which it is. If we give it to the head of Major Crimes, people will wonder why such a heavy gun. But he trusts you. So I said, 'Okay, have it your way, Eddie.' But Sam, you've had this over a week. People are asking questions. Don't make it into something it's not. I know what you think of Eddie. He took your job. Don't stab him in the back."

Holding back a laugh, Sam realized that Vicky Duran's feelings for the state attorney went way beyond professional. The poor woman was in love with him.

She had her fingers clamped around Sam's coat sleeve now, like talons, digging in when he started to move. "Don't. If you ruin his chances, Sam, you won't be happy working here."

He raised his eyes to hers and she dropped his sleeve.

He came in closer, conscious of his size, and of her moving backward a step, bumping the desk. He said quietly, "Better hope he takes you with him, Vicky."

Sam was twenty minutes late meeting Dina for lunch. She had chosen the restaurant downstairs from her accounting firm, a walnut-paneled place with a three-tiered salad bar and classical music coming out of hidden speakers. Walking in, smoothing his wind-blown hair, Sam bypassed the maitre d' and went to Dina's table, located to one side under a painting of a Bahamian fishing village.

The waiter came over and he ordered iced tea, nothing else.

Dina's lunch was already on the table, a fillet of grilled fish. She had eaten it into a square, apparently, then had cut off the corners to make a perfect octagon.

Sam asked, "What's up?"

"Thank you for tearing yourself away from the office," Dina said.

"Sorry. I got here as soon as I could. Are you okay?"

"Yes, fine." Her olive green suit made her skin sallow, and the brown shadows beneath her eyes might have been painted on. She stirred cream into her coffee. "I was thinking of going to Tarpon Springs next weekend. Would you mind?"

He smiled a little, trying not to show his annoyance. He turned the cut-glass salt shaker around and around. "Dina, I told you. I have a trial starting Monday."

"I know that," she said. "I don't expect you to go with me. I'll fly to Tampa. Nick can meet me at the airport. He says Dad's a little better. He was asking for me the other day." Her mouth twisted into a smile. "*Pou ineh i Constandina?* Maybe this time he'll remember who I am when he sees me."

She'd last been in Tarpon Springs at Easter, a month and a half ago, but not only to visit her father. Nick had told Sam that whenever Dina went home she would pick up some potted flowers from his nursery and take them out to the cemetery.

The waiter brought iced tea in a frosted glass. A thin wedge of lime sat on the rim.

Sam said, "Sure. Go ahead. You want to take Melanie along?"

Dina shook her head.

"That's fine. We'll make do." He tore open a blue pack of fake sugar and stirred it into the tea. He didn't know what she wanted him to say. "Go up anytime you like. You don't have to ask my permission."

As he lifted the glass he noticed the way her attention seemed focused on a spot past his chair. "What's the matter, Dina?"

She shifted her eyes to his, then said, "I've made an appointment with Frank Tolin for five-thirty this afternoon, for both of us. Frank will tell us if we have grounds to file a lawsuit for wrongful death."

Carefully he replaced his glass on the table.

Dina smiled, then said, "I believe that is the correct term, isn't it? Wrongful death?"

His mind finally caught up to the meaning of the words. "A *lawsuit*? Against *whom*, for God's sake?"

"The bar where Matthew had been drinking. He wasn't twenty-one. He didn't have an ID, even a false one. They broke the law, and they should be held accountable. We can sue Harley-Davidson if there was a defect in his motorcycle. And the city of Miami Beach. Did anyone ever ask if the road was properly maintained? And what about the owner of the truck? It was changing lanes—"

"Hold it." Sam lifted his hands. "When did you see Frank Tolin?"

"I haven't yet. I called him this morning, we discussed it briefly over the telephone, and he said to come in. Five-thirty is the only time he has available till next week. You're not in trial this afternoon. There's no reason we can't go."

"I can't believe this."

Dina asked, "Do you have some objections to Frank Tolin? I've noticed that since you left his office you never mention his name."

"You want to sue Harley-Davidson?"

"The motorcycle is still around. We can have it examined. A friend of Matthew's bought it, and it's still in his garage till he finds the money to—"

"Forget it."

Her dark eyes were on him, accusing.

"Dina. Listen to me." He dropped his hand over hers, which stiffened under his fingers. "Honey. Whatever Frank told you over the phone, if we file a lawsuit—which I can't imagine he'd advise us to do—the chances of winning, much less collecting damages—"

"I don't give a damn about the money. It's the principle. People can't be allowed to get away with this."

"With *what*?"

"With destroying our son. What was his death if not wrongful? And Matthew wasn't the only one destroyed. What about us? You're morose and edgy. Melanie's grades are terrible. My career is in tatters."

"Dina, I am familiar with personal injury law. We are not—"

"You've never done a wrongful death case. Have you?"

He spoke slowly, his forefinger accenting the words. "We are not going to spend money we do not have to file a lawsuit begging a jury to compensate us for an accident caused by the negligence of a nineteen-year-old who chose to drink, who chose to exceed the speed limit on a souped up, fifteen-thousand-dollar motorcycle at four o'clock in the—"

"He didn't choose the result."

"No. He didn't. That was just tough luck. He's not around to see the consequences, but we are. And that's our tough luck. I'm not going to lay the blame on somebody else. There's already too goddamn much of that these days." Sam picked up his tea, then put it down. He turned sideways in his chair and forced his breathing to slow.

When he glanced at her again, Dina said, "You're worried how it might appear, I suppose. What people would say if the next state attorney for Dade County sued the city of Miami Beach—"

His angry, warning look stopped her in midsentence. Then he added quietly, "The answer is no."

"You astonish me," she said. "Your only son is gone and it causes barely a ripple. You'll show someone his picture in our photo album next year, or in ten years, and say, 'This was our son Matthew.' And they say, 'Oh.

What a shame.' Yes. What a shame. Tell me, Sam. Is it that you didn't care, or are you afraid to admit you loved him?"

Sam swirled the ice in his tea, then took a swallow. "Great set of alternatives you're giving me. I'm either an unfeeling bastard or a total coward." As he watched, the color drained from her face, and she stiffened, hugging her arms over her chest. "Dina?"

She turned her cheek away from his hand and took a deep breath, then another. Her voice, when it came, was calm. She smiled. "You know, Sam, I grew up believing in God. It's easy to do if nothing bad has happened. Well, here's what I think, now that I'm older and presumably wiser: If there is a God, he got bored with us a long time ago, and now he's busy elsewhere. The innocent perish and the wicked are raised up, but don't wait for the Almighty to balance the accounts. I don't know if there's eternal justice or not, but I can tell you this. Here on earth we'd better make our own. That's what you do, isn't it, Sam? Hand out justice, or try to. Your own substitute for God. Well, guess what? Our son is dead. And the funny thing is we're dying, too, and you just don't care."

Laughing suddenly, she raised her fingers to her lips. "I said it. Dead. Usually I can't get the word past my teeth. Matthew is dead. His flesh is rotting in a coffin, and by God some point should be made of it. He is *dead*. I wish you would acknowledge that fact. And I would dearly love it if someone would simply say, 'I'm sorry.'" Her eyes gleamed with tears.

He took her hand. "Dina, no. You think a lawsuit will fix everything. Believe me, it won't. Let me call Dr. Berman."

Her smile wavered. "I have tried Dr. Berman. I have taken the pills he prescribed. I have said prayers to a God in whom I no longer believe. I have considered going back to Tarpon Springs to live. I have even thought of not living at all. That would be effective, certainly, but a little extreme."

"Oh, Jesus." Sam leaned on an elbow, knuckles supporting his cheek, which had grown some stubble since he had shaved at five-thirty this morning.

"I want—need—a resolution. I don't know what will happen after I talk to Frank, but I'm going to keep that appointment, whether you go with me or not."

Sam could see it: Dina sitting in the leather wing chair in Frank Tolin's office, weeping. Sam had never shown much pity during Matthew's life. He had yelled at Matthew, then at Dina for taking Matthew's side, the two of them forming an alliance against him. And Sam was still demanding that she make a choice: her husband or her son. It wasn't fair.

"All right," Sam said. "I'll go with you."

"No." She aligned the corners of her napkin and smoothed it flat on the table. "You've told me how you feel. Tonight—if you have time, or if you're interested—I'll tell you what Frank said."

"Jesus. You wanted me to go. I'm saying I will."

Anger flashed across her face. "Is it too much to ask that you treat me as a wife, rather than as another of your obligations?"

Stunned, he didn't reply.

For an instant her emotions seemed to hang like a stone at its apogee, then her features sank into something like despair. "I love you, Sam."

He nodded. "I love you, too, Dina."

She laughed self-consciously, picked up her purse from the adjacent chair, then held it in her lap, studying the gold clasp. "We nearly lost each other once, didn't we? I wish I knew why; I'd fix it. I've been a terrible mother to Melanie and such a burden to you."

"No. Don't say that."

"Have we lost each other, Sam?"

"How could we?"

"Why do I feel it, then? As if you're somewhere else?"

"I'm not. I'm right here."

Her dark, shadowed eyes lifted to his. "Sam, please. Don't lie to me. I've been your wife for twenty-two years. Do you think I don't know what's in your heart? Come with me if you want, or not. But please, don't lie to me anymore."

c h a p t e r
eight

"**C**ome on, baby. Open up."

"I'm not letting you in." Ali snapped her cigarette out of her mouth and blew smoke toward the door. The white paint chipping off around the bottom showed a pukey shade of pink underneath. Dark smudges circled the deadbolt and doorknob. Her roommates were pigs. It was weird, she thought, how she'd never noticed it before.

"Don't make me stand out here in the hall, Ali. I'm not gonna hurt you. I want to talk, that's all, I promise."

"Forget it, George." Through the window she had seen him jumping out of his Mustang convertible. Strutting up the walk in his fucking Tommy Hilfiger shirt, trying to look good. Like it would matter.

"I'm sorry for what happened. Jesus, if I could take back that whole night. I was totally wasted. I didn't know what was going on."

"Yeah, right. I was crying, you asshole. Were you *blind*?"

"You let me do it, Ali. You wanted me to."

"In front of God and the world? With *three* guys?" Ali made a little scream of frustration. "I didn't even want it with *you*! What do you think I am?"

"Okay, okay. Look, I can understand being mad, but you're overreacting. You want the police to arrest me, put me in prison the rest of my life? If I'd been the only one, would you be doing this?"

"Shut up, George."

"No. You wouldn't. So it's not me you're mad at." There was a silence; then he said, "Maybe you don't believe this now, but I swear to you, Ali, I swear on . . . on anything holy you could name that I care about you. I've been out with other women, but you've always been special, baby doll."

She laughed. "That is so pathetic. George, go away. Caitlin will be here any minute. And the police are coming, too. They're escorting me, so you'd better leave."

George knew she was going to the state attorney's office. Ali had told him when he called her half an hour ago. She wouldn't have answered but the caller-ID showed her agency's number. He had used their phone, the fucker, and now here he was. It was true about Caitlin, but not about the police escort.

"Go away!"

A low moan came through the crack at the door frame, like his lips were pressed to it. "If I could explain to you, tell you straight to your face how sorry I am. Take your hand. Like friends. Haven't we been friends, at least? Please, I'm begging you."

The sound of his voice descended toward the floor, followed by a thud. "Jesus, I don't believe this. I'm on my knees to you, woman. Ali, I was stoned. We were making love, then Marquis pushed me out of the way—"

"You held me down, you shit." Ali rushed forward and slammed her fist on the door. "Then you let Marquis Lamont do it to me. And then Klaus, who is even *worse*! I had to have stitches, and don't you *dare* tell me it wasn't your fault!"

Eyes stinging, she ran across the small living room and grabbed a kitchen towel off the back of a chrome-legged chair. She pressed her face into the cloth and cried. The towel was damp and reeked sourly. She hurled it into the sink, where it sank in dishwater and sent a palmetto bug scrabbling across the counter. Ali went to the faded plaid sofa and dropped heavily on one end of it, drawing up her knees and resting her cheek on them. She remembered a year ago, carrying up her boxes and her new clothes, the apartment shiny as in a TV ad with a housewife holding a mop and smiling at her kitchen floor.

"Are you crying, Ali?" She heard a soft knock. "Hey. Are you all right? Oh, baby. You're in there alone, forgetting all the good times we had. Remember Key West? Ali? It was great, wasn't it? Don't throw it all away. Jesus, I'm *sorry*!"

Lighting a cigarette, she watched the door. George Fonseca out there begging. Sounding like he meant it. She wondered if the prosecutor, Samuel Hagen, could sue just Marquis and Klaus. Put them in jail and threaten George, something like that. Make him really sorry. When they were going out George didn't used to be so horrible. She wondered if he had changed, or if he'd always been a total sleazewad.

"Ali, please—" She heard footsteps coming up the stairs, a pause, then George mumbling, "Hi. Just waiting for Ali."

He must have gotten to his feet. The landing out there was small, with stained green carpet and two doors leading off it. A Mexican couple lived across the hall. Ali heard keys jingling, then a soap opera on Spanish radio turned way up, then a door closing. The neighbor was illegal, so he wasn't likely to call the cops. Not that Ali was afraid of George Fonseca. In all the time they'd gone out, he'd been nice. Until that night at the Apocalypse.

She pawed through her black leather backpack for a mirror and checked her makeup. She wet the tip of her forefinger and rubbed away the splotches of mascara under her eyes.

George said, "Ali? You listening? I talked to Marquis. I said, 'Marquis, maybe you could get Ali a part in that movie.' And he said, 'Sure, tell her to come see me.'"

"You're a liar," Ali said. She tossed her compact into her bag. "The stars don't hire people, and Marquis Lamont isn't even a star. And it's a low-budget flick anyway. Terrorists taking over a cruise ship. How lame."

"Baby doll, you're being stupid here. I mean, you're

not thinking this through. Okay, forget Marquis. You're a model. Klaus Ruffini could get you some bookings. Think about it."

"I have. He's a total turd." She added, "Worse than you, George." She picked up her cigarette from where she had laid it across an empty Diet Coke can. Crossed her legs, swung her foot. Waited. Maybe she could forgive him after all, depending on how long he groveled.

There were dull thuds on the door, as if George was banging his forehead on it. "What the hell do you want?"

She screamed, "You do not give me to your friends, George! You do not screw me in front of a roomful of people. Nobody does that to me!"

"I fucking said I was sorry, for God's sake!"

"Sorry you got caught! Sorry you might go to jail!"

She could hear him breathing.

Finally he said, "I don't have any money, if that's what you're after."

"Fuck you. Who asked you for money?"

"Listen to me. Klaus might be a turd, but he's a very rich turd. He'd pay you to drop this. He would. I could talk to him."

Eyes closing, Ali dropped her head to the back of the sofa and groaned.

"Let me in, I'll call him right now."

"I said no." She got up and stood by the window, parting the dusty miniblinds to see out. Where the hell was Caitlin? Ali glanced at her watch. Twelve-forty-five already. They'd be late.

George was saying, "You've got the man by the shorts, if you'd just realize it. Ali, you know that project on First Street? Grand Caribe? He's into it big time, him and some high rollers. Nobody's gonna let him run it from jail. If he gets hit with a rape charge, he's in deep caca. Use your head for once."

"I am not a *whore*!"

"Go ahead. Make your point. Then what? People talk for a while, then they forget and they're on to the next thing, and where are you? Oh, yeah, the girl that banged three guys in the Apocalypse, what was her name? On the other hand, however, say you snag ten, twenty grand off of Klaus. You go to New York, make him get you some bookings up there. You'd be set. I've learned something about life, baby. If you have money you are never a whore."

Raising the miniblinds, Ali looked both ways along the narrow street. Two guys in nothing but swim trunks and sunglasses rolled by on skates. Still no Caitlin.

The doorknob rattled. "Jesus! Talk to me, will you? I could kick this door down, but I'm trying to be nice." A wooden bang reverberated through the apartment.

Ali watched the lock, hoping it would hold. "Stop it! I'll call 911. I mean it!"

"Yeah? Tell them about that stash your roommate has in her closet." The door groaned and thudded, and Ali backed away. "We're gonna talk one way or the other." The molding creaked.

She sprinted into the tiny kitchen, skidded in her clogs, and threw open a drawer, metal clanging inside. She found a twelve-inch serrated bread knife and sped back across the living room. "Stop that! I've got a knife, a big one. If you come in here, I swear to God I'll kill you!" The door bounced. "Don't! I'll cut you in pieces like dog food!"

A surprised laugh came from the hall. "Jesus. You're such a bitch, you know that? What the fuck, wasting my time." His voice faded, then his footsteps returned. His palm hit the wood and Ali flinched. "You're on coke and you pop heroin. Nobody would believe a word you said."

"And you deal! Everybody knows it. If you don't leave I'll tell the police what you do!" Ali heard the toot of a horn and ran to the window. A blue Toyota was double-parked. With some effort she cranked open the jalousies. "Caitlin!" she yelled through the screen. "Watch out! George is up here!"

"Don't fuck with me, Ali."

His voice was right behind her. She spun around with the knife, ready to strike. But he was on his side of the door, his voice hissing through the crack.

"Some people I know would definitely take exception if you open your mouth about certain matters. Do you understand what I'm saying? I hope you like the Everglades, baby, cause you might be taking a trip out there real soon."

And then his feet were thudding down the stairs.

Flying over MacArthur Causeway bridge, Caitlin checked the rearview mirror again to make sure no one was following. George Fonseca's Mustang had roared out of the parking space at the curb, but she was afraid he had doubled back. He hadn't, and she took a deep breath, trying not to show she was nervous.

In the passenger seat, Ali was reaching up to tap ashes out the partially opened window. Her eyes were obscured by silver-framed sunglasses with lenses the size of quarters, her lips shone with gloss, and her red hair was a flaming cloud around her head. She wore a black miniskirt, patterned thigh-high hose, and a long-sleeved leotard that glimmered like mercury. No bra. Caitlin wondered if she ought to lend Ali her jacket. She herself didn't intend to go upstairs at the state attorney's office, only to wait in the lobby.

Ali smiled through an exhalation of smoke. "George was so pissed off. God, you should've heard him screaming."

"I heard enough." Caitlin looked at her. "Are you stoned?"

"No, but I could use a Xanax." Ali held up her palms. "Kidding! Caitlin, I was kidding. I haven't done anything since that night, honest. I don't know what happened to me, but it's weird. I'm all—" She lifted her hands and splayed her long fingers. "Boing! Wake up!"

Caitlin said, "Could I have a drag off that cigarette?"

"What? No, you said you quit."

"I did, but I'm about to climb out of my skin."

"Really, Caitlin. You shouldn't. They say it gives you wrinkles. Out it goes. Say bye." After a last, deep lungful of smoke, Ali flicked the cigarette through the crack and rolled up the window. "Why did I ever go out with him? I was out of my mind." She shook her head. "That's it. Over. I'm finished with men. They're trouble, that's for sure."

A resolution like that wouldn't last long, Caitlin knew, but at seventeen, Ali needed all the resolve she could get.

"Make sure you tell Sam Hagen everything George said to you. The threats, everything."

"Somebody from his office knocked on my door this morning," Ali said. She opened her bag and rummaged through it.

"Whose office?"

"Mr. Hagen's. I pretended not to be home. He goes, 'Miss Duncan, I know you're in there. Miss Duncan, we need to talk.' It was a creepy old guy with a limp. Not *old* old, but his hair was white. I looked out the window when he left. He was wearing a guayabera, but his name isn't Spanish. He put his card under the door. On the back it says to call him." She held it up. *Dale Finley, Investigator, Office of the State Attorney.*

"Did you call?"

"No way. The detective with the Beach Police—what's his name? With the accent?"

"Detective Ryabin."

"Right. He told me not to talk to anybody—except Sam Hagen."

"That's probably a good idea."

Ali gave a casual shrug. "A reporter from the *New Times* wants to interview me. Plus Channel 7 and the *Miami Herald* left messages. My mom called. She was drunk, as usual. She goes, 'Call *Sixty Minutes*. Call *Inside Edition*.' No way. It would screw up the trial. You hear about that all the time on TV. But maybe after it's over I could sell my story." Ali flipped up the cover on the visor mirror, took off her sunglasses, and checked her makeup. "Should I get a lawyer, do you think? What about Mr. Hagen? Does he do that?"

"No. He's a prosecutor."

"But he's a lawyer, right?"

"Very much so," Caitlin said. "He's yours, but only for the criminal proceedings."

"Brilliant." Watching her image in the mirror, Ali said, "Speak to my lawyer, George. No, Mr. Ruffini, I cannot talk to you. My lawyer advised me against it." She laughed and put her sunglasses back on.

Caitlin said nothing. Ali Duncan was floating on a

giddy rush of excitement, the star in a drama that the rest of the world didn't care about, except as a passing example of sordid excess.

Just two days ago Ali had come trembling to Caitlin's studio, not knowing whether to go back home to her mother or tell the police it was all a mistake. And Caitlin had rushed in with the answer Ali had wanted most of all. *Of course you didn't deserve that. You've done some dumb things, but you're a decent person at heart.* First Ali had sobbed. And then she had become angry.

Glancing now at the girl beside her, Caitlin didn't want to talk her out of it. Ali D. had snapped into a young woman Caitlin had never seen before.

Maybe the case wouldn't be filed at all, if Frank was right about the city manager whispering in the state attorney's ear. But that information had come from Marty Cass, who was hardly reliable. And anyway, Sam Hagen, for all his faults, couldn't be bought. If Ali had the guts to go through with this, Caitlin could, too.

She blew out a little puff of air and resettled her hands on the steering wheel.

And if it came out about her affair with Sam, she would deal with Frank somehow. And if, by some remote chance, anyone learned about Matthew—well, that was in the past as well. It would hurt Sam and Dina to know it, but they could work out their own problems. And nothing could hurt Matthew anymore.

The expressway rose high over the Miami River, over the rusty freighters and boatyards and small white houses with tile roofs. Far to the west, heavy gray clouds were forming over the Everglades, where the sprawl of asphalt and concrete finally ended in wetlands.

"Let me give you a hint about Sam Hagen. I know him. Well, I used to. He practiced law with Frank a few years ago."

"Frank?"

"Frank Tolin. You met him Saturday."

"Oh, yeah. Your boyfriend."

Caitlin glanced at her, then said, "Listen, Ali. Sam isn't going to be impressed by the fact that you're a model. He doesn't like South Beach, the club scene, or the fashion industry."

"Why not?"

"He doesn't, that's all. Be polite, be ladylike, and watch your mouth. Try to be respectful. He'd appreciate that."

Above the sunglasses, little creases appeared in the smooth skin between Ali's eyebrows. "Wait a minute. *I'm* not the one who committed a crime. Why do I have to suck up to the prosecutor? Sam's supposed to be on my side."

"Don't call him Sam. It's Mr. Hagen. He is on your side, but I've seen how you act around people you want to impress—men especially."

"What do you mean, how I act? I don't act."

"Ali, you do. You laugh too loudly and you talk too much. Don't try it with Sam Hagen. He isn't like the people you're used to. He has a low tolerance for bullshit. And you ought to wear something over that shirt. Take my jacket."

"God! I'm nervous enough and now you start criticizing me. How I talk, what I'm wearing. Thanks a lot." Her voice shook.

Caitlin said sharply, "I'm trying to help you."

"Why should you?"

"Well, excuse me to hell and back. I didn't have to drive you over here."

"I didn't ask you to." Ali stared straight through the windshield, thin arms crossed tightly over her chest. "Just drop me off and leave. I can get home by myself."

Caitlin guided the car off the exit ramp. "You'd be somebody's lunch."

They waited at an intersection for the light to turn green. The state attorney's office was in the five-story, salmon-pink building to their right. No one was visible through the heavily tinted glass.

Ali said, "Caitlin? I'm sorry. Okay? I mean, I'm like really scared about this."

Caitlin looked over at her, then reached across the seat. "It'll be okay." She squeezed Ali's hand. The bones seemed as fragile as a kitten's.

"Damn." Ali sucked in a breath. "It won't do any good.

Klaus Ruffini convicted of rape? Like it would ever happen." She laughed shakily. "Or Marquis either. And they'll say George was my boyfriend once, so it wasn't rape at all. I could do what George said and collect a pile of money to shut up about it."

"Is that what you want?"

Ali's head was moving slowly back and forth. She said quietly, "I remember everything they did to me. They think I don't, but I do. They are going to be very sorry they ever saw me."

The light changed, and Caitlin drove past the criminal court building, slowing while people crossed the street. The sky was saturated with blue.

"Ali—what I told you about how to deal with Sam Hagen? Never mind. Just tell him what happened. He'll listen to you."

When she was Ali's age, Caitlin was modeling for a department store in Pittsburgh to make extra money for high school. After her stepfather came into her room one night, her mother told her she'd have to leave. Caitlin stayed with a married cousin in a trailer and slept on the sofa bed. At eighteen she was sharing an East Village walk-up with a friend who had won a contract with the Wilhelmina agency in a "silky hair" contest. Caitlin had some head shots taken, made the rounds, and finally an agency signed her. They put her smiling face in a rack on the wall with her stats: height 5′8″, size 5/6, bust 34, waist 24, hips 34, shoe 8, hair blond, eyes green. Then her European sizes in French and German. Another clone of Cheryl Tiegs.

During the day she rode the subway, noisy and crowded, to her appointments, where she was turned down more often than not. If she had no bookings, she didn't eat. But at night she might be picked up in a limo and given champagne on the way to dinner at restaurants where the prices were printed on his menu, not on hers. She waited tables, made floral deliveries, walked dogs, froze in the winter, kept her energy up on cocaine if it was offered, and stole from delis when she was hungry.

Men with money liked to have models around, and the

agency gave the girls invitations to parties in apartments overlooking Central Park or the river, with antiques, thick carpets, original art, catered food, and, in those days, crystal bowls of cocaine on polished tables. In a penthouse on Park Avenue, Caitlin stumbled into an immense bathroom with a marble floor and a wide, silk chaise where a senator with a pelt of white chest hair lay with two teenage models, his ruddy, glistening member ludicrously erect. She used the toilet, then left. They never noticed. That winter a lawyer for Chase Manhattan Bank woke her at dawn, said he'd forgotten his wife and kids were coming back from Disney World at noon. He sent a fur coat by way of apology, and when Caitlin refused to see him again he sent someone to retrieve it. The man reached into her closet and she knew better than to object.

Most people in the industry did their jobs and went home. Caitlin joined the club scene: models and photographers and designers partying with rock stars and other celebrities, going from club to club in limos, getting drunk, getting stoned, dancing until sunrise, then snorting or popping whatever they needed to get through the shoots scheduled for eight o'clock in the morning.

Caitlin found work. Her book grew thick with tear sheets from catalogs and magazines, and clients began to ask for her by name, paying up to $5,000 a day. She flew a dozen times to Europe—a hair color commercial in Paris, runway shows in Milan, shoots in Spain, Sweden, Greece. One cosmetic company had rights to her eyes, another to her hair, and a hosiery company owned her legs. She felt just as fractured inside, aware that who she was depended on what the camera might record at any given moment.

She married a TV producer and divorced him when she found him with another man. She passed out in a shoot for Richard Avedon that had taken two weeks to arrange. She was arrested twice for DUI, evicted from several apartments, and had an abortion and a miscarriage. A doctor told her she would never conceive again. Her heroin use ended after she nearly died of an overdose. Her agency kept it all quiet.

In Miami no one cared that her career was in decline; the town was hungry for any kind of celebrity. As she closed in on thirty, there were fewer fashion ads and more products—a deodorant, a cruise line, the female half of a couple having dinner at a hotel. Then an ad for Correctol, smiling and stretching in her nightie as if she'd had a good night's sleep for a change. Caitlin began to imagine the inevitable progression: grocery shopping, laxatives, dentures, then incontinence pads, and then what? Coffins?

At the clubs she kept it down to an occasional line of coke with her friends. She drank too much. She thought seriously of suicide.

Frank pulled her back from the edge. Not a perfect white knight, but he saved her, then stuck around. Some days were hard, others weren't so bad. She wanted to take photographs and make a living at it, although being an artist of any kind was risky, and the competition was murderous. Of her earlier days, she could almost swear they had happened to another woman, or in a book she had read a long time ago.

Caitlin had told Sam about her life. Bits and pieces, what she thought she could afford to give away, and then everything in a flood of words and tears. Sam's arms around her, his warm breath in her hair. But in the end it was too much for him. A man with a responsible job, a wife, and two children.

But he would listen to Ali. Caitlin was sure of that, if she knew anything at all about Sam Hagen.

On the ground floor Ali gave her name through a glass window, then she and Caitlin found places to sit. Several dozen chairs faced front, bolted together in long rows. The room was crowded and noisy with people. A couple of young Hispanic cops in dark blue city of Miami uniforms stared openly at Ali. Even in Caitlin's jacket, two sizes too big, she had that effect.

Five minutes after they had come in, Caitlin felt Ali's fingers clamp around her forearm.

She whispered, "It's him. The guy outside my apartment this morning."

A man with a bristly white crew cut stood in the open

door to the lobby. A scar ran through his bottom lip to his chin—as if it had been slashed with a knife—giving him a tilted, off-center cleft.

After a minute he came over, walking with a limp. A waist holster made a bulge under his loose-fitting guayabera. He looked down at Ali, who stared back up at him. "Miss Duncan."

She nodded.

"Good afternoon. I'm Dale Finley. I work for Edward Mora."

"Who?"

"The state attorney." He made a slight smile, then glanced at Caitlin. His eyes were icy blue with flecks of yellow. "Who are you, a relative?"

"A friend."

"What's your name?"

"Why?"

"Because I asked you."

She shrugged. "Caitlin Dorn."

There was a flicker of recognition. "Were you asked to appear, Miss Dorn?"

"No."

"What are you doing here?"

"I came with Ali. Does it matter?"

"Not at the moment." He held an arm toward the lobby. "Let's talk for a minute, Miss Duncan."

She took Caitlin's hand. "You come, too."

"Miss Dorn can sit right here. We won't be long."

Ali raised her chin. "I don't have to talk to you at all. Detective Ryabin said for me not to talk to anybody but Sam Hagen." She raised an eyebrow. "I assume you know Detective Ryabin?"

Whatever Finley thought of her response, he made none of his own. He put his foot on the chair adjacent to hers and leaned over so she could hear him, crossing his arms on his knee.

He smiled at Ali. "I bet you're tough, aren't you? That's good, because with the men you're accusing, why, there might be half a dozen defense attorneys, all itching to get at you. We need to know in advance that you can take the pressure, that you're not going to give up halfway through a trial."

She laughed. "I won't."

"Good." He nodded, then came closer. "Once this case is filed, if it is, they'll want to know about you. Your sexual practices, your boyfriends, the drugs you take, everything. We need to know about it first, so before Mr. Hagen sends for you, put your thinking cap on. That'll make it go a little faster, if you're ready with your answers when he starts asking questions. Some people say it's like a trip to the dentist, but if you don't hold back, you'll be out of here before you know it." The scar through his lip whitened when he smiled.

Ali stared up at him.

He said, "We've got police reports and statements by a number of witnesses. Some of them say you were a little tipsy. Maybe you don't recall the events as clearly as we'd like. I don't care, myself, but Sam Hagen's not as forgiving as me when people want to file a case, then change their story when the going gets rough. You have to be straight with us. Can you do that?"

She nodded.

"That's great. I wouldn't want to see you charged with perjury." He patted her arm. Then he turned toward Caitlin. "Miss Dorn. I might have to pay you a visit, ask you some questions. I'm afraid you can't get any special treatment from this office."

"Excuse me?"

"Aren't you dating Mr. Hagen's former law partner?"

"That's none of your damned business."

He smiled and straightened up, taking his foot off the chair, leaving a dusty shoe print. "I appreciate you ladies taking the time to talk to me. Mr. Hagen is busy right now. He'll send someone down in a while to get you, Miss Duncan. See you later."

Dale Finley limped out of the waiting room and vanished in the direction of the elevators. Caitlin looked back at Ali. She was taking deep breaths, and her eyes were fixed on Caitlin, burning with indignation and betrayal.

"I told you. They won't do anything. I knew it. They wouldn't care if I walked out that door."

"Stay here. I'll be back." Caitlin abruptly grabbed her purse and stood up.

"Where are you going?"

"To find out what the hell is going on."

chapter
nine

The reason Sam had not been able to reach Adela Ramos, he discovered when he returned from lunch, was that Adela Ramos had been on her way to his office. She had brought her brother with her. She wanted Sam to explain to him why the jury had acquitted a guilty man. Adela had tried to explain it herself, the American system of justice was difficult to understand.

Idelfonso García and Adela sat side by side on the sofa. Joe McGee, Sam's co-counsel on the case, sat in a chair facing them, Sam in another. García worked construction, and it was hard for him to take time off. He had worn a suit and a white shirt and a tie, showing these lawyers he was worthy of some respect.

He wanted to know: If Luis Balmaseda had confessed, why had the judge not allowed the jury to hear it? Had the judge been paid off? Perhaps the jury had found Balmaseda not guilty because he was an American citizen and Adela was not. Did the life of a four-year-old boy mean so little to them?

García's thick wrists stuck out past the hems of his coat sleeves. He could have crushed a brick in his sunburned, muscular hand, but he gently held his sister's in it. He had moved Adela over to his place because she didn't want to live in the apartment where Luis Balmaseda had murdered her son.

For the last fifteen minutes or so, Sam had been explaining the exclusionary rule, not calling it that, but telling Idelfonso García that if the police made mistakes in gathering evidence, they couldn't use what they found, including confessions.

"Nobody was paid off," Sam said. "The judge didn't want to exclude Balmaseda's statement, but he had to. The rule is meant to protect ordinary citizens from the police, and we all have to follow it. As a prosecutor, there are times I'd like to take shortcuts, believe me. But if I did that, I'd be breaking a law I'm supposed to uphold."

Sam spoke the words, but they sounded condescending to him. Even absurd. Carlito Ramos, this man's nephew, his sister's only child, was dead.

García thought about it for a while, not convinced, but sensing the futility of argument. Finally he said, "I told your friend—" He nodded toward Joe McGee. "—that Luis has been calling Adela on the telephone. When I answer he hangs up. If Adela answers, he uses bad language with her. I don't want to say in English." Ramos had a heavy accent, but he spoke slowly, as if it was his nature to take his time, being careful.

McGee said, "Mr. García, you could change the number. Or get Caller-ID. There are ways to block the calls."

"Why do I have to pay for Luis to stop? The police should put him in jail. They say they can't."

"Well, Mr. García, they will if you prove harassment or if you get a restraining order. Then they can put him in jail if he makes threats, or if he hangs around your apartment. If he follows Adela, that sort of thing." For an instant McGee's eyes met Sam's. If Balmaseda had walked into the room right now, either of them might have slammed him against the wall.

Adela spoke up. She looked a little better than she had ten days ago. She wore lipstick, and her long dark hair spilled down her back from a gold clip at the top of her head. "The policeman, Robin—" She meant Ryabin, Sam realized. "—he coming to my brother house for say . . . about arrest Luis."

Sam said, "Here's what I want you to do. Go straight to see Detective Ryabin. Tell him I sent you. Make out a police report."

"*Sí*. He say the same." She looked at her brother. *"Después de salir de aquí, vamos a la policía."*

An anguished expression fell over García's face. He shook his head. "I knew Luis before Adela did. I brought him to meet her. I introduced them."

She touched his arm. *"Shhh, Idelito. No es la culpa tuya."* She was telling him it wasn't his fault. How could he have known it would turn out this way? Sam remembered Luis Balmaseda: good-looking guy, nice clothes, some money to spend on a pretty woman like Adela. She would have fallen in love with him. But what quirk of psychology had made her put up with the abuse he handed out? To take it for months and months, not telling anyone, even her brother, who obviously cared for her.

Adela nudged him, then stood up, tucking a bra strap under her neckline, adjusting her shoulder bag. She extended her small hand to the prosecutors. "Thank you, Mr. Hagen and Mr. McGee."

García didn't speak. He held the door for Adela. Joe McGee said he would take them downstairs.

After they left, Sam sat alone in his office for a while, feet sprawled in front of him, too tired to move. He couldn't count the number of times that scene had been played out in one fashion or another, so many sets of victims and survivors of victims. They were all, himself included, caught in a clanking, inefficient machine that ran on habit, custom, and lack of any reasonable alternative. Not exactly a substitute for God, as Dina had said. And she wasn't entirely right about the guilty being raised up, either, although yes, it did happen. Just often enough to make people cynical. Sam knew he would lose faith entirely if he dwelled on the ones that turned out badly. Most of the time—he was confident of this—the system worked all right. He won nearly all his trials, and the accused were sent to prison. Sometimes survivors would stay in touch. One set of parents gave him a new tie every Christmas, a thank you for convicting the man who had raped their daughter, then blinded her with a pencil. Six ties so far, nineteen to go—unless the guy got out early on parole.

Dina had heard too many of the bad stories. Too many

descriptions of the unspeakable things a person could do to another human body. Sam knew he shouldn't have burdened his wife with it.

Four hours from now he would be walking into Frank Tolin's office to hear Frank tell Dina the same thing he had just told Carlito Ramos's uncle: I know you're feeling bad, and the system sucks, but there isn't a damn thing I can do for you. I share your loss.

Sam went over to his desk, picked up the telephone, and punched in Frank Tolin's number, which he still remembered. He announced himself to a receptionist whose voice he didn't recognize. She put him on hold.

Then Frank came on the line. "Sam. How's it going?"

"Well, I'm not sure. I'd like to know what you discussed with Dina relative to a wrongful death suit. She told me about it over lunch today. I can't say I approve."

After a few seconds of silence, Frank said, "There was no intention to hide anything from you, Sam. Dina called me this morning, and I assumed you knew about it."

Frank's office was on a corner, with floor-to-ceiling windows that gave a view of Biscayne Bay. Frank might have his feet propped up on his desk right now. Ostrich skin cowboy boots, twelve hundred bucks.

"This is a lousy idea, Frank. Were you aware she spent most of last October in a hospital?"

"Yes, I'm aware. It isn't uncommon, Sam, to seek help after the death of a child. Dina sounded perfectly competent to me."

"She is," Sam said. "Now she is. We've got our lives back, and I'm doing my damnedest to keep it that way. I don't want my wife going through any more emotional trauma like she—"

"Sam, I've done this for years, counseling people who've lost loved ones. I know just how you feel."

"You fucking do not know how I feel." There was only silence on the line. He said more reasonably, "Did you tell her we had grounds to file a complaint?"

"Of course not. Listen. Matthew had been drinking at a club that shouldn't have served him. That's all I know. Dina wants to see what can be done, if anything. I'll talk to her. I think she needs to get it out of her system. Let her do it. You've handled the loss in your way; let her do it in hers."

"I'm telling you here and now, Frank, I don't want to file a lawsuit, and I don't want you raising her hopes."

"No, no." His voice was soothing. "I'm going to listen to what she has to say, that's all. And don't jump in. Just let her talk. If I advise against legal action, Dina might accept it better if you don't say, 'I told you so.' "

Sam nearly hung up.

"You know, Sam, we didn't end our professional association on the best of terms, that's true, but I still consider us friends. We go back, buddy. Don't worry, I'll take care of Dina. It's the least I can do."

He could imagine Frank Tolin signing papers with his Mont Blanc at the same time he was telling Sam what buddies they were. *How far back, Frank? Bien Loc?* Frank a second lieutenant and Sam a specialist, fourth class. In the thickly forested hills outside Bien Loc their platoon had come under heavy NVA artillery attack. Gunships put down covering fire, and the men were ordered to fall back. The place was a hell of smoke and explosions. Tolin lay in a gulley with his arms over his head, leaving a gap in the line. Nobody noticed but Sam, who dragged him by his web belt to the Huey and threw him aboard like a duffel bag. The chopper barely made it out. Frank never mentioned the incident again. Now what? Gratitude after all these years?

Sam made himself reply, "We'll see you at five-thirty."

He heard a disconnect and slammed down the phone. Almost immediately it buzzed.

He swept it up. "What?"

It was Gloria. "Sam? I noticed Adela Ramos leave a while ago, with her brother. I wanted to remind you about Duncan."

"I haven't forgotten." He rubbed his forehead. "Send her up."

"Someone else wants to talk to you first. Caitlin Dorn. She called awhile ago from a phone downstairs. She was insistent. Rude, if you want to know."

His mind reeled. "Caitlin Dorn? What does she want?"

"She refused to say. I told her you didn't have time to

talk to anyone else, but she made me promise to mention it to you." Gloria waited. "Sam? Are you there?"

"Yes. Send them both up. I'll see Miss Dorn first."

Sam met them in the small waiting room outside Major Crimes. Alice Duncan was as he had expected: a tall, skinny attitude problem with a God-awful choice in clothes. It was hard to tell her age. She asked if she could smoke. He said no.

He led Caitlin through the maze of corridors on the second floor. He had recovered from the shock of seeing her again after three years. Three years except for the time he had passed her by accident in the art museum. Then he had ducked behind a divider until his heart had stopped pounding. Now he could not imagine what she wanted.

She kept up with him, just off the point of his left shoulder, and neither of them spoke. Sam could see people glance at her as she swept past. Caitlin had a way of moving, a syncopated, chin-up, long-legged stride that originated in the hips, each foot firmly planted, blond hair swinging with each step. She wore tight jeans and a black pullover with the sleeves pushed up. Her eyes were slightly narrowed, and Sam felt himself tensing for the mayhem to follow.

He shut the door to his office. "Have a seat."

She tossed her purse onto a chair. "What was the meaning of the welcoming committee downstairs?"

"You want to tell me what you're talking about, or do I have to guess?"

"Dale Finley, your investigator, whatever he is. He scared the hell out of Ali. He said you were ready to throw her in jail for making a false report. I can understand defense attorneys intimidating a victim, but not you. Not the prosecution."

"Hold it right there." Sam lifted a hand and kept it raised. He would corner Beekie Duran about this, but he couldn't do it now. "What did he say, precisely, to make you conclude that he intended to frighten Ms. Duncan?"

"Oh, Jesus, don't be such a goddamned *lawyer*." Caitlin began to pace, and the office seemed to quiver with her energy. Her hair swung around her face when she turned.

"Ali wanted to walk out of here, the hell with all of you. Was that what you had in mind? Then you keep her waiting half an hour to give her plenty of time to think about it."

"Keep your voice down," Sam said sharply.

Caitlin came over to him, furious but in control. "I heard you have no intention of going after the men who attacked her. Is it true?"

"No. It isn't. Who told you that?"

"Someone I know."

He leaned a little closer. "I'd like a name, Caitlin."

She said nothing, then shrugged. "Martin Cass."

Sam frowned. The name was familiar. "I met him at Frank Tolin's office a few years ago. What's your connection to Martin Cass?"

"I'm doing an advertising brochure for him for a big development project. Not his project. Klaus Ruffini's. Well, isn't this a coincidence? The same Ruffini that you're supposed to be prosecuting."

"What about Marty Cass?" Sam repeated.

Caitlin said, "Oh, Marty is generally a self-aggrandizing blowhard, but he knows everybody on the Beach. Including Klaus. Marty says the city manager persuaded the state attorney not to prosecute. I thought he was full of shit, but now I wonder, after the reception we got downstairs."

His mind grasping at the implications of this, Sam couldn't think of what to say.

Caitlin misread his hesitation. "It is true. My goodness. Saint Samuel is playing in the dirt with the rest of us."

"What are you doing here, Caitlin?"

"Dale Finley asked me the same thing," she said.

"Now I'm asking."

She looked at him steadily, then said, "Ali Duncan is my friend."

"Your friend got herself into some trouble," Sam said. "I'm attempting to find out what happened. Whether you believe that or not, I don't give a damn. If you have something to add, then do it. If not, I'll talk to Ms. Duncan."

Caitlin's green eyes were blazing. "Okay. You want

facts, try these. George Fonseca came to Ali's apartment just before I arrived. She wouldn't let him in. He suggested that she'd be smart to take money not to testify. When she said no, he tried to break her door down. He said if she talked about the drugs he's been dealing, she'd wind up in the Everglades."

Sam said, "Did she call the police?"

"There was no time."

"She can call from my office. If Fonseca did what you describe, he committed a felony."

Caitlin stared sullenly at him. She obviously hadn't expected this response.

Sam said, "Before I talk to Ms. Duncan, it would be helpful to know what you saw at the Apocalypse that night."

Abruptly turning away, she paced to the window, arms crossed under her breasts. Her narrow waist was circled by a silver belt. She had aged some, but not much. Still the small, neat jaw, smooth skin, and generous mouth. A nose that tilted upward, which she had once complained was too short.

"Are you going to call me as a witness?"

"Not if I don't have to," he said.

"No, I suppose not."

She was smirking. Caitlin Dorn had become damnably hard-edged, Sam thought. He asked, "What about the incident at the Apocalypse? Was Alice Duncan assaulted or not?"

"Ali."

"What?"

"She calls herself Ali. She doesn't like Alice."

"Ali, then." He was still waiting for an answer.

Caitlin nodded.

"You're certain?"

"Yes. Yes, she was." Caitlin exhaled through her teeth. "I said so to the police. Didn't you read my statement?"

"All twenty-five words of it. You were there, you confirmed that Ms. Duncan was sexually assaulted. I want to hear it from you. What happened?" Sam sat on the edge of his desk and straightened his suit coat. He put his hands on his thigh.

Caitlin looked back at him for a second, then walked

to the wall where his diplomas and certificates hung, then to the cluttered bookshelves. She pivoted slowly, taking it all in. The boxes stacked in the corner, a coffee stain near the door, a scratched metal cabinet, law books, a heavy desk, a photo of his daughter, another of Dina, framed newspaper clippings of cases he'd won, the two conference chairs, the battered sofa.

She wore canvas shoes with open toes. Thin straps wound around her ankles. The jeans clung to her slender legs and outlined her derriere. He was aware of the scent of her perfume. It seemed familiar. Her hair gleamed, pale gold.

She glanced over her shoulder. "I expected a grander office for someone in your exalted position."

He said, "I work for the state."

Smiling, she faced him fully now, her weight on one hip. He could see a curve of breast at the low neckline of the blouse. Her eyes swept over him.

He shrugged. "My hair's going gray. I've gained a few pounds. Anything else different?"

"No. You look . . . substantial. The ideal prosecutor."

"Is that a compliment?"

"If you like."

She walked over to the window, looked closely at it. She fitted the tip of her forefinger into a concavity in the glass. "What was this, a bullet?"

"A .38. It clipped a chair and ended up in the wall."

She smiled, her tongue touching for an instant the lower edge of even white teeth. "Were they aiming at you?"

"No. I came in on a monday a couple of years ago and found it. Just another weekend shootout in Overtown."

"You can't get it fixed?"

"I don't want it fixed," he said.

"A good conversation piece."

"It's to frighten defense attorneys."

"Or your witnesses."

Then he noticed the diamond on a thin chain that twinkled in the hollow at the base of her throat. She had once said she wasn't the type to wear diamonds. Maybe Frank Tolin had bought it for her.

"Why were you at the Apocalypse?" Sam asked, closing in on the subject again.

Casually she said, "Freelancing for a magazine. Fun on the South Beach party scene. No candid photos of a rape, unfortunately."

"So you still have the negatives?"

"Yes. I didn't print them. I didn't think it would be appropriate if they were published." She added, "You won't find much of value."

"What happened, Caitlin?"

"Ali's outside. Ask her. She's been waiting long enough."

Sam got off the desk and turned one of the chairs toward her. "I'd rather talk to you."

She glanced at the chair, then at him. "If you're not going to call me as a witness, what difference—"

"You want to help your friend or not?" Sam sat in the chair facing hers and held his hand toward the other one. "Please."

Giving Sam a cool look, she crossed the room, pulled the chair around so it was at more of an angle, then sat down.

He said, "Tell me about the place where it happened. Some kind of room off the main party room?"

"Yes. Upstairs in the VIP room there's a sort of alcove. It had a couple of chairs and a table with drinks on it, bottles, extra glasses. There's not much light, only a small sconce on the wall."

"Before the incident, did you hear any conversation between Ali and any of the men involved?"

"Not really. The usual stuff. Kidding around. It was hard to hear anything with the music coming from downstairs." Caitlin gave him a look. "What do you mean? Was she propositioning anyone? The answer is no."

"She wasn't on Ruffini's lap? Kissing him?"

Caitlin let out a breath. "Yes. She shouldn't have, and she knows it now. I think she was trying to get a reaction from George. I guess she succeeded."

Sam asked, "Are they involved?"

"They used to be. Not anymore."

"Did you come with anyone?"

"No."

"Had you been drinking?"

"I wasn't drunk."

"Caitlin. What had you been drinking, and how much?"

"Soda and lime. I can't work and drink at the same time. And no, I wasn't on anything else." She laughed, stretching her arms over her head. "I've even stopped smoking, aren't you proud of me?"

Sam looked at her awhile. She crossed her legs and swung a foot. He said, "What about Ali?"

"She had champagne. A few glasses. I don't know how many."

"Any drugs?"

"Sam, she wasn't wasted." Caitlin closed her eyes for a second, then said. "She had some coke in the bathroom downstairs. She didn't say so, but I could tell. This was earlier, around midnight. And she took a pill of some kind just before she came into the VIP room. She told me about that later. She said George gave it to her. That was before I came up. George always has something in his pockets."

"When did you go upstairs?" Sam asked.

"About three o'clock."

"When did she go into the alcove with George?"

"About an hour later. We got to the hospital at a quarter of five."

"How far were you standing from where it happened?"

Caitlin looked around for a reference point. "From that wall to the other. Fifteen feet?"

"All right. What happened after that?"

She bit down on her lips, then released them. "I wasn't paying much attention at first. I was talking to somebody. I had already shot some pictures, a dozen or so. But then I noticed Klaus Ruffini taking Marquis Lamont back there, pushing him along. They were laughing. And then I saw her on the table. And George on top of her. It was dark, but I knew what they were doing. I only saw glimpses, because people were in the way. I didn't know, at first, that he made her do it. Then he—George—"

Caitlin glanced up toward the ceiling, taking a breath. "George got off and he held her down while Marquis stood between her legs."

"What did you see?"

"He was moving his hips. It took him thirty seconds. What did I have to see?"

"Then what happened?" Sam asked quietly.

"Then Klaus—Klaus turned her over and used a bottle of champagne. Cristal." She laughed shakily. "How could I have noticed that? But I did. It was unopened. The cork—you know—it's held in with metal and wire. Ali was screaming, but I thought maybe it was the music, because it couldn't be *real*. Not that; not people I *knew*. And besides, no one was doing anything to stop it." She laughed, pushed her hair off her forehead, then let her hand fall to her lap.

"It was real. And I—I couldn't move. I couldn't. Like I was made of stone, or dreaming. And then Ali started to throw things, and George told her to get out, and I followed her, and she was on the floor—" Caitlin's voice broke. "Oh, God. Sam, I keep seeing her like that." She pressed the heels of her hands into her eyes. "I hate it. I hate it all."

Still slouched in the adjacent chair, Sam ground his teeth together. He listened to the hum of traffic through the window for a while. An ambulance wailed by, heading for the public hospital down the street. Finally he spoke. "I told you about the time I saw the guy in my squad get killed by a sniper in Vietnam. Remember?" When she didn't respond, he said, "Caitlin?"

She lifted her head, blinking as if coming out of the dark. Her face was pale.

"The sniper aimed, and I watched him; then I saw a guy twenty feet away from me drop. I told you."

She nodded.

"Two weeks in the field. I froze. It happens, but I felt bad about it for a long time. I didn't let it happen again." He had never told her what he had done in the madness that had exploded later. Had never told anyone.

He said, "You still taking pictures on the streets? Real life, all that gritty stuff?"

She cleared her throat, then said, "Yes."

"I ran across your name in the paper a few months ago. You had an exhibit at the art museum downtown."

"Oh, well. Me and a bunch of other local photographers. You're in the paper all the time. Samuel Hagen, chief of Major Crimes, quoted again." She laughed.

"But you're doing all right?" he asked.

"Oh, sure. I'm busy."

"That's good."

They were silent for a while. Sam wanted to ask her how it was going with Frank Tolin, but he caught himself. He watched a jet go in and out of a cloud, then vanish past the edge of the window.

Caitlin asked, "And you? Are you all right? You and Dina. With Matthew gone, I mean. It must have been so awful."

"For a while. It's better now." Sam said, "I should tell you this. We're going to talk to Frank this afternoon about a wrongful death suit. In case he mentions it to you. But we don't expect it to go anywhere. Matthew made his choices, like everybody else."

"Oh, Sam. I was such a coward," she said. "I wanted to call you, come see you, something. I didn't know how. I wrote you three different letters and tore them all up. Nothing I could say would be enough."

"Don't worry about it."

Caitlin had turned toward Sam, and her hand lay on the arm of the chair. Her nails were bare and clean. She still wore a silver Celtic ring with loops of filigree. "Did you know I did Matthew's composite?"

"What's that?"

"The photos he showed to the agencies. You know. Dressed in various clothes, different looks. But besides that, I took some studio portraits of him. Good ones. They really are. And if you—if his mother—if you want, I could make copies."

"No, we've got pictures." Then he added, "Thanks."

"I have a show in a gallery on Lincoln Road next month. I was thinking of showing some of his photos. Would you mind?"

Sam smiled. "Are they nudes?"

"Well . . . a few. But they're so powerful."

"I'd rather not, but that's your business. Matthew did a lot of things I don't necessarily approve of."

"I could tell you about him, Sam. He said you and he didn't talk to each other a lot. He was a terrific kid. Well,

I'm sure you know that, but he may not have told you much about his life—"

"Caitlin." He raised a hand.

"I'm so sorry."

Sam stood up. "Let's go find Ms. Duncan." Caitlin's eyes followed him as he crossed the office. He opened the door and waited.

Her lips compressed. She picked up her purse and walked out.

He could have blamed Caitlin. The way she used to look at him, that sideways glance just short of provocation. She must have picked up on his troubles with Dina, the way women sense that kind of thing. But Sam would never have touched her as long as she was involved with Frank. She knew that. He had assumed she was trying to needle Frank, to make him jealous. Another reason not to be stupid. But Sam worked late, hoping to catch a glimpse of her, and she knew that, too. He smelled her perfume in the hallway when she left, and his head swam with wanting her.

When he left Frank's office it was primarily because he hated the work, but also because of Caitlin Dorn. He ran into her a few times in the next year or so, being friendly, asking her out for coffee, talking about this and that. Then he heard she and Frank split up. A week later he knocked on her door.

Caitlin opened it wearing a long T-shirt, nothing else. Her eyes widened. He stood there, not saying a damn thing, till she put a hand around his wrist and drew him inside. He took her standing up against the wall, his arms under her thighs, her legs around his waist, her sucking on his tongue, then they were on the floor and he was screwing her there, too, slamming into her, everything sticky and wet. He could have fucked her in her mouth, up the ass, between her breasts, all of which, and more, he had eventually done. Her apartment had smelled of cigarettes, dirty laundry, and a cat box. There were dishes in the sink and photographs jumbled everywhere. The breeze had belled the curtains inward and cooled the sweat and sex on their bodies where they lay panting on the floor.

* * *

Just past five o'clock, the state attorney stood by his bookcase, making what appeared to be piano chords with his right hand on one of the shelves. Glancing at his fingers, he rubbed them lightly, producing dust that swirled downward, visible against the deep blue of his suit.

Sam had just explained why arrest warrants should be issued in the Duncan case.

"Well. I'd been told there was nothing to it," Mora said.

"You were misinformed."

"Apparently so." He made a slight smile. His round cheeks were smooth and taut. "Who's going to take it from here? Somebody in the Sexual Battery Unit?"

"No, I'm taking it. I'll appoint co-counsel."

"And do we have a press conference scheduled?"

"Not yet. You want to do it?"

Mora lifted an arm. "No, by all means. It's your case. What about bond on the defendants?"

"I want a hundred grand on each of them. And Ruffini's passport."

"This will be something to see. TV satellite trucks lined up outside. Press conferences every afternoon, live at five." Walking past his desk, Eddie Mora drummed his fingers across its surface like hoofbeats. "Did you tell Miss Duncan we're filing charges?"

"I said thank you for coming in, I'd get in touch."

"Then I suggest you tell her that we decline to prosecute."

Sam kept his voice low and even. "I've already told my staff to draw up the arrest warrants and find a judge to sign them."

"Before you consulted me."

"What do you want, Eddie? You told me to handle it. Now you don't like the result."

Mora shot him a malevolent glare. "I thought you'd be impartial. I was wrong. You're using this case as a vehicle for some kind of personal vendetta."

"Not remotely true." Sam leaned his weight on the back of a chair, pressing down so he wouldn't pick it up and smash it over Eddie Mora's desk. "I wondered about that, Eddie. Why you'd give it to me. My son is dead and I'd walk away from a case that took me anywhere near South Beach. Am I reading it right?"

Eddie Mora made a laugh of disbelief. "No. You are not reading it right. What I thought, Sam, was that you, with your experience, would see, as well as I do, that if we proceed, this office will waste six or eight *fucking months* on a case that we *can't win*, where we will *blow* the fucking budget, be accused of harassment or racism or politics or *all* of the above, because no matter what the *fuck* you tell me, the witnesses are *totally* unreliable. Little Miss Duncan will change her fucking mind, and we will all look like publicity-grabbing, incompetent fucking *idiots*!" Eddie Mora's face had turned red with rage.

For several seconds the two of them stared at each other. Then Sam said, "Anything else, Eddie? I've got to be someplace at five-thirty."

"No. That's it."

The meeting was over.

On his way out Sam left a message for Eugene Ryabin, and they finally connected by car phone in heavy traffic on Flagler Street.

"Tell Chief Mazik the warrants have been authorized in Duncan. You want to come by early? We can discuss procedure."

Ryabin's chuckle came over the line. "Such service I get from you."

"Not for free." Sam swung into a parking garage and lowered the window to grab the ticket from the machine at the gate. "Do you know the name Martin Cass?"

A pause. "Yes. Real estate. A small man, big mouth. What has he to do with this?"

"I'm not sure. See who he knows at the city manager's office. And another thing. Ms. Duncan says our Italian friend is involved in a project called the Grand Caribe. I think Cass is working on promotion. See what you can find out."

Ryabin said it might take him a few days; Sam could buy him a beer.

Sam wheeled into a space and cut the engine. The Duncan case was going to be filed. He knew without doubt that any chance he had of taking over Eddie Mora's job was now lost, and had been lost from the moment he let Caitlin Dorn into his office. Unless he could find out why the state attorney had really wanted this case to disappear.

chapter

ten

George said, "This place is worse than you can imagine. I never been in a place like this, man. It's like in the movies. The food sucks, the toilet stinks. And they pack you in with like eight or ten guys, gold teeth, massive B.O. One of them says he wants to do things to you that you wouldn't even let a woman do—"

"Hey." The lawyer's fat fingers, interlaced on the table, tapped up and down. "My heart bleeds. Look, I was told to come down and see what you want. I assume you would like to arrange legal representation. Do you have a method whereby you can pay the fees or no?"

"Yeah. I mean, I will. First I have to get out of here."

The lawyer shifted as if to stand up.

"No, wait. I want you to talk to Alberto for me. I couldn't, you know, on the phone. I mean, it's probably bugged or something."

"Bugged. They don't bug the fucking phone."

"Can you talk to him?"

"In what regard? If I could know, it would be of some help here."

"Ask him if he'd go the bail, all right?"

"The bail." The lawyer smiled. "He would risk a hundred grand for you?"

"Listen to me. Alberto said if I ever—*ever*—needed a favor, to ask him."

"That's the way he expresses himself. He's a very friendly person. But not that friendly. I don't think so."

"He's gotta help me out, man."

"He don't gotta do nothing. You're in jail, that's your fucking problem."

"Man, you're an asshole, you know that?"

"For two hundred an hour, why not? Pardon me, but I have other matters to attend to."

"Wait. Sit down. It's not good for Alberto, me being in here, okay? I know things."

"What things might that be?"

"You know what I mean."

"Yeah? I'll tell him you said so."

George said, "No. Jesus, I don't mean *that*. I mean, what if I get beat up? Or stabbed? Then I'm in a coma and say something by mistake?"

"What a moron."

"Listen, dammit. I'm not asking him to give me the money, not like *give*. And it's not a hundred grand, it's ten, which is the bondsman's fee. That's nothing for Alberto. There's no way I'd skip town and stick him with the whole hundred, so don't worry about it. I'll pay interest, naturally. Ten, twenty percent. Whatever. Think of it as an investment."

"You got no money for a lawyer. No money for bail. Tell me. Where's the money to repay a loan?"

"Klaus Ruffini. You know who I mean?"

"Yes. So?"

"Klaus will pay me if I can get Ali to drop the charges. I know he will. Then I pay Alberto back. Okay? Give me two weeks. Three at the outside."

"And how will you persuade the girl to change her mind?"

"I got ways."

"You got ways." The lawyer wiped his eyes. "I love how you put it, George. Do you propose to *whack* this girl? Break her legs, perhaps?"

"No. Oh, man. I wouldn't do that to Ali. Come on."

"Enlighten me, then. What ways?"

"I'd talk to her. I tried already, but I lost my temper. You do that with a woman and it's over, man. Now I know my mistakes."

"I see. You believe she would respond positively?"

"Yeah. She likes me."

"You gang-bang the chick and she likes you?"

"I didn't mean to."

"No, it slipped and fell in."

"Would you—oh, fuck. *Fuck!* I didn't mean to, all right?"

The lawyer put a finger to his lips. "I will give you five seconds of free legal advice. When other people may be walking past the door, refrain from screaming that you didn't mean to do it, because they might conclude that you did it."

"Sorry."

"I'm impressed you have such rapport with women, George. All right. I'll talk to Alberto." When the lawyer stood up he was smiling. "In person. I want to see his face."

Rocking slowly in his big leather desk chair, Norman Singletary studied the young man who was staring morosely out the window at blue sky and clouds from forty-six stories up. Handsome kid, thirty years old. Paying a price for stupidity.

"Marquis, I hate to plead a case like this. It's not too late to change your mind."

"No, it's way too late, Mr. Singletary."

"You know, I was looking forward to a few rounds with Sam Hagen. I was his division chief when he first started, did I tell you that? Lord. That's almost twenty years ago. He's a heavyweight now. Not a stylish fighter, but he can go the distance and put you away if you don't watch yourself." Singletary gave a low chuckle. "I don't enjoy the new guys near as much."

The figure at the window gave a weary sigh. "My wife's about to divorce me. I might get kicked off the movie. I don't have money for a trial. Between your fees and the bail, I can't do it."

"Hagen and I have had, oh, a dozen good bouts since I left. I think we're six to five."

Marquis Lamont glanced around. "That makes eleven."

"One was a hung jury. The defendant was knifed by another inmate before the retrial. That doesn't count."

"Who's ahead, you or him?"

The phone buzzed and Singletary reached over to pick it up. His secretary said, "Mr. Hagen on line two, sir."

"Thanks. And Doreen? Could I trouble you for some refills?" He lifted his empty glass toward Marquis, who shook his head. "Just mine."

Singletary pressed the button. "Sam? It's Norman." He smiled. "Yes, it has. Too long. How's it goin'? . . . Yeah, I'm just fine." He laughed. "Yeah, I hear you. . . . Well, what I called about. . . . Right. I've had some discussions with my client. He's here in my office. I want to pass a couple of ideas by you. All hypothetical, you understand."

Singletary kept an eye on Marquis, who had paced across the office and was now coming back. "I could tell you the work my client does with young people in the poor neighborhoods, but you know all that. What I want to say is, Marquis Lamont is the wrong man to put on trial. . . . Well, that's true, but hear me out. Let's say there's a fine young man, a family man, who goes to a nightclub in a strange town with some people he doesn't know very well."

Marquis sank onto one end of the L-shaped sofa and put his head in his hands.

"Now, at this party they give him free drinks, and they pass around some cocaine—not his thing, but he doesn't want his new friends to think he's not with the program. So all right. He's having a good time. The music is hot, everything's cooking. Then a young lady dances with him, rubs herself up against him. You know, Sam, there are girls who like to do it with celebrities, and this young man is a celebrity, in a small way. Now what if someone at the party were to say, 'You know that girl you were dancing with? She wants you. Come on, have some fun. Look, there she is. She's ready.' "

Doreen came in with another diet cola and lime in a crystal rocks glass. As Singletary talked, he squeezed the lime, then patted his fingertips on a cocktail napkin.

"Our young man is led into this, Sam. For the amusement of the people, you understand what I'm saying? A circus act, but he doesn't see that. My investigator spoke to a witness who recalls hearing someone at the party, maybe a wealthy foreign gentleman, say he would pay a large sum of money to see the big nigger fuck the white girl. And let us say the young man foolishly accepts what has been offered. But he can't even get it up, he's so far gone, whereupon he is pushed aside, and the foreign gentleman assaults the young lady with a champagne bottle. Our young man is horrified. He staggers away, goes into a corner, and throws up. Now, how can any reasonable person conclude that he had the requisite intent to commit a crime? Nevertheless, two weeks later the police arrest him for sexual battery, and the state demands a bond of one hundred thousand dollars."

Singletary reached into a desk drawer for his flask of Bacardi and poured. He moved a swizzle stick and the ice tinkled in the glass. Slumped on the sofa, Marquis Lamont was staring upward at the ceiling.

"Tell me, Sam. How many years of his life should our young man spend in prison? Would you not prefer that he testify against those who instigated this crime? . . . Well, I think a dismissal of the charges would be appropriate, yes."

Listening to Hagen's response, Singletary chuckled. "He wasn't so drunk he can't recall who did what. If you work with me on this, you might get a fast guilty plea out of the other two. Unless you *want* a trial. A trial would look mighty good on TV. Maybe that is what you want."

He sipped his drink.

"This case wouldn't have been filed if not for Marquis. . . . Damn right, and I'll say so to the national media, if I have to. . . . Race certainly is a relevant issue, and I'd be shirking my duty to my client not to raise it."

He listened to Sam Hagen tell him he was full of shit.

"Then what do you suggest? . . . Maybe, but only if there's a withhold of adjudication."

Elbows on knees, Marquis gazed fixedly at Singletary, waiting.

"Uh-huh. . . . I'd appreciate that, Sam. Next week is fine. . . . Take care, now." Singletary hung up.

"Did he say he'll do it?"

"He'll consider it."

Leaping to his feet, Marquis raised a fist. "All right!"

Norman Singletary's voice rumbled across the room. "Mr. Lamont. What I have just conveyed to the prosecutor was a bucket of horse manure. I know it and he knows it. And yet it is the dance we all do in this business. If you are saved from prison, it won't be because Samuel Hagen likes the way you played at Florida State, but because he can use you. You are expedient. You are not innocent. In fact, you should be ashamed."

"What?"

"Ashamed. For playing the fool. For sucking up to no-account trash in their fancy clothes, with their fancy ways. For believing for one drunken, self-deluded moment that they wanted more from you than the chance to snicker behind your back."

Marquis Lamont stared at the carpet.

Singletary took a sip of his drink, then unfolded his glasses and put them on. "Did you bring my retainer?"

"Yes, sir."

"Don't you hang your head in my office, you hear me?"

Marquis Lamont took a check from his wallet and handed it across the desk. A certified check for $25,000. "Mr. Singletary?"

He glanced up, looking over his glasses.

"Six wins to five. Who's got the six, you or him?"

Jerry Fine, a partner in the firm of Cohen, Kaplan, Porter, Wolfe & Berkowitz, had come to Klaus Ruffini's house to discuss the criminal charges against him. Collar open and jacket off, Fine sat on the terrace in the shade of a canopy in a metal-framed, blue canvas butterfly chair from the fifties, his knees level with his chest. The house was sleek and white, with yellow metal lattice over the windows and tubular red railings on the second level. Fine could see Biscayne Bay and the Miami skyline a few miles west. The sun glittered like bits of glass on the turquoise water.

One of several persons who seemed not to have a defined function at the house had brought Jerry Fine a vodka and soda in a heavy, chilled glass. Others came and went. The guy who served as Klaus's bodyguard and Tereza's masseur was lifting weights by the pool, watching the naked girl swimming around in it. Another model in a thong bikini, sound asleep or comatose, was working on a sunburn. A fat, bald man dressed completely in black, except for a red scarf at his neck, carried some swatches of fabric over to Tereza Ruffini, who waved him away. She was in the middle of an argument with Klaus.

They were circling a white limestone table screaming at each other in several different languages. Rather, Tereza Ruffini was screaming. Klaus was laughing. A very jolly guy, Fine had observed. Klaus had straight brown hair that flopped over his forehead and bright blue eyes. He was barefoot, wearing khaki pants and a faded shirt with palm trees on it. At thirty-four, three years younger than Jerry, he was already getting soft in the belly. His wife Tereza was tall and skinny, with black hair so short it looked like it was painted on her skull, and an incredible pair of hooters. Jerry Fine couldn't pick up even the English words they shouted at each other because someone had put a CD of Little Richard on the stereo inside, and the massive speakers were blasting through the open French doors.

The law firm that Jerry Fine worked for was the largest, most powerful in Miami. They took care of all the Ruffinis' legal matters when they were in the States. Otherwise, the couple might be found at their houses in Milan, Aix-en-Provence, or Geneva. Tereza designed clothes; Klaus managed the multinational chain of boutiques where they were sold. He also played with real estate. Cohen Kaplan billed nearly a million dollars a year to handle his deals, his proposed deals, his traffic tickets, and the occasional shakedowns—of which this alleged rape could be the latest.

Jerry Fine did not like defending people accused of sordid crimes like rape. He had a master's degree in tax law and a CPA. He preferred financial crimes: tax evasion, embezzlement, or bank fraud. Cohen Kaplan's clients did not commit rape. But Jerry Fine would defend this case, sordid or not. It would cost Klaus a quarter million for a trial, possibly twice that. Jerry Fine could think of no reason to enter a plea. He would assemble a team of private investigators and experts in forensic evidence, psychology, and jury selection. But first he had to discuss the case with Klaus. So far Klaus had only slapped him on the back and told him not to worry.

At an hourly rate of $300, sipping a second vodka and soda, and watching the naked girl climb the ladder and dive into the pool, Jerry Fine was in no particular hurry. As Little Richard gave way to the crooning of the Platters, Fine took out his portable phone and conducted some other business while Tereza and Klaus finished theirs.

Finally, Klaus came over and sank into the yellow butterfly chair beside Jerry Fine's blue one. Tereza had already begun another argument with a blond woman in heavy, black-framed glasses. Her assistant designer. Or her interior decorator.

Klaus put a hand on Jerry Fine's thigh. Fine had learned that Klaus wasn't queer; he simply liked to touch people. "Jerry, you know what? George Fonseca wants $50,000 and he will make the Duncan girl dismiss the case. What do you think?"

Jerry Fine looked at him, then said, "No. It's a felony, called witness tampering. Besides, only a judge or the state attorney can dismiss a case."

Klaus nodded in the direction of the man lifting weights. "You know what Franco says?" He moved closer to Fine and whispered, "Franco says we should put her in a bag and throw her into the ocean. We can use my boat."

"For the love of God."

"Why do you take so seriously everything, Jerry? I'm kidding!" He laughed. "Did you see the prosecutor, Samuel Hagen, at the bond hearing? More serious than you, even. Like a cowboy, so tough. Jerry, come to dinner with Tereza and me tonight. The Strand, okay? The art director of *Vanity Fair* will be there." Klaus could make these abrupt turns in conversations.

Jerry Fine said, "Let's go inside. We need to talk."

Then Tereza came over, followed by the bald guy in black whining that he needed her signature. He made Jerry Fine's skin crawl. Tereza looked down at Jerry through impenetrably dark sunglasses with rhinestones on the frames. She said, "Hello, baby," then leaned over and kissed him on both cheeks. He could see straight down her shiny turquoise dress. It was one of her own creations, which she wore with white high heels and pink anklets. Now the stereo was pumping out "Shake Your Groove Thing." Two girls by the pool were doing some disco moves in their swimsuits. Tereza screamed, "Stop it! Stop! Now!" The music went off. "I can't stand that. It's horrible."

As she signed her name to six different pieces of paper, Tereza glanced at Jerry Fine. "Tell my idiot husband to pay the *puttana bugiarda* who says he raped her."

"Jerry won't let me." Klaus slid his hand up his wife's bare leg. "Jerry says it's a crime to pay her."

"How much does she want?"

"I don't know, Tereza *mia*. I haven't talked to her. I haven't sent anyone to talk to her."

"Now it's too late! Look what you have done!"

"Will you miss me when I go to jail?"

"No. You make me insane. I will be happy."

"But you love me. Insanely." Klaus pinched her thigh.

"They have taken your passport," she pouted. "You can't go to Paris with me. You can't go anywhere. *Non potrai andare da nessuna parte con me!*"

He was laughing. "I don't want to go anywhere. I like it here. The tourists are leaving, the weather is perfect. At this moment Miami is heaven. I could stay forever."

Tereza turned her sparkly sunglasses toward Jerry Fine, "I tell you who is behind this. Claudia Otero. *Feccia di una ragazza!*" She spat out the words. "Claudia has her show the same night as me next week. I bet you she's the arranger of this. Klaus, did the girl model for her? Maybe Claudia paid the girl to lie."

Klaus shook his head. "No. Claudia likes dark models. The girl was pale, and too much red hair." Then he grinned. "Look at my wife, how excited she is."

"*Sta'zitto*, Klaus." Tereza grabbed Jerry Fine's arm. "You know who she is, the bitch? Her sister Amalia is married to the Dade district attorney. What's his name?"

Jerry Fine said, "Edward Mora? He's the state attorney."

"Right, right. Amalia, his wife, is the sister of Claudia. I heard this from I forget where."

"I don't see what you're driving at."

"Of course you see it," Tereza said. "Claudia told the district attorney, her brother-in-law, to arrest Klaus."

Jerry Fine smiled. "I don't think so."

"I'm hungry," Klaus said. "Let's go to Nick's at the marina."

"You have a cook," Fine said, annoyed. "If you're hungry we can eat here."

Tereza knelt and put her forehead on Fine's shoulder. "You have to do something about her, Jerry. Hire a private detective."

Fine said, "Let me see if I follow this. You're suggesting that your business competitor told her sister to tell the sister's husband, the state attorney, to file this case against your husband, in order to put you out of business."

"Yes. Why not?"

"No, Tereza. Trust me. No."

"Who is saying these things against my husband? You know who? Claudia's friend, Sullivan. And she is forty-two years old and he still sleeps with her. You know him, Klaus. The model for Armani in *Uomo* this month."

Klaus said, "I'm hungry."

"Jerry, find out about this."

To shut her up, he said, "Okay, Tereza."

With a gasp, she noticed her watch. "*Dio!* I have to meet the buyers from Macy's ten minutes ago!" She kissed Klaus on the mouth. "*Ciao, caro.*"

He reached up and squeezed her breasts. "*Ciao, bella.*"

"*Va bene. Andiamo.* Let's go." She headed for the house, trailed by the blond woman and the fat homosexual in black.

Jerry Fine said, "Klaus, we need to talk."

Klaus propped one bare foot on his knee. The toes were pedicured, but the sole was gray with dirt. "You know what? Miami was getting a little boring. Same, same, same. And now it's very interesting."

"I hope you find prison interesting, Klaus."

"It won't happen. Come on. Let's go have lunch at Nick's."

"What do you mean, 'It won't happen'?"

"You worry so much." Klaus began to rub Jerry Fine's

chest, a strong, side to side motion. Sweat broke out on Fine's neck. He would have shifted away but this chair was shaped like a sack. Klaus said, "Tereza worries also. She is crazy. Claudia Otero this and that and so on. But you know what? When Tereza is crazy, she makes love like—oh, God, you should see." Laughing, Klaus sprawled in his chair. "No, I won't let you see that."

Fine said, "Have you done something you don't want to tell me about?"

"No, Jerry." Klaus's mouth twitched upward. "But I know something about a boutique soon to be in Havana, special to the tourists, next door to Benetton."

"Moda Ruffini? I didn't know you and Tereza were in Cuba."

"Not us. Claudia. Don't tell Tereza."

"What in hell are you doing?" Fine could hear his voice rising. "I'm your lawyer. You pay me to worry. And I'm telling you. If you don't get serious about this, Sam Hagen is going to nail you to the fucking floor!"

Klaus laughed. "This is for me like a movie, so exciting."

Jerry Fine tipped back his drink and finished it off.

From the door a young man in bicycle shorts yelled to get Klaus's attention. *"Du, Klaus, diese Nervensäge von Vertreter ist wieder an der Tür! Was soll ich ihm sagen?"*

Klaus frowned but didn't answer.

"What is it?" Fine asked.

"He wants to know if he should tell Marty Cass to go away."

"Who?"

Klaus shouted back at the young man, then said, "For you, Jerry, I'll let him in. Marty Cass put money, not so much, in the Grand Caribe, and he thinks now he's my partner. After the red-haired girl made up those lies, Marty said he was a close friend of Hal Delucca, and nothing would happen."

"Holy Christ. You didn't bribe the city manager."

Ruffini's blue eyes widened in surprise. "No, never." Then he said, "It's funny, Jerry. People do things for me all the time, and they ask for nothing. Isn't that strange?"

It was the way the world worked at these heights, Fine thought. People of lesser status doing favors for those higher up, some kind of natural obeisance hard-wired into the human brain, perhaps. Or a hope that beauty, sex, and power could be vicariously obtained.

Hal Delucca, along with a few other gushing syco-phants in city hall, had supported Klaus's pet project, the Grand Caribe. Delucca himself had cut the ribbon on phase one. So far only a twelve-story time-share apartment building had been constructed. The model under glass in Klaus's office showed a Caribbean-theme village with shopping, restaurants, water slides, a la-goon, and a mega-hotel. The village would be as much fun as the real Caribbean, but cleaner, with no guilt-inducing Bahamians or Trinidadians gazing through the fence.

Klaus Ruffini squeezed Jerry's knee. "I didn't ask Marty Cass to talk to Hal Delucca. He did it because he thinks he's my partner, to help me."

"You're telling me Delucca went to the state attorney?"

"He said no, he didn't. But now I look bad to the city of Miami Beach because of Marty Cass, and I don't get my zoning approved. Look. Here he is." Klaus settled into his chair.

Coming across the terrace was a man in his late thirties dressed in open-weave shoes, linen slacks, and a green silk shirt. He carried a small leather pouch and a portable telephone. His eyes were hidden behind expensive tortoise-shell sunglasses. He ducked under the edge of the canopy. "Klaus! How's it going?"

"Say hi to Jerry Fine. Jerry's my lawyer."

"Hi." Marty Cass shook Fine's hand.

Klaus smiled up at him. "How is Uta, your fantastic and beautiful wife?"

Cass hesitated, then said, "We split up. You didn't know?"

"Oh, that is so sad." Klaus laid a hand on Jerry Fine's arm. "Uta was sleeping with another man. A model, very young and blond and good-looking. Of course Marty would throw her out."

Marty Cass's face twitched. "Klaus, have you got a minute? This is business."

"Sure. Talk. Jerry knows all my business. I hire Jewish lawyers, Marty. Very sharp." Klaus waved toward a chair. "Sit."

Marty Cass pulled up a plastic pedestal chair upholstered in blue-and-white stripes. His ponytail curled under at his collar. He put his bag and telephone on the terrace floor, then dropped his sunglasses to his chest, dangling from their cord. His eyes looked as if he'd stayed out all night in a smoky bar.

"A couple of things," he said. "First, I've got people to take care of on the Grand Caribe brochure. The photographer's been hounding me for days. Bitch, bitch, bitch."

"How much?" Klaus said.

"With her, the printer, the production people . . . five grand."

"Okay. I get you a check before you leave."

"Great," Marty said. "Now, the other thing—"

Klaus smiled. "You know what? The city commission will vote next week on the zoning. They will tell me no because now I've been falsely accused of raping that red-haired model. A terrible thing! You said the city manager would help me. You promised."

"I know, I know. Hal tried, but the state attorney took it the wrong way. Hal says Mora filed the case for spite, the Cuban bastard. I did my best for you, Klaus. Look, they haven't voted yet. I could talk to them for you."

"I'm thirsty. Dominique!" Klaus shouted. A woman at an umbrella table across the terrace put down her copy of *Vogue* and uncrossed her legs. She wore leopard print toreador pants and a gold bikini top. "*Apporte-moi un coca, ma petite, et le même pour mon copain.* Marty, you should see the Coke machine. It works on nickels. Why did you come, Marty? To tell me what I know already?"

"It's about the rental property you wanted. Let's iron out the details, then I can do the contract and bring it back for you to sign."

"What rental property?"

"The apartments, Klaus, The Englander."

"I don't recall this."

Jerry Fine knew what property. So did Klaus. The tax

department at Cohen Kaplan had said Klaus could buy it if he wanted, but it was overpriced.

Marty Cass's nervous smile reappeared. "The Englander. Sixteen-unit on Drexel Avenue, held at present in the name of Tolin Associates. I've been trying to get in touch with you all week."

"Ahhh." Then Klaus shrugged. "I don't know. With my other problem, which you said you would fix, I'm not in the mood anymore."

"You wanted it, Klaus. It's perfect. The location, everything."

Klaus's bare foot bounced on his knee. "But the property belongs to someone else. You have only ten percent, so why do you care?"

"I told you all about this."

"Tell me again so Jerry can hear."

He made a little shrug in Fine's direction. "I have ten percent. My partner Frank Tolin has the rest. He owes me money. He says he can't pay—which is a lie, by the way. So we'll settle up when the apartments are sold. My own partner. We were supposed to be in fifty-fifty, and he screwed me down to ten percent."

Klaus looked at Jerry Fine. "I find out that four years ago the building caught on fire. Jerry, would you advise me to buy a building like that? It might collapse, don't you think so?"

Marty Cass protested. "It was rebuilt, Klaus. New roof, everything. It's in great shape. Back to the original art deco design."

Dominique came clattering out in her black high heels and toreador pants with two green glass bottles of Coca-Cola. Marty said thank you, then set the bottle on the terrace.

Klaus said, "Okay. Maybe I do want the building."

"It's a good deal, Klaus."

"If I buy the building, what would you do for me?"

"Do?"

"Do you think I'm a nice guy?" He smiled.

Perplexed, Marty Cass replied, "Sure. A very nice guy, Klaus."

"Do you like me?"

Cass shrugged. "Yeah, sure. You're funny. I have a good time at your parties."

Jerry Fine looked across the terrace, out toward Miami. He wondered what would happen if he got up and left. He could see his law firm's building among the others downtown, shiny blue and white.

Klaus said to Marty Cass, "Would you help Tereza with her show next week?"

"Okay. What do you want me to do, some promotion? Call some people?"

"No. She needs someone to help her set up the chairs."

Marty exhaled, glancing at Jerry Fine, who said nothing. "Why not? We're all nice guys here." He laughed.

"And would you help clean up afterward? Please? For Tereza. You know. She's so tired, planning for her big show. We can talk about the apartments if you promise to help Tereza."

"Jesus. Sure, okay."

"And would you kiss my ass if I asked you to? If I promised to buy the property, would you kiss my ass right now?"

Marty made a high-pitched whinny and glanced around. The other half-dozen people on the terrace were watching. The naked girl, who had wrapped a towel around herself, hid a giggle behind her hand.

"I'm not going to kiss your ass," Marty said. "Kiss mine."

Gripping the curved metal frame of the chair on either side of his knees, Klaus pulled himself up. He took out his wallet and counted five hundred-dollar bills. "Okay, here's a deposit, which I give to my attorney in escrow. Not enough. I need more cash. Dominique! *Va, cherche-moi encore de l'argent!*" Klaus pointed. "Jerry, write a contract. You have paper? Good. The Englander Apartments. Address, such and so. Seller—Tolin Associates. Right? Yes. Purchaser, Ruffini Properties. Price—" He looked at Marty Cass. "I forgot the price. How much?"

"Six hundred."

"Six hundred thousand dollars, all cash, standard terms, and so on. Okay?"

Marty stared up at him from his chair.

"Okay or not?"

"Jesus. You're kidding."

"Does this look like kidding? Am I kidding you?" Klaus dropped his trousers and his blue jockey shorts, holding on with both hands to keep them from falling down entirely. The hem of his palm-tree shirt hung just below his groin. The pink tip of an uncircumcised penis bobbled as he turned his back toward Marty, who pressed himself against the chair.

Klaus wiggled his fanny. "Marty, you want me to do something for you? Okay, do this for me. It's clean. If you kiss it I'll tell my attorney to write the contract. Jerry, did you hear what I said? Call your office, get the legal description. Do it!"

Muttering darkly to himself, Fine flipped open his portable phone and punched in the number. Dominique came clopping out onto the terrace again, carrying several banded stacks of hundreds.

With loathing, Marty Cass braced his hands on his thighs, and took a breath. He gritted his teeth, then reached out to lift the hem of Klaus Ruffini's shirt.

Quickly Klaus whirled around, pulling up his pants, laughing. "My God! He would do it! Oh, no!"

Cass stumbled out of the chair, nearly weeping with rage. His voice was choked. "You lousy fuck. May you rot in hell."

"Marty, I was making a little joke. I'm sorry. I didn't think you would do it." Klaus was laughing and trying to zip his pants at the same time. "Go with us to Nick's for lunch. Okay? Watch the boats, have a drink with us. Come on." He put his arms around Marty Cass.

"Go to hell, you dago bastard." Marty Cass violently pushed him away, grabbed his bag and portable phone, and ran across the terrace. Laughter came from the onlookers. Klaus hid his face in his hands and sank to his knees, a parody of remorse.

Jerry Fine closed his telephone. He felt dizzy, and the sun reflecting on the bay made shards of light that hurt his eyes.

"Everybody!" Klaus rebuckled his belt. "Let's go to Nick's. I am starving." He paused beside Jerry Fine and rubbed his shoulder. "We'll get a separate table from the rest, okay? Then you can tell me how to save myself from Edward Mora."

At the door he called, "Jerry! Come on."

After a moment, Jerry Fine struggled out of the butterfly chair and followed him across the terrace.

chapter
eleven

The press conference in *State* vs. *Ruffini, Lamont, and Fonseca* was held just before noon, in time to be edited for the midday news and rebroadcast in the evening. Sam Hagen stood at a cluster of microphones in a blaze of light, the state and U.S. flags behind him. He swept his gaze around the room and denied that the sexual battery charges had been filed for political reasons. This was not part of a plan to stop development of the Grand Caribe Resort. A crime had been committed, and the defendants would be brought to trial. Sam was flanked by two other assistant state attorneys he had named as members of the prosecution team: a woman from the Sexual Battery Unit and Joe McGee, on temporary loan from the Felony Division.

Insiders in the state attorney's office knew what was going on here. Edward Mora might be leaving. Whoever he recommended as his interim replacement, Sam Hagen would be running for state attorney in the fall. The battle was starting now, in front of these cameras.

"Mr. Hagen, the girl is seventeen years old. Is there any indication that the defendants realized this? Did she present herself as older?" A local TV reporter in the front row had stood up so he could get himself on video.

Sam heard the unstated question, *What kind of girl is this?* He said, "I don't know what they thought. Whether she looked fifteen or twenty-five, does it matter?" Sam waited a beat for emphasis. "No one deserves to be the victim of such a brutal attack."

"What can you tell us about her?"

"Well, first, I admire her courage. She's willing to testify against people who could influence her career. The young lady is a native of our area. She's been modeling for about a year, and she hopes to pay her way through college. That's all I'm prepared to tell you at this time."

Florida law prohibited publication of her name. Sam had begun to refer to Ali Duncan as *the victim* or *the young lady*. He didn't want details of her life to show up in the press—not yet—although sooner or later the media would sniff them out. For now, she was the girl next door.

A reporter from the *Miami Herald* asked about evidence, and Sam gave a brief overview, keeping his response as nonspecific as he could and refusing to give the names of any witnesses.

The story had hit the national news the day before, but only in the form of a ten-second announcement on NBC that actor Marquis Lamont, along with two other men, had been arrested for an alleged sexual assault on a model in a Miami Beach night club. An entertainment news show had asked Sam for an interview, but he had refused to talk to them. Klaus Ruffini had not been mentioned except as a co-defendant, and George Fonseca not at all. The only in-depth coverage was local, although a pale young woman in black had come from New York to do a story for *Women's Wear Daily*. Eddie Mora's predictions of media bedlam had been wildly off the mark.

The state attorney himself was absent. He had gone to a Cuban-American Bar Association meeting, tending to his own political fortunes, making sure he kept the local exile community happy so they didn't scuttle his chances to go to Washington.

"How did the girl get into the Apocalypse at age seventeen?" someone asked.

Sam replied, "She was let in by the management. Most clubs are careful about this, but there are a few that cause problems." He glanced around at his prosecution team, then said, "We've talked to Chief Mazik of the Miami Beach police department about a joint effort to identify and prosecute those owners and managers who don't control the doors or who permit the use or distribution of narcotics on the premises, usually in the rest rooms or the so-called VIP rooms. This is not, and I stress this, a judgment on Miami Beach nightlife as a whole. Most of the clubs and restaurants are great places to go, an asset to the community."

As several reporters called out questions, Sam lifted a hand, then said, "You know, what concerns me, as a prosecutor and a resident of Dade County, is the idea that because we rely so much on tourist dollars, we have to excuse things that most other communities wouldn't put up with. The attitude that people with enough money or sophistication ought to be indulged. This has consequences, particularly for our young people. What do they learn when we say that not everyone has to be held accountable to the same rules? I see forty thousand felony cases come through this office every year, and I can tell you that most of those defendants think that somehow the rules just don't apply to them."

After a few more questions Sam checked his watch, apologized for having to cut it short, and thanked everyone for coming.

Avoiding the lunchtime crowds in the elevators, Sam took the stairs to the ground floor with Joe McGee and Lydia Hernandez. Lydia, from Sexual Battery, was a petite young woman with frizzy blond hair. Hustling down the stairwell in her flats, she said that the motions demanding blood samples would be personally served on the defense attorneys in the morning.

Joe McGee rounded the landing. "Good. We won't have a whole lot of time. Fonseca's lawyer says he's going to ask for a speedy trial."

When he reached for the handle of the heavy steel door, Sam told him to wait a second.

"I had a phone call this morning from Norman Singletary. He says Marquis Lamont isn't so sure now he wants to plead out."

McGee groaned. "Oh, man. We're offering the moon. What does he want?"

"A not-guilty verdict," Sam said. "He doesn't want to plead to anything. If we lose him as a witness, someone has made it worth the risk."

"Klaus Ruffini," McGee concluded.

"Probably."

"Son of a bitch," Lydia said. "How much do we need Lamont?"

McGee said, "We'll be okay if the witnesses don't crap out."

"Let's see what happens between now and the arraignment," Sam said. "Then I'll have another talk with Norman. Threaten some serious jail time. That might change Lamont's mind. Or we give him immunity from prosecution and force him to testify. We're in for a rough ride, boys and girls."

Sam opened the door, and they walked into the lobby, then out the rear entrance of the building, squinting in the bright light. Wind tossed the tops of the trees and chased tattered pages from the newspaper across the parking lot.

Joe McGee was grinning. "I feel a little sorry for Marquis."

"Why, for God's sake?" Lydia demanded.

"Well, he isn't getting much media coverage. He's probably going, 'Hey, where is everybody? You mean I'm not big enough to have all the TV networks down here? Nobody wants to put me on the cover of the *National Enquirer*?' " McGee jerked his head toward the Justice Building. "Sam, you coming over to the cafeteria?"

"No, you two go ahead. I've got a meeting."

Sam's silver Honda was parked in a private space. As he approached he noticed someone leaning against the fender, a white-haired man in a tan sport jacket and knit shirt. Dale Finley. Sam hadn't seen Finley since telling Beekie to get him off the investigation team in the Duncan case.

Finley came a couple of steps closer with his uneven gait.

"You're looking for me?" Sam took his keys out of his pants pocket.

"I caught the press conference on TV," Finley said. "All that about setting examples for our young people. Very inspiring."

Sam stuck the key in the car door. "Excuse me. I'm late for an appointment."

"With Gene Ryabin." Finley smiled, and the scar across his chin pulled at his lower lip. "I asked your secretary."

"What do you want, Finley?"

"Cut to the chase." Finley's scalp gleamed through the bristly white crew cut. "Detective Ryabin, so I have been given to understand, has been making inquiries about Martin Cass. What reason? I pondered this. Then I remembered that Mr. Cass is an associate of a businessman from Italy currently residing on Miami Beach. And Mr. Cass has been heard to remark that he personally asked Hal Delucca, the city manager, to persuade the Dade state attorney not to proceed on a certain sexual battery case involving the said Italian businessman."

Finley's pale eyes, which had been taking in the movement of people through the parking lot, fixed now on Sam Hagen. He said, "I know what you're thinking. You're mistaken, but I won't argue with you. Consider this, though. If you fuck up his nomination, he will stay here, and you can't beat him in an election, not in Dade County, *amigo*."

Sam opened his door. "Stay out of my sight, Finley."

"It could be an interesting trial," Dale Finley said. He watched Sam take off his jacket and put it on a hanger behind the front seat. "The lead prosecutor asking questions of the witness, then the defense asking the witness did she ever spread for the prosecutor."

As Sam slowly grasped what Dale Finley was saying, he felt a wave of fury build, then sweep through him. He turned slowly around, wanting to get his fists around Finley's lapels.

"You don't have to be concerned anybody's going to run out and blow bells and whistles." Finley gave a slight shrug. "As long as we understand each other."

He turned and limped across the parking lot toward the state attorney's office, the sides of his sport coat lifting and falling in the wind.

Waiting for Ryabin, Sam stood outside the Criminal Investigation Unit looking down into the terrazzo-floored lobby. A piece of publicly funded art hung just below him, suspended on thin cables from the high ceiling. The sunlight pouring through the windows glowed through

blue and green glass disks and bounced off turquoise,
brown, and maroon rods and wires bent into weird shapes.
Every time he came over here he tried to figure out what
it was supposed to mean, beyond the $85,000 it had cost
the city. Up where the eyebolts screwed into the walls, the
plaster was getting rust-colored and flaky. That much
money could have fixed the leaks in the roof.

Sam leaned his elbows on the railing. Maybe it was seaweed. Occasionally maintenance would pull out a Styrofoam cup, like the ones that washed up on the beach.
Ryabin had told Sam he'd seen an open-mouthed inflat-
able doll in black fishnet stockings caught among the
wires. Nobody had consulted the rank-and-file before the
scaffolds went up to install the thing.

Behind him the door opened, and Eugene Ryabin
emerged in a white-on-white shirt with French cuffs. His
holster and badge were on his belt. He pressed the down
button on the elevator.

"I apologize for keeping you waiting," Ryabin said. His
accent turned his last word into *waitink*. "We're interviewing a girl who says a man she met last night, a student from Holland, beat her up." He shrugged. "The
tourists are striking back."

They took the elevator to the lobby.

Sam said, "I ran into Dale Finley just now. He's aware
you've been asking questions about Marty Cass."

"Where I come from," Ryabin said, "they had men like
Dale Finley on the police force. He would have used pli-
ers on a suspect's testicles. What did he say to you?"

"He assumes I'm out to get Eddie Mora, and it would
be better if I lay off. Let Eddie go to Washington, then I
can win the election in November."

"Do you think Eddie asked him to approach you?"

"I don't know," Sam said. "It isn't Eddie's style. Finley
has a reason to act on his own. If Eddie gets some national
attention, Finley will be back in action. He can forget the
stuff we give him—rounding up witnesses, taking statements, serving warrants. He probably got off on working
for the CIA, before the Cubans broke his legs."

Beyond the automatic glass doors a long walkway
slanted to the street. Among the trees between police
headquarters and city hall, bums sat or lay on white

concrete benches. Their ranks were thinning out now that warm weather had set in. Soon the sun would melt asphalt, turn puddles into steam, and leave the Beach prostrate and panting. Sam loosened his tie. He had left his jacket in the car.

He said, "Finley told me I'm wrong, by the way. Eddie wouldn't commit political suicide over this case. Meaning he wanted it dumped for the reasons he gave me—the girl is lying, the witnesses cancel each other out, and we'll bust the budget on a sure loser."

Ryabin's heavy brows lifted. "You believe him?"

"I might, except for the way Finley came at Ali Duncan. He tried to make her run, Gene. Just before she was supposed to talk to me, Finley tried to scare her off."

Ryabin walked in silence for a while. The top of his head was about level with Sam's shoulder. Then he said, "Why did Eddie Mora give you the case? That, Sam, has made me curious."

Sam watched a mixed-race Hispanic woman coming out of a market across the street, pulling a small child by the hand. Bleached hair. No bra. Filthy white T-shirt knotted at the waist. She staggered enough for him to realize she was drunk.

"For whatever reason, Eddie wanted this case to go away. He thought I'd rubber-stamp his decision not to prosecute. I wouldn't want to get sucked into South Beach."

"Because of Matthew."

"And because I wanted Eddie's job. Call it a bribe if you want to. It feels that way to me now."

Ryabin looked at him.

"Eddie said he would be grateful. And I was ambitious. I wouldn't question a damn thing."

They waited on the corner for traffic to pass. Washington Avenue had two lanes each way and parking meters at the curbs. A few scraggly palm trees were stuck into narrow, grassy medians. In the space of a few years, Sam had seen the neighborhood shops die off one by one: the old barber shop replaced by a chic salon, the diner by a restaurant that charged twenty bucks for a plate of sushi. High rents were killing off the old places, and chain stores were taking over; ugly but profitable card-board glamour.

"I have a question," Ryabin said.

At a break in the traffic they dashed across the intersection. When they reached the other side Sam said, "What's the question?"

"What is Dale Finley using to get your attention?"

After a second or two, Sam said, "He knows about me and Caitlin."

They turned north. "Who told him?"

"I don't know, Gene. He asked around."

"Is this another reason you took the case? Because of Caitlin?"

"Christ, no. I didn't read the incident report till after I told Eddie I'd handle it."

A guilty grimace deepened the lines on Ryabin's face. "I interviewed her myself at the Rape Treatment Center, where she took Miss Duncan. I'm sorry. I should have called you."

Sam waved a hand. "Forget it."

"I see her sometimes, walking with her camera. I say hello. She says hello." Ryabin added, "You never told Dina."

"No. She met Caitlin when I was working at Frank Tolin's office, and I didn't want to tell her. I still don't. She had a rough time with Matthew's accident. And then I imagine my daughter hearing about this from some kid at school who read it in the paper." Sam laughed. "Caitlin never told Frank, either. And now Dina's consulting him about a wrongful death suit. The whole thing has infinite possibilities for blowing up in someone's face."

Ryabin nodded. "And what is Dale Finley going to do, light the fuse?"

"Not if I leave Eddie Mora alone."

"Will you?"

"That would be the intelligent thing to do."

They were silent for a while, walking. They had decided on a bar a couple of blocks away that served sandwiches. Ryabin said, "So. What next? Do you let Eddie Mora go to Washington, to solve crime in America for us? Perhaps work his way into the Oval Office in eight years?"

"I frankly don't give a shit."

Filling his lungs, Ryabin rested his fingertips lightly on the starched front of his shirt. "You should come lie on the beach, Sam. Get a tan. Relax."

"You really get a kick out of this place, don't you?"

"I know. Reading the newspapers you think Miami *is* worse than the South Bronx. But look. Sunshine. The blue sky, the lovely young people." Ryabin nodded toward a threesome of girls skating past on long honey-gold legs, backpacks over their shoulders.

Blue sky and sunshine. Enough of it to blind you, Sam thought. Palm trees and bare skin and the endless, blinding glitter. Rushing over the causeway, climbing the stairs to Caitlin Dorn's apartment, hearing the summer downpour outside the open window by her bed, believing things could be so simple.

"Do you still want to know about Martin Cass?"

"Sure. Tell me about Martin Cass."

Ryabin said, "Thirty-six, born in Queens, father a trumpet player on the *Tonight Show* with Jack Paar. Attended but never finished City College. Real estate license with Tropic Realty and Investments. They say he made a sale three months ago, one condo unit. He married a year ago—a German named Uta Ernst, but she's not living with him at present. His secondhand BMW was repossessed last month, and he is overdrawn at First Union Bank."

Sam looked at him. "Very good."

"He was the realtor for the building where Caitlin lives," Ryabin said. "The Englander Apartments. Frank Tolin bought it from Anna. You remember."

Anna was Ryabin's wife. Four years ago Anna had owned the Englander. She had inherited the apartments from her sister Rivka, who had died when the building burned. Another tragedy for the women Eugene Ryabin had brought out of the Soviet Union.

Ryabin had suspected arson, but without a motive or suspect, the case eventually died. Frank Tolin poured money into the place, and by the time Sam left his office, Frank was still complaining that it had been a mistake. Bad luck, he had said. Ghosts.

Ryabin continued his recitation. "Marty Cass has

coordinated publicity for Miami Beach civic groups—unpaid, but good for making contacts. He knows the city councilmen, the mayor, the heads of the departments. He pretends to have money. Now he's claiming partnership with Klaus Ruffini."

He paused to move around a man shouting through the open door of a small gift shop with a display of gay postcards and T-shirts in the window.

The man's hair had gone a little wild, and his pants hung so low his plaid shirt had come halfway out. He was carrying a limp, leather-covered Bible with pages edged in gold leaf.

"What is so hard about that, my friends? Man was made for woman, woman was made for man. It's simple. It's in the Bible. Man for woman, woman for man. Is that a difficult concept for you to understand?"

A muscular man with a shaved head, heavy work boots, and tight denim shorts slit up the sides came out of the shop, unlocked his bicycle, and steered it into the flow of traffic.

"What a freaking circus," Sam muttered.

"You know, Sam, in this city, if you act important, and maybe even fool yourself, and you do it with flair, and you wear the right clothes, and you have a good tan, people will believe you."

Sam could vaguely picture Marty Cass from more than four years ago: the perpetual smile, the jaunty little ponytail, the silk sport jacket.

"From what I've heard," Sam said, "the Grand Caribe is Ruffini's answer to Disney World."

"Yes, like an island in the Caribbean." Ryabin smiled. "I went to the sales office for the condominium, which already is built. They told me there's too much of Europe here, too much trying to be Cannes or Portofino. The Grand Caribe is more Miami. There will be buses to and from the discount malls, the cruise ships, and Orlando. And of course room for a casino, which sooner or later the voters will approve."

They stopped walking, having reached the place they had agreed on for lunch.

"Ruffini must be out of his mind," Sam said.

Ryabin's eyes danced with evident amusement. "No! Klaus Ruffini understands American culture very well."

They went into Pogo's, a dark, wood-paneled dive with dusty windows and faded posters of old Miami Dolphin games, where a cold draft could still be had for under two bucks. By now the plainclothes cops who usually came in for lunch had gone back on duty. A slender black woman in a gauzy Indian skirt wrapped over a swimsuit sat on a bar stool speaking into a portable telephone in a language Sam couldn't place. There was a small lightning bolt tattooed on her left breast.

They took a table in the back and ordered sandwiches. The waitress brought their drinks. Iced tea and a beer. The air conditioner buzzed in the wall.

Ryabin took a cigarette from his pack. "Don't move away yet. The city commission is going to vote no on the Grand Caribe." His gold lighter flamed, illuminating his lined face and throwing shadows upward from his tangled eyebrows.

Sam picked up his beer. *"Nastrovye."* He closed his eyes and took a few deep swallows, then set the glass back on the wooden table in the ring it had left. He rubbed his forehead for a while.

"Edward José Mora went to Harvard Law School," he said. "Did you know that?"

"No." Smoke wreathed Ryabin's head.

"Eddie graduated near the top of his class." Sam stretched out his legs. "I was about midway down the list at the U. of Florida—which is not a bad school, by the way."

Ryabin sipped his iced tea.

"He clerked for a justice of the U.S. Supreme Court, and he married a woman whose father owned half the sugar plantations in Cuba."

"Is that so?"

"And Edward Mora, who learned Spanish from Berlitz, and who is so fucking preppy he buys his toilet paper from Brooks Brothers, would be delighted to see Klaus Ruffini in prison. One would think."

"Yes. One would," Ryabin said, and smoked his cigarette.

"And one also wonders, Detective, why Eddie Mora is associating with a lowlife like Dale Finley."

Ryabin sat looking at Sam Hagen for a while. Finally he smiled broadly, and the gap between his front teeth showed. "I thought—forgive me—that you were going to leave it alone."

Sam picked up his beer. "I thought so, too."

c h a p t e r
twelve

In the entrance hall of the Cathedral of St. Nicholas, an old woman in a flowered dress sat reading the Bible on her knees, smoothing the pages with pale, twisted fingers. She looked up and smiled when Dina Hagen came in. Light reflected off her heavy glasses.

"*Kalispera, Constandinamou.*"

Dina nodded. "*Kalispera, kyria.*"

She put money into the box for a candle and carried it into the small, overheated room where two dozen or more were already burning. She lit the candle and wedged it into the sand, then crossed herself, right to left, and kissed the icon of the Blessed Virgin.

An hour ago she had kissed her father on the forehead and told him she was going to take a walk. She had left him in his chair on the back porch, gazing dimly through the screen, his feet in slippers. Aunt Betty was clattering dishes in the sink. *Go,* she had said. *I'll look out for him.*

No one was in the sanctuary. Dina walked slowly up the red-carpeted aisle, her hand trailing along the wooden pews. Each arch and curve of this church were familiar to her, the white marble and gold trim, the icons, the crystal chandeliers, the walls vaulting upward to a sky-blue dome. God himself was painted on those upper reaches, and farther down, his prophets. The names of all four of Dina's grandparents were written on stained glass windows. When her father died, he would be remembered on a plaque or pew, along with her mother, already gone. Matthew's name was carved on a granite bench outside.

As a girl, Constandina Pondakos, like her friends, had dreamed of being married here in a long, white dress. There would be flowers at the altar, the smell of incense, the ancient liturgy, everyone dancing afterward. But the priest said no, not unless her fiancé converted. Sam explained to him that yes, his mother had been Jewish, but he wasn't religious at all. Father Demetrious had shaken his head, the long, gray beard moving across the black robe and heavy silver cross. *My son, believing in nothing is worse than being a Jew.* Sam would have to become Greek Orthodox. Or Catholic, if he preferred. Insulted, Sam had stubbornly refused, on principle, he said, even when Dina begged, then threatened to give back his ring.

She had married him anyway, love outweighing pride. Now, on principle, Sam was resisting the idea of a lawsuit: Matthew had been to blame for his own death. Sam was wrong, of course, and in the end he would be glad Dina had insisted. He would understand. He knew the horrible perversities human beings were capable of. He had seen the smashed bones of the child who had been thrown through a window to his death. And he had brought charges against the men who had raped that poor girl on South Beach. Those were his causes. Dina would fight for hers, and eventually Sam would understand.

At the altar she knelt before the icon of the Blessed Virgin with the infant Jesus Christ and made the sign of the cross.

"Panagiamou, anapafse tin psihe tou agapimenou pediou—" Mother of our Lord Jesus, bless the soul of my beloved son—"

Dina's words trailed off. Who was listening? Only oil and canvas. Mother and child in two dimensions. And God, if he was here at all, was no more substantial than the painted image on the rotunda a hundred feet above her head. There was more help on earth. Yesterday, Friday, she had gone to Frank Tolin's office for the

second time. Sam didn't know. She'd had no appointment, but Frank had seen her anyway. He had sat beside her on the sofa, and his secretary had brought
them tea. Don't blame yourself, he said. Matthew
had been pulled into a swamp, that life on South Beach,
the clubs, the drugs, the easy sex. Frank listened until
his floor-to-ceiling windows went dark and he had to
turn on the lights. Dina had nearly fallen to her knees
in gratitude. He had performed a miracle, of sorts:
since that day in his office she had not felt one twinge
of pain.

Dina suddenly tensed. From behind her had come a
whisper. An echo.

She silently mouthed his name: *Matthew*. But how
could he follow her here, into this place? What did he
want?

Beyond the altar the silent faces of the apostles
and the Holy Family gazed back at her. Jesus lifted a hand, palm outward. St. George, in his armor,
raised his sword. A white dove carved of marble
perched on a corner of the pulpit, wings lifted as if in
flight.

If she turned around, she might see Matthew in the
shadows in the back of the cathedral, under the icons
of the saints. Last night he had come into her father's house while she slept upstairs in the small
room that had been hers as a girl. One moment asleep,
the next awake, trembling, hearing only the cric-
kets in the backyard. The moon shone blue-white
through the window and fell across the bed, holding her
there as if moonlight had weight and substance. She
saw the glass doorknob turn, turn. Then a face in
fragments, abraded to the bone. Her screams had
brought Aunt Betty, bathrobe flapping, running into her
room.

Dina closed her eyes tightly. Of course he wasn't
real; she knew that. The laughter she heard at night
wasn't real. Or the door that closed on the other side of
an empty room. Nor was Matthew's face when it
had appeared in her bathtub, his hair lifting and falling
with the movement of the water. The worst had been
yesterday, leaving Frank Tolin's office. Alone in the

elevator she had heard the hollow drip of liquid, then a gush. Looking down she saw a pool of blood, foaming and surging, sticky and red, sucking at her feet, swirling into vortices. When the door opened, the blood flowed into the crack. Gone. Not a drop of it on her shoes.

She whirled around, heart leaping. There had been a flutter, like birds' wings, and now a shadow seemed to pass in and out among the white columns along the side of the cathedral.

Above the doors were the faces of the saints, dark, bearded men with heavy-lidded eyes and long, tapering fingers at their hearts.

As in a dream, she struggled to move her lips and whisper, *Matthew*. The light in the cathedral dimmed, then brightened—a cloud passing over the sun, nothing more.

Steadying herself on a pew, Dina got up and walked out of the sanctuary. The old woman again looked up from her reading and smiled. *"Kalinichta, koritsimou."* Good night, my dear.

"Kalinichtasas, kyria."

Dina went down the broad steps to the street. A faint smell of brine and seaweed came from the sponge docks. Main Street was just ahead, curving down a low hill, with its tidy shops and old-brick storefronts. If only they had come to live here, instead. Sam could have opened an office in town, and Dina would have hers close by. Melanie would do better at the church school. And Matthew would not have been destroyed.

Last Monday in Frank's office, Sam had sat impassively, hardly speaking. Then Frank had said the case should be investigated, and Sam had argued, until Dina had begged him to stop. Of course, Sam believed that nothing would come of it; let him think what he wanted. She had realized, in the cold light of perfect vision, that she was the stronger one. She could redeem their son; Sam could not. Such terrible knowledge, because now she knew how utterly alone she had become.

* * *

On her way back to her father's house Dina walked a street too far and found herself at Spring Bayou, at the top of the stone steps that led down to the water. Palmetto palms grew on either side of the steps, and a sidewalk fronted around the bayou, which was shaded by pines and oaks.

Dina walked out onto the concrete platform. The gray-green water threw back reflections of the clouds. A cool breeze arose, winding its way from the Gulf. Her skirt pressed close to her thighs, then fluttered.

On Epiphany Day three Januaries ago, Matthew had been one of sixty or so young men who dove for the cross. After services in the cathedral ended, the people, thousands of them, marched to Spring Bayou. The archbishop in his miter led the way, his gold-embroidered robes sewn with bells. Behind him came the bishops and the priests with censers; children in native costumes; marching bands; and then the crowd, the crush of people.

The boys went out into the bayou in small boats to form a semicircle around the platform where Dina now stood, which at the time was decorated with flowers. It was cold that day, and the boys shivered in swim trunks and white T-shirts. Lovely, innocent young men. Tensed and ready, they fixed their eyes on the archbishop. He said a prayer, then dipped the cross into the water, once, twice. The third time he flung it high, and at the same moment a girl behind him released a dove. It soared upward, white ribbons streaming from its feet, wings beating against the clear blue sky.

Before the cross touched the surface, there was a huge splash of young men diving for it. Dina could still see the flashing arc of Matthew's bare legs and extended arms. Other boys came up, took in air, and dove again. Watching them, holding her own breath, Dina clutched at Sam's arm. Matthew could be drowning!

Then he burst to the surface, mouth open, gasping, water streaming over his face. In one upraised hand he held the cross. The people cheered. Dina jumped up and down like a girl, laughing, hugging Sam. Matthew scanned the crowd, smiling when he saw her, his hair dark and wet on his forehead.

The other boys carried him on their shoulders to the archbishop, who took the cross from him and blessed him. It meant Matthew would have a long and happy life.

c h a p t e r
thirteen

Under a brightening sky, Sam Hagen picked up his pace. Pushing himself a little, keeping a steady rhythm. He ran the usual route, four miles in a long rectangle through the subdivision where he lived. Brookwood. No brooks, no woods. Only flat terrain with curbless streets and houses on a common theme, worth two or three hundred grand apiece. Blank windows and empty yards at this hour, the Sunday paper lying in driveways. There would be an article, with pictures, about Eddie Mora. Someone in Washington had leaked the story about his being Michigan senator Phil Kirkman's choice as running mate. Kirkman, needing some minority blood on the ticket. Edward José Mora. A little young, said the commentators, but the V.P. hopeful on both tickets this election year would be a sop to minorities.

Sam breathed the damp, heavy air in and out and concentrated on the ground ahead of him. He wore an elastic band on his left knee and five-pound wrist weights.

As a kid, when he'd run through his father's orange grove or around the track for football practice, the rhythm had been enough, the joy of blood rushing through his veins and the earth blurring under his feet. There wasn't much joy in this, the slow pounding on asphalt and concrete, but not doing it made him feel vaguely dissatisfied with himself.

He had awakened before dawn, not used to sleeping

alone. Dina was in Tarpon Springs with her father. She had called yesterday morning to say she'd made it safely, which was the drill whenever anybody went out of town. Sam had asked how Costas was. *Fine. He's fishing off the dock. Pick me up at the airport Sunday at four-thirty.* Then she'd hung up as he was in the middle of saying, *Tell the old man to catch a few for me.*

She was still incensed that Sam had given her a hard time about taking two thousand dollars out of their savings account. She hadn't asked, just carried the cash to Frank Tolin on Friday as a cost deposit. Then she told Sam about it as she was packing a bag for the trip. He'd been irritated, said he was going to call Frank and get it back. And Dina had calmly looked around from her closet and said no. *Would you rather I get more Prozac from Dr. Berman? Would that be easier?*

He had to admit her mood had improved, if anger could be called an improvement on depression.

Last Monday afternoon, Frank Tolin had explained how difficult a wrongful death suit would be in a case like this. The city, which had maintained the street, had immunity from prosecution. Uncle Andy's, the bar that had served Matthew, was still in business, but did they have enough assets to pay a judgment or the insurance to cover it? And even if Matthew's Harley, nearly new, had been defective in some way, had the defect contributed to the accident? Dina had been undeterred; Frank promised to look into it. He never said he wanted a two-thousand-dollar cost deposit.

What irritated Sam most was that out of professional courtesy, if not good manners, Frank should have discussed money with the father of the decedent before he asked the mother for two thousand dollars. Sam had thought Frank was doing this as a favor. *Hey, buddy, we go way back.*

The brake on Sam's temper was realizing it had been partly his own fault: He had made it clear this was Dina's undertaking, not his. He had gone with her just the one time. He didn't care to see that office again, where he had made no success of private practice. And he didn't want to see Caitlin Dorn, if she happened to drop by. He had imagined Frank showing him and Dina out just as Caitlin came breezing in.

Rounding the corner past some pine trees, Sam ran directly at the sun. A few trees still lay in the underbrush, toppled by the hurricane; the lot was tangled and overgrown. Sam took a deep lungful of air and expelled it slowly, then again to ease the stitch in his side. He wondered if he was at the age where a man could drop in his tracks, sprawling on the pavement a half mile from home. There had been times when he would have welcomed it.

He stretched out his arms, feeling the pull of the wrist weights, and finally the burn in his muscles.

Since showing up in his office, Caitlin Dorn had reappeared in his thoughts. That Dale Finley knew about her made Sam churn with helpless fury. He felt vulnerable, caught in a lie no longer relevant. They hadn't been careful, three years ago. Finley had found out; other people could, too.

If Caitlin testified, one of the other prosecutors would do the questioning, Sam had decided. If she ever got to the stand. She might swear in a deposition she had seen nothing. Sam had seen witnesses fade out. Indignation over a crime only lasted so long, when it had happened to someone else. Then a witness would start thinking about other choices. Caitlin could be offered an assignment for a major fashion magazine in Italy. If she didn't look out for herself, who would? Loyalties were fleeting on South Beach.

Fleeting everywhere.

Open-handed, she had struck a glancing, ineffectual blow across Sam's cheek, then tried to shove him off her. He pressed her wrists into the mattress. "What in hell's the matter with you?"

"I don't want to hear it. How much you love me. Next you'll tell me you've been thinking of a divorce." She turned her face. "Don't ruin it, okay?"

He laughed, astonished. "Don't you trust anyone?"

When Sam slowed in his own driveway, breathing through his mouth, hands on hips, the muscles in his legs were trembling. Sweat soaked his shorts and T-shirt. He picked up the Sunday paper, then went inside to shower and change.

Before going downstairs to make coffee he looked in on his daughter. The blinds were shut tightly, and in the near-dark he could make out Melanie's shape, her hair tangled on the pillow, and the pink curve of her hand. A bear with half its fur gone lay upside down on the carpet. Fourteen years old, and she still slept with her bear. Sam quietly closed the door.

Three years ago, neither of the kids had known how close he had come to running away, packing what would fit in his car, signing over the house to Dina, paying alimony, child support, it didn't matter. He'd been alive again, leaping, breathless, the blood pounding through his body. If he couldn't live honestly, openly, then what was the point?

He had come close, but couldn't leap that far. Sam had always thought of himself as having some standards in this world. He wanted his children to know he wasn't like the parents of some of their friends: those adults who permitted anything and demanded nothing; who drank and overdosed; who told their kids what a sad, rotten business life was; who overspent and whined and slept around with the abandon of teenagers.

Matthew had never known about his father's infidelity, but he had heard the angry voices behind the bedroom door. He had seen his mother turn her back in icy silence. Had seen Sam come home late from work, then change into his running shoes and be gone. Matthew had carried a grudge for unnamed sins.

Melanie, if she had known, would have been all right. She had always been more forgiving, more placid and steady. The one who swept up the bits of shattered glass from the back porch after her brother had come home at dawn, stinking drunk, sixteen years old. Sam had seized him by the front of his jacket, and they had stumbled, both of them, into the sliding glass door while Dina sat on the kitchen floor and wept.

Last night Sam had awakened to noises from Matthew's room. Grumpy and squinting, he had found Melanie there, going through photographs and papers that her mother had been organizing into folders for Frank Tolin.

Sam had ordered her to get back to bed.

He had watched her go obediently down the hall, a plump girl in a big lavender sleep shirt. At the end of the hall she turned and looked at him. *Night, Dad.*

Sam felt bad about yelling at her, and he had his knuckles on her door, about to knock, but he didn't know what in hell he would tell her. He went back down the hall to Matthew's room to turn out the light.

On Frank Tolin's instructions, Dina had been organizing Matthew's school records, yearbooks, snapshots, crayon drawings and handmade Mother's Day cards, reports from his psychiatrists and counselors—a sad exhumation of every scrap of information she had saved, and she had saved them all. Sam refused to take part. It terrified him beyond explanation. Dina pierced him with her own: *You'd rather believe in accidents. It lets you off the hook, doesn't it?*

If this wrongful death suit were ever filed, Frank Tolin would recreate Matthew Stavros Hagen as he had never existed in life. Maybe he had a few problems, but really, don't all our teenagers go through rough times? The defense wouldn't dare alienate the jury by ripping into the dead boy's parents, sitting side by side at the counsel table holding hands and weeping. In his final argument, Frank might show the jury a series of framed photographs. Mr. and Mrs. Hagen's son at birth, at age two, age five, ten, and so on. Here he is in his Cub Scout uniform, here on his soccer team. And here, the happy family on vacation in Colorado. But the last frame would be blank. Frank would walk slowly past the jurors holding it in his hands. *How do you measure a parent's grief, ladies and gentlemen, as you look at this empty frame?*

Love quantified. Grief translated into cash. The deeper the grief, the higher the recovery. Sitting in Frank Tolin's office, jaw clenched, Sam had found the idea revolting.

At the door to Matthew's room, Sam reached in to turn off the light but dropped his hand by his side. Dark blue carpet. Single bed, chest of drawers, desk and bookcase.

Dina had taken the lurid posters down, but other than that, it was the same as when Matthew had moved out, a year and a half before he died. Now there were some open boxes on the floor, and neat stacks of folders and envelopes on the bed.

Sam used to get sick with rage, opening this door, the chaos hitting him in the face. Clothes that lay where they'd been dropped, a beer bottle on the windowsill, school papers crumpled on the desk. Three thousand dollars' worth of stereo and video equipment, CDs scattered on the floor. A bass guitar and amp, used for a month then forgotten.

Matthew standing barechested in the center of the room, laughing, his face contorted and shiny with tears, the barrel of a Colt pistol at his temple. *Hey, don't worry I'll blow my brains out, Dad. I don't have any, remember?*

Sam was twenty years old when he flew home by army transport to see his father, Lewis Hagen, for the last time. The old man was lying wasted to bones on white hospital sheets, his belly tight with a swollen liver, and his eyes yellow and filmy. It made Sam queasy, although he had seen worse where he had just come from.

The eyes rolled to see who was there. "Hey, Sammy." Then a dying man's reedy voice. "It's my boy." The nurse looked around and smiled. Lewis said, "Damn. Don't he make a picture?"

Sam's parents had divorced before he could walk. He and his mother, born Lily Hirsch, had lived with her elderly aunt in Borough Park, Brooklyn. When he was ten, his mother died and none of her family could take him.

The neighbors came by to say how sad it was, how terrible for Lily's son. Sam sat with his great-aunt and her adult children on the mourning bench and drew himself in, numb with misery, while relatives whispered in the kitchen. Impossible, they said, to give him to his father. Lily's shame, the man no one ever mentioned. She had gone to Miami Beach, a trip with her parents. A pretty woman, but almost thirty. How they met—who knew?— but they had to marry. Of course it hadn't lasted. Lily came home with the boy and kept house for her parents till they passed away, and now what? Who would take him? Not so smart, this one. Too quiet. She had insurance. That would help.

Sam's cousins glared at him from across the room, kicking the heels of their shiny shoes on the horsehair sofa, making their opinions known. Three days later, Lewis Hagen showed up in a coat too thin for New York in November. He was a towering man with a wide face, an older version of the black-and-white snapshot Sam had seen by accident in his mother's dresser drawer. After her death the picture had vanished, and he'd been afraid to ask where it had gone.

There were discussions in the front room with the door closed. Shouts. Outrage and threats. Finally, Lewis Hagen tossed Sam's bag into the trunk of his car and told him they were going to Winter Haven. "You know where that is, kiddo?" Sam shook his head. "It's in Flor'da." Lewis was driving a Ford convertible with red upholstery and dings in two fenders. He squealed the tires taking off, and Sam looked backward until they turned the corner and the house was gone. His father lit a cigarette. He had freckled, sunburned hands. "I'm sorry about your momma. She sent me your picture. I should've wrote you, and I'm sorry about that, too."

They stopped at a motel in New Jersey and picked up a woman named Fay who had kept Lewis Hagen company on the trip north. It took two days to get to Florida, stopping overnight with Fay's relatives in North Carolina. By the time they reached Georgia the top was down on the convertible, and Sam took his coat off. The second night he lay under a blanket in the backseat, the wind roaring around him, and watched Fay's fingernails scratch through his father's thick brown hair, heard her singing with the radio. The telephone wires along the road rose and fell, and the moon passed overhead. It would be years before Sam found out that his mother's life insurance had been worth nearly fifty thousand dollars and that Lewis had pissed it all away.

At sunrise they rolled into the scraggly yard of a concrete block, ranch-style house. A grove stretched out behind it, rows and rows of bushy trees and hard, green citrus, the land gently rolling, the dirt gray and sandy. Lewis Hagen made a living off oranges, tangelos, and grapefruit. If the crop was bad, he did auto repair work. He drank; he couldn't keep a woman; and he lost more and more acreage a year to citrus blight or freezes. He was a brutal man, not for the enjoyment of it, but because that was what he himself had known.

At school, Sam was tormented for his accent and his shy, clumsy manner. Finally Lewis Hagen took off his belt and beat him. He couldn't stand a whiner. If Sam came home again with bruises and hadn't knocked the crap out of the other boy, he'd catch it again. By the time Sam reached junior high his voice had settled into Florida Cracker and no one dared touch him. His arms and legs were muscled from climbing up and down ladders carrying canvas bags of fruit. His hands were calloused, and the thorns on the branches drew blood. Like his friends, Sam learned how to use a shotgun and a .22 rifle. He got his restricted drivers license at fourteen and learned to drive on the jouncing, sandy roads between the orange trees. He wore his hair in a crew cut and played tackle for the Winter Haven Blue Devils. A big boy, six-two, two hundred pounds, still not big enough to whip Lewis. Sam might have earned a scholarship, but he studied just enough to stay on the team. There was no point in going on; he would own the grove someday.

Lewis worried about the communists. He was opposed to antiwar protesters and forced integration and would get drunk worrying about it, although there were no hippies in Winter Haven, and the Negroes made few demands. He would get drunk to ease the pain from the shrapnel he still carried. He showed Sam his Purple Heart and let him hold the Luger he'd taken off a dead German soldier.

He mortgaged the grove, then stayed too drunk to make the payments. Sam worked thirty hours straight during a hard January freeze, tended the smudge pots, hired pickers, yelled at them, pushed them hard, nearly failed his senior year, but took care of the bank. When Lewis signed another mortgage that spring. When Sam screamed profanities and threw a bottle of Jack Daniel's into the yard, Lewis went for him. Sam knocked him down. Lewis got up, spat out a mouthful of blood, and hit Sam in the stomach. They continued like that until Sam saw that his father would die before he stayed down. Sam was the first to stop. But something had shifted, and Lewis Hagen left the running of the grove to Sam, then seventeen.

In the summer of 1967, Kenny Davis, last season's Blue Devils quarterback, was drafted into the army. In February they sent his body home in a steel coffin and gave his mother a folded flag. At the funeral somebody gave a speech about patriotism and there was a 21-gun salute. Sam and four other boys on the team got drunk that night and the next day drove to the recruiting office in Tampa and signed up, ready to go after graduation. Lewis shook his hand and told him to be careful.

Vietnam was even hotter than Central Florida, and wetter. Sam found himself running through tangled, steaming underbrush, with an M-16, two ammunition belts, a Claymore mine, and half a dozen fragmentation grenades. Sliding down a wire out of a chopper. Churning up a hill in the red mud through the rain that drummed steadily, without letup, on his helmet and poncho. Sam was halfway through his second tour before he slowed down and saw what it was. After his lieutenant, talking on the radio next to him, pitched backward, a neat red hole through his eye, the back of his head gone. After Sam saw body bags by the hundreds loaded on the same C5As that had arrived with hundreds of fresh troops. After Sam's squad chased a Cong guerrilla out of the jungle. Sam raked the thin walls of a hut with automatic rifle fire, then went inside. He put a boot under the body and turned it over. A boy about thirteen. He had known when he pulled the trigger, but he couldn't stop.

A couple of months later, Lewis was in the hospital for the last time, and Sam took emergency leave. He wore his uniform with three service ribbons, a unit crest, and a combat infantryman's badge, and on his left shoulder the 101st Airborne patch, the Screaming Eagles. His boots and belt gleamed.

Lewis smiled: thin lips pulled back over protruding teeth. "Damn. Look at this boy. Ain't he something else?" He lifted his hand to cradle Sam's face in his dry palm. Sam barely held himself together. He pulled up a chair and sat down, and told his dad it looked like the war had turned around all of a sudden. They had the North Vietnamese on the run now, nearly pushed back across the DMZ, and it wouldn't be long before all the guys would be coming home.

c h a p t e r
fourteen

This late in the season, fashion shoots in Miami often began at dawn to avoid the heat of midday. Caitlin waited in the tiny open-air lobby of the Century Hotel to join the caravan to the site. The production van led the way, followed by a rented Lincoln carrying the client and his people, and then by Caitlin in her car, crammed with her equipment. Ali Duncan, who would help Rafael Soto with makeup, sat in the passenger seat with a camera bag on her lap. Two models followed Caitlin in their car, and Tommy Chang's Jeep brought up the rear. Today would be the last shots for the fall catalog of Narragansett Traders, a Boston sportswear company. Caitlin got the job because they liked the work she'd done for them last year.

Now her camera was set up on some flat ground fifty yards or so from a ten-foot-high ridge of white sand and rock, which had been tossed there years ago by dredging machines. Virginia Key was home to scraggly woods, a nudist beach, some rundown boat shacks, and the Central District Treatment Plant, the county's main sewage facility. Low, concrete buildings lay toward the west beyond a chain-link fence. There was no odor, or else the residents of Fisher Island would have raised hell. That exclusive piece of ground lay just north, a landscaped, Mediterranean fantasy of red-tiled roofs and yachts tied to private docks. Miami Beach was out of view beyond it.

Caitlin had a crew of three today: two photo assistants

and Rafael Soto. She would have no problem paying
them. This was the last day of a four-day shoot at fifteen
hundred per, before expenses. Not great, but not bad, either. Caitlin had known top fashion photographers to pull
in twenty-five thousand a day. They would shoot dozens
of rolls. But she had never seen Richard Avedon waiting
around next to a sewage plant to do sportswear for a
catalog.

Caitlin and the art director stood under her umbrella
and went over some photos from yesterday, which they
had taken at a marina. She heard the crunch of gravel and
glanced up. Frank Tolin's green Jaguar was parked next
to her own car. The door was opened, a flash of chrome
and glass in the early morning sun.

The art director's expression turned sour under the brim
of his red baseball cap.

"He's a friend of mine. He won't be in the way." Frank
had come to shoots before, but only when invited. She
didn't know what he was doing there. Two nights ago
they had argued, and she hadn't heard from him since.

He walked around the Jaguar with a cup of coffee from
McDonald's and sipped it as he propped one booted foot
on the bumper. He knew to stay where he was. He con-
tented himself with a nod in her direction.

Caitlin sent the boys to check the exposure. Tommy
Chang had brought a friend from photography class to
help out. Jean-Louis scurried up the rocky hill with the
meter. Blond coils of curly, sunbleached hair bounced on
his head. He and Tommy were dressed about the same: no
shirts, baggy shorts, big sneakers. Tommy, whose bandanna kept his hair from blowing into his eyes, was at-
taching the Polaroid to the telephoto. The people from the
catalog company and the production staff, average age
well under thirty, stood around talking, waiting for the
models.

When the art director went to check on something,
Caitlin crossed the road to talk to Frank.

He finished the last of his coffee and tossed the cup into
some weeds. "I'm not going to stay," he said. "I told
Marty Cass I'd meet him this morning." Frank smiled
with one side of his mouth, his mustache tilting. "He's

going to push me to sell the building to those Jordanians he found the other day."

"Well. Why not?"

"You'd have to pay rent on your apartment."

"Did you come to tell me that?"

"Oh, Catie. That was intended to be humorous. No, what I came for was to apologize. Our disagreement the other night should never have happened."

She laughed. "Disagreement?" It had begun with a petty snit over flowers he had sent her, which she had neglected to thank him for. It had ended in profanities and mutual shoving, till she left in a fury, her car screeching out of the parking lot ten floors below.

Frank's eyes closed for a second in acknowledgment. "Yes. More than a disagreement. You deserve a proper apology. And here I am. Seven o'clock in the morning, hat in hand, so to speak. I'm sorry. I am immensely—galactically—sorry. You didn't call. I was worried, so I went by your place last night. I nearly came upstairs. A juvenile reaction, but I wanted to see you. In the end, dignity held."

Fatigue showed in the shadows on his face. He had a long, narrow face, almost foxlike. He was lean everywhere, with a flat middle, practically no rear end, and long legs corded with sinew. There was nothing to ease the bumps, she had once told him. If they were together for too long, she would come away bruised. Now she felt she was veering toward the edge again, the place where all she wanted was to be left alone in an asexual, ageless state of feeling nothing at all.

She said, "I can't talk now."

But Frank was looking past her, shaking his head and smiling.

A male model had just come out of the Winnebago in deck shoes, sailing shorts, and a crewneck sweater. Rafael had pinked his nose and cheeks to simulate the effects of sun and a brisk wind off the North Atlantic. Trailed by one of the costumers, the model started climbing the rock pile. Caitlin could see his underwear through a rectangle cut out of the back of his sailing shorts, and bare skin showed through a missing piece of sweater. The fabric samples would be kept on file. The garments were held together with safety pins.

Frank said, "All this has ruined me for men's fashion magazines."

"Caitlin!" Tommy Chang was waving at her. "They're ready to roll."

"Gotta go," she said. "Talk to you later."

"Wait." He grabbed her wrist. "Take this thought with you. I want us to live together."

She made a disbelieving laugh.

"I'll sell my condo." He tightened his grip on her arm. "We'll find a place together. Something new and untouched. We'll be the first ones to live in it."

"Oh, Frank. It wouldn't work."

"How do you know? Have we spent more than a week in each other's company?"

"I have to go."

"Think about it," he said.

With no more answer than a shake of her head, Caitlin hurried back to her camera.

Bracing one foot on a pitted white rock, the costumer smoothed the model's collar with a straight pin—she had a mouthful of them—then jumped kangaroo-style down the hill. Caitlin looked through the lens. The wind was ruffling the model's hair. He was a nice-looking guy, blond and collegiate.

"You get laid a lot, Jeffrey?" The art director liked to keep them loosened up. He was a pudgy guy in faded green hiking shorts and a Nine Inch Nails T-shirt.

Someone started talking about a new restaurant in Moscow called Santa Fe, and how the steaks weren't bad if you wanted to pay fifty bucks, but you couldn't get decent salad at any price.

Caitlin called out, "Turn your head to the side a little bit, like that. Okay. Great. A little lower. Now look out to sea." The camera whirred and clicked. Tommy Chang changed camera bodies, giving her a fresh roll. Jean-Louis ran to check the exposure again, and Caitlin took a series of the model sitting down with an arm draped over one knee.

Then the art director called a break to use the bathroom in the van.

Frank had wandered nearer, hands in his pockets.

Caitlin said quietly, "I was thinking, as I lay in bed at three o'clock this morning trying to sleep, that I might go to New York next month with Rafael. He's leaving for the summer. We could drive up together."

"New York. Why?"

"When you hang around Miami too long, Frank, you lose your edge. There's nothing here except people who see each other all the time at the same places, and all they can talk about is each other, with absolutely no sense of loyalty or perspective, while they try to avoid the worst thing that can happen to them—boredom. I'm so tired of this scene."

"It's all a scene, baby. Wherever you go, it's a scene. New York is worse, or don't you remember how it was?"

"I could see some exhibits. Take classes. Talk to people who are doing what I want to do."

"Which is?"

"Taking real pictures. Not making them up. Not—" She lifted an arm toward the bottom of the rock pile, where the next models had come out, two girls in turtleneck shirts. Their hair was perfectly disarranged, as if they had been walking on the beach.

Unnecessarily, Caitlin checked to see if there was fresh film in her equipment cart. She said, "Maybe I could even go overseas and work freelance for one of the news services for a few months."

Frank said, "You could be a war correspondent in Bosnia."

She glared at him.

He spread placating hands. "Mind if I ask what you intend to do for money? Manhattan ain't cheap."

"I know people. Last summer I stayed in Miami and nearly starved to death. I might just as well be poor there as here."

"Would I let you starve?"

She laughed. "How much do I owe you already?"

"I've lost count. You know, it's a little hard to believe, sweetheart, that there's no work to be had in all of South Florida."

"There's work. I know of an import-export company

that wants pictures of the company officers in the board-room for the annual report."

"Does it pay?"

"Weddings and bar mitzvahs pay," she said.

"Yes, but those are boring."

"My God. You can be such a bastard. I think you should leave now."

He stood silently for a moment. The wind lifted a strand of dark hair on his high forehead. "I'm sorry. You're making me crazy, you know. How do you expect me to feel? Do you think I'm happy you won't be around? It scares the hell out of me, thinking about you going to New York. You might never come home." The strong white light showed every line and sag in his face. "We've been together a long time, Catie. Good or bad, but we've stayed together. I love you."

The last words came out as a whisper, and his mouth made a lopsided smile. Caitlin noticed that his lips were chapped. *How weak and unattractive,* she thought. *Begging like that. I wish you'd just go away.* And then, embarrassed by her thoughts, she turned to a clipboard hanging from her tripod, where notes for the next series of photos had been written.

"I wouldn't live there permanently," she said. "I can't stand the cold anymore. And I'll be back over the summer as well, for depositions and the trial. Sam Hagen says I'll be one of the witnesses." She had told Frank about talking to Sam. Not everything. Only that she had gone to help Ali Duncan.

Cupping her hands, Caitlin yelled to Tommy Chang. "Take those reflectors about twenty feet down the ridge." She watched him toss the silver circles into the air and catch them. His black hair flowed down his back.

Frank sat on a folding metal chair and extended his legs. "Sam looked pretty good on TV."

She shrugged. "I suppose so." A segment of his press conference had been shown on the eleven o'clock news Friday night. She and Frank had seen it in his bedroom as they undressed after coming back from dinner. They had never made it into bed. Frank asked about the flowers he'd sent, and whether she took his gifts so much for granted that a thank-you was optional.

Now Frank sat with his fingers laced behind his neck. He tapped Caitlin's calf with the toe of his boot. "You know what I read in the paper this morning? Eddie Mora's on the list of possible running mates for Senator Kirkman. That means Sam Hagen could be our next state attorney, if he runs for election. What do you think about Sam as state attorney?"

Still holding the clipboard and pencil, Caitlin kept her eyes on the notes she'd made. She was deciding how to respond. Finally she said, "I think he'd do a good job. He could probably win an election."

"Sam's a great guy." Frank reached out to hook the back of Caitlin's shorts and pull her toward him. "Did he remember you?"

"Of course. Let go, Frank, I'm working."

Last night they and another couple, a client and his wife, had gone to Pagliacci, a supremely chic restaurant in Coral Gables. Three hundred dollars for dinner. Almost half her rent for the month, if she had to pay rent. Frank had gone to the men's room three times, coming back with his nose red. On the way home they fought about it. He told her he was tired, that he had needed it, that she should shut up. Later she'd been brushing her teeth when Frank turned on the nightly news. She caught the words *state attorney's office* and *sexual battery prosecution,* and she came out to see. And there was Sam in a roomful of lights and people. It only lasted a few seconds, but long enough to tell her that of course he couldn't have given all that up for her. Even so, she had expected, as Sam Hagen had led her to his office last Monday, and closed the door, that he would show some flicker of interest. He was a man, and she was still attractive. And they had been lovers, after all. Three years wasn't that long ago. But she had seen nothing in his eyes. Nothing.

"Hey, folks! Heads up!" The art director came out of the production van with a bottle of water, yelling for everybody to snap it up, let's go, he had a plane to catch at noon.

Caitlin called, "Jean-Louis, I need you over here, *s'il vous plaît.*" He trotted toward her umbrella, curls bouncing, eager as a puppy.

"Frank, I have to shoo you away."

The two leggy, sun-ripened girls trudged up the hill, hips swaying, one of them grabbing the other's arm to keep from slipping down. The backs of their bodysuits were cut out and clipped with clothespins. This would be a shot from the waist up, featuring the necklines of the body suits. The girls' legs were bare, and they wore sandals.

"Tommy?"

"Right here," he said.

"Go get me some water, will you?" Caitlin asked. "Lots of ice."

She brought the camera into sharp focus, and Jean-Louis held up the meter and called out the exposure. Caitlin yelled that the models were too shiny. The assistant costumer, who had stepped just out of camera range, came forward to pat a sheen of sweat off their faces. Apparently they wore dark-tinted contacts. They weren't squinting in the bright sun.

The art director yelled, "Hey! Lean back so we can see the snaps on the crotch."

The blond model laughed. "You want me to unsnap it?"

"Yeah, show us some bush."

Their slender figures were crisply outlined against the pure blue sky. They posed one way then the other, side by side then apart. Smiling into the lens, then away.

The art director was dancing. "Give it all, girls. Pump it. Pump it up."

Tommy Chang washed his hands in the production van bathroom, dried them on somebody's old T-shirt, then came out to fill Caitlin's water bottle.

One of the models sat at the makeup mirror with Rafael Soto. She had her mouth open while he went around it with a lipstick brush, and her face was pointed up at the TV behind the driver's seat. She was watching a tape somebody had made of a soap opera. There was a model with short blond hair reading a magazine, and the guy model was in the back changing clothes again.

Ali Duncan stood at the table wiping off Rafael's hot curlers and things, and Tommy had to move around her to get to the fridge. "Hey. What's up?"

She put her blue eyes on him for a second. She didn't talk much to guys anymore, which was understandable. She would hang out with Rafael Soto, but that was different.

Tommy filled Caitlin's insulated container with ice, then poured in some Evian and screwed the lid back on. He noticed the box of wheat crackers. Lowfat, no salt. He took a handful of Chips Ahoy instead. The van was like a little house, everything all crammed in together. He leaned against the counter and looked at Ali again. Her hair was in a red braid down her back, and there were curls around her face where it had come loose.

He went over to stand next to her. "Are you supposed to be the new student of the master?"

She stared at him.

"That child is a genius," Rafael declared. He winked at her, then tossed the little brush into his makeup case and came back with a big one. He flicked powder all over the model's face.

Tommy went over to see what he was doing. "Why's her mouth brown like that?"

"It isn't *brown,* it's *natural.* She has to look like your basic girl next door, so as not to distract from the clothes. This is catalog, not editorial." Rafael's glasses were like red letter O's, and the lights on the makeup mirror slid across them when he moved.

"A few years ago," he said, "I was on a shoot with Helmut Newton, lots of white skin and black lipstick and death-ray eyes. Catalog is something of a reversal, but you take what you can get in this trade."

"Yeah, I guess."

The dark-haired model was looking at herself in the mirror, tilting her head this way and that. She smiled. "*Divino.* Rafael, you are fabulous." She kissed the air beside his cheek.

"*Gracias,*" he said. "The manipulation of reality to create the illusion of truth."

She gave him a puzzled look, then went into the back to change. The guy was still back there, but Tommy had noticed that models didn't mind getting undressed in front of each other.

He moved out of the way when he heard the door

opening. It was Caitlin's boyfriend, Frank, who stepped up into the van and asked if he could get some coffee.

"In the pot," Rafael said, waving a comb. "Carmen, honey. *Ven aca, mi amor.* Let's make you beautiful." The model on the sofa went over and sat down and started talking about a guy she was going out with. Rafael told her the guy was a total jerk, was she crazy?

Tommy ate another cookie. Ali was packing used makeup sponges into a plastic bag. He spoke to her so nobody else could hear. "I'm sorry about what happened. I guess you don't want to be reminded and all, but I wanted to, you know, tell you." His face was getting hot. "That's it."

Her hands stopped moving. She laid them flat on the table, then looked at him. "I've been meaning to tell you something, too. You have chocolate on your upper lip."

He brushed at his mouth, laughing a little.

"Eurotrash, if you want my opinion," Rafael was saying. "At least they shaved their legs. The agent must have told them to. You have to tell these girls, the Germans especially, about personal hygiene."

The guy came from the back in long pants and a windbreaker, said hi, then went out.

Ali went over to Caitlin's boyfriend. "Excuse me? Frank? I mean, Mr. Tolin? Can I ask you a question, as a lawyer?"

"Sure." He was stirring some sugar into his coffee.

"Somebody came by my apartment yesterday who said he worked for Klaus Ruffini's lawyers, and he wanted to take my statement. I tried to call Mr. Hagen but it was Saturday. I told the guy to go away. Was that all right?"

He nodded. "You don't have to talk to anybody unless Sam Hagen says so. Call him tomorrow, let him know what happened."

"Yeah, I will. Thanks."

Frank Tolin went over to see Rafael put makeup on the model.

Ali picked up the magazine the model had left, then plopped down in one of the bench seats at the table.

Tommy slid in across from her. "Hagen. He's the prosecutor."

"Uh-huh." Ali's head was bowed over the magazine.

She had a pink shirt on with a thin gold chain. He could see the pulse in her neck.

He said, "Yeah. Caitlin said you and her went to see him. How'd it go?"

Ali lifted her face. "All right."

"That's good."

"They're friends from a long time ago," Ali said. "She told me all about him first, so it was okay. I have to see him a few more times, but I don't mind. Except he wants me to move back home."

"Are you going to?"

"No way. Me and my mom do not get along. And how would I get to work? I don't have a car."

"I do." He ate the rest of the cookie, then brushed his thumb across his mouth. "I mean, if you need to go somewhere I could take you. I've got the red Jeep. That's my car. I guess you saw it already."

She only looked at him, then started reading the magazine again.

Tommy asked, "Did you ever meet his son? The one that died?"

"Yeah, a couple of times. He was nice. A little wild, but he was okay."

"Know what I heard?" Tommy would have mentioned Charlie Sullivan by name, but Rafael was there. "Somebody told me he was hittin' the drugs. Some serious shit."

"Yeah, I know," Ali said.

"Stupid, man. Stupid."

"I know," she said. "Well, I tried coke, but not anymore. Stavros was doing crack, which is the *worst*. George Fonseca got him started on that, plus heroin."

Tommy heard the clack of a brush getting thrown onto the table at the makeup mirror. Rafael said, "For your information, children, Stavros was *not* a junkie. He wasn't *that* messed up. He was a delightful, intelligent young man."

Frank Tolin was eating a wheat cracker. He said to Rafael, "How well did you two know each other?"

The way he asked it made Rafael stare at him through his round, red glasses. Then he turned his back and started looking for something in his makeup case.

Frank glanced at Tommy and Ali, then left the van. He was whistling through his teeth.

When the door closed, Rafael said, "Why she's in love with him I fail to comprehend." He held his hand over the model's eyes and sprayed her hair.

Ali settled back into the corner with the magazine.

Tommy said, "So. You Rollerblade."

She turned a page. "Yeah. How'd you know that?"

"I saw you a couple of times at Lummus Park. You're pretty good." She looked over the top of the magazine. He made the cookies into a stack, then a line of four. "Maybe you'd like to go out sometime."

"Thanks, but I'm busy."

Tommy could feel himself blushing. "No, I mean, we could, like, meet there and skate. At the park." Her blue eyes were on him like spotlights. He shrugged and looked back down at the cookies.

"People might talk about you," she said.

He laughed. "I don't give a damn. And they'd better not say anything about you either."

"Sometimes they do, right to my face."

"If you were with me, they wouldn't. I wouldn't let anybody bother you."

Ali laughed, but not like she thought it was stupid, what he'd said. "Well. Thanks." He noticed that she had dimples.

For the last series of photos, Caitlin set up her camera close to the shore for a view of Fisher Island's greenery and red tile roofs. These would appear in the background to give the impression that the models were in the Mediterranean.

She glanced around when Frank handed her the ice water she'd asked for ten minutes ago.

"Where's Tommy?"

"Hitting on Ali Duncan," Frank said.

Jean-Louis nodded and laughed. "Man, I thought he didn't have the guts to talk to her. I bet him five bucks he wouldn't."

"Well, go tell him to get his fanny out here, will you?" Caitlin flipped the mouthpiece open on the container and drank. It wasn't hot yet, but in another month summer would set its teeth and not let go till late October.

"Aren't you supposed to see Marty Cass?" Caitlin said. She picked up some Polaroids that Jean-Louis had just taken.

"Marty can wait." Frank took them out of her hand and laid them on the cart. "Before the little rascals come back, I want to know: Was George Fonseca giving heroin to Matthew Hagen? Ali and Tommy were talking about it." When Caitlin stared at him, he explained, "It matters for the lawsuit I'm doing for the Hagens."

"I thought it wasn't going anywhere," she said.

"So far, no, it isn't, but if I find a defendant who isn't out of state, insolvent, or immune from judgment, then maybe I'll file it to see what happens. But if Matthew was not only drunk but nodding off because he'd been shooting smack—"

"What are you going to tell Sam and Dina?" she asked.

"That depends on what you tell me," Frank said. "Was he or wasn't he?"

Caitlin finally said, "He'd had some problems, but I don't think he was seriously hooked on anything. He was trying hard not to be. Don't tell them if you don't have to."

Tommy and Jean-Louis came running out of the van. Tommy came over to get the exposure meter, and Jean-Louis picked up one of the big reflectors on the ground near the models.

"Get over there!" The art director was jabbing at his watch. "Places to go, things to do, people."

Looking through the lens, Caitlin focused on a young man and a girl in matching windbreakers, both smiling. The girl was leaning lightly against his chest. Caitlin pressed the shutter and the camera clicked and buzzed, two frames per second. The art director came over to check the angles, then shouted for the models to stand in another position.

"Catie? I have to go."

"Okay." She looked through the viewfinder and pressed the shutter release. "I'll call you later."

"We'll talk about what I asked you before."

"All right."

Tommy told her to wait a second, the sun was going behind a cloud.

Frank said, "You don't remember what I asked you before."

She turned around and made a guilty smile. "I'm sorry."

"Come live with me. I'll buy us a fantastic place. You can have your studio right there if you want."

He was happy, she could see that. She knew she'd have to tell him no. "We'll talk about it later," she said.

A motion caught her eye. The brim on the art director's hat had turned toward the production van. Now the client and the costumer looked in the same direction, and so did the woman they were talking to.

Then Caitlin heard someone wailing.

Rafael Soto was at the door of the Winnebago, swinging from the frame. He took the steps down, walked a few feet, then sank to the ground.

Everyone ran to him. Caitlin pushed through. "Rafael!" She knelt beside him. "What happened?" Looking up she saw Ali Duncan's wide-eyed face at the door.

Rafael pressed into Caitlin's shoulder. "He's dead! Oh, God. Oh, God. They shot him."

"Shot who? Rafael, *please*."

He sobbed. "Sullivan. He's dead. I called the agency about the job tomorrow, and they told me. Someone shot him. Oh, my God, he's dead."

chapter
fifteen

At Pier Park, the southernmost point on Miami Beach, a long mound of sand ran parallel to the beach as a storm break. A boardwalk had been constructed along the top of it, and sea oats had been planted to keep it from blowing away. Just past the point where the sea oats ended and the ground sloped gently toward the ocean, lay the body of Charlie Sullivan. A Canadian couple out walking at dawn had at first thought he was asleep, then began to wonder how he could breathe with his face in the sand.

Sam Hagen was not the assistant state attorney on call, but Detective Eugene Ryabin beeped him. When Sam arrived there was yellow crime tape across the entrance to the boardwalk and an officer posted. He showed his ID, went under the tape, and climbed the wooden steps. From the top he could see a group of about a dozen Miami Beach Police detectives and uniformed officers gathered in a ragged semicircle twenty yards up the beach. Through the gaps between them he glimpsed a prone figure which he assumed to be the remains of Charlie Sullivan. The body, clad in tan slacks and white shirt, lay on a diagonal axis, legs pointed roughly toward the water, head near the grass-covered dune.

On the beach uniformed officers kept the onlookers back about fifty yards on either side. A few tourists had their cameras out. Crime scene techs walked slowly back and forth, picking up a soda can here, a cigarette butt there. Two news photographers had their telephotos trained on the activity, and a helicopter from a local TV station was hovering overhead, not quite close enough to be a nuisance.

As Sam descended the steps, Ryabin noticed him and waved him over. Sam could feel the sand going over the tops of his leather shoes. Nobody was going to get castings of footprints from this terrain.

A thin, young-looking man in a plaid sport shirt and casual slacks squatted beside the body—David Corso from the Medical Examiner's office. The police wouldn't touch the body until he had finished his examination.

Sam stopped beside Ryabin.

"Anything so far?"

Ryabin shook his head. "Nothing." The word came out as *nothink*. "No witnesses, nobody coming to us to say he heard gunshots. No footprints, no weapons, nothing left on the sand. The money and credit cards were still in his wallet."

The wind was lifting Charlie Sullivan's blond hair, and the sun shone through it, turning it golden and silky. There was a dark red entry wound at the base of the skull. Dr. Corso, his hands in latex, brushed aside the hair and pressed a thumb on the hole. Sam felt his scalp prickling. Blood had seeped into the sand. The bullet had gone all the way through the skull.

"Fabric," Corso announced. His fingers combed through the dead man's hair. "There's fabric around the wound."

Hands braced on knees, Ryabin leaned over to say, "Fabric?"

"Fabric, fuzz, cotton. Green, I'd say." Corso held up a piece and squinted through his rimless glasses. "It's charred, probably from the gun, wouldn't you think?" Corso's rail-thin physique, thick glasses, and mop of light brown hair often caused others to peg him for a computer nerd rather than a ten-year veteran of the M.E.'s office.

Ryabin gestured. "Look down the back of his shirt."

Corso did so. Some blood had oozed down the sides of the neck, not much getting on the shirt. He retrieved several irregularly shaped bits of tattered fabric, dropped them into a plastic bag, then slit the shirt halfway down, not finding anything more. The skin on Charlie Sullivan's back was pale and bloodless.

An older detective on Ryabin's shift said, "The shooter could've wrapped the barrel to keep the noise down. Possible?"

Ryabin agreed that it was. He told one of the crime techs to get an evidence tag. And to bring something to lay under the head when they turned the body over. He didn't want sand in the wound, and didn't want to lose any fabric samples that might still be present around it.

After a piece of plastic tarp had been laid next to the body, Corso stood up and motioned for the nearest officer to help him. He was a burly kid in his twenties who flexed his hands a couple of times before he touched the corpse. Together he and Corso pulled on an arm and shoulder. Rigor mortis had set in. For a moment the face seemed to cling to the sand, then come away slowly, a mass of glistening red and purplish brown. The jaw and forehead were still intact, teeth exposed but twisted. A clump of something meaty slid out where the mouth and nose used to be.

"Holy shit," someone said. More profanities followed, including a remark about the ultimate blow job.

Taking a sharp breath, Sam concentrated for a few seconds on the ocean. Morning light shone through the breakers as they crested and curled. The tide was out, but wind whipped up the foam. Beneath the salt smell of the Atlantic lay the darker scents of blood and human waste.

When he looked back he noticed the red circle on Charlie Sullivan's white shirt. The bullet had gone into the chest but hadn't exited the body.

Sam asked one of the crime scene techs, "Did you find any shell casings?"

"Uh-uh. Shooter probably had a revolver, or he picked them up, which I doubt, because it's black-ass dark out here at night."

The shirt was some grade of cotton that said money. Likewise the thin gold watch. One slip-on shoe was upside down beside its foot, and the socks were tan like the slacks, patterned with white squares.

Sam had seen dozens of corpses, and they all looked peaceful to him, like sleeping children. Even the worst of them, the most brutally slashed or bludgeoned, seemed to have passed beyond pain to a state of ultimate serenity. He liked to think so.

Two detectives were arguing across the body whether the slug still in it was a hollow-point or steel-jacketed. One of the uniforms said it had to be a hollow-point to blow out the face like that. He mimed holding a gun, arm extended, barrel at the back of another cop's head. "Steel jacket's going to sail right through the fucker."

The other cop said, "Yeah, but we got stippling on the wound there. Means the barrel's right up against the skull, no place for the gases to go but straight into the head. That can blow out your brains, too."

"I don't see powder on the shirt," noted a cop positioned near what remained of Charlie Sullivan's head. "The shooter was at a distance shooting into the chest. He pops him, then puts another one in the brain to make sure. Was this person in the drug trade?"

"He was a fashion model."

"No shit."

"Yeah, I seen him around. I work off-duty, I seen him at the clubs."

"If I had a body like that my wife would go wild."

"This guy, now when he says, 'Gimme some head,' he means it literally."

Laughter.

"Oh, Jesus. That's sick."

"A model? Come on. He's a faggot. A jealous lover did him in."

"Maybe he was out here with another guy."

"A quickie on the beach, why not? I see it all the time."

"Yeah, but his pants are still up."

"Hey, you going to go down on a guy then shoot him?"

"I ain't goin' down on a guy *period,* my friend."

"You're wrong. I can't see the jealous lover scenario. If it was a jealous lover, he would've got stabbed in the nuts, something vicious like that. I say drugs."

Someone told a story about three dealers taken out last week over in Miami. Hands tied, popped in the back of the head.

Ryabin lit a cigarette, cupping his hand around his lighter. He snapped it shut and inhaled deeply. Gesturing with the cigarette, he told Sam that Sullivan had lived on the other side of the park in Portofino Towers.

There were several high-rise buildings to the west, most of them luxury condominiums. Ryabin said, "There's a doorman. He could have seen him leave with someone. We'll talk to the neighbors as well."

Sam said, "It's not a drug-related killing."

"I would agree with that," Ryabin said.

"But not done on the spur of the moment, either," Sam said. "The shooter knew where he lived. May have known him well enough to entice him out here in the dark."

Corso was taking more photographs. All the medical examiners had their own camera equipment, rather than rely on the police. When Corso finished, he gave the camera to one of the uniformed cops to hold. He put on a fresh pair of gloves and unbuttoned Sullivan's shirt to make sure the hole in the fabric lined up with the hole in his chest.

The skin was mottled purple where the blood had settled, sinking to the lowest point. Now that the body had been turned over, the dark side was on top. He'd been in full rigor mortis two hours ago when a squad car had responded to the scene. Dade County M.E.'s didn't take core body temperature to determine time of death; it was notoriously unreliable. Sam assumed that Charlie Sullivan had died sometime last night, a brilliant deduction, and not much more could be added with certainty. An autopsy would show the angle at which the first shot had entered the chest. This would help determine the height of the shooter and the distance.

Using a scalpel, Corso slit the pants open far enough to decide that there had been no other injuries. He checked the dead man's hands, looked at the fingernails, then removed his watch and jewelry. He put these into a plastic bag, which he handed to one of the detectives, who sealed it. The on-scene examination was over.

Now the police photographer was panning slowly, taking pictures of the crowd with a telephoto lens. A shooter who denied he was in town could sometimes be located in a crime scene photo. In the background a couple of high-school age kids were tossing a Frisbee.

Sam's eyes swept across the faces, then backtracked.

There was a man in shorts and a faded yellow T-shirt sitting on the end of a wooden beach lounger. He looked familiar. Slender, late twenties. He had short dark hair, red-framed glasses, and high-topped canvas sneakers. Sam studied him for a minute trying to decide where he had seen him before and finally remembered. He was the hair and makeup designer Caitlin used for most of her fashion shoots. Sam had met him a couple of times at her apartment. Rafael . . . The last name wouldn't click. The way he sat, with his hands clasped between his knees, and his eyes fixed on the sand, told Sam he had not come here out of mere curiosity.

Soto. Rafael Soto.

Stripping off his gloves, Corso tossed them into a brown leather bag and put his camera in after. He took out a green tag and checked off instructions to the technicians at the morgue who would prepare the body for autopsy. Corso leaned over to slip the tag around Sullivan's wrist. His work here was finished. Now the police photographer closed in to take his own views of the body. The van would arrive shortly to pick up the remains.

Sam told Ryabin about Rafael Soto.

Ryabin's pale, pouchy eyes fixed on the young man, who was now standing with his hands tucked under his armpits as if he were cold. Ryabin asked, "He and Charlie Sullivan were an item?"

Sam didn't know.

"We should ask him."

"You go," Sam said.

As Ryabin trudged through the sand, the wind ruffled his white hair and flipped his tie over his shoulder.

"Mr. Hagen!" He scanned the crowd and saw a pale, skinny arm waving at him, a girl jumping up and down. Ali Duncan. She lifted the crime tape and scurried across the sand, followed by a young man in an unbuttoned plaid shirt with the sleeves cut out. He had long black hair and a bandanna around his head. A uniformed cop yelled at them to stop, but Sam motioned that it was all right, let them come.

Ali Duncan's china-blue eyes were wide as she peered around him toward the body of Charlie Sullivan. From where they stood not much could be seen. The cops' legs blocked the view.

"He's dead, right?" Her lips drew back in a grimace. "Who did it?"

"They don't know. How did you hear about this?"

She couldn't drag her attention off the scene. "Oh, my God. He was going to testify for me. Maybe George shot him. Or Klaus's bodyguard." She pulled in a deep breath. "What am I supposed to do now?"

Sam took her shoulders and turned her around. "Don't panic. This probably has nothing to do with your case. We've got too many other witnesses." He heard the assurance in his voice and wondered if she believed it. "I want you to talk to Detective Ryabin when he has a minute."

The young man put his hand on her shoulder. "I can stay." He was a tall, well-built kid with Asian features.

"That would be nice," she said, then realized introductions were due. "Mr. Hagen, this is Tommy Chang. He's a friend of mine."

Just then Sam spotted a woman in a khaki baseball hat running down the beach, making a wide circle around the crime scene. Her sneakers splashed through the edge of an incoming wave, and her long legs carried her quickly up the slope into the looser sand. Frank Tolin was following behind, trying to keep up. Caitlin was a good thirty yards ahead of him. She stopped beside Ali Duncan.

She looked at Sam through her sunglasses, then said to Ali, "I got here as soon as I could finish. Where's Rafael?"

Ali pointed. "He's talking to Detective Ryabin."

"Why?"

When she started up the slope, Sam gripped her arm. "Caitlin, don't interfere."

"Why are the police talking to him?" She was frowning behind the dark tint of the glasses.

Frank finally caught up, winded. He nodded at Sam. "Hey, buddy. What's going on?"

"Homicide. A model by the name of Charlie Sullivan, shot sometime last night, early this morning. No witnesses so far."

Eugene Ryabin was giving Rafael Soto his card. Soto

uncrossed his arms long enough to take it, then made a pattern in the sand with the toe of one sneaker.

Caitlin said, "Go tell him not to talk to the police, Frank."

"Sweetheart, I'm not his attorney."

Abruptly she sprinted away, ducking under the crime tape. She put a protective arm around Rafael Soto's waist. Sam couldn't make out the words, but he could hear her voice at an angry pitch. Soto shook his head. Eugene Ryabin nodded to Caitlin Dorn, almost making a bow, then moved away. He glanced toward Sam, then went back to where the other detectives were still gathered around the body.

Ali Duncan made a disbelieving laugh. "Get real! Rafael could never hurt anybody." She walked over to see what was going on. Her Asian friend followed.

Frank Tolin glanced around at Sam. "Caitlin has a real soft spot for the fuckups of this world. The woman has no sense whatsoever."

Frank was dressed in jeans and cowboy boots and a hundred-dollar button-down shirt.

"Let's talk," Sam said.

He led Frank Tolin toward the water's edge. The sand was firmer there, and a few yards farther out the waves were clawing at the beach, churning the broken shells. A sheet of water edged by frothy bubbles surged up the slope, then fell back. Seagulls screamed overhead, beating against the onshore wind.

"This is about Matthew's wrongful death case," Sam said. "You asked Dina for two thousand dollars as a cost deposit, which she delivered on Friday. Don't do that again, Frank. I'm on the point of wanting it back. Don't ever go around me like that."

Frank seemed surprised. "Buddy. Come on."

"I'm not your buddy, Frank."

"Take it easy." The wind played with Frank's hair, which was still black, hardly any gray. He had a thin mouth with deep creases on either side, and a high, jutting nose. Sam wondered how much force would be needed to break it.

Sam said, "My wife trusts you to do a decent job for her. That's all we've got here."

"I told Dina to discuss it with you. She said she would."

"No. You should have talked to me. You know she isn't well."

Frank lifted his arms helplessly, then let them drop against his thighs. "I'm sorry."

Sam exhaled heavily and looked out to sea. "What have you found so far?"

When a wave slid toward him, Frank backed up a little, and wet sand clung to the heels of his cowboy boots. He said, "The club is still there, same owner. It's doing good business, so I assume there are assets."

After a minute Sam made a short, soundless laugh. "There was a case," he said, "when I was in your office that year. A teenager, a girl, had been hit by a car while she was riding her bicycle. She was still alive, but her brain had turned to oatmeal. One of the defenses, when it came time for the jury to consider an award for damages, was that the girl had been a slacker. Bad grades, bad attitude. Smoked pot, skipped school, ran away from home. The point being, of course, that on a monetary scale, she rated pretty low. I will not put Dina through that. She thinks the sun and stars went out when Matthew died, and the last thing she needs is a bunch of lawyers arguing over how much her son was worth to her."

For a few seconds Sam watched a cruise ship that was just sliding over the horizon. He said quietly, "Whatever you have to do, avoid a trial."

"What I hope for is a settlement," Frank said. "If there's some liability insurance, I'll make a demand. They'll pay something. Dina will have made her point. That's all she wants." Then he added, "This has got to be tough for you. I sincerely regret any misunderstanding."

"Take care of Dina. Let's leave it at that."

Sam turned around and walked back up the slope. Sand had sifted through his socks and it gritted on his skin with each step. He didn't let himself look in Caitlin Dorn's direction.

Sam had parked his car, with its front end pointing toward the ocean, on the one-block street just south of Penrod's Beach Club. Sunday mornings there wasn't much activity, just a few kids on surfboards, making the best of the lethargic waves. Sam unlocked the door and reached in to take the OFFICIAL BUSINESS, STATE ATTORNEY'S OFFICE sign off the dashboard. He was halfway out of his jacket when he heard the squeal of tires.

A candy-apple-red Cadillac convertible, vintage about 1948, had come to a bouncing stop at the intersection behind him. Sam could see a massive grille, a bulbous hood, and long, rounded fenders with skirts. The car remained motionless for only a second before it shot around the corner, white sidewall tires cutting a hard left to turn up the narrow street. The sun reflected in two bright pulses off a split windshield. The headlamps were cat's-eyes, covered halfway down in chrome.

The man at the wheel wore a Hawaiian shirt and a white panama hat. Another man sat in the passenger's seat, and there were three young women in the back. When the driver slammed on the brakes, the women pitched forward, then fell back against the seat, giggling.

"Jesus," Sam muttered. Then he recognized the driver. He had last seen him making bond at the county jail.

Klaus Ruffini grinned up at him. "Samuel Hagen! I thought it was you."

Sam finished taking off his jacket.

"You ever see a car like this one?"

"Not lately."

"The man who sold it to me said it belonged to Jayne Mansfield, the movie star with the bleached hair and the big tits. You believe that? I don't either, but I don't care. It's a great car." He patted the seat, which was upholstered in white leather. "Completely restored, like new."

"Yeah? Well, moon-disk hubcaps didn't come in till the late fifties. You ought to get your money back." Sam still held his jacket. If he opened his door to reach the wooden hanger in the backseat, the edge would hit the Cadillac's fender. "How about moving the car back?"

Ruffini's boyish face became serious. "May I ask a question? You came to see Charlie Sullivan, the place where he died, am I right?"

"Your lawyer would tell you not to talk to me."

"Like on TV! Anything you say can be used against

you in a court of law!" Ruffini laughed and turned around to his companions. The girls giggled again. The male passenger only stared through a pair of orange, reflecting sunglasses. He had heavy shoulders that connected to his head without benefit of a neck. His T-shirt had a PLANET HOLLYWOOD logo on it.

Ruffini draped an arm over the wooden steering wheel. "Do you carry a gun?"

"No. I'm not a cop."

"You look like a cop. A plainclothes detective."

"What do you want, Mr. Ruffini?"

"Nothing. To be friendly. Someday when this is all over, let's go out to dinner. I'll tell you all about my life. It's not easy. You might think so, but I have my troubles. You know what?" Ruffini reached across the space between the two cars and gripped Sam's wrist. "You should send your wife and daughter to Moda Ruffini. They can have a dress, whatever they want. Later, after the trial. Now would look bad, but later."

Sam pulled his arm away. "Is this a joke with you?"

Ruffini was still talking. "Someone told me you have a wife and daughter. And once you had a son. May I express my sympathy for your great loss? I have a son, Francesco, who is eleven, but he's in Milan with his mother. He isn't Tereza's son, you see, so we don't talk about him so much in front of Tereza. But not what you think! I was married to his mother, who was a relation to Louis Malle. You like French cinema, Mr. Hagen? I don't. Made so cheap, and very depressing."

"Move the car," Sam said. "I need to open my door."

"One of my troubles," said Ruffini, "is the girls who come after me. Like this red-haired girl, saying I did things. It's a lie. You know what she wants. Money. They all do. She'll come after me for blackmail. Will you arrest her when I prove this to you, maybe on a videotape?"

Sam flung open his door. It caught the Cadillac on the front fender and left a silver crease in the shiny red paint.

"Hey!" Ruffini leaned out, looking at the fender, then at Sam. "What did you do?"

"I told you to move the fucking car."

"I could sue you."

"Go for it." Sam slid through the narrow opening, started his engine, and shot Klaus Ruffini a black look as he pulled out of the parking space.

c h a p t e r
sixteen

When Rafael Soto showed up at the police station at one o'clock, Gene Ryabin took him into the interview room, a small beige cubicle with a table and two chairs. They spent the first fifteen minutes bullshitting about New York. Soto had grown up there in a Puerto Rican neighborhood in East Harlem. Ryabin said his wife had been born in San Juan, and he'd lived off upper Broadway after emigrating from Prague.

Sam and a Miami Beach detective watched from behind a two-way mirror. Rafael Soto sat on one side of the narrow table in a chair with a molded blue plastic seat. Ryabin had a chair with wheels, and gradually he had rolled around to the same side of the table. Both men were facing the mirror. There were some gauzy curtains over it.

Ryabin had left his pistol and holster in his desk drawer. His jacket was off and his tie was loosened. He asked Soto if he wanted anything. A cigarette, coffee, a soda? Soto said he didn't, thanks anyway.

"Oh, I almost forgot. Anytime we bring someone in here, for any reason, we have to ask if they want a lawyer present." He shrugged. "Bureaucracy. What can you do?"

"I don't think that's necessary," Soto said.

"Good. But if at any time you want a lawyer, let me know, okay?"

"Okay."

Ryabin slid a pen and a legal pad across the table and asked Soto to write his full name, address, Social Security number, and so on. For the file. And to make a list of his friends and co-workers. And the same for the decedent.

Five minutes later, Soto had his head bent over the paper when Ryabin asked, "The doorman at Charlie Sullivan's building says you came by a few nights ago."

Without looking up, Soto said, "Yes, to get some things of mine."

"What things?"

"A few CDs. Some clothes."

"He says you were arguing in the lobby."

"No, that isn't true."

Ryabin took the paper and pen away and slid them to the other end of the table. "When was the last time you saw Charlie Sullivan alive?"

"That night, I guess."

"You guess."

"It was that night."

"What day of the week?"

"Umm." He looked upward, and the fluorescent fixtures made bars of light in his red-framed glasses. "Wednesday."

"How long did you know Charlie?"

"Everybody called him Sullivan."

"Okay. How long?"

"We knew each other for a few years, you know, to say hello to. We met in New York. Last year he bought a condo on the Beach and spent more time here."

"You were boyfriends?"

Soto ran a finger along a scratch in the Formica tabletop. "That sounds so . . . trivial."

"I apologize," Ryabin said. "When did the relationship get to be more than, 'Hello, how are you?' "

"Last fall. November, I think."

"When did you split up?"

"March. More or less. I mean, it didn't just stop. We saw each other for a while, although it wasn't the same." Soto wiped a knuckle under his nose.

"Did he find someone else? Was that the reason?"

Sam recalled that Rafael Soto had given his age as twenty-seven. He was a graceful, slender man, and behind the silly glasses were a pair of melting brown eyes. Luis

Balmaseda, who had murdered his lover's child, had possessed the same delicate male beauty.

"There was always someone else, Detective. That's how he was. I knew that before we got involved."

"You were in love with him?"

He nodded.

"And you say you didn't care that he was promiscuous. Is that the way it is with you guys, Rafael?"

There was a silence as Rafael Soto stared at him. Then he said, "How it is, Detective, is the way it is with any human being. We're all the same. You people are the ones who don't get it."

A chuckle rumbled out of Ryabin's squat chest, and the gap in his front teeth showed. "I know if I'm finding my wife doing another guy, I would care."

"No, I did care, but—"

"You didn't like it, did you?"

"I might not have liked it, but I didn't *shoot* him, if that's what you're implying."

"But he deserved it."

"To die like that? Sullivan was outrageous in many ways, and I suppose he made some people angry, but he didn't deserve that. He grew up in Southwark—that's the bleakest part of London. He almost didn't survive it. Yes, he was promiscuous and often cruel, but he could also be kind and generous. He had many friends. You don't know. It's so easy to make judgments from where you are, in a police station, but really. You don't know." Soto wiped his cheek. "I'm sorry. Do you have a tissue?"

Ryabin gave him a handkerchief and watched while Soto blew his nose.

"How do you become involved with a man like that, knowing in advance what he is?"

"We don't always choose whom we fall in love with, Detective."

Ryabin waved for Soto to keep the handkerchief, then leaned back in his chair and knitted his fingers across his belly. "If I went with you to your apartment, would you have a problem with showing me around?"

"Why?"

"Why not? You don't have something you want to hide, do you?"

Soto said, "Is this proper procedure?"

"Of course. If you show me around your apartment voluntarily, I don't have to get a search warrant."

The brown eyes widened. "A search warrant?"

"Not if you help us out."

Soto glanced at the glass ashtray at the end of the table against the wall. "Could I have a cigarette after all?"

"Sure." With some eagerness Ryabin pulled his pack out of his shirt pocket and lit one for Rafael Soto, then himself. Soto inhaled deeply. His hands were shaking. Ryabin slid an ashtray down from the end of the table.

Settling back in his chair, Ryabin propped a foot on the edge of the table. "Rafael, are you HIV positive?"

Soto frowned. "No."

"You're sure? Maybe a present from your late friend?"

"I said no. Sullivan was always careful. So am I."

Ryabin said, "Tell me about the others. Who was he involved with?"

"Several people."

"Several who? The names."

"I don't know names. Arnold somebody, the head bartender at the Clevelander. A dozen models, mostly men, but some girls too. One of Madonna's personal fitness trainers whose name is something like Igor or Boris. A gay cop—would you like *his* name? There was a novelist with a wife and two kids." Soto tapped his cigarette on the rim of the ashtray. "Claudia Otero, the designer. She was his steady girlfriend, I guess you could say. Uta Cass was a more recent acquisition, a plaything, really. Her looks aren't up to his usual standards, but she's very inventive. And there would be others he'd pick up and drop."

"He wasn't particular."

"Oh, you're wrong. He was very particular."

"This Uta Cass. She's the wife of Martin Cass?"

"Sullivan didn't mind."

"Maybe her husband did."

"To say the least. Uta told me they got into a fight about Sullivan."

Behind the mirror, Sam Hagen wrote quickly, trying to catch it all. The lights were dim, and he had left his glasses in the car. He couldn't read his own writing.

Ryabin asked, "Have you ever met Martin Cass?"

"Yes."

"Where?"

"Around. South Beach is a very small town. Caitlin and I—Caitlin Dorn—we were working on a project for him. Well, it's really Klaus Ruffini's project, the Grand Caribe Resort, which is going absolutely nowhere, now that Klaus is in trouble. Not that I care. The Grand Caribe was obscenely tasteless. It would have ruined the Beach." Soto exhaled impatiently. "Isn't it obvious who wanted Sullivan out of the way?"

"Tell me," Ryabin said. "Maybe not so obvious. I don't have the benefit of your inside knowledge, Rafael."

"Any one of those men who assaulted Ali Duncan. Klaus Ruffini more than the rest."

"Why is that?" Smoke drifted around Ryabin's head.

"Because his wife, Tereza, hated Sullivan for being such good friends with Claudia Otero."

"The designer."

"Yes. Claudia gave Sullivan his first real boost into international modeling. He was faithful to her, in his way. But Claudia and Tereza are constantly at each other's throats. One season Tereza somehow stole Claudia's best designs before they were shown, and she put on her own show with knock-off copies. Claudia has never forgiven her for that."

"Did Sullivan ever sleep with Tereza?"

"God, no. He thought she was the lowest of the low."

"How is it that Charlie Sullivan and Klaus Ruffini can be at the same time in the same room at the Apocalypse?"

"Well, that's South Beach. Hypocrisy refined to an art form."

Ryabin moved in closer. "What were you doing around midnight last night?"

"I told you. I was at home watching TV. Then I went to bed after the news because I had to get up early. Excuse me, but do I need a lawyer?"

"I don't know. Do you?" Ryabin shrugged. "Right now we're only asking some questions. Would you say you need a lawyer?"

Soto hesitated, then shook his head. "No, it's okay."

"What time did you meet Miss Dorn this morning?"

"About six o'clock. I left my car on the street outside

the Century Hotel and rode in the production van, and she followed."

"Do you own a gun, Rafael?"

"Me? I've never fired a gun in my life."

"I didn't ask you that. I asked if you owned one."

"No."

"The doorman at Sullivan's building says you and he were screaming at each other on Thursday. Not Wednesday. Thursday. Three days ago."

"All right. Thursday. But we weren't screaming at each other."

"The doorman is lying?"

"We might have raised our voices."

"What were you arguing about?"

Soto gave a nervous laugh. "Nothing important."

"Rafael. Don't get an attitude. You want to wait in the holding cell with three or four teenage gang members from Liberty City who I have in there at the moment, then okay."

He drew in his shoulders. "You can't do that to people."

"In here, I can do anything I want to. Don't make me prove it. Now, an answer, please." Ryabin's forehead creased into deep horizontal lines. "What were you and Charlie Sullivan fighting about?"

Soto twisted his cigarette into the ashtray. "I'd like to leave now." When he started to get out of his chair Ryabin gave it a sharp kick. Soto stumbled and sat down hard. He crossed his arms tightly over his chest.

"I asked you a question." Ryabin's hand came down on the table with a sharp crack. The ashtray bounced.

Soto's voice trembled. "He . . . he wouldn't give back my Etta James CD."

Ryabin raised an eyebrow.

"She's a blues singer."

"What did you watch on TV last night?"

"A movie. On my VCR." When Ryabin continued to look at him, Soto added, "I believe it was Hitchcock. *The Thirty-nine Steps.*"

"Yes, I've seen that. It's very good. What is your video club?"

"It's . . . Blockbuster. No, I borrowed this one from a friend."

"What did you do after the movie, Rafael?"

"I went to bed."

"Five minutes ago you told me you watched the news. So now you're watching Hitchcock?"

"No. Both. I don't remember." He was trembling. "Are you going to arrest me?"

"Is there a reason we should arrest you, Rafael?"

"I didn't kill him!"

"All we want now is your help." Ryabin patted his arm. "That's all. Tell me. Didn't you and Sullivan live together at one time? Then he told you to get out?"

Rafael Soto lifted his eyes and seemed to look through the curtains, past the glass, and into the small, dark room where Sam Hagen and Ryabin's partner on the case were listening to this. "When can I go home?"

"Soon. We're almost finished."

Sam got up. He knew that Gene Ryabin had only begun. He would ask the same questions again in a different form, add new ones, and pick the answers apart. Then start over.

The detective was leaning back in the chair, with a foot propped on the edge of the desk. He took his pencil out from between his teeth and said, "What a fuckin' weenie."

Sam lifted his jacket off the back of his chair.

"You comin' back for the rest of the show?"

"No, I've got to pick up my wife at the airport." Sam put his notes into his coat pocket. "Tell Gene I think he's spinning his wheels with Soto."

The benches in the lobby downstairs were made of concrete and supported by glass blocks, fitting the neo-deco style of the police station. Caitlin Dorn sat on one of them, staring through the big windows at Washington Avenue. Her hat lay beside her on top of a canvas bag. Sam walked across the terrazzo floor, his heels echoing. When he sat on the other end of the bench she barely glanced up.

"You're the one who told the police who he was," she said. "Aren't you?"

Sam said, "What do you expect? To have certain people excluded because they happen to be your friends?"

"Rafael couldn't kill anyone."

"They have to ask."

Her green eyes were on him now, cool and disapproving. "What evidence do you have against him?"

"I can't discuss that." Sam leaned his elbows on his knees.

"What are they doing to him, Sam?"

"Talking. Don't worry. Nobody's going to hurt him."

"Promise me."

"I promise."

Sam remembered he hadn't shaved this morning. He wondered if he looked as worn out as he felt.

Closing her eyes, Caitlin let her head fall back. Her throat was exposed, a long, pale line. "Love could never turn to hate for him, Sam. He isn't made that way."

He said, "Why don't you stick around? Rafael might like to see a friendly face when he comes downstairs."

"I will. I told him I'd wait." She opened her eyes, then focused them on the ceiling. She blinked. "What is that supposed to be?"

He looked up at the sculpture hanging over their heads. "Those colored glass disks are the souls of officers killed in the line of duty. The crumbled-up wire represents crime."

"You're making that up."

He smiled, then glanced around the lobby. "Where's Frank?"

"He had an appointment," she said. "It's all right if you talk to me."

There was more humor than defiance in her voice. For a moment their gaze held. Her smile faded.

"Caitlin—" Sam frowned through the windows, past the neatly trimmed grass to the silently moving traffic on the street. He spoke quietly. "I have to discuss you with my wife. She knows I was involved with someone, but she never knew who it was. You're going to be a more central witness now for Ali Duncan. Our past might not come up, but it could. I'd rather Dina hear about it from me."

He turned to look at Caitlin, unable to tell what she was

thinking. "I wanted you to know. Dina doesn't plan to mention it to Frank. We should have found some other lawyer to handle the wrongful death case, but she wanted Frank to do it, and I'm reluctant to overrule her. Maybe you should talk to him—unless you already have."

"Are you serious? Of course I haven't." Caitlin made a husky laugh. "What are you trying to do, ease your guilty conscience?"

"I don't feel guilty, Caitlin."

"Yes, you do. You're sorry as hell. It makes me sick, how sorry you are."

Sam stood up. "I have things to do. Rafael should be down in a couple of hours."

"See you around."

He was halfway across the lobby when he heard her call his name. He let out a breath, then turned.

Caitlin was reclining back on her hands, swinging one crossed leg. Her body was long and curved, her bra so silky he could see the outline of nipple under the T-shirt. "I'm not sorry," she said quietly. "It was very good. You have to admit."

The officer at the reception desk was talking to a couple who needed directions to the convention center.

Sam looked back at Caitlin. "I never denied that."

With a flicker of a smile and a langorous motion of her body, she sat up, resettled her chin in her palm, and resumed looking through the window. "Good-bye, Sam."

chapter
seventeen

In the kitchen, Melanie couldn't hear what they were saying upstairs in their bedroom, just some muffled words now and then. It was raining, and water drummed in the downspout and whispered on the terrace roof.

She stared into the microwave and watched the numbers counting down from thirty seconds to zero. There was a piece of frozen chocolate cake in there. She had made it herself from a mix last week. Then her mother stuck it in a plastic bag and put it in the freezer, and now there were fold marks on the frosting.

The house had been quiet all day, with her dad gone to a murder scene, then not getting home till he went by the airport first to pick up her mom. Now it was almost dark outside, and the two of them were having a talk. *Why don't you go downstairs and watch TV, Melanie, your mother and I have to talk.* She wondered if they were talking about a divorce. Probably not, because they had been much nicer to each other ever since Matthew died. Maybe they were in bed. *Welcome home, darling. I've missed you.* That wasn't likely either. They hadn't been getting along *that* well.

The microwave made three beeps.

The frosting was too hot and dripped down the sides. Melanie took a bite anyway. She finished the cake quickly, then put another piece in the microwave. When that one was ready, she looked at it. "You're disgusting," she said aloud. "Don't eat that." She grabbed the salt shaker and sprinkled salt all over the frosting so she wouldn't be tempted, then dumped it into the garbage.

School would be out in two weeks, and she still had not lost one pound. This weekend had been a total black hole. She was supposed to be studying for her finals, but hadn't done anything but play her CDs with the headphones on and her door locked.

It was totally quiet upstairs. Thunder grumbled in the distance. The rainy season would be here soon.

Melanie put the cake back into the freezer, then left the kitchen. She climbed the carpeted stairs, her bare feet making no sound. She slowed going past her parents' door. There were voices coming from inside.

He was talking about someone called Finley. Making trouble. He wasn't going to let that son-of-a-bitch call the shots. And she said that was the real reason he had told her all this, because he couldn't stand not being in control. Then he said no, the only reason was that he didn't want her to be hurt. She laughed and said he should have thought about that three years ago.

Melanie moved a little closer to the door.

Her mother said something about irony. How ironic that they would meet again this way. "A witness in a rape case. What was she doing there? Does Frank know she goes to places like that?"

"She was taking photos. She's a freelance photographer, Dina."

"You believe that, don't you?" Then a laugh. "I've got to say I'm surprised at your choice. I thought she would be one of the lawyers in your office, someone actually worth worrying myself sick over. But this. It's almost funny. A middle-aged man falling for a blond model. How . . . cliché."

"Okay, fine. We've discussed this enough—"

"I mean, when I met her at Frank's office I thought she looked trashy."

"That's enough!"

For a while there was silence, then her mother said calmly, "Are you still in love with her?"

"No. Drop it."

Melanie closed her eyes and stepped back from the door, but she could still hear them. Her father saying he didn't want to discuss it any more. She leaned against the opposite wall, her heart sinking.

Then he said the word *lawyer* and Melanie stiffened. Hiring a lawyer. They must be talking about a divorce.

Biting her lip, she put her cheek to the door.

"I won't do it, Sam. I'm perfectly satisfied with Frank. I trust him. . . . Of course I don't intend to tell him. If she wants to, that's between them."

Melanie could hear a drawer opening, then closing. Then the closet door. Her mother might be unpacking from her trip.

There was the rumble of her father's voice. Then she answered, "He did know about it. . . . Because I told him." A drawer slammed. "Why? Because I was wretchedly, miserably alone and unhappy, and he begged me to tell him what was wrong. I wanted him to understand. He was old enough."

"Was this your way to get back at me? To take my son? Turn him against me?"

"Don't you dare blame me. You brought this on yourself, Sam. The only way you ever approached Matthew was with anger and intimidation."

"That is absolutely not true. I can't believe this. What utter, monumental selfishness!"

"Selfish! You who went out and screwed another woman—"

"Dina, shut up. Melanie's downstairs."

"What are you afraid of? Let her hear. It might do her good to know what her father is. Matthew knew the truth. I think we should all discuss it together, don't you? *Melanie!*"

The word turned to a cry, then a thud. There was silence for a while.

His voice sounded like he was trying not to cry. "What have we done? Oh, God. Dina, what have we done?"

Then a tired laugh from her mother. "Go get me my pills and a glass of water. Sam, please. I would have preferred not to know about this, but now that you've told me—" She laughed. "I don't care anymore. I really don't."

Then his voice, and then hers. She said, "Take the damn bottle with you, then. Give me two of them. I don't want to dream tonight. . . . I want to sleep and not wake up, and if I don't wake up for a year, it will be too soon."

One bare foot in front of another, heel and toe, Melanie moved silently down the hall toward her room. She didn't want to think about this anymore. Maybe she'd try to study her French. She was behind in all her subjects. She would study her French, then math, each for an hour, then listen to one CD, then go to bed.

The door to Matthew's room was open an inch or two. She stopped. With one finger she pushed the door inward.

In the faint light coming through the window she could see the shoeboxes full of pictures on his bed and a stack of papers beside them. Her mother had been going through everything to take to the lawyer.

She sat on the floor with her arms around her knees and cried for a while, wiping her face on her T-shirt.

A little later she heard the door to her parents' room open and close, then her dad going downstairs. Then nothing, then a clanking noise. He was working out on the back porch on his weight machine. Melanie closed her eyes, trying to decide how she felt. Whether she should hate his guts or not.

She got up and went over to the window. It was still raining and the yard was dark now. Her mother hadn't been out there in a couple of weeks, and everything was getting overgrown, looking wild.

Matthew had never mentioned their father's affair. He did say that all parents screamed at each other. He'd heard his friends' parents do a lot worse than theirs, so she shouldn't worry about it, he'd told her.

She sat on the end of the bed and put her elbow on the windowsill.

One night, Matthew woke her up by tossing pebbles on her window. He wanted to take her riding on his motorcycle. He had a dark red Harley-Davidson 1300-cc low rider. It had black fringe on the seat and on the handlebars. She sneaked out of the house and met him down the block.

He was six feet tall and really handsome, in a funny way. He had straight, thick eyebrows that almost met, a sharp nose, and lips as full and red as a girl's. His wavy, dark brown hair came to his shoulders, and he would tie it back when he rode. That night he gave her his extra helmet to put on. He wore jeans and boots and a T-shirt with no sleeves. He had wide shoulders and ripply muscles in his stomach.

The street lights on the MacArthur Causeway slid across the chrome, and the palm trees whipped by in a blur. Then a blue police light flashed from behind them. She saw Matthew turn his head, saw him smile. He yelled *Hang on!* She tightened her arms around his waist and screamed as they shot forward. They went in and out of cars, around a corner, and got away.

He parked in front of a restaurant on Ocean Drive. People at the sidewalk tables watched him when he took off his helmet and shook his hair free. Some girls he knew came over and kissed his cheek and called him Stavros, his middle name, which he used for modeling. He put his arm around Melanie's shoulders and introduced her. He didn't say, *This is my little sister.* He said, *This is Melanie. My sister.* It was perfect.

Coming back they went the long way, over the Julia Tuttle bridge, black water below them on either side, the tires singing on the metal grid. Behind them the bottoms of the clouds were getting pink, but they made it home before the sun came up.

She couldn't believe it when they told her he was dead. He died crashing his motorcycle, and at his funeral she wished, for one crazy minute, that it could have happened on that night when he took her riding.

chapter
eighteen

Thursday morning, Sam Hagen delivered the final argument in the manslaughter prosecution of a plastic
surgeon. The victim was an aging actor on a Mexican
soap opera who had come to the defendant's clinic in
Little Havana for liposuction of his jowls and belly.
As a surprise for his wife, he asked for penile augmen-
tation surgery as well. The doctor failed to note that
the patient was on blood thinners for a recent heart
attack. In recovery, he died of massive internal bleeding while the doctor, whose license had been suspended the month before, debated whether to call for an
ambulance.

The defense attorneys argued that the victim misled the
doctor about his heart problem. And even if the doctor
was wrong in not running tests, his negligence didn't sink
to the level of a crime. The widow had a cause of action
for malpractice, but how fair was it to put the doctor in
jail? Very fair, the jury decided. They came back in
twenty minutes with a verdict of guilty. Sam Hagen was
kissed by the grateful widow, made a short statement to
the media, then left the courthouse trailed by two new assistant state attorneys, young men in their twenties, who
carried the files and in high spirits made numerous jokes
and puns about the type of surgery the doctor had performed. His mind on gloomier matters, Sam paid them
little attention.

They walked the short distance to the state attorney's

office, going around the metal detectors at the rear entrance. At the elevators Sam leaned a shoulder against the wall and waited for the doors to open.

He noticed a stocky Hispanic man hurrying across the tiled lobby and recognized him a second later. Idelfonso García, the uncle of the dead Ramos boy. He wore a cheaply made brown suit and a plain shirt open at the collar.

Sam nodded in greeting. "Mr. García."

"Mr. Hagen, how are you? I been calling for two days, and your secretary told me you have no time to call me back, so I said to myself, well, I think I'll go see him face to face."

The messages García had left said he wanted to discuss the murder case against his sister Adela's former boyfriend. Again. Sam had already returned two of García's calls last week, and now he was making more of them. Sam had explained to him why the jury had acquitted Luis Balmaseda. He had talked about evidence and reasonable doubt. He had instructed García and Adela Ramos to make a police report if Balmaseda was harassing her. He had called the Miami Beach Police to make sure it was a priority. He didn't know what else to tell him.

"Sorry I couldn't get back to you. I've been in trial."

He introduced the two young lawyers, and Idelfonso García mumbled a hello, then said, "They work with you?" When Sam nodded, García said, "Luis has been calling Adela again. He says to her how much he loves her and wants her back. The man is crazy. He killed her son, and now he wants her back."

Sam said, "I advised you to call the police, Mr. García. Have you?"

"They don't do nothing." García's voice was soft, but anger lay like coiled steel beneath the words. "Luis is scaring her. He follows her and he cries. He says he loves her so much. He is sorry for killing Carlito."

The two young men glanced at each other.

The elevator doors opened and Sam gestured for García to get on. "Come upstairs."

García said, "I told Adela, 'Let Luis come close to you. Let him talk. And put this in your purse.' " From his coat pocket, García withdrew a microcassette recorder. He held it up in his big, work-roughened hand. When he hit the play button a tinny, hollow male voice sobbed from the speaker.

"Adelita, discúlpame, no intenté que Carlito se muriera, te juro. Que Diós me condene si miento. Yo estaba fuera de mi mente por celos de ti."

Sam knew one of the young lawyers was bilingual. "What does he say?"

"He says he didn't mean for Carlito to die, may God send him to hell if he's lying. He wants Adelita to forgive him. He was jealous. That's why he did it."

The elevator doors opened. No one moved. One of the young men quickly stuck a foot across the tracks as the door began to close again. They all got out.

García's expression was triumphant. "You take this to the judge. Tell him to get the jury back. Make a new trial. This time the filthy son of a bitch, he's going to die for what he did."

The three or four people in the hall were staring at García. Sam hesitated, then said quietly to the young lawyers, "Gentlemen, why don't you come into the conference room with us. And on the way I'd like you to decide what our legal options are."

Exchanging glances with each other, they followed Sam and García down the hall. The conference room was furnished with a few steel tables and some folding chairs. Windows gave a view west toward the justice building and the county jail behind it.

When they had all sat down, Sam looked from one of the young men to the other, waiting.

The bilingual lawyer glanced at García, then said, "Well, I think we've got a double jeopardy problem here, Mr. Hagen."

Sam asked the other man his opinion.

"I regret to say it's the same. The defendant can't be brought to trial twice for the same offense."

"What does this mean?" demanded García.

Sam said, "It's our system of criminal procedure, Mr. García. Once the jury has spoken, we can't ask them to reconsider, no matter what new evidence we find. We have only one chance to put a man on trial."

He was outraged. "This makes no sense! Luis Balmaseda is guilty."

"We know that, but there's nothing we can do about it now except prosecute him for stalking Adela. This is a different offense. I'm sorry."

"But I have proof!" García looked around the table. "He murdered Carlito. He said this."

"Tell Adela to come see me," Sam said. "I'll talk to her. And meanwhile, don't you do anything we're all going to regret. Do you understand what I'm saying?"

García's face darkened. "You don't care to do nothing. What kind of place is this? You let murderers go free."

"It isn't us, Mr. García. I wish I could do what you ask, but I can't. It's the law."

As if the words he wanted to say were bile in his throat, Idelfonso García swallowed several times. Abruptly he picked up the tape recorder from the table and walked out of the room.

For a long moment no one spoke.

Finally, Sam stood up and gave the two younger lawyers a weary smile. "There it is, gentlemen. We can get a conviction for a botched penile enlargement and we let murderers go. What do you think about that?"

The two young assistants rose silently and gathered the manslaughter files they had laid down on the way in.

Sam arranged to meet Eugene Ryabin at the downtown campus of Miami-Dade Community College. Ryabin had located Tommy Chang, who had agreed to talk to him. In four days the police had no real leads in the murder of Charlie Sullivan, only a list of people who might have wanted him dead. One of them was George Fonseca. A restaurant manager on Ocean Drive had contacted the police to report that two weeks ago Fonseca had to be restrained from attacking Sullivan. He didn't know what the dispute was about, but did recall that a young Asian man had been sitting at the table. The manager described him, and Ryabin thought it might be Tommy Chang, whom he had met at the murder scene on Sunday.

Tommy Chang might give Ryabin something to work

with this afternoon, when George Fonseca would appear at police headquarters. Fonseca's attorney had agreed to routine questioning—in a spirit of cooperation, he had said. This would be touchy, as the murder victim had been a witness against Fonseca in another crime. The attorney would call foul if questions veered too close to the sexual battery case. Sam had cautioned Ryabin that inquiries would have to relate only to the murder of Charlie Sullivan.

Sam arrived at the college just as classes changed, and the wide plaza outside the main building teemed with students. They dressed in the ubiquitous uniform of the young: shorts, jeans, T-shirts, sneakers. Their voices were loud and cheerful, their faces a variety of ethnic types.

He stood in the plaza in his dark suit, and the students flowed around him as if he were a rock in a babbling stream. He thought of Matthew, who had promised, finally, to enroll for a semester. Sam was going to pay his books and tuition, even his rent. Whatever he needed. But Matthew let the deadline for registration pass, and Sam told him he could earn his own damned tuition if he wanted to go to college.

Among the bobbing heads, Sam noticed a white one. Gene Ryabin was coming through the atrium, smiling as if buoyed by so much vitality and youth. He spotted Sam and pointed toward the fountain. Water poured down a low, slanting wall of roughly made concrete bricks, then filled a shallow, nearly flat basin, lapping at the opposite end. They met under the shade of a tree growing from a circle of ironwork.

Ryabin reported on his progress in questioning Martin Cass, whose wife had been one of Charlie Sullivan's conquests.

"None, I'm afraid. Mr. Cass is avoiding me." Ryabin sighed. "I'll have to find something to arrest him for. Maybe traffic tickets, does that sound good?" He touched Sam's arm. "Here's Tommy coming."

Sam recognized him, the boy with Chinese eyes. His long black hair was tied back in a cord, and he had a book bag slung over one shoulder.

Ryabin introduced himself, then said, "This is Sam

Hagen from the state attorney's office, the prosecutor on Miss Duncan's case."

Tommy Chang extended a hand. "Yeah, we met. Hi, how're you doin'?"

They found seats at a red-painted metal umbrella table. The rush of students had let up. Ryabin asked Tommy about himself, his classes, his interest in photography, and his work with Caitlin Dorn. Then Ryabin asked how he had happened to meet Charlie Sullivan. On a photo shoot with Caitlin, Tommy replied.

"You went with Sullivan to a restaurant on Ocean Drive," Ryabin said.

"Right. He said he'd tell me about fashion photography and modeling. I mean, that was the only reason I went. He tried to come on to me, but I told him I was straight, so he left me alone. We talked for a while, but then he, like, flipped out and told me to leave. It was weird."

"The manager says George Fonseca caused some trouble?"

Tommy nodded. "He was driving by and saw Sullivan, and he jumped out of his car and started screaming at him because Sullivan was going to be a witness for Ali. Then they got into an argument about Claudia Otero. She's a fashion designer from New York, and Sullivan was, like, I guess her boyfriend."

Sam remembered the name Claudia Otero. Rafael Soto had mentioned her, one of Charlie Sullivan's many sexual partners. He said, "Why did they argue about Claudia Otero?"

Tommy said, "George said the reason Sullivan was going to testify was because Claudia Otero put him up to it. She supposedly hates Tereza Ruffini, Klaus Ruffini's wife. Tereza's a designer too. George thought that Sullivan was trying to help her. I guess his theory was that if Klaus is convicted of rape, it would hurt Tereza's business."

Ryabin asked, "What did Sullivan say about Klaus Ruffini?"

"Nothing much. He didn't like him, I know that."

"He didn't give the reason?"

"No. He just got into it with George. George said he

would bust him in the teeth. Then Sullivan told George he'd kick his ass. They weren't just talking. They were going to fight. Then the manager came out and told George to leave."

"What happened after that?" Ryabin asked.

"We talked some more. Sullivan invited me to a party his agency was giving, then he became very insulting and told me to get lost."

"Why did he do that?"

"I have no idea."

"Is there anything else you can remember about the conversation?" Ryabin asked.

Tommy didn't say anything for a while. He brushed a leaf into one of the holes in the red wire mesh the tabletop was made of. "Yeah." He looked over at Sam. "George also accused Sullivan of trying to get back at him because of your son."

"My son? Matthew?" Sam exchanged a glance with Ryabin, whose brows had risen a fraction of an inch.

"They didn't, like, mention *you*. They said Stavros. Ali says that's your son, right? He was a model?"

"Yes. Stavros was his middle name. What did they say?"

"Well, George said Sullivan was still pissed off about Stavros, that's why he was going to testify against him. And Sullivan said no, that wasn't it, but I asked him after George left. He told me that Stavros died in a motorcycle accident, and the way he talked, it sounded like he blamed George for it." Tommy shrugged, then said, "According to Sullivan, George got Stavros hooked on drugs. Heroin."

The sounds of the plaza seemed to recede into nothing. Sam stared at Tommy.

"I guess you didn't know."

"What else did he say?" Sam asked.

"That Stavros was doing coke and meth also. This was in the context of Sullivan warning me to stay away from drugs, which I don't do. Sullivan didn't either. He was angry at George for getting your son into it. He said to talk to Caitlin Dorn. I asked her. She said the same thing. That he—your son—was doing heroin."

When Sam said nothing more, Tommy looked back at Ryabin. "That's all I can remember."

Ryabin thanked him, gave him his card, and instructed him to call if he thought of anything else. Tommy Chang shook their hands, then walked away, going through the wide opening that led to the inner courtyard of the main building.

Sam turned around and stared at the traffic that passed without letup between the plaza and the old tile-roofed post office across the street. Matthew had lied to him, lied to Dina. Had promised her that he didn't do this, had never, would never.

Charlie Sullivan had spent nearly two hours in Sam's office telling him about the attack on Ali Duncan. In an offhand way he had mentioned Matthew. But he had said nothing about heroin. Sam had known about the heavy drinking. He assumed grass and cocaine, the drugs of choice on South Beach. He had not suspected needles and searching for veins.

Maybe it wasn't true. There had been no signs of this. Nothing. Not this. Or maybe Matthew had tried it a couple of times, and Tommy Chang had assumed too much.

"Sam—" Ryabin patted his coat pocket for his cigarettes, but didn't take them out. He said, "Forgive me if I'm asking you a difficult question. What do you think was going on between Matthew and Charlie Sullivan?"

Sam looked at him, then made a short laugh. "Going on? Nothing. They knew each other. They were in the same business. Maybe they were friends, but that's the extent of it. I have no doubts about my son in that way, Gene."

Ryabin shrugged. His attention seemed to be on a group of girls in shorts walking by, laughing and talking in Spanish. Their dark hair gleamed in the bright sunlight. Ryabin watched them, the morose expression on his face not changing. He said, "Tommy Chang said Sullivan blamed George for Matthew's death. Why would there be blame unless he cared for him in some way?"

"All right, maybe Sullivan was interested. Matthew was

a handsome kid, but he wouldn't have responded, any more than Tommy did. He would have seen what Charlie Sullivan was like."

"Even so," Ryabin said, "Sullivan hated George Fonseca. And so I ask, why? If it was a mutual hatred, we might have something. A motive. Not only that, but now that Sullivan's dead, he can't testify against Fonseca. So. Two motives."

"I think there's more in this connection to Claudia Otero," Sam said. "We know Sullivan was involved with her. Rafael Soto confirmed it. And that angle leads us to Klaus Ruffini."

"True." Ryabin gave in and tapped a cigarette out of his pack. "We'll pursue it with George Fonseca this afternoon, if his lawyer allows us." He clicked his gold lighter. His fingers were stained brown with nicotine. "And as for Matthew, I'll have to bring that up as well." With an eye on Sam, Ryabin slid the lighter back into his pants pocket. "You understand," he said.

"Sure."

"You're the lead prosecutor, but may I suggest that you not be in the same room?" Ryabin said. "If Fonseca knows who Matthew was, we might not get straight answers."

"So I'll sit behind the mirror again."

Sometime during the year before Matthew died, Sam had come to the apartment he rented with two of his friends, half of a duplex south of Fifth Street in a shabby neighborhood. The grass in the yard was dead, and there were rusting security bars on the windows.

Eleven o'clock in the morning, Matthew came to the door barefoot, squinting and unshaven. Sam wanted to take him to lunch. To talk. To find out what was going on with him, since it had been weeks since they had seen each other. The apartment, predictably, was a shambles. Beer cans on every horizontal surface. Open pizza boxes. A girl asleep on the sofa in her underwear.

Matthew came along reluctantly. They went to the News Café and sat indoors, where it wasn't as crowded. Matthew refused to take off his sunglasses. He crossed his arms over his lean stomach and barely touched his food. He said they'd had a party last night, the apartment wasn't usually so messy. Yes, he had work. He was a waiter in between bookings. Yes, he was paying his bills. No, he wasn't on coke. Yes, he was using condoms. *Jesus, Dad, get off it.* When Sam said he'd arranged a job for him as assistant manager of a music store downtown, Matthew was insulted. No, he said. He liked modeling. He was doing what he wanted for the first time in his life. Sam filled the ensuing silence by talking about his own work. But they couldn't connect. Eventually they argued. Sam told him he was a disappointment to him and to his mother. That as soon as he got himself straightened out, they would have something to talk about, but until then, they had nothing to say to each other.

Matthew looked across the table through his sunglasses, then smiled. *You're such a hypocrite, telling me how fucked up my life is. Why don't you take a good look at your own, you phony?*

It was three months before they spoke to each other again. Matthew would come home occasionally, but at times when Sam was likely not to be there. Dina held Sam responsible for the rift and begged him to relent. Finally he told Matthew he was sorry they had argued, he'd been out of line. Both of them came close to tears. Sam embraced him. But gradually the old resentments rose again to the surface, and relations between them remained cool.

He was aware now, too late, that Matthew had known the truth about him, had seen clearly his failings, his infidelity. Sam would never know if Matthew had forgiven him for that or had ever seen him as more than a pompous, judgmental fake.

It seemed now to Sam that Matthew's death might not have been an accident but a choice. From his boyhood he had tended toward gloomy introspection. Dina had once found a book of poetry on his desk, a bookmark at a page, and a certain passage underlined. *I am half in love with easeful death. . . .*

Matthew had not found joy in family, in school, in work, in love, or even in what George Fonseca had offered: the hazy oblivion of narcotics. He had been looking for meaning on South Beach, with its shoddy values and pitiless judgments. Blue sky and sunshine, then the long, dark night. One more drink. Another half-turn of the accelerator on the handlebar. Easier that way.

Thinking of this brought Sam to the point of utter despair and sent a wave of black depression washing over him, threatening to pull him under. If Matthew had lived, would he have been happy? He might have suspected sooner or later in his adulthood, as Sam did now, that he had been wise at nineteen to send his motorcycle hurtling into the darkness.

The lawyer was a heavy, obnoxious man named Don Gessing. Sam had seen him around the courthouse on drug cases. He seemed to have a steady South American clientele.

Joe McGee, assigned to the prosecution team on the Duncan sexual battery case, sat opposite Gessing at the interview table. McGee had a pen and a legal pad with notes on what to ask about. It had been decided that he would go first, then Detective Ryabin would follow up.

Ryabin sat at the end of the table, opposite George Fonseca.

Gessing, facing McGee, knitted his fingers in front of him. He had a ring on each hand and a diamond Rolex on his wrist. "My client is here voluntarily in the spirit of cooperation to help you with a murder investigation. No inquiries on any other matter. Mr. Fonseca will answer about fifteen minutes' worth of questions, then we're done."

McGee got right to it. "Mr. Fonseca, where were you between about eight P.M. and three A.M. last Saturday night, Sunday morning?"

In his tight T-shirt, George Fonseca looked like he had overpumped at the gym. His thick forearms were covered with dark hair. He said, "I was out with friends. We went to dinner at Lario's, then to the clubs. Chili Pepper, Club One, Amnesia."

"Could you give me the names of your friends?" There was a tape recorder on the table.

Fonseca gave the names and addresses of three people.

"And they were with you the entire time?"

"That's correct."

"We have a report from the manager of the Seahorse Grill that you and Charlie Sullivan got into an altercation a couple of weeks ago."

"A discussion. I wouldn't call it an altercation."

"The young man with Sullivan called it a fight."

"Call it what you want," Fonseca said.

"Do you know Tommy Chang?"

"No."

"He was the young man at the table," McGee said. "Had you ever seen him before?"

"No."

"You know a woman named Claudia Otero?"

"I heard of her."

"Who is she?"

"A fashion designer from New York."

"Have you met her personally?"

"I might have. Probably."

"She was intimate with Charlie Sullivan?"

"Correct."

"Did you ever see them together?"

"Yeah, I probably did, at the clubs and whatnot."

"And in the conversation with Sullivan at the Seahorse Grill you mentioned her as a rival to Tereza Ruffini. Tell me about that, Mr. Fonseca."

The lawyer put a hand on George's arm. "No. You don't mention the name Ruffini to my client, Mr. McGee."

Joe McGee said, "This isn't about the sexual battery charges, Mr. Gessing. It's to elicit what Mr. Fonseca might know about a rivalry between Tereza Ruffini and Claudia Otero, as a possible source of information about Klaus Ruffini and Charlie Sullivan."

Gessing said, "You don't hear? I said no questions on that topic."

McGee lifted a sheet on his legal pad to see what was

written underneath, then said, "What is your personal relation to Claudia Otero?"

"I don't have one. I know her. That's it."

"What do you think of her? Do you like her? Dislike her?"

"I don't have any feelings one way or the other."

"Did you and Charlie Sullivan ever discuss Ms. Otero or his relationship to her?"

"Nope."

"Mr. Fonseca, have you ever been arrested for or charged with possession of any form of controlled substance?"

He glanced at his lawyer, who nodded slightly. The roll of fat around his neck rested on his collar.

"Possession of cocaine. That was like two years ago, and the charges were dropped." He looked at Gene Ryabin. "The Miami Beach Police Department planted it in my car, and I had a witness see them do it."

The lawyer glanced at his watch.

Ryabin said, "Mr. Fonseca, you also mentioned in your conversation with Charlie Sullivan a young man named Stavros. Who is he?"

"A model. One of his boys."

"Meaning . . . ?"

"One of his boys. You know. His boyfriends. Sullivan swung both ways. Stavros died last year. Not AIDS. It was a traffic accident."

Ryabin sat without speaking for a few seconds, then asked, "How well did you know this young man?"

"I saw him around the clubs. I didn't know him."

"Do you know his last name?"

"All I heard was Stavros. That's all I know."

"Did you provide him with cocaine or heroin?"

The lawyer said, "Don't answer that, George. What's the point of this, Detective?"

Ryabin asked, "Mr. Fonseca, do you know if Stavros was shooting heroin?"

Don Gessing shifted his weight. "Okay. You can answer that one."

Fonseca said, "Yeah. He was doing it. A lot of the models are into smack. It's a fad. Recreational use, you know? You see it around a lot."

"Where do they get it?"

"Not from me."

"From where, if you know."

"Used to be they'd have to drive over to the black section." Fonseca glanced at Joe McGee, then shrugged. "Liberty City, like that. It was dangerous. Not now. Now you can get high-quality dope all over the place. But I don't know where they get it. Not from me."

Ryabin said, "Sullivan accused you of causing Stavros's death. Is this why he was going to testify against you?"

"He never told me that."

"Tommy Chang heard you say it."

"No, I never said that. Stavros didn't O.D., he ran his motorcycle off the causeway and broke his neck. He was a loser from the word go, man. I had nothing to do with it."

The lawyer pushed himself out of his chair. "Okay, folks. That's it. George, we're done here."

While Gessing held the door for George Fonseca, then lumbered out after him, Sam Hagen leaned heavily against a wall in the adjoining room. He savagely pulled at the knot in his tie. The two MBPD detectives who had been taking notes looked around.

One of them asked if he was okay.

"Yeah. I'm all right." Sam wiped at his forehead with the heel of his hand.

"You sure? You don't look so good."

The other cop said. "No, you don't. You got some pain? I had chest pains last year. Doctor put me on nitro. Don't fuck around with that, Hagen."

"No, I'm okay. I need some air. Tell Gene I'll be right back." Leaving his suit coat on the back of his chair, Sam left the room and walked quickly down a narrow white hallway to the outside door. It clanged open on the parking garage, third level. The wind blew through the open sides, stirring the fumes. An unmarked car made a turn down the ramp, tires squealing.

Sam's shirt was wet with perspiration, sticking to his back. Hands braced on the low concrete wall, he stood staring north, seeing nothing but the red, shimmering veil of his own rage.

If he had taken another exit to the ground floor. If he had come face to face with George Fonseca on the street—

Sam gripped the edge of the wall so hard his fingers ached. He wanted Fonseca. Wanted to slam his head into the sidewalk. Make him bleed.

Fonseca's attorney would call. Within a week, probably. He would want to talk, not necessarily about possible murder charges against his client, but about the sexual battery case. He would be sniffing around for a deal. The state was obligated to make some kind of offer. Not a plea-bargain but a good-faith offer so that trial could be avoided. *I offer your asshole client a fair trial. I offer the maximum of twenty-five years.* Sam knew he ought to get off this case. So said the rules. Not kosher for the prosecutor to have it in for the defendant.

He exhaled, then again, as though he'd been running up stairs. It took him a while to realize that Gene Ryabin was standing a few feet away.

Ryabin's pouched eyes were directed at the few cars moving slowly past on the narrow street below. "I'm going to go talk to George Fonseca's alibi witnesses. Do you want to come along?"

"No, I've got things to do. Call if you find anything worthwhile."

Elbows resting on the wall, Ryabin flicked his cigarette past the edge. The wind swirled the loose ashes. "People such as Fonseca, they don't last too long. Something always happens. They make bad decisions. It all balances out in the end."

"You think so."

"I prefer to think so," Ryabin said.

Sam laughed. "Jesus. Too late for some things, though. Some things never balance. Unless Fonseca was the one who shot Charlie Sullivan. That has a nice symmetry to it." Pushing away from the wall, Sam said, "But it puts me in a quandary. Do I send him to the chair or give him a fucking medal?"

Ryabin's mournful eyes turned on Sam. "I don't know."

"I don't know either, Gene. And I'm losing the ability to pretend I do."

c h a p t e r
nineteen

Sunday morning had come to be almost sacred to Frank Tolin. He liked to sit on his eighth-floor terrace overlooking the marina at Coconut Grove, read the paper, have another cup of coffee, and think of anything but his law practice, his investments, or the various other baying dogs that snapped at him the rest of the week.

Caitlin was sitting cross-legged in the living room, just inside the open sliding glass door, going over some photographs for her show next week at the DeMarco Gallery. He could hear her humming to herself. She still hadn't given an answer about living with him, and that annoyed him. Other than that, they'd had a good weekend so far.

From this height, Frank could see the skyline of Miami a few miles north, and the misty green expanse of Key Biscayne to the east. Sailboats, sport fishers, and motor yachts criss-crossed the bay. Sea grasses alternated with sand, making bands of green, bright blue, and turquoise. Occasionally he would spot the dorsal fins of dolphins. The last thing Frank wanted was to have his Sunday invaded by Marty Cass.

Marty rang up from the lobby and said he had a signed offer on the apartments. It wouldn't take fifteen minutes. While Frank went to change out of his bathrobe, Caitlin let Marty in. When Frank came back out, Marty was on the terrace. He'd taken over the lounge chair in the shade. There was a trellis overhead that filtered out the sun.

Frank's mood was improved slightly by knowing that as soon as the apartment building was sold his association with Marty Cass would be over. He pulled up a chair and sat down.

"You've got a great place here, Frank. What a view. This condo must be worth half a million now." The trellis reflected in Marty's sunglasses, white grid and yellow flowers. "You wouldn't have some coke around? Share with a friend?"

Frank said, "Caitlin and I are going out to lunch. How about showing me the offer?"

Marty said, "I live in a one-bedroom condo that I paid fifty grand for, six blocks off the water, and you've got all this. Why is it that some people have the luck, Frank?"

He smiled. "Too bad you didn't get Klaus Ruffini's signature. Maybe you should've offered to blow him." The grin under the sunglasses vanished. "That incident about you kissing his ass is making the rounds, but don't worry. Most people don't believe it."

"Hey, Frank." Marty raised his middle finger.

Frank gestured toward the leather portfolio that Marty had dropped on the patio table. "The contract."

Just then Caitlin came out with a glass of iced orange juice for Marty, who had his grin back on, telling her she looked like a million. The ponytail stuck out from the back of his head like the letter *S*. Frank wanted to rip it off.

His mistake—Frank knew this now—had been to take a partner. Marty Cass, being in real estate, had the contacts, but Frank had put up the money; Marty was all mouth. Frank should have known better. His father had been in the oil business in West Texas. Never made much, but he had done all right, till he let some other men invest with him. He died of a heart attack a few months after losing it all. He had told Frank to join the army and get some GI benefits, since there was nothing he could pass on to him. Except one piece of advice: Assume people are going to screw you, because they will if you let them.

Frank had found this to be true. His partners in the law office were always fighting among themselves. He would go over the books at night, keeping them honest. The secretaries would run up personal phone calls, steal the office supplies, and take two hours for lunch if they could get away with it. Frank's first wife had cheated on him when he'd been away in the army. The second stayed married to him till he made some money, then hired a son-of-a-bitch divorce lawyer to take it away. Later she had the nerve to come after him for an increase in alimony. He had her followed, caught some interesting photographs of her with a married man. She dropped her claim. Frank's kids were another disappointment. None of them wrote or called except as a prelude to asking for money. He generally ignored them.

Frank said, "Sweetheart, Marty and I have business to discuss. You want to close the door, please?" He tossed the portfolio into Marty's lap.

Caitlin gave him a look and slid the door shut harder than she needed to.

Marty took out what looked like several copies of a standard form contract. He leaned over and handed the papers to Frank. "Four-seventy-five, all cash above the mortgage, which nets us about two hundred thousand."

Frank tossed the contract back at him. "You've got to be kidding."

"We won't get better in this market. Sign it," Marty said. "I'm not asking, I'm telling. And we're going to work out our shares. I want fifty percent, Frank. That's one hundred thousand. And I want it net."

Frank gave a slow smile, not believing this. "Marty, I don't know whether to laugh or to toss you over the side."

"Yeah, Frank. Laugh. You've screwed me too long. Four years. We were supposed to be partners, fifty-fifty. We signed our partnership agreement, if you recall, giving you ninety percent *on paper* because I was having problems with the IRS. Four years, you've taken ninety percent of the rent. The building has doubled in value and now you want ninety percent of the profit. No way."

"And I paid ninety percent of the operating expenses," Frank said.

"No. Not true. I put in my time. Now I want my share. Sign the contract."

"Fuck the contract," Frank said. "And fuck you. I don't need to sell the property. You want out, I'll give you twenty grand, right now."

"One hundred. Cash. You've got two weeks. After that, I'm going to the police."

Frank stared at him.

Marty sipped his orange juice.

The buzzing behind Frank's eyes got worse. He said, "You're out of your mind. That was four years ago."

"Is there a statute of limitations on murder?"

"It was an accident."

"Tell that to Detective Eugene Ryabin. It was his sister-in-law that burned."

Frank came out of his chair so fast Marty spilled his juice down his silk jacket. The insulated plastic glass hit the terrace with a clatter.

"You're in this too, Marty."

Marty slid out of the lounge chair and around the table. "I didn't pay the guy. You did. He knows who you are. And I know where he is. I saw his name in the paper. He's been arrested for armed robbery on South Beach. You think he won't turn you over to save himself some time in prison? The police would love to get your ass, big attorney like you. This is no bullshit, Frank. You screw me, I'm taking you down."

Marty's shit-eating smile had turned into the rictus of a man who wasn't sure if he had the other guy by the balls or if he would get his hand chewed off.

They were eight floors up. Frank thought of seizing Marty Cass by his neck, pitching him over. Watch him get smaller and smaller, bounce on the landscaped lawn below, then lie still.

"I want what's mine," Marty was saying. He sounded strangled. "Do that, I'll never contact you again. Okay? Fifty thousand in two weeks, the rest within a month. No arguments." He sidled around to the glass door. "I'll give you twenty-four hours to decide." He slid the door open, went through it, then quickly shoved it closed.

Dizzy with rage, Frank went over to the railing and looked down. After a while he saw Marty Cass's foreshortened figure walk quickly across the parking lot and then out toward the street. The tops of the trees seemed to tremble in the wind. His thoughts were murderous. The blood gurgled and boiled in his head.

It took him a minute to realize someone was saying his name. He looked around.

It was Caitlin, frowning. Standing there in her white shorts and pullover, hair shining, looking cool, as if this were any other day and he'd only been having a nightmare.

"Frank, you're pale as a ghost. What's wrong?"

He wanted to bury his face between her breasts. He dropped into a chair, breathing hard. "Come here." He pulled her down to sit on his lap.

"What on earth is the matter with you?"

He clung to her, his head on her shoulder, then told her he was in trouble. Marty Cass was trying to extort a hundred grand.

Four years ago, Marty had come to him with a deal on an apartment building on South Beach. The Englander, where Caitlin lived now. A rundown place in a borderline area, but the Beach was hot, and prices were going up fast. The owner couldn't make up her mind.

"Marty wanted to burn the place because the land was worth more than the building. Not destroy it, just do enough to make the owner want to sell. I told him it was a crazy idea," Frank said. "He did it anyway, paid an illiterate Marielito to start a fire in the trash area, make it look like kids or crack addicts had done it. The man was drunk, who knows, and the fire got out of hand. The owner died. A woman."

Caitlin said, "She *died*?"

"It was an accident. The trash area was outside her apartment. She was asleep, and the smoke got her before anyone knew she was still in there." Frank rolled his forehead back and forth on Caitlin's shoulder as if he could rub the pain out. "Marty's asking for money. The son of a bitch is trying to blackmail me for something I didn't do!"

Caitlin's arms fell away. "My God. Rivka. Wasn't that her name? Some of the old tenants still talk about her. How she died in the fire."

"It was an accident," Frank said. "It wasn't supposed to happen."

Caitlin got off Frank's lap and went over to stand at the railing of the terrace, leaning her elbows on it, eyes closed. Her mouth moved. *Oh my God. Oh my God.*

Frank stood beside her. "When I found out, I wanted to call the police. Someone had to arrest this guy. But Marty said I'd be charged as an accessory to murder. He had me boxed in."

"Frank, you have to go to the police."

"I can't do that."

"You weren't there. You didn't know!" She took his shoulders. "What can Marty do to you? He can't prove you were involved."

"I wasn't *involved*." Frustration was clawing at his throat.

"If you let him do this, it's like admitting guilt, Frank."

"No. It'll be okay. I'll pay him. I have to, then it will be okay." Frank threw his arms around her. "Oh, Catie. I'm so glad you're here."

She drew away. "What happened four years ago? Did the police question you? I mean, they knew you wanted to buy the building, didn't they?"

"No. Marty never told the owner I was interested. He had a listing on the property. After the fire, the relatives inherited the building, and they decided to sell. I made an offer. That's all anyone knows."

"Why did you do it? Why did you buy the building?"

He looked at her blankly.

Caitlin said, "Why, Frank? After someone died."

After a second, he said, "It was terrible, what happened, Catie, but there was nothing I could do."

"I guess it was still a good deal," she said. The breeze came up and lifted her hair. The shadows from the trellis played on her face.

He reached out a hand and touched her arm. "Catie. Come on. This wasn't my doing. It was Marty. He pulled me into this, and now I've got to pay for it."

She glanced around at the plates and glasses on the table, then started picking them up. "Tell me it's true, Frank. Tell me that's how it was." She leaned down to pick up the glass Marty had knocked to the terrace.

"It is, I swear to you." He took the juice glasses out of her hand and put them on the table. He slid his arms around her waist and breathed in the scent of her hair. "Oh, Catie. How can you even ask? After what I went through, living with this, sick about it."

She seemed to be watching the sailboats out on the water. Finally she said, "Let's not talk about it now."

He followed her into the house. "I wouldn't lie to you. Is that what you think? That I'm lying?"

"No. I don't know." She held up her hands as if warding him off. "Please, Frank."

His living room was a wide expanse of ivory carpet and modern furniture. Her photographs lay in rows on the carpet. Enlargements. Color, black-and-white. Fifty or more. She had laid them out in the order she wanted them to be hung in the gallery. Now she started picking them up.

"What are you doing?"

"I should go," she said. "I have a lot to do for my show next week."

Frank felt like somebody had rammed a fist in his gut. "Damn it, I wouldn't lie to you. What's the matter? Why don't you believe me?"

She spun around. "All right. You didn't know what Marty was doing. That's not it. You bought the building. I remember what you said at the time. You told me what a good deal you were getting. You were happy."

"I wasn't happy she died."

"No, it didn't affect you at all, did it?"

"We're not going to argue. Not now." He took the photos and dropped them back on the floor. "Catie, let's forget this for a while." He pulled her close, tried to kiss her. "Please, sweetheart."

She knocked his arms away. "Don't." She started picking up her pictures again. There were eight-by-tens on the floor, and bigger prints, many of them mounted. She had told him it had cost her nearly a thousand dollars for the processing. She expected him to pay for it, which he had done without protest, wanting her to be happy.

He laughed. "I ask for some understanding, and you turn into an ice cube. You wouldn't be having a gallery show if it weren't for me."

"I know that." She bent to her photos, lifting them carefully, placing them in a pile. "Frank, I mean it. If we talk about this now, we're both going to be sorry."

He lifted his hands. "Okay. Off limits. Gotta find another topic. Can't talk about that one."

On the floor were photos of a skinny black woman

taking a bath with a green garden hose. More of Caitlin's candid camera shit. *A damned high-priced hobby,* he thought to himself. Models and people on the street. And a black-and-white series. Old men and women. Kids. And nudes, some of Matthew Hagen.

"A pretty boy. He looks like Dina," Frank said. "Her eyes and mouth." He walked along as Caitlin stacked the photos. "I've seen too much of Matthew Hagen lately. His mother brought me two boxes full of memorabilia. She made me sit through every photo, report card, and crayon drawing he ever made. I've heard things I didn't want to know."

"You shouldn't have taken that case," Caitlin said.

Frank smiled. "Dina used to go into his room when he was asleep and sit by his bed and watch him. I'm serious. She likes to talk about how her perfect little boy was destroyed by the forces of evil. It's very Freudian, if you ask me."

"He was her child," Caitlin said. "She loved him."

"Oh, Catie." Her back was turned. He closed his eyes and put his arms around her waist, his forehead on her shoulder. "Marry me. Don't just move in. Let's get married. We can adopt a baby. Is that what you want?"

"Don't, Frank." She put the photos on the coffee table.

"I would, for you," he said. "Marry me. I'm going crazy without you. Wouldn't that be nice? To have a child of our own?"

She smoothed her hair down, then knelt to stack the last of the photographs.

Two more of Matthew. Sam Hagen's kid in the buff, leaning on his hands, looking out a window. Back view, tight ass, every muscle defined. A perfect, nineteen-year-old body.

Frank said, "I need an answer."

She frowned. "It wouldn't work. Leave me alone, Frank. I want to go home."

He grabbed her arm and pulled her to her feet. "You'll go to New York and stay with your fairy friend, won't you? But you won't live with me. I'm only good for what you can get out of me."

The photographs had slipped out of her hands. She

cried out, dropping to the floor, touching them as if they'd broken. "Shut up, will you? Just leave me alone."

He went over to the coffee table and picked up the photographs she had put there. "I should have a few of these for my place. I've paid for them already, haven't I?"

She rushed toward him, and he held them over his head.

"Come on, Ms. Dorn. Fair's fair. I bet I've paid the equivalent of a thousand bucks apiece for these, if you count rent, equipment, and every other God-damned expenditure I've made on your behalf." He looked at the photo of the black woman playing in the garden hose. "This is what you call fine-art photography? You're dreaming." Caitlin reached for them and he swiveled away. "Now this one of Matthew ought to go over big with the gay crowd on South Beach." He sent it spinning to the floor.

"Stop it!"

He glanced at a photo of Matthew lying on rumpled sheets, light coming over one shoulder. "What am I seeing? This is your apartment."

She pulled the picture away. "You're crazy. I took this at a studio."

"Uh-uh. No. These are your sheets. I ought to know your sheets. What was Matthew Hagen doing in your bed?"

"I took the sheets to the studio!" She reached for the photograph. "Give me that."

He pulled it away. "What a terrible liar you are, baby. I know how the light comes in your room. Just like that in the morning. Right? Right? Would you look at the sleepy smile on this kid. I bet you wore him out."

Her eyes glittered with tears. "Please, Frank. Give me the damned photo."

Frank was struck by the hilarity of it. "You told me Sullivan was doing him. Did you have a threesome?"

"Oh, God. No." She bent over as if he'd hit her in the stomach.

"How was it? He was a kid. Let's see . . . Fifteen years younger than you. Those young guys can go all night, can't they? Oh, that's naughty. Does Sam know? What did you do, Ms. Dorn? Get Matthew into bed because you couldn't have his daddy?"

Her mouth was open, and finally the words came out. "I despise you. I've never really seen that till right now. What have I been *doing*? Staying with you, all these years, like I was your fucking *whore*!"

He ripped the photograph down the middle.

Her fist came toward him faster than he could react. Stunned for a moment, Frank touched his inner lip with his tongue, tasting salt and heat. She ran, but he grabbed her arm. Then he slapped her. He kept slapping her while she yelled at him. Her hands were up and her hair was flying around her face. She was screaming profanities.

He screamed back. "I know about you and Sam Hagen. You didn't think I knew, did you? Cunt." He shook her. "Lying bitch. You fucked him. Didn't you? Answer me!"

"Yes! Yes, I did and I loved it! You're nothing next to him! He should have left your sorry ass in Vietnam!"

They spun to the floor, crashing into the end table. A lamp went over. She groped for it, raised it above his head. He deflected the lamp, then pushed her to the carpet, hit her again.

Caitlin's nose was bleeding, a smear of red on her cheek. Frank dragged her across the living room, opened the door, and shoved her through it. He came back with her purse and an armful of clothes. She was on her knees in the hallway, crying. He slammed the door and locked it.

Finally, silence.

Frank sat on the sofa and wept.

chapter
twenty

In the bedroom where her roommate let her keep her clothes, Ali rummaged through a box for a top to wear. She had a job today, handing out announcements on Ocean Drive for a party at one of the clubs.

Big smile. *Hi! Party at the Gear Box on Thursday. It's gonna be fun!* And the manager had told her not to give them out to obvious tourists or anybody younger than twenty-one; it was a waste of paper.

Ali was trying to ignore her mother, who was in the living room folding Ali's sheet and blanket from the convertible sofa, acting motherly.

Her mother's voice came through the half-open door. "He talked to me for the longest time. He was so *nice,* not like a lawyer at *all.* I know y'all would take to each other."

She worked in a bank. She'd taken the morning off to drive all the way to South Beach. Ali had noticed her mother's breath smelled like mints, meaning she'd probably had a drink already. "Honey? Can you hear me in there?"

"I sure can."

"Well?"

"I don't *want* to sue them right now. Mr. Hagen says wait till the trial is over."

"Wait? Why on earth would he say that, sugar?"

Shugah. Peggy Duncan hadn't lived in Charleston for twenty years, but every time she got that sticky

South Carolina drawl in her voice, Ali knew she wanted something.

Ali said, "If I sue them now, their defense attorneys would bring it up at the trial. I'd look mercenary. That's what Mr. Hagen says."

"Oh, Mr. Hagen. All he cares about is winnin' another case. He doesn't care about *you*. What if he loses? Then how are you gonna convince a civil court jury to pay you? That's what Mr. Barnett told me. Bring that girl in here *right now*. Let's get a settlement out of those boys while we still can."

Pushing aside the nighties hooked on the back of her roommate's door, Ali studied herself in the mirror. She had put on a pink top that showed her midriff. Nice with the white shorts, but her shoulders would freckle. She pulled it off, put on a white T-shirt, and tied that in a knot under her bust. Then changed into a pair of green shorts. Then wiggled into her knee pads.

Her mother was still talking.

". . . three or four hundred thousand dollars. A million. Those men have money. Klaus Ruffini has more money than *God*. Excuse me for saying this, sugar, but if you don't watch out, they're gonna have their way with you again, right in the courtroom."

Ali tried on hats and finally went with the tropical print billed cap, good with red hair. She pulled her ponytail out the back of it.

"Are you gonna be poor the rest of your life? Live like this?"

"No. I'm going to be a famous model."

"Oh, baby."

As if her mother had never heard anything so pitiful.

Ali dumped her house key, wallet, lip gloss, and sunscreen into a fanny pack and clipped it around her waist. Before leaving, she would take a bottle of water out of the fridge, too, so she wouldn't have to spend money when she got thirsty. But she knew a couple of the waiters at the Booking Table Café. They would probably slip her a soda. She took her in-line skates and a pair of socks into the living room to put them on.

Now her mother was in the kitchen wiping off the stove with a dishcloth. She wore her uniform for the bank, a blue skirt and a white blouse with a bow, but it made her look too heavy. Her hair was dyed red, the same shade as Ali's. She hung the dishcloth over the spigot on the sink.

"Honey, you're such a pretty girl. You're as pretty as the girls in the magazines. But the Ruffinis know everybody. What work are you gonna get round here now?"

"I have a booking next week." Ali dusted off the bottoms of her feet and put on her socks. "A back-to-school catalog for Macy's, so I guess my career has some life in it after all."

"Oh, baby. A catalog? And it's June. The season is over. What are you gonna do this summer?" *Summah.*

Ali shrugged. "I don't know. Hand out party announcements?"

The front door opened, and her other roommate came in: a blond model named Helga from Frankfurt, wearing a short, flowered dress and carrying a backpack. She had a tattoo around one ankle. Ali told her she had some mail.

"Hi. I'm Ali's mother, Peggy Duncan." She was smiling so big her gums showed. "My goodness, you're *tall.*"

Helga looked at her. She glanced at Ali and then went into her own room, shuffling through some letters.

Ali glared at her mother as she finished putting on her skates. They were shiny black with hot pink closures like ski boots. "I have to go." She skated to the refrigerator for her bottle of water, zipped it into her bag, then glided back to pick up the party announcements—five hundred of them about the size of postcards, printed on bright yellow paper.

Her mother put on her jacket and smoothed it over her hips. "Tell me somethin'. How much do you get paid for this?" She put her purse strap over her shoulder.

"Ten dollars an hour." They went into the hall and Ali locked the door.

"Ten dollars. I swear, I don't understand you one bit."

Ali held on to the balustrade one-handed, carefully picking her way down the steps, which were surfaced in scraps of tile, pink and turquoise and white.

Her mother was right behind her. "This is what I was thinking. You could write a book. Look at the people that made money off of O. J. Simpson. Get a ghostwriter.

Everybody does it. People would love to read about Marquis Lamont. It could be a bestseller."

"Ma, nobody cares about him."

"Well, maybe he isn't real famous, but if you did a book, Marquis might even help you. He'd get lots of publicity."

At the sidewalk Ali spun around. "I am not going to write about what they did to me! I don't even want to talk about it!"

"You don't have to scream at me." She sounded hurt. When Ali started off on her skates, her mother trotted behind in her pumps, holding her purse against her side so it wouldn't bounce. "Now what am I supposed to tell Mr. Barnett? He says you have a claim for damages. You ought to make them pay. What good will it do if they just end up in jail? You can use the money to do something for yourself. You could go to college."

Ali curved around a man walking his dog. "Ma, please. Stop following me."

"I spent two hours of *my time* consulting with an attorney about you. Trying to help. I drove all the way down here—"

"I don't care!" Ali skated faster. "Leave me alone!"

At the corner she looked back and saw her mother leaning against a light pole, her chest rising and falling. Then her mother cupped her hands at her mouth. "You'd better think about it, Miss Priss! Nobody's gonna do a thing for you but yourself in this world!"

Ali waited for a car to pass, then skated off the curb and across the intersection.

On the terrace of the News Café, his usual place for lunch, George Fonseca drank a beer and watched Ali Duncan handing out pieces of yellow paper to people on the sidewalk. He knew what it was for, a party at the Gear Box, which he had been hired to plan. But Ali wouldn't know that.

She hadn't spotted him among the tourists and regulars who filled the restaurant and spilled out onto the sidewalk at closely packed umbrella tables. He sat at a small table on the terrace just behind four women with English accents. The skin on their arms and thighs looked like raw beef.

He watched Ali spin around on her skates. If he went over to talk to her, just to say hi, how's it going?, he would be thrown in jail. At the bond hearing the prosecutor, Samuel Hagen, had looked at him as if he were garbage, then said to the judge, *Would the court instruct Mr. Fonseca that any attempt to contact the victim will result in immediate revocation of his bond.*

Even on the terrace, with a ceiling fan whirling overhead, George was sweating. This was only the first of June, and the temperature was already over ninety degrees. He pushed away the remains of his grilled tuna sandwich, which tasted like a piece of wet cardboard. He had no appetite. Alberto had called him last night, wanting to know if he was going to get paid back for putting up the bond, or what. Had Ruffini come through? Where was the ten grand? George had told him not to worry; he'd have it next week.

Ten grand plus another thousand in interest so far.

George had considered, but only for a minute, getting out of Miami. He didn't think he could get far enough. When it was all over, then he would leave. Maybe go to California, start over. He had heard someone say, *You go to L.A. if you want to be somebody, to New York if you are somebody, and you're in Miami if you used to be somebody.*

He leaned to one side to see around the sunburned Englishwomen. Ali Duncan was down the street fifty yards now, still handing out party announcements. And talking to another skater, a guy with a red bandanna around his head. No shirt. Dark tan, long black hair. He looked Japanese. But he was too tall to be Japanese. Ali was smiling at him. George finished his beer, remembering where he'd seen the guy: having lunch at the Seahorse Grill with Charlie Sullivan, now deceased. George wondered if Ali's new buddy was gay.

They skated across the street, weaving between the cars, then hopped up on the wide sidewalk that curved through Lummus Park. They zipped past the swings, where little kids were being pushed by their mothers, then around some sea grape trees. They sat on the coral rock wall bordering the beach for a minute; then the guy started showing off. Somebody had left a plywood ramp, and he was skating backward off it, doing a turn in the air. He stood about six, six-two in the skates. He wouldn't be as strong as George, but he'd be quick. George thought he could probably take him down.

George unfolded his portable phone, pulled up the antenna, and got the number of the state attorney's office from information.

"Let me talk to Samuel Hagen. He's one of your prosecutors."

He waited. Another female voice said, "Major Crimes."

"Is this Samuel Hagen's office? . . . Is he in? Let me talk to him. . . . Never mind my name. Tell him it's regarding Ali Duncan's case . . . *Duncan* . . . No, I'm not a reporter. . . . A possible witness, okay? Tell him that."

The waiter came by and cleared the table. George ordered another beer. Then in the phone he heard a man say he was Sam Hagen, and who was this?

George cupped his hand around the mouthpiece to keep out the noise. "This is somebody interested in the Duncan matter. I have a hypothetical question for you. . . . It doesn't matter who I am. Here's the question. In a criminal case, and you've got more than one defendant, what if you decide you want to get one of them to testify for the state? What do you do? Offer to drop the charges?"

There was silence on the other end. Then Hagen asked if this was George Fonseca.

He remembered now that Hagen had heard his voice at the bond hearing. "Yeah . . . I haven't made up my mind, but I've definitely been thinking about it, if we could work something out. What about dropping the charges? . . . Wait, hang on a second."

He stuck a finger in his ear. Three Harleys had pulled up to the curb. The engines went off and the guys dismounted in their boots, black helmets, and black T-shirts that said DAYTONA BIKE WEEK. They were probably dentists from Iowa, down on vacation.

George said, "Okay, I'm back. . . . Look, I'm trying to work things out, that's all. What's your problem? . . . No, I don't want to go through my attorney; the guy's a bloodsucker. . . . Listen, okay? . . . Why not? I won't say we had this conversation. . . . It's only a hypothetical question at this point, all right? . . . No, listen—"

With the click of a disconnect in his ear, George wanted to throw the phone across Ocean Drive. *Unethical to talk to you.* Hagen had also said he was going to call George's lawyer and let him know about this. And if anything was going to be worked out, the lawyers would do it. *Fuck.*

For a while he watched a blond woman in a thong bikini skating down the middle of the street between the cars. She got to where Eighth Street plugged into Ocean Drive, turned her back toward the intersection, and stood there on her skates making her butt cheeks jump. Drivers tooted their horns and people stared. She was a little fat, George decided. Good legs, but a fat butt.

Pulling a small address book out of his wallet, George flipped it open. He dialed Klaus Ruffini's number. One of his lackeys answered the phone. George told her who he was. Klaus wasn't there. George asked the number for his car or his portable. The woman asked for George's number. Maybe she could find Klaus. Maybe Klaus would call him back.

"Maybe you can kiss my ass," George said. "Tell him to call me."

The waiter brought another beer. George talked to the women at the next table. Turned out they were from Australia. Schoolteachers. Finally the phone made a soft *brrrp.*

It was Klaus Ruffini. George said, "Yeah. I've got a problem. No. *We* have a problem." He turned his chair so the women couldn't hear him.

"I'm getting pressured in relation to this bond. . . . You know what bond. Plus my lawyer is costing a fucking fortune. The point is, I could use your assistance. . . . Twenty thousand. . . . Look. I am not going to jail, all right? . . . Well, fuck you very much. . . . Then I don't have anything to lose by pleading guilty at the arraignment next week, do I?"

Over the phone came a long sentence in Italian. It didn't sound friendly. George said, "Listen to me, Klaus. My lawyer has been in contact with the state attorney. . . . No, not Mora. The other guy. Hagen. They might offer something on the charges. Maybe even drop them in exchange for my testimony.... Because I'm gettin' pushed to the fuckin' wall here."

Klaus told him to hold on. Judging from the noises in the background, Klaus was probably having lunch at a sidewalk café. Maybe he was in the next block. He heard people yelling at each other in Italian. A woman's voice. Then Klaus. Then the woman again.

Then Klaus came back. He said he would have somebody contact George in the next day or two.

George pushed in the antenna, folded the telephone, and picked up his beer. He took several deep swallows. His heart was about to jump through his ribs.

Through the crowd on the sidewalk, and past the cars, he could see the park. Kids skating. An old Jew in a black coat and hat, reading the paper in the shade. Some tourists walking toward the beach with swimsuits on. He watched for a while, but Ali Duncan was gone.

c h a p t e r
twenty-one

Caitlin's photographs remained inside Frank Tolin's apartment after he locked his door. Caitlin called that night about them, but he hung up on her. With no alternative, she reprinted the black-and-white negatives in her studio on Lincoln Road. The color work she took to the lab, which charged extra for a rush job. To pay for it, she sold the diamond pendant Frank had given her.

On Wednesday afternoon when she returned to her studio, her equipment was gone. The enlarger, the developing tanks, the lenses and filters, telephoto and tripod, two camera bodies, film and developing paper—everything but her boxes of negatives and prints.

There was an envelope on the work bench with a letter typed on Frank Tolin's law office letterhead: *The photographic equipment on the premises, purchased by the undersigned, has been seized to repay monies owed by you to same. . . .*

Caitlin screamed aloud what Frank could do with his letter.

That same afternoon she found an eviction notice on her apartment door giving her thirty days to vacate. She ripped the paper into pieces and threw it into the garbage. She still had her old Nikon. She would wear rags if she had to, but she wouldn't go back to him if he begged on his knees.

Frank had done that before. Begged her. Sobbed. Wept with his arms around her knees. *Oh, God, baby, I'm sorry.*

Please don't leave me. I need you, Catie. Hours of this. Phone calls. A soft knock on the door late at night. Or dozens of flowers and pages-long letters of apology. Until she gave in. And for a while, months sometimes, they were good together. Caitlin could usually tell when it was about to get bad. She would say so, and Frank would understand, and they would give each other some room. This time she had waited too long, till breaking away turned ugly.

She had gone back to him before, when the breakup had been uglier than this. Believing him had been easier than arguing. But not this time. There would be no going back. It was over. Over. Since Sunday she had repeated that to herself like a mantra to make sure that it came true.

Now Caitlin and the gallery owner, a woman named Paula DeMarco, stood by a table in the rear of the gallery going through mounted photographs for the show on Friday night. They arranged and rearranged, deciding what to put where. Paula was in her late fifties, overweight, and plain. Her arms, bare in a sleeveless black shirt, danced with muscle. She herself was a sculptor, married to an art dealer. In another week she would join her husband for the summer on Long Island.

Caitlin, nibbling on a thumbnail, nodded toward a street scene. "Maybe it should go there, with the night shot of Collins. Or maybe not."

Paula took a long look at her. "What is this? Nerves? Come on. You've had shows before."

"These photos are so simple. I'm not sure how well they'll go over."

"Simple? They're more real. They don't try to be clever, if that's what you mean." Paula allowed one further compliment. "These are okay, kid."

"Do you think so?"

"Jesus. What a question. Would I show them if they weren't?" Putting on her bifocals, she made an arrangement of four shots of models halfway through their makeup. "There. How's that?"

The gallery, on Lincoln Road a few blocks west of Caitlin's studio, was a narrow rectangle with big windows, polished wood floors, and stark white walls. On them had been hung three huge red abstract canvases, a collage or two, and some fabric pieces. In the middle of the room was a piece of art that resembled a stack of weathered boards. There was some sculpture, but not by Paula, who sold her pieces in New York. It was all very avant-garde and frighteningly expensive.

Caitlin felt her beeper buzzing at her waist, and glanced at the display screen. A 547 exchange. She frowned, then remembered what that was. The state attorney's office.

"Use my phone," Paula said, waving her toward the office.

Sam Hagen answered on the second ring. He wanted to see her regarding Ali Duncan's case as soon as possible, preferably this afternoon. Caitlin told him there was no way she could drive to Miami; she was working on her show. He said he would come to the Beach. When she told him it wasn't convenient, he told her to name a time. She let out her breath and told him after five, at the gallery.

She didn't want to see Sam Hagen. Didn't want to see anybody.

In the tiny bathroom in the office she checked her face. The harsh light over the mirror made her look washed out and tired.The swelling in her upper lip was gone. She pushed back her hair. The purple mark on her cheekbone was hidden under makeup. A long-sleeved linen shirt covered the bruises on her arms. She closed her eyes for a minute.

If he noticed, he would ask. And she would lie. Sam Hagen wasn't the kind of man to let it go. He might call Frank. And then? Frank would tell Sam about her and Matthew. But Frank wouldn't know what he was talking about. He would twist it, get it wrong. Sam wouldn't understand any more than Frank had. It would be worse with Sam. He wouldn't become violent. But it would be worse.

Caitlin leaned on her hands on the sink, her hair falling around her face, thinking of the deceptions that people had to practice on each other. And Paula had just said her photographs were becoming more real. She had to laugh.

While Paula attended to customers, Caitlin finished the display. Forty-two photographs, many showing ordinary scenes of South Beach, but more of the fashion industry.

Models talking, smoking, being made up and dressed and told where to sit or stand. There was one of Matthew Hagen at a marina, his dark hair at jaw level. Loose white slacks and shirt slashed, pinned, and clipped. Tourists in the background staring. He was making faces, laughing at himself, a mixture of innocence and sensuality. The final shot appearing in a German magazine had been in color. Stavros with his sultry glare pasted on, slouching at the railing of a motor yacht. Slick and impersonal, worthy of being tossed into a trash can after the magazine had been read.

There would be one nude of Matthew in a section devoted to portraits. Caitlin had done a study in black-and-white of his back and hips. His face was turned into the pale arm that circled his head. His hair was longer, flowing in waves to his shoulders. The photo had been taken two weeks before his death. She had not reprinted the photograph of Matthew in her bedroom.

Caitlin wrote notes, made measurements, and walked along the white wall and two movable partitions where on Friday morning she would place the pictures. Then she and Paula discussed prices and double-checked the text in the gallery guide. Finally, Caitlin placed all the photos between sheets of paper in the wide, shallow drawers of a cabinet in the office.

When she came out it was just after five o'clock, and Sam Hagen was in the gallery looking at one of the big canvasses, ten feet by ten feet. His back was to the room. He had turned up his shirtsleeves. White shirt and dark slacks against a background of vivid red. Wide shoulders like the pediment of a building, supported by columns of muscle resting on solid hips and legs.

He turned around as she approached. He had loosened his tie, an exquisite silk one with an abstract pattern of leaves. He had told her once he never wanted for ties: the parents of a girl whose murderer he had sent to Death Row kept him well supplied.

For a long moment neither of them spoke. He had a way of looking at people: unblinking, intense. The first time she'd met him it had unsettled her. She had laughed and told him he had to be scary as hell in a courtroom.

Caitlin held her tote bag in both hands, bouncing it lightly against her bare shins. "Did I keep you waiting?"

"A few minutes. Where are your photos?"

"They go up next week."

"Maybe I'll come see your show."

"Should I expect you?"

He said, "Probably not." He tilted his head toward the street. "Can I buy you some cappuccino?"

"Make it a cold beer, I'll say yes."

"I'd prefer that myself," he said.

Outside, Caitlin put on her sunglasses. All ten blocks of Lincoln Road had been closed to auto traffic some years ago. Trees had been planted, fountains and benches put in. The mall was quiet now, but by sundown the dinner crowd would be out in force.

After a bit of discussion they walked east toward Lyon Frères, the French deli where one could sit at small tables inside or out. Better inside this time of day, with the sun still blazing and the temperature stuck at ninety. Caitlin had dressed for the heat in sandals and a short cotton skirt. Her blouse had long sleeves, but linen let the air through.

"How's Rafael doing?" Sam asked.

"Still shaking. He lost Sullivan, then you guys smacked him around. How do you think he's doing?"

"They don't believe he did it," Sam said.

"You should tell Rafael, not me." She added, "At least he isn't going to agonize over Sullivan anymore. I'm not happy Sullivan's dead, but it sets Rafael free, at least that."

"I understand he's going to New York," Sam said.

"We both are. He has a job doing hair and makeup for a studio photographer. He'll be staying with his sister in the Village, and they said I could take the couch." She tilted her head up toward Sam. "I'll give you my number so you can get in touch about coming back for depositions and the trial. Would the state pay for an airline ticket? I'm a little short of funds these days."

"We could work something out." He walked for a while, then said, "Sounds like you and Frank have split up again."

"The way you put that, Sam. As if it's just another in a long, boring series."

"It isn't?"

"No. *C'est fini.* Kaput. Dead, buried, and unmourned."

Sam didn't reply to that. He said, "And what are you going to do in New York? Fashion photography?"

"Whatever strikes my fancy."

"You don't have a job?"

"Not yet."

"Kind of risky. If you're so short of funds these days."

Caitlin smiled. "Risky? A few years ago, Sam, I went to a conference at NYU on women in photography. By mistake I stumbled into a lecture by someone who had been in rural Pakistan. She'd been attacked for taking photographs of the way women live over there, and she was planning to go back. That's risk. She was risking her life. And I? I was taking pictures of pretty people in pretty clothes. Do you understand what I mean?"

Sam was looking at her. "Yes, I think so."

"Well, after the lecture was over, people gathered around to speak to her. I couldn't move out of my chair, I was so stunned. That isn't too strong a word for what I felt. Stunned. I knew that my life would change. But it didn't. And it hasn't. And here I am, thirty-five years old, still taking pictures that have no past and no future, and therefore, as far as I'm concerned, not much of a present."

With a hand on her elbow he guided her out of the way of two teenage boys on skates, their open shirts flapping behind them. The surface of the road was smooth, painted in wide, diagonal stripes of black and white. The paint had begun to fade.

Sam said, "New York. Well, you've got enough talent. I wish you the best, Caitlin."

The words were right, but she had no idea what Sam Hagen really thought. He could have been sorry to see her go. Or relieved. Or he didn't give a damn. She let out a breath. "What do you want to talk to me about? I don't have much time."

"Ali Duncan's case," he said.

"You mean what happens now, after Sullivan?"

Sam nodded. "I want to know why he died. If the other witnesses think he was killed to keep him quiet, they'll start losing their memories of what happened at the Apocalypse, and then I have no case."

She raised her hands, then let them fall. "I have no idea who shot Sullivan."

"But you know the people involved with him. Martin Cass's wife, Uta Ernst. She was one of Sullivan's sexual partners. Cass refuses to be questioned about the night of the murder. What do you think? A viable suspect?"

Caitlin took a while to frame an answer. She knew Marty Cass was a blackmailer. He had arranged an arson accidentally resulting in the death of Rivka Levitsky, the sister-in-law of a Miami Beach homicide detective. Say so, and Marty would implicate Frank. And Frank had his own stories to tell.

Finally, Caitlin said, "Marty Cass is basically a whiner. He might want Sullivan dead, but I don't think he's got the nerve to shoot anybody." That much was true.

They walked, passing under the shade of a live oak growing in a patch of grass edged by a low pink wall.

Sam said, "When you came to my office two weeks ago, you said something that stuck in my mind. Cass told you the Miami Beach city manager was going to ask the state attorney not to prosecute. Do you recall that?"

She hesitated. "It wasn't Marty Cass who told me. It was Frank, who got it from Marty. Frank said Marty told him the Beach didn't want the case prosecuted because it would create a bad image. The state attorney would investigate for the sake of appearances, then drop it."

Sam's expression was impenetrable.

Caitlin went on, "Of course you wouldn't prosecute. Nobody would believe a girl like Ali Duncan. In fact, everyone wanted her to be quiet and go away. Like Dale Finley from your office. The creepy man with the scar across his chin. After he got through with Ali, she wanted to run out of there. But how is this connected to Sullivan's death?"

"I don't know," Sam said. "Maybe it isn't."

And if there were a connection, Caitlin thought, Sam wouldn't tell her. She glanced at him as they walked. His face was shadowed with fatigue, as if he hadn't slept in days. The lines in his brow had deepened.

She stopped. "We passed Lyon Frères half a block ago."

Sam's gray eyes were fixed on her. He said, "Sullivan was sleeping with a rival of Klaus Ruffini in the fashion industry, Claudia Otero. What do you know about that?"

"It's true. Sullivan and Claudia were lovers for a long time. She's been married twice that I know of, and never gave up her affair with Sullivan. But do you think Klaus would have Sullivan killed because his wife and Claudia hated each other? That's a stretch."

"Last Sunday," Sam said, "on my way from the crime scene, I ran into Ruffini. He stopped his car and spoke to me. There were four people with him. Three girls and a muscled, black-haired guy who looked like a bouncer."

Caitlin said, "Franco. His bodyguard."

"Ruffini seemed . . . unconcerned that he might go to prison."

"Cocky?"

"That's a mild word for it."

"Obnoxious? Flaming asshole?"

"Close," Sam said. "He acted as if he couldn't be touched."

"Well, that's Klaus."

The water in the fountain nearby sprayed upward from a circle of copper and splashed merrily into a shallow basin painted the turquoise of a swimming pool. Caitlin waited for Sam to speak.

"What can you tell me about Claudia Otero?" he said.

Caitlin thought for a while, then said, "She's damned good at what she does. Very tough businesswoman, too. She's in her forties, but you'd never guess." Caitlin held her hand level with her forehead. "About this tall, five-five or so. Black hair, brown eyes, skin like milk. I've taken her picture a few times, freelancing for local magazines. She wouldn't remember me."

"Is she Spanish?"

"Originally Cuban, I think. She has friends in Miami, but most of the time she's either in New York or traveling in Europe. She runs with a very fast crowd. Lots of money and influence in the fashion industry. Everyone knows her."

"I'd never heard of her," Sam said.

"That's because you're not in the fashion industry. It's another world, Sam. Very insular and self-referential. People amusing themselves with dressing well and eating well and gossiping about the celebrities they know. You've never heard of Claudia Otero, and I'd be willing to bet she can't name the vice president or tell you how much a gallon of milk costs, or even gives a damn."

Stepping around Sam to see up the street, Caitlin said, "Her store is on the next block. You want to take a look?"

They crossed the mall and headed west again, staying under the awnings and flat roof extensions that shaded the storefronts. The sun wouldn't set till around eight o'clock.

The boutique was called Otero, decorated in black and gold. The mannequins in the window had dark, chopped hair and impossibly long, slender legs. They wore capes and micro shorts, or four-inch heels and dresses that clung and shimmered.

"She likes to use Spanish themes in her designs," Caitlin said. "That silver outfit with the matador cape is eighteen hundred dollars."

"Jesus. No thanks." There was a list of cities in a corner of the window. Sam was reading it. "Is this a chain store?"

She laughed. "Not at these prices, but essentially, yes. Claudia has them scattered throughout the U.S. and Europe. One just opened in Tokyo. Most of her business is in a less expensive line for department stores. Bloomingdale's, Saks, Lord & Taylor."

Caitlin could see Sam's reflection in the store window, hers next to it, half a foot shorter, a thin blonde in big sunglasses and a skirt to mid-thigh, a canvas bag on her shoulder. He had his arms crossed over his chest, one hand at his chin. He wore a watch with a brown leather strap and a plain wedding band. She let herself look at him. The height and size and angles. The curve of bicep under his sleeve. He could lift her easily. He had done that. Had swept her up and over his shoulder, carried her into her bedroom, and tossed her on the bed. She bounced, giggling, then watched while he unbuttoned his shirt, undid the cuffs, and unbuckled his belt. Starting with the arches of her feet and ending when he smoothed back her hair and kissed her forehead, Sam had touched her till she was dizzy from desire, and words spilled from her lips. *Please please Sam now oh God yes do it please.* He had entered her slowly, an agony, his solid weight pressing her into the mattress as if keeping her from flying into space. His breath on her face, mouth poised over hers. She had tightened around him and cried out. If a hurricane had brought the ceiling down, she wouldn't have known it.

Caitlin realized Sam was looking at her, and she was glad for the sunglasses. A few seconds went by before he asked, "Where is Claudia Otero at present?"

"Gone. She had a show this week, but she didn't attend. I think she went to London for Sullivan's funeral. I don't know when she'll be in Miami again. They say she's heartbroken."

Caitlin moved from under the awning. "I don't have time for a beer, Sam. I really have to go."

Sam stayed where he was. He asked, "Who are her friends in Miami?"

"Friends?"

"Claudia Otero's. You said she had friends here."

"I don't know who they are. Every Cuban alive must have friends in Miami." Caitlin came back a few steps. "There was a lot of Spanish spoken at her grand opening party."

"For this store?"

"Yes, by invitation only. The area was marked off with potted plants and barricades. There was a Cuban salsa band. Models and agents and celebrities all over the place. Gloria Estefan showed up, but she didn't sing. My God, there must have been three hundred people here."

"When was this?"

"I don't remember. It's been a few years. I was here taking pictures for *Beach Life* magazine."

"Could I see them?"

"What does this have to do with Ali's case?"

"I don't know yet," he said. "How about it? Your studio's just down the street. I remember you keep copies of photos you take."

"Well, the studio is closed. I moved everything to my

apartment, and it's a total jumble. Besides, I don't keep prints that old."

"What about the negatives? Contact sheets? Or that issue of the magazine?"

"I doubt I still have them."

Sam continued to look at her, his eyes giving nothing away. Finally he said. "That's all I want, Caitlin. To see the photographs."

Smiling a little, she put a hand on her hip and walked back to him, then turned her head, gazing along the sidewalk through her sunglasses. "I don't really believe that," she said, "but it's all you're going to get."

He laughed. "Three years and you'd still like to slap my face, wouldn't you?"

"Well, Sam, it *was* rather shallow, what you did, but then, affairs with married men are usually shallow and pointless, so I shouldn't complain." As she pivoted she said over her shoulder, "You can wait for me downstairs on the porch."

c h a p t e r
twenty-two

Caitlin Dorn lived off Meridian a few blocks south of Lincoln Road, in a pale yellow art-deco building with a blue stripe at the top. Over the door a semicircle of bas-relief letters read ENGLANDER APTS. Shade trees grew in the yard, and a low white wall ran around the property. Beyond the wall was a sidewalk, a narrow street with cars parked at the curbs, and more apartments on the other side.

Sam sat in a folding aluminum chair on the porch watching the street. A car would go by. Then a bicycle. Less often somebody would walk along the sidewalk. One of the tenants of the building would come through the gate occasionally, home from work. There was a line of about a dozen chairs, all of them facing outward so people could do what Sam was doing, sit in the shade and look at this small patch of the world. He stretched out his legs and the chair creaked a little. He thought about finding a deli on Alton Road for a beer, then decided he was too tired to move.

The old man three chairs down was throwing bits of bread into the yard for the birds. Nobody else was on the porch, just the two of them. Occasionally the muffled clang of a pan or rush of water in a sink would come through the open windows of the corner apartment. Somebody was cooking dinner.

Caitlin had gone upstairs about fifteen minutes ago to look through boxes of photos and negatives. She'd said it would take her a while. Sam was trying to get clear what exactly he hoped she would find. Photographs of a party three or four years ago at an overpriced dress shop owned by a *cubana* fashion designer who used to sleep with a man whose brains had spilled out through his handsome face last Saturday night. Charlie Sullivan, the main witness on a rape case that Eddie Mora, the *cubano* state attorney, had wanted to ignore. Other facts shifted through Sam's mind. Beekie Duran, Eddie's deputy chief of administration, hadn't wanted Sam involved. Dale Finley, ex-CIA spook, had threatened to expose Sam's affair with Caitlin Dorn if Sam made trouble for Eddie. None of these facts hung together, but Sam continued to play with them as he sat looking out at the street.

A flutter of wings and a piercing squawk made him glance to his right. A mockingbird was hopping around near the old man's bony feet. He wore frayed corduroy slippers. Death not too far off, the old man frail as a bird himself.

Sam looked back at the street. In the gaps between the overhanging trees, the sky was still bright blue. He shifted in the flimsy chair. There was a legal pad in Sam's briefcase on the front seat of his car. He thought about getting up. He could make some notes, see the details on paper. He had saved some cases by picking at details. Going after faint threads of possibility. Answers wouldn't come easily or fast, but they would come.

"Arthritis?"

Sam glanced around.

The old man gestured toward Sam's hand, which now Sam realized he had been massaging. "I said have you got arthritis?"

"No. The joints ache sometimes, that's all."

"My wife has it in her hip. The doctor says she needs a replacement, but she won't do it. My knees are bad, but I don't have it in my hands, thank God. I'm a scribe at Temple Bet Aviv."

Making a noncommittal response, Sam shifted again in the chair. His backside was getting numb. He wondered how these people could sit here like this all day, doing nothing. The old man had a plastic bag on his lap with slices of bread in it. He reached in, pinched off some bread, deftly rolled it into a ball, and flicked it into the yard. A bluejay screamed and went for it. The mockingbirds rose up in a flurry of wings.

Forcing his thoughts back on track, Sam went over the manner of Charlie Sullivan's death. The shooter had known what he was doing. He'd been methodical, exact. Maybe a paid hit. Or maybe Sullivan had known the shooter well enough to walk onto a deserted beach at midnight with him, expecting some fast sex. Didn't want to bring the guy up to his apartment for some reason.

The M.E. had retrieved fragments of a .45 hollow-point from Sullivan's chest. Sullivan had been dead, or dying, when he hit the ground. Then the shooter had fired into the base of the skull. Charlie Sullivan's casket in some London funeral chapel would be closed. Nobody would see that face again. It wasn't there anymore.

Metal scraped on concrete. The old man was moving his chair to get farther into the shade of the roof overhang. His cane slipped off the arm of the chair and clattered to the porch.

Sam went over and picked it up.

The old guy tilted his head up to see Sam through a pair of thick, black-framed glasses, and his mouth was open. Cords stretched down his mottled throat like the neck of a featherless chicken. "Thanks."

Nodding, Sam walked back to his own chair. He didn't want to get into a conversation. These old people could chatter on forever about their aches and pains, the lousy government, the Spanish moving into the neighborhood.

"I've seen you." The thin voice pursued him. "You used to come visit Caitlin. What's your name?"

He turned. The old man was still looking at him through the glasses. "Sam Hagen."

"I'm Harold Perlstein. I live here." He jerked a thumb at the open jalousie windows behind him.

"Nice to meet you." Sam sat down. Stared into the street. Wondered how many other people in this building knew she'd had her married lover here. Wondered if any of them had told Frank Tolin about it. Not that it mattered, now that Caitlin had broken it off. Again. Sam assumed she'd go back to Frank eventually. Thinking about it irritated him, so he didn't think about it.

Sam rubbed his forehead, trying to remember if he'd brought all the files he needed from his office, or if he'd have to go back in tomorrow or Sunday. There was a trial on Monday. Armed robbery, a career criminal prosecution. Sam had used the phone in his car to call home. Melanie had answered. Dina was still at work. He'd said to expect him about seven, seven-thirty.

A thought careened out of nowhere. *Please, God, don't let it be that Matthew knew who Caitlin was.* Then Sam realized Matthew couldn't have known. He'd never have come near Caitlin. Matthew had been judgmental about that sort of thing, in a curiously old-fashioned way for a kid. He would have despised her, and he would have skewered Sam with it. *Hey, Dad. Guess who I saw at a club last night?*

Harold Perlstein's chuckle broke into his thoughts. The old man's bony arm was extended toward the walkway. A glossy black bird with an iridescent purple sheen to its feathers was pecking at the edge of the concrete. Ugly bird. Big shoulders and a sharp beak. It didn't hop; it stalked.

"That grackle. He's the one. He sits outside our window every morning. He shakes his wings and yells, 'Up, up, you lazy bums.' "

The old man's chest was sunken, and his head seemed too big for his shoulders. Age spots dotted his face. The glasses sat on a curving nose. Behind them the eyes were faded blue. Still laughing, he held out the plastic bag and asked Sam if he wanted a piece of bread for the birds. Sam replied that he didn't, thanks. He checked his watch. She had been up there almost half an hour. He thought about going to ask what the problem was.

Caitlin had the southwest corner on the second floor. Apartment 12. The two brass digits would be beside the door, which last time Sam had been there had been painted pink. All the doors were various shades of pastel.

The breeze had stopped and the trees were still. Nothing moved. Sam was hot, tired. He leaned on his open palm, sleep dragging at his eyelids.

A telephone rang shrilly inside Perlstein's apartment. Then a woman's voice. Loud, as the voices of the hard-of-hearing are loud. She said hello, then must have recognized the person on the other end. *Ahhh, ja. Vus machts du, Shayna?* Yiddish. Asking her friend how she was doing. Then she switched to English with a New York edge to it. Brooklyn, maybe.

The voice reminded him of his great-aunt Sheila. Married to Hyman, who'd come straight out of somewhere in eastern Poland. Hyman was dead by the time Sam was in elementary school. Never spoke much English, but he made good money in the wholesale button business. Enough to buy the brownstone in Borough Park. *Vus machts du, Shmuel?* Hyman would ask him that when he came home from school.

The house had been dark and quiet. Thick curtains at the windows shut out the street noise. Dark wood floors, heavy furniture, a tall, gilt mirror in the entrance. All the mirrors had been covered after his mother died. Aunt Sheila made him wear his suit, which he had outgrown. His wrists went past the sleeves. She put a yarmulke on his head and gave him slippers for his feet. The visitors washed their hands on the front porch with water from a pitcher. The women loaded the kitchen table with food, then came over to hug him. Their bosoms were soft and wide, smelling of roses. The men squeezed his shoulders. Earlier in the temple the rabbi had chanted the mourner's prayer. *Yisgadal v'yiskadash sh'may rabo*—The only part Sam could recall, and he didn't know what it meant.

Birds fluttered closer to the porch, squawking. They pecked at the ground where the old man had thrown pellets of bread. Sam turned away and pulled in a breath. He was dizzy with heat and fatigue.

He didn't know what the hell he was doing here. He would look at the damned pictures if Caitlin could find them, then go home and work on his case. Cross-examination of defense witnesses. Now he remembered. He had left the deposition transcripts on his desk. For a while Sam weighed whether to go by his office on the way home.

He remembered Charlie Sullivan in his office, sitting in one of the battered chairs facing the desk. Blond hair combed back just so. Chiseled features, full lips. And the smooth British accent. *I knew your son, Mr. Hagen. A terrific guy. I was so shocked to hear of his death.*

Sam had been afraid of this; he knew it now. When Matthew had said he wanted to go into modeling and live on South Beach, Sam had made some jokes. Lame ones. Matthew hadn't laughed. He'd called him narrow-minded. Probably right. But Matthew had never given him a chance to prove otherwise. He had taken that last ride, sailing beyond the reach of understanding or forgiveness for either of them.

Sam decided to leave the transcripts on his desk till tomorrow. It didn't matter. He had tried hundreds of cases. After a while they all ran together, but the moves were the same. A long line of criminal defendants, like a carnival shooting gallery. Knock them down, they come back around. Whatever Sam Hagen did, the cases would come and go, and the inhabitants of Dade County, Florida, would continue to murder, rape, and rob each other. For a while, Sam sat and wondered what he could do with himself if he lost the election. Victoria Duran would not make life pleasant at the office. He could keep his head down and his mouth shut. Or leave. To go where? And do what? Open his own office? Defend the same bastards he'd been trying to convict for eighteen years?

Slowly Sam became aware of a sweet, yeasty smell drifting through the open windows. The smell had been working its way into his consciousness for a while, he realized. Bread baking in the oven. And another smell besides the bread. Roasting chicken. Sam's stomach was an empty pit.

"Smells like Shabbat in there," he said half to himself.

Perlstein looked around, a bread ball still balanced on his thumb. He considered Sam through his glasses, tilting his head. "You're Jewish?"

"No. I used to be."

"Used to be. How does a person used to be Jewish?"

"My mother. We lived in Brooklyn with her aunt and uncle. She died when I was ten. God, the way they cooked. As if we'd never eat again."

"So what are you now?"

"I'm not religious."

"That can be fixed. A bar mitzvah, even at your age."

Sam smiled and shook his head. "I don't think so."

Perlstein aimed the bread so the smaller birds could

reach it. His fingers were remarkably deft, with quick, sure movements.

He saw Sam looking at his right hand, then looked at it himself, turning it palm up. The dark stains on the thumb and first two fingers had worked their way under the nails.

"Ink," he announced.

Sam nodded. "Right. You said you were a scribe."

"Good memory. I thought you weren't paying attention. Temple Bet Aviv, Third Avenue, not the oldest congregation on Miami Beach, but close. The rebbe is pushing eighty. These days we're lucky we get a *minyan*. You know that word?"

"A quorum, isn't it?"

"We're going to have to start counting the ladies, God forbid."

"A scribe," Sam repeated. "What do you write?"

"Write?" The old man studied Sam as though he couldn't decide if he were serious. "The Torah. I write the Torah. I copy it. I make new scrolls."

"By hand?"

"What should I use, a copy machine? A typewriter? Please. Not even a ballpoint pen could I use. No, no. You have a new congregation, you need new scrolls. I use ink made the way it was since the beginning. And not paper. Parchment, from the skin of a kosher animal. The scrolls will last a long time. Hundreds of years, who knows? This may be the last one I do. The eyes are going. The hands are all right, but I don't see as good as I used to. God takes us piece by piece, if we live long enough."

The branches shifted and cast spots of light and shade on the yard. The colors had changed, turning more golden as the sun moved farther down in the sky.

Bracing both hands on the arms of his chair, Harold Perlstein stood up. He shuffled to the edge of the porch, upended the bread wrapper, and shook the last crumbs into his palm. He flung the crumbs into the yard. Birds descended on them. Chuckling, Perlstein dusted his palm on the front of his shirt.

It had been almost three years since Sam had climbed the stairs to Caitlin's apartment. He went to the correct door and knocked. The door was no longer pink but white. Even so, the same apartment. Second floor, southwest corner.

Her voice said to come in, it wasn't locked.

Sam came in. Caitlin knelt among half a dozen cardboard boxes at the far end of the room. There were more boxes stacked along the wall and on the table. The living room doubled as a dining area, with an opening leading to a tiny kitchen. She turned to look at him, and pushed her hair back from her face.

He said, "It's hot out there, and Harold Perlstein was driving me crazy."

"Close the door, don't let the cat out." Caitlin stood up. "I'm sorry. I should have brought you something to drink. I didn't realize this would take so long."

The apartment was cool and quiet. An air-conditioning unit hummed. Green plants hung at the windows, and the late afternoon sun came through and made a patch of light on the opposite wall. There were framed photos and prints Sam hadn't seen before. She had a different sofa. The same tabby cat watched him from the end of it.

Sam asked, "You find anything?"

She said, "Negatives and contact sheets and two magazines that ran some of the photos." She stepped over a box. "I have some beer. Or sodas. Whatever." Her earrings rotated slowly. Silver ovals. She crossed her arms, trying to be casual about his being here.

"A beer would be great," he said.

"Sit down, why don't you?" She went into the kitchen. He heard the refrigerator open, then a cabinet. She called out, "On the table. See those two magazines on top of the boxes?"

"Yes."

"I've marked the places. They both have stories about Claudia Otero."

Sam took his glasses out of his shirt pocket and sat down in the armchair by the window. The chair had a back that came up just behind his head, and a roomy seat. He shifted to pull a small batik pillow from under his hip and toss it to the couch. The cat stopped licking its paw and looked at him, then resumed, closing its eyes.

The first magazine was an issue of *Vanity Fair,* which

contained an article about the South Beach scene, with Claudia Otero's grand opening included as an example of how hip the Beach was getting. A new boom in fashion and modeling. People coming from all over. The article began with a typical candy-colored photo of Ocean Drive. Palm trees, blue sky, hotels like iced pastries. Then on the next page a photo of a woman on the back end of a turquoise '58 Caddy, holding on to one of the outlandish tail fins. Claudia Otero was, as Caitlin had described, a black-haired beauty. Next page: pictures of nightlife, the clubs. Claudia's boutique, her standing out front in tight pants and a short sequined jacket with padded shoulders, hair pulled back like a Spanish dancer. In the text, names were mentioned, the usual run of celebrities. A couple of minor actors. A rock singer. A writer. Sam turned another page. More shots of South Beach as a destination for the young, tanned, and prosperous. He went back to the photo of Claudia Otero. She looked familiar. He'd never met her, but he had the feeling that if she walked through the door, he'd know her.

Caitlin came out with two beers in mugs frosted with ice. She kept them in the freezer, he recalled. "Thanks." He drank deeply, then wiped a knuckle across his upper lip. The cold liquid seemed to seep into his body like water on dry sand. She put a couple of coasters from Club Deuce on the end table, and he put his mug on one of them. She slipped out of her sandals and sat on the end of the couch, one leg under herself, the other swinging.

Sam settled back. The next magazine was *Beach Life*. Same topic. Caitlin's name in small type credited her for the photos. Sam spotted Charlie Sullivan in the background of one of them. Linen suit, open collar, teeth and hair shining. In another photo George Fonseca had his arm around Claudia Otero's waist, grinning at the camera. Curly black hair, black leather vest.

"George Fonseca is a friend of hers?"

"Not particularly. He planned her party. Her PR person probably hired him."

"Did he bring his goodies?"

"Everyone brought their goodies." Caitlin laughed and rolled her eyes. "You could breathe hard and get high off the dust in the air."

There were five other photographs in the article, and the captions contained quite a few Spanish surnames. Sam didn't recognize any of them, but he asked Caitlin if he could borrow the magazines.

She told him he could, then said, "You probably ought to see the contact sheets, too." Leaving her beer on the end table next to his, she crossed the room and sat on her heels beside the boxes. Her narrow skirt rose up her thigh, and her bare toes spread out on the carpet. "Where the hell did I put it? Ah. Here." She found what she was looking for, then went over to her desk to rummage in a drawer for a rectangular magnifying glass.

The contact sheets consisted of two sheets of developing paper with tiny photos shot directly from strips of black-and-white negatives. Attached was a piece of paper with a list of frame numbers and the names of whoever was in the shot. Sam removed the paper clip.

Caitlin sat down again. "I was shooting with two cameras that night, one with color film, the other black-and-white. I don't know where the color negatives went to." She took off her earrings. They made a bell-like jingle when she tossed them onto the table. The cat came over and bumped its nose into her chin. She tilted her head back, laughing a little, then stroked her hand along its flank. The cat curled up on her lap, the tip of its tail twitching.

Through the magnifying glass, Sam swept over one photo, then the next. Celebrities, models, and less important people who hadn't made it into the magazine. Sullivan reappeared. So did George Fonseca. And the man who'd been mayor of the Beach at the time. People smiling at the camera. Good teeth. Glasses of champagne.

Sam backed up a few frames. Claudia Otero. She was with another woman, both smiling. He moved the contact sheet closer to the light coming through the window and looked again. The women's heads were touching. Arms around each other's waists. He checked the list. Frame 23. *Claudia and Amalia (her sister).*

He took a while to let this sink in. Claudia Otero had looked familiar. Now he knew why. She was enough like her sister to be a twin. Her sister was Eddie Mora's wife. Amalia Otero Mora.

"What did you see?"

Sam asked if she had the negatives.

"Why? Did you find something?"

"I'm not sure yet."

"Yes, you are, you'd just rather play prosecutor." She lifted the cat off her lap and went back to the boxes on the floor.

Sam had met Amalia Mora maybe half a dozen times since Eddie had been appointed state attorney. Eddie kept his personal and public lives separate. He and Amalia had come to Matthew's funeral. She rarely appeared at the office. A pretty woman, mid-thirties, dark hair, spoke perfect English. Cultured, well dressed. Not as flashy as many of the Cuban women in Miami. Her father had owned sugar in Cuba, pre-revolution.

Caitlin returned with negatives pocketed in a clear plastic sheet.

Sam said, "This list that goes with the photos. Where did you get the names on it?"

"From the people in the pictures. I had a tape recorder with me and before I took the picture I'd ask who they were, and I'd record it."

"Some don't have last names."

"Some people don't like to say."

He considered that as he drank his beer. It was smooth and cold. She used to keep a six-pack of bottled Amstel in the refrigerator. He sank farther into the armchair, his body heavy as poured cement. He put his glasses back into his shirt pocket.

The air conditioner compressor went off and he could hear the cat purring. Caitlin was scratching under its chin. After a while her eyes lifted, seemed to focus somewhere on the carpet, then move to Sam's face. Her irises caught the color of the plants in the window, and the light made them shine. Her blond hair fell from a center part, framing her face. Sam lifted his mug and took another swallow.

Her bedroom door was open, a corner of the bed showing. A bedspread. The bed was made, or maybe turned down at the head, where he couldn't see it. The same blue curtains at the window. Her dresser. A pair of shoes, one turned on its side, carelessly kicked off.

He finished his beer.

Caitlin sipped hers. "Can I get you a refill?"

"No, I should go. A couple of aspirin, that would be good."

She looked at him for a few seconds, then put down her mug. "Sure." He watched her walk into the kitchen: long muscles in her legs, a slight sway to the hips. A few seconds later ice cubes dropped into a glass. He wondered if she still kept bourbon, decided not to ask. He could have used a bourbon more than the beer.

She came out of the kitchen. Moving in that way she had. Bare feet. Bare legs to the hem of her skirt, halfway up her thighs. He could feel a pulse in his temples, tightness in his groin. He wanted to slide his hand under the hem till he found her flesh. Pull her panties aside, if she was wearing any.

Her fingernails lightly grazed his palm when she gave him the aspirins. She stood so close he could see the stitching in the seam of her skirt. She wore a long-sleeved shirt, and her hand was tanned, the skin paler and delicate at the wrist.

He took the glass of water from her.

Her laughter was breathless. "I never thought you'd be in this room again. I would have shot you if you had come through the door."

He tossed the aspirin into his mouth, then swallowed some water. He held the glass for a minute, debating where on the table to set it, not to make a ring. The table was made of some light wood. He put the glass on a section of newspaper.

"I'm sorry, Caitlin." He let out a breath. "Jesus. I said that the last time I was here, didn't I?"

Across the room the plants behind him were casting an odd shadow on a window-shaped patch of sun. Harold Perlstein and his wife were probably sitting down to dinner. Sam decided he would run a few miles when he got home. Then have a couple of drinks and something to eat and stretch out in the family room. Watch some TV.

"I don't want you to be sorry, Sam."

Her voice was soft, and memories rolled over him in a black and hopeless wave. He could walk out and nothing would have changed. Or he could stay a while longer. Turn around and sink into those green eyes. Say the right words. Pull her into his lap. Kiss her. She was waiting for him to do that. He could hear it in her voice. She wouldn't shy away if he touched her.

He had known all this before he had climbed those stairs, without knowing it consciously. And now the blood was roaring in his veins. He knew what it was like to touch her. Breasts that fit perfectly in his hands. Inside she was warm and slick. He knew the sounds she would make when she came. They weren't strangers. He could take her to bed. And then walk out and pretend it hadn't mattered to either of them.

The moment ebbed. He could feel it flowing away from him. Saw the room come back into focus.

He checked his watch, made a noise. "I've got to get going." He picked up the mug and took it into her kitchen.

When he came back out, Caitlin stood by her desk sliding some enlargements into a big white envelope. She glanced over her shoulder. "While you were downstairs I found some portraits of Matthew. I'd like you to have them."

Sam was at a loss. "What am I supposed to do with them?"

"Take them with you. Frame them, put them in an album, I don't know."

"Thanks, but we've got plenty of photos of Matthew."

"Not these."

"What are they, the nudes you said you took?"

"No, Sam. They're black-and-white portraits. His face. There are a few of him standing up, but he's got a pair of jeans on." She folded back the flap. "I'll show you." She grasped the edges of several sheets of photographic paper and pulled.

"I said I didn't want them, Caitlin." The words had a bite he hadn't intended.

They looked across the room at each other. She let the photos drop back inside the envelope. "Fine." She laid the envelope on the table. "What are you afraid you'll see?"

"No. You're wrong," he said. "You don't do that, Caitlin. You don't push photographs of a man's dead son in his face."

She evidently hadn't considered that. She nodded.

"Forget it." Sam looked around, trying to remember

what he had to take with him when he left here. He spotted the magazines and contact sheets and negatives in the armchair. He picked them up, stood there a second, then dropped them back on the seat.

He said, "I want to ask you something. About Matthew." He turned around and looked at her.

She crossed her arms over her chest, raised one shoulder in a shrug. "All right."

"You knew him pretty well. You told me you did."

"I suppose so."

Sam felt like he'd run up several flights of stairs. "Was Matthew gay?"

Her eyes widened a little. "Gay?"

"Come on, Caitlin. You know what I'm talking about."

"Why are you asking that?"

"Yes or no?"

She continued to look at him. "No. He wasn't."

The witness was lying. Sam moved in a little closer. "Then would you mind telling me what Matthew was doing with Charlie Sullivan?"

"Oh, Sam. What you're thinking—" She shook her head. "No. It wasn't—" Her eyes closed, then opened. "He and Sullivan had a brief relationship, but for Matthew—"

"Brief." Sam laughed. "Well, that's all right, then. Brief. But Charlie Sullivan's relationships were always brief, weren't they?"

"Sam, please. You need to understand this."

"I do understand." He raised his hands. "Details are not required."

"For God's sake, he wasn't gay!" she shouted. "And if he was, it wouldn't have been the damned end of the world, but he wasn't. Can't you listen?"

There was silence for a moment. Sam said, "All right. Tell me."

She raked her fingers through her hair, then said, "When Matthew came to South Beach, he wanted to be a model, not for the most mature reasons in the world, but that's what he wanted. Except he didn't know how hard it would be. He wasn't prepared for that. The hard work, the rejections. He met Sullivan, who was everything he dreamed of being. A top international model. A celebrity.

People fawning all over him. Sullivan had looks, he had money, he traveled. He was older. Sophisticated. And incredibly seductive. Whatever Sullivan wanted, he could usually have. And he wanted Matthew."

Sam stared at the wall.

Caitlin went on, "What Matthew felt for Sullivan—I don't know, call it hero-worship. Loneliness, confusion. Sullivan took advantage. Then it was over, and Matthew was sick about it. He's your son. He had your values to contend with as well as his own. It happens to people, Sam."

"In this environment, I'm sure it does."

"Don't judge," she said sharply. "You have no right."

"Yes, Caitlin. I goddamn well do have a right. My son was sleeping with another man and shooting dope. Heroin. Another little surprise. Yes or no?" Sam waited for a response. "Yes or no, Caitlin?"

"Smoking it, more than shooting, and he was stopping, Sam. He was."

"Why in hell didn't you tell me?"

"Me? How could I have?"

He brought his voice back down. "No, you couldn't have. If there's any fault here—and there's plenty—it isn't yours." He picked up the magazines from the armchair and rolled them into a tight tube. "I'm glad someone shot the perverted son of a bitch. I might have done it myself, if I had known this. Matthew couldn't tell me, could he? Christ, no. I'm the last person he would have come to."

Her cheeks were blazing with color. "Matthew wasn't a boy anymore. He had to work it out on his own. He would have, Sam. Please believe that."

Sam noticed through the jumble of plants in the window that the clouds were starting to turn pink. With the roll of magazines he pushed aside a cascade of philodendron leaves.

"It doesn't matter what I'd like to believe. I know how it was. Matthew and I, at some point, stopped connecting. I told you some of what we went through, so maybe you can understand. A lot of fathers and sons, that's the way it is. I said, okay, Matt, if that's what you want, you go do your own thing. And he did. I figured we'd get past all

this one day. Then he takes a ride off the deep end. I don't
know why he turned out the way he did. His sister's nothing like him, and she has the same parents, so how do
you figure? I can't go back and fix it. What I said, how I
handled it. He's gone. I lost him a long time ago."

A muffled noise came from the sofa. Sam looked
around. Caitlin was sitting on the edge of it crying. "Oh,
God." He walked over to her. "Caitlin, what is this?"

She took a napkin off the end table. It still had the imprint of his beer mug in it. She pressed the napkin to her
eyes with her long, slender fingers.

"What's this about?" He touched her hair, let his hand
move to her cheek.

She turned her head. In a thick voice, she said, "I want
you to go."

"Caitlin."

"Please. Get the hell out, will you?"

He looked at her a while longer, then went over and
picked up the negatives and contact sheets and stuck them
in the pages of one of the magazines. He glanced across
the room as he closed the door. For a second her eyes cut
toward him, then she crossed her arms tightly over her
chest and turned away.

chapter
twenty-three

Sam was halfway across the MacArthur Causeway when he got the call, Gene Ryabin telling him that George Fonseca had been found shot to death. At a break in traffic, Sam made a U-turn and sped back toward Miami Beach.

The location was a parking lot outside a boarded-up motel on the northern end of the Beach, just off Collins Avenue. The last half mile Sam found himself behind one of the gray Ford sedans from the M.E.'s office. It splashed through a pothole near the sidewalk, then drove slowly to the rear of the lot, its headlamps sweeping over six Miami Beach police cruisers and a crime-scene van. Dense Australian pine trees grew wild along the perimeter of the property. Beside the two-story motel, lights had been set up to illuminate the scene, a blaze of white.

Dave Corso got out of the sedan with his camera and flash unit and waited for Sam. "What is this, Hagen? You get all the Beach homicides now?"

"Looks that way," Sam said. "This could be related to the one from Sunday, Charlie Sullivan."

"The model without a face."

"He was a witness on a sexual battery case I'm prosecuting, and today's victim was one of the defendants."

"No kidding. First a witness, then a defendant. Be careful. They might go for the lawyers next." Corso looked around. "Who's the lead detective? Ryabin again?"

Sam nodded, and Corso went to see what was what before he got started.

The hotel was called Pelican Harbor. No pelicans, no water, except for the scummy rainwater in the swimming pool behind a low chain-link fence. The faded pink paint was decorated with graffiti, and sheets of plywood had been bolted over the lobby windows. The swooping concrete portico dated the construction from the 1950s, before this part of Miami Beach had slid downhill and stayed there.

For a minute Sam stood with his hands in his pockets watching the activity around the red Mustang. A routine patrol from the north district had spotted the car in the parking lot about five o'clock, then noticed it again an hour later. The man behind the wheel seemed to be asleep. The officer drove over to check it out. The driver was dead, shot once in the thigh, once in the stomach. They ran the tag. The car was owned by George Fonseca.

The crime-scene techs gathered what evidence they could find, which didn't amount to much: a tiny vial of brown powder in the glove compartment, a cellular phone in the front seat, and several beer bottles on the floor. These items would be dusted for prints. The pitted asphalt parking lot held no fresh tire tracks or footprints. Several officers had started canvassing the immediate area for possible witnesses, so far without result. No one had heard gunshots.

Ryabin had given him this information by phone, and now Sam walked over to take a look. A head of dark curly hair rested on the edge of the open window. The windshield was spattered with blood, and the police lights coming through the glass cast a weird, dappled pattern inside the car and on George Fonseca's face. The dark brown eyes were half open. His mouth and nose were smeared reddish brown. There was blood and what appeared to be vomit down his shirt. He had a lapful of blood and a chunk missing out of his right thigh, just above the knee.

Pulling back from the window, Sam continued to stare at the body, trying to sort out his thoughts. As if he'd willed this murder into being, here was the corpse. Half an hour ago he had imagined such an end for George

Fonseca, not precisely this scene, but something similar, proceeding from a desire as sharp and compelling as sex, a need to inflict pain. Not by gunfire, that would be too quick. Sam had wanted to use his hands. But this had happened without him. He felt distinctly ambivalent: both responsible and cheated.

Flashes of light came from the other side of the car. The medical examiner was taking photos through the passenger's door, which the police had opened. Then he let someone hold the camera while he put on his gloves and walked around to the driver's side. He spoke to one of the techs. "You guys finished over here?"

"For now. You want to open the door, doc, go ahead."

"You do it. He might fall out."

The fingerprint technician was a big man with a trimmed blond beard. The door came open, a screech of rusty metal, and George Fonseca's body began to tilt sideways. While the tech leaned on the door, the officers took a quick vote and the losers put on latex gloves. Grunting and cursing, they maneuvered the body out of the bucket seat, past the steering wheel, and onto the asphalt. Fonseca was slightly curled up, neck twisted to one side, more or less his position in the Mustang.

Sam forced himself into a dispassionate consideration of the evidence. There were no powder burns on the pant leg. The shooter must have been several feet away, aiming either through the open window or open passenger's door, which he had the presence of mind to close before leaving. But if he'd wanted to kill Fonseca, why not one neat shot into his head? These shots—one in the thigh, one grazing the gut—seemed rushed, even unplanned.

Corso aimed his camera. Light flashed for an instant on the long gouge across Fonseca's abdomen. Again at another angle. Right thigh: flesh missing, bone exposed. More shots, side and top. Fonseca's face, the smears of blood and vomit.

One of the plainclothes detectives stopped popping his gum long enough to ask, "What'd he do, hurl his lunch?"

Corso sat on his heels beside the body. "Did you guys find any drugs in the car?"

"Yeah. Little bottle of smack in the glove compartment,

inside a flashlight. Looks like smack, anyhow. No works, though."

A young patrolman said, "You mean he O.D.'ed?"

The fingerprint tech laughed. "He was fuckin' *shot,* man. He might've O.D.'ed, but it ain't what did him in."

Corso returned his attention to the body, lifting the eyelids, going through the routine. Petechial hemorrhages could indicate strangulation, though that didn't seem to apply here. He levered down Fonseca's arms, which resisted. "No obvious needle marks."

"Maybe he snorted it," someone said.

Another cop agreed. "It don't take more than a piece of tinfoil and a lighter."

Someone laughed. "You can't overdose that way."

"So the guy that killed him had a syringe."

A young officer with a blond crewcut asked, "Hey doc, why'd the shooter blow him away if he was overdosing?"

Corso looked up. "Well, that's for you to find out, isn't it?"

Holding a magnifying glass, Corso got closer to Fonseca's nose and mouth. "I can't tell if we've got a nosebleed or a brachial hemorrhage. Bullet might've nicked a lung." He pressed on the jaw to open the mouth and flashed his penlight inside. "Not much blood in here. Looks like it's coming from the nose. That's odd."

Sam asked, "Why is it odd?"

"Because a heroin overdose doesn't give you a nosebleed." Corso pushed his rimless glasses up a little farther with his wrist; his gloves were bloody. "It makes you go to sleep. You might twitch a little, but that's it."

"What about coke?"

"No, not with coke either. Or any opiate or morphine-based drug, or any synthetic that I know of—meth, PCP. You want a list?"

"What else could have caused this?"

Corso glanced up at Sam. "You don't usually ask me for opinions at the scene, Hagen."

"Yeah, I know, but how about it?"

"I don't like to give opinions at the scene," Corso muttered. His hands dangled between his knees as he sat silently on his haunches. "I think he was sick, but I don't know from what, and I don't know at this point if it made a difference. These gunshots weren't necessarily fatal. He might have survived if he'd made it to a hospital, but I'd say the man bled to death. Wait for the toxicology report, will you?"

Sam said, "That's going to be five or six weeks. Can you push it?"

"For you, I'll ask the toxicologist pretty please."

"How soon can I get an autopsy report?"

"Call me tomorrow. He's scheduled for the morning. I'll have him done by noon." Corso raised his hand. "It won't be written, okay? Come on. I've got a life."

He took off Fonseca's jewelry: a heavy gold watch, an ID bracelet, a gold chain.

The blond cop said, "Damn, look at that watch."

"It's a fake," Corso said.

Sam asked if the wallet was still in the back pocket.

Corso took it out, held it up, then bagged it. With a short, curved pair of scissors he started slicing through Fonseca's clothes, matching holes in the garments to bullet holes in the body. As the clothes fell away, a stench of body wastes hung in the unmoving air. Corso gestured with the scissors. "The victim urinated and defecated all over himself. Consistent with a toxic reaction to something, okay? But don't ask me what." He stood up and took some photographs. Grit and pine needles stuck to Fonseca's back when they rolled him over. His genitals and buttocks were mottled red-purple from livor mortis, and smeared with feces.

Sam looked around for Gene Ryabin, and saw him watching the crime-scene technicians examine the interior of the Mustang. The backseat and floors were buried under yellowed newspapers, food containers, and crushed beer cans. After a cursory examination the techs would roll up the windows and take the car to the police garage, where they could go over everything with tweezers and a magnifying glass.

Ryabin noticed Sam and told him to come look at what they'd found. He held up a bag sealed with red evidence tape. There were some misshapen pieces of lead inside. "We found these on the floor. Whatever is in the side door we'll dig out at the garage, and there's a bullet hole in the seat. So. At least three shots, and the shooter had terrible aim."

Moving out of his own shadow cast by the spotlights, Sam put on his glasses. He felt the fragments through the thin plastic. "What's your guess? Forty-five's?"

Ryabin made a gap-toothed smile. "As with Charlie Sullivan? Maybe ballistics can make a match—although you are aware, Sam, how many forty-five-caliber handguns there are in Dade County, and how many of those shoot hollow-points." He gave the bag to one of the uniformed men.

"What now I am wondering is why, if the same person did both these gentlemen, he chooses first a witness, and then a defendant on the same rape case. Is this logical?"

Sam said, "Fonseca called me yesterday."

"Did he?" Ryabin's bushy eyebrows rose.

"He offered to testify against Klaus Ruffini if I made a deal. I think he was looking for his own deal."

"Money from Ruffini not to testify," Ryabin concluded. "Did you offer him a plea?"

"Sure, to put him away for the maximum. He didn't like my attitude," Sam said. "I told him to have his attorney call me. I didn't hear back. You might want to talk to Ruffini's bodyguard. I think his name is Franco."

"We've met." Arms crossed just above the curve of his belly, Ryabin said, "Here's another possibility for a shooter. Asking around, I'm finding out Fonseca had no money for bond."

"Who put it up for him? Not Ruffini."

"No. Alberto Gusman is the name I've been given. A midlevel trafficker who was, I believe, Fonseca's source. He and Fonseca share the same attorney, Don Gessing."

Sam said, "And you think Fonseca could have leaned on Alberto Gusman, and Gusman pushed back."

"It's a theory," Ryabin said.

"But what motive did Gusman have to kill Charlie Sullivan? Sullivan had nothing to do with drugs," Sam said.

"You believe the same person killed them both."

"Don't you?"

"So many complications." Ryabin sighed. His heavy beard had broken into stubble this late in the day. "Better not to assume anything yet, although I think what you do,

Sam, that the bullets came from the same forty-five-caliber semiautomatic pistol."

"How soon can we get an answer?"

"A few days."

They watched a couple of officers unfold a tarp and spread it over the naked body lying on the asphalt parking lot. A carcass now.

"Gene, I wanted to prosecute the son of a bitch," Sam said. "I was looking forward to it."

"What now?" Ryabin asked.

"The case is still on. I'm not too fond of Klaus Ruffini, either, and I'd be particularly annoyed if somebody shoots him."

Sam told Ryabin to come over to his car for a minute. They sat in the front with doors open and the dome light on, looking at the contact sheets he'd borrowed from Caitlin Dorn. Ryabin lit a cigarette and blew smoke into the darkness.

Pointing at one of the frames, Sam said, "This woman with Claudia Otero is her sister, Amalia Otero Mora. Eddie Mora's wife."

"Give me your glasses. I'm going blind." Ryabin held them a few inches over the page, squinting through one of the lenses. "Lovely women. Both of them. I like women with dark eyes. Did Eddie ever mention to you that Charlie Sullivan, now deceased, was sleeping with Amalia's sister?"

"It must have slipped his mind," Sam said.

Still studying the tiny photographs, Ryabin said, "How wonderful to be so rich and to know so many people."

"Fabulous."

"Yes. Fabulous people, a fabulous party." Ryabin moved the contact sheet, following the lines of negatives printed on it. "George Fonseca is here."

"He planned the party," Sam said.

"And look. Hal Delucca, our city manager." Ryabin added, "Before he became our city manager. That's how you get elected on Miami Beach, Sam. You go to parties given by rich foreigners." Ryabin went to the next contact sheet. "Here's Marty Cass."

"Show me. I met him a couple of times at Frank Tolin's office, but that was a few years back." Sam put on his glasses. Cass was a short man with a big smile, his arm around a former mayor of Miami Beach who had eventually gone to prison for tax evasion. "Yeah, this is Marty. I remember the ponytail."

Ryabin gazed for another moment at the small, grinning face in the photograph, then tossed the contact sheet aside.

Sam remembered that Marty Cass had handled the sale of the Englander Apartments, where Ryabin's sister-in-law had burned after telling him she'd never sell the building. The fire department had called it arson. Ryabin had never accused Marty Cass, but neither had he forgotten.

They got out of the car just as an unmarked Dodge van turned slowly into the parking lot, its headlights sweeping over the people watching from the sidewalk, then illuminating the trees at the property line. Two men got out and rolled a gurney over to George Fonseca's covered body. They slid the body onto a board, lifted the board to the gurney, then loaded the van and slammed the door. Onlookers parted to let the van through, and it turned south on Collins, heading for the morgue.

It was late when Sam got home. He'd bought a beer along the way. Coming in through the garage, he threw the empty bottle into a trash can, let the automatic door down, and went into the house through the kitchen. He flipped on the light.

Melanie, in a pink nightshirt, was standing at the refrigerator, pouring herself a diet soda. She looked at him, not speaking.

He reached out and ruffled her hair. "Hey, how's the kid?"

"Stop it, Dad." She jerked away.

"Jesus." He reached past her for a beer out of the six-pack on the bottom shelf. "Am I still on your shit list for unnamed crimes, or is this a phase of adolescence?"

Dina's voice came from around the corner in the dining room. "Melanie, are you still up? I told you to go to bed an hour ago."

"I'm thirsty, do you *mind*?"

Sam said, "Hey. Watch your mouth."

Melanie dropped two ice cubes into her glass. "Wow, Dad. You just used the word *shit,* plus you took the Lord's name in vain. Can I do that?"

"No." He twisted the top off the beer and flipped it into the trash. "Do what your mother told you. Get upstairs." He watched her go, then turned off the light. A dim rectangle of yellow fell across the kitchen floor from the dining room.

Dina sat at one end of the long, polished wood table, which was stacked with files and tax manuals. The dark windows looking out on the backyard were behind her. The chandelier was off. She had put a lamp on the table, and her fingers were flying over the number pad of her ten-key. The paper spit out of the machine in a steady rhythm. *Click-click-click, ca-thunk. Click-click, ca-thunk.*

Beer in hand, Sam leaned against the side of the entranceway from the kitchen. "Did you get my message?"

She didn't look up. "The one that said you'd be home two hours ago?"

"It took longer than I thought."

Dina was still in the clothes she had worn to work, a black skirt and red silk blouse. Her gold bracelet glittered as her arm moved, and her earrings swung. She'd been to a salon last week, had her hair cut and colored. It was parted in the middle and stood out from her head in dark, heavy waves. She was wearing makeup again. No more pills. Up early, working late.

He took a long swallow of beer. "What's going on with Melanie? Is she failing her classes? Has she got a crush on some boy who won't look at her?"

"God knows. She refuses to discuss it. I told her, fine, stay in your room and brood. Come out when you can behave properly."

Sam asked, "What is that you're working on?"

"It's for the lawsuit."

Which could only mean *Hagen* vs. *Harley-Davidson, et al.,* still unfiled and unlikely ever to be filed.

He caught a glimpse of himself in the windows, the darkness beyond making a mirror of them. He looked like shit. He pulled off his loosened tie and walked back to the kitchen to throw away the empty bottle.

Her voice followed him. "Who died, Sam? What was it? A robbery? A fight of some kind?"

"George Fonseca," he said.

"I know that name."

"A defendant in the Duncan sexual battery case." Sam came back with another beer and sat down in one of the upholstered side chairs. The lamp reflected in the tall cabinet that held the china they never used anymore. He could see Dina's profile in the glass.

"Fonseca. Yes, the ex-boyfriend. How did he die?"

"He was shot. Twice." Sam took a swallow of beer. "Not neat, but effective. He bled out pretty fast. I think he was twenty-six years old."

She laid down her pencil. "Charlie Sullivan was shot twice."

"Correct. With a forty-five-caliber handgun. It could be the same shooter."

"Who?"

"No idea."

The corners of Dina's mouth turned up. "Does Ali Duncan know yet about George Fonseca? She'll be ecstatic."

"Ecstatic?"

"One down, two to go. Only Ruffini and Lamont left now."

"I don't think she expected any of them to get the death penalty."

Dina made an impatient noise with her tongue. "Nothing would have happened to him. He wouldn't have been found guilty."

Eyes closed, Sam rubbed his forehead with the heel of his hand. "You know, Dina, I'm damn good at my job. I would not have lost this one. I promise you that."

She looked at him another moment, then turned back to her papers. She ran her finger down a column of numbers.

"What is that?"

"I have an appointment with Frank tomorrow morning." Dina clipped a stack of papers together and set them aside. Other little stacks were spaced evenly on the table.

"Christ. What the hell is this? What is he making you do now?"

"He isn't making me do anything. This is my idea." She lifted another stack of papers out of a file. The adding

machine started up again. *Click-ca-thunk, click-click.*
"I'm reconciling Matthew's checking account, which he
never attended to. He received almost twenty thousand
dollars when he turned eighteen by cashing in the savings
bonds we purchased for him. When he died he had less
than three hundred dollars. Where did it go?"

"He spent it."

"On what? He bought his motorcycle with his earnings
from modeling." She shook her head. "Someone stole it."

"Stole it?" Sam paused with the beer halfway to his
mouth.

"Yes. If not outright theft, then a fraud of some kind.
You remember, Sam. He was talking about investing in a
business. Someone must have taken his money in a spurious deal. They robbed him."

Sam lowered the bottle to rest on his thigh. $20,000.
Not so much money for a kid in a fast crowd on South
Beach. Matthew could have run through that amount in
weeks. He could have spent it on clothes, clubs, parties.
He could have snorted it, drunk it, even shot it into his
arms. "Dina, it doesn't matter anymore."

She wet her thumb and flipped through a stack of can-
celled checks. "I'm going to trace every one of these.
Someone as good as held a gun to his head and emptied
out his bank account. Frank says we can sue whoever did
this."

"Oh, Jesus," Sam muttered softly.

Her eyes lifted to pin him with a dark stare. "I'm not
asking you to get involved. You've made your position
clear. I'll take care of it. Frank may require your signature
on a document, but otherwise, you needn't bother."

Sam finished his beer, then put it on the table. He
picked it up again, wiping off the circle of condensation.
He said, "I've been thinking about Matthew lately. It may
surprise you, but I do think about him, Dina. I don't dwell
on it, but sometimes . . . he comes to mind." Sam took a
breath to ease the tightness in his chest. "There was a lot
about him I didn't know. But I wasn't aware of it at the
time. Not knowing, I mean."

She wrote down some figures with her mechanical pencil. Dina had neat handwriting, very precise. She'd had

her nails done. Lengthened, painted. Whatever women did to their nails.

He set his bottle on the carpet beside his chair. "Did Matthew ever talk to you about Charlie Sullivan?" Dina looked up. "Did he ever mention the name?"

Twin lines appeared between her dark brows as if she'd drawn them there. "Not that I recall. He knew that man? How?"

There was no point to this, Sam thought. No reason to tell her. He said, "Around South Beach. Matthew knew him from modeling. One of the witnesses on Ali Duncan's case told me they had met."

"So? I don't see the importance."

He shook his head. "It isn't important."

She sighed. "Sam, you're drunk. Why don't you go to bed?"

He laid his arm out on the table and clenched and unclenched his fist, easing the stiffness. "Today I was thinking about the time I took Matt fishing up at Crystal River. Don't know why I thought of it. How old was he, fourteen?"

"Fifteen. It was his birthday. June twenty-first."

"That's right. It was. We used your brother Nick's camper. A long weekend, just Matt and me. It was great. Shit, I don't think we caught anything, but we had a good time. Did he ever tell you about it?"

"Yes, Sam."

"We used to be buddies. He said that. 'Hey, Dad, we're buddies.' So what happened? I swear to you I don't know. One day we're okay; then there's a wall between us, and he grew up on the other side of it. He was always closer to you. What was he like, Dina? What . . . was my son like?"

Dina smiled. "You're really asking that. He was perfect. He was—life. Everything." The lamp made a circle of light on her files, the machine, and her arm, sleeved in red silk, lying across the papers. "Matthew would have been twenty years old this month. Twenty." She was silent for a while, then said, "I can't talk about him now."

Sam dropped his hand over hers. "Never mind." He stood up, steadying himself on the back of the chair. "Let's go to bed. How the hell long has it been since you and I have gotten into bed at the same time? How long has it been since we made love? I'll bet you have that tallied up somewhere. Do you?" He laughed. "You'd better hurry, or we'll be in the debit column again."

There might have been an exhalation of breath. "Go on. I have to finish this," she said. "I'll be there soon."

Somewhere in the night he saw Dina sitting at the dining room table with a .45-caliber pistol. Loading it, metal clicking on metal. Her fingers moving quickly, precisely. Pressing bullets into the clip. Hollow-points. Click. Click.

What are you doing, honey?

I have to balance the accounts.

No, no. Let me do it.

Sam saw himself looking down the barrel at a beautiful blond man, felt the weight of the gun. Then an elongated boom, slow motion. Then aiming at George Fonseca. Pulling the trigger again, feeling the heavy steel shuddering in his hand.

Heart slamming against his ribs, Sam sat up, disoriented.

Dina was a shape under the blanket. He stared at her for a while. She breathed peacefully, a hand curled at her cheek. He remembered his dream, and his body trembled. A sudden, horrific thought had shaken him to the bone. Making no noise, he pushed back the blanket and got out of bed.

Tying his robe, Sam went downstairs to his study, a small room off the living room. Dina's antique mantel clock ticked softly as he passed by. Three thirty-five A.M. He closed the door and turned on the desk lamp. The key to his gun cabinet lay on top of the bookshelf across the room, out of sight. The cabinet, six feet tall, was paneled in oak. He opened the decorative door and inserted the key.

Past the inner walls, made of steel, were his single-shot .22 from boyhood, a double-barreled twelve-gauge, a restored Mauser, a .357 Winchester hunting rifle with a scope, a .38 Smith & Wesson chrome-plated revolver in a leather zipper bag, and his Colt pistol, military issue. The pistol was in a wood box. Also in the cabinet were bluing, machine oil, rags, brushes, and boxes of ammunition to fit the various firearms. Sam pulled the .45 rounds off the shelf. Neat rows of bullets. One box of steel-jacketed rounds, two of hollow-points, plus another half full. He couldn't remember how many rounds were in there, last time he looked.

He opened the box that held his .45. The pistol was there along with three clips, all loaded, nine rounds each. He took out the gun. Not so heavy now, but it would weigh close to two pounds fully loaded. He checked the chamber. Empty. Checked the action, pulled back the slide, fired it dry, then did it again. The clicks were loud in the quiet room. He shoved in a clip with the heel of his hand, sighted down the barrel. Then unloaded, rechecking the chamber. He smelled the barrel and ran his hands over the crosshatched wood grip and the smooth, gray metal, looking at his fingertips afterward.

Nothing. It was clean, only the faint scent of oil. Sam sat heavily in his lounge chair. "You're crazy, that's what."

If Dina walked in here right now, asking what he was doing up at this hour, playing with his guns, he wouldn't know what to tell her. He would feel ridiculous as hell.

This pistol had been smuggled out of Vietnam by way of a friend in transportation. Sam had carried it in combat. Had used it. Maybe he had stolen it because he'd thought it was lucky. It had saved his life a couple of times.

Now he looked down at the Colt, which he still held by the grip. He got up, put the pistol back into its box, returned the box to the cabinet, and locked the door.

c h a p t e r
twenty-four

For an art exhibit on Miami Beach in the month of June, long after the season was over, Caitlin's show wasn't doing too badly. She allowed herself another glass of champagne. Her photographs looked splendid, mounted on the high, white walls. Five or six had already been sold.

Paula DeMarco, the gallery owner, had planned the usual wine and cheese and crackers. Caitlin had run her charge card to the limit having the show catered with champagne. She was wearing loose slacks and a hand-painted vest, looking properly artsy. On South Beach, image was everything.

Now she was in the middle of an interview with a freelance writer for *Ocean Drive* magazine. He wanted to know how a fashion model could make the leap to art photography. Then he asked what other top models she'd worked with. And wasn't it great that the Beach was acquiring some of the cultural ambiance of New York? Caitlin said yes, she'd heard about a new restaurant opening up on Collins where the waiters were all transvestites. Very East Village, didn't he think? Then he asked if she had any shows this summer. She said there would be an exhibit in Soho, a gallery on Mulberry Street. A lie, and he probably knew it but wrote it down anyway. Surely, before the summer was out, she *would* have a show somewhere. The reporter had a camera and asked to take her picture.

Sipping her champagne, Caitlin glanced past him toward the door. A young couple going out, a trio of men coming in. Catching herself, she muttered *idiot* under her breath. She knew what she was doing, for the hundredth time tonight: looking for Sam Hagen. The more rational part of her brain told her this was the last place he'd show up.

"Caitlin, I *adore* your photographs!" A model agent she'd known for years gave her a fumbling hug. The woman was high or drunk, possibly both. "But I knew you had talent. Didn't I say that? Didn't I?"

"Thanks," Caitlin said. "They're for sale." *For less than you paid for those ugly shoes,* she added to herself.

The woman grabbed the reporter's shoulder. "Brian! My God, somebody told me you'd gone to L.A."

Caitlin slipped away, nearly bumping into Rafael Soto around the other side of a divider. He was speaking Spanish to a good-looking man about thirty. Caitlin took the cigarette out of Rafael's hand and filled her lungs.

Exhaling smoke, she said, "Thank you so much."

He took it back. "That's all you get. Caitlin, this is Julio. Julio, *esta loca es mi amiga preciosa,* Caitlin."

"Hi," said Julio. He had eyes as dark as Rafael's, and perfect teeth.

"Hello. Did you come willingly tonight, or did Rafael twist your arm?"

"Please?"

Rafael did a fast translation, then said, "Julio just moved here from Paraguay. He speaks no English, so I'm showing him around."

"He's gorgeous. Should I say congratulations?"

"Not yet, but stay tuned." Behind the red-framed glasses, Rafael's eyes shifted across the gallery. "Oh, God. Your ex just walked through the door."

Caitlin glanced around. Frank Tolin was looking at her. He smiled. Then picked up a gallery guide and walked toward the first grouping of photos as if he had actually come here to see them.

"Have him thrown out," Rafael suggested.

She turned her back. "He'll leave if I don't speak to him."

Rafael chattered on, but Caitlin didn't hear him.

Frank's presence in the room intruded like speakers turned up to high volume. In the past ten days, Frank had left so many pleading messages on her voice mail she'd lost count at fifty. He had sent flowers. She refused delivery, but they kept coming. Two days ago she'd found all the equipment Frank had taken from her studio stacked up neatly outside her door. She sold it all to pay some bills. She was packing up, finishing leftover jobs, and calling old contacts in New York. In two weeks she would be gone.

"Caitlin, Hiii-ii-iii!"

A tall, black-haired girl in a short white dress was coming toward her, arms extended. If Caitlin hadn't noticed Tommy Chang next to her, she wouldn't have known who it was. Ali Duncan.

Caitlin gave her a quick hug. "What are you doing here?"

The day after George Fonseca's murder, Ali had gone back to live with her mother. She'd told Caitlin that Sam Hagen had practically forced her to. "Tommy drove all the way up to Broward County to get me tonight." She patted his chest. "Isn't he sweet?"

Tommy blushed. His long black hair was tied back with a beaded strip of leather. This was the first time Caitlin had seen him in long pants and a new shirt.

Ali smiled at Caitlin through the dark glasses. "I'm not afraid to be on South Beach. All these people around? Nothing's going to happen. I had to see your show, Caitlin. It's so genius!" The black, wedge-shaped wig was short in back, longer in front, with heavy bangs across her forehead. Her sleeveless white minidress skimmed her perky little butt and high breasts. Waving toward the linen-draped table at the rear of the gallery, she pouted prettily with a mouth made scarlet by glossy lipstick. "Go get me some champagne, Tommy. Please?" When he was gone, she said quietly, "He is really nice, but *so* protective you would not believe."

How easily she ordered him around, Caitlin thought. How readily he complied. One of them would eventually suffer when this romance ended, and it wasn't likely to be Ali Duncan.

Caitlin scanned the gallery. Frank Tolin had wandered

to the candid photos of models on a runway, pretending to study them. Acting casual. Hands in his pockets. Wearing the Armani double-breasted suit she'd picked out for him last year in New York. His eyes shifted to meet hers, piercing.

Quickly she turned back to Ali. "Are you working?"

"Yeah. I'm doing okay. I got a booking in Fort Lauderdale. It's like, nobody heard of me up there, so it's cool. My mother is driving me crazy, though." Ali took her cigarettes out of her tiny purse, then fished around for a lighter. "I am still in total shock about George."

"That's a strange reaction," Caitlin said.

Ali lit her cigarette, and for a second her blue eyes flashed over the top of her sunglasses, making sure Tommy wasn't on his way back. "I didn't want George to *die*. I was trying to tell Mr. Hagen it wasn't George who was the worst, but he won't listen. He's so, like, *Be quiet, Miss Duncan, what do you know?*"

Her elbow on a hipbone, she took a long drag on her cigarette. "God, I can't stand living like this. Caitlin, why am I putting myself through hell for a bunch of cops and state attorneys who only want to use me? Like, to chase Klaus Ruffini out of South Beach. And Mr. Hagen was on a TV interview show on Sunday, did you see him? I'm his most visible case. The reporter said that. And he goes, 'Mr. Hagen, are you going to run for state attorney?' Ha. Is Mickey a mouse?"

"Ali, they won't let you drop it."

"I *know*. I said I was sick of this, and he gives me this really mean look and says it doesn't matter. It's not *my* case anymore, it belongs to the state of Florida." She made a muffled scream through clamped teeth. "I wanted to show George, and now I *can't*. Oh, damn. Damn. Why'd he have to get *shot*? It isn't *fair*." Her lips trembled. "I didn't want him *dead*."

Frank had moved closer, no longer pretending to look at the pictures. He stood silently and stared.

Caitlin took Ali's arm and walked her slowly around a group of chattering social types, all of them munching on hors d'oeuvres. She found a place along the windows that faced the side street.

"Ali, you did the right thing. You were so brave."

"Brave. Yeah. Try stupid. I should've gone to see Tereza Ruffini when she asked me to." Ali laughed. "Now she's out of the country and it's too late, and I'm modeling for Kmart."

Tommy came back with her champagne and another glass for Caitlin, who held it without drinking. Her hands were trembling slightly. As if her vision could extend at all angles, she saw Frank behind her, watching. Waiting till she was alone. It was nearly nine o'clock now, and the crowd in the gallery was thinning out.

When a male friend of hers, a graphic artist, started a conversation, Tommy and Ali drifted away, hand in hand, to look at the pictures. The graphic artist owned a production company in the design district in Miami. They got into a friendly argument about digital cameras and manipulation of imagery. Caitlin stupidly had to ask him to repeat what he had said. She couldn't concentrate.

Then Frank was standing beside her. He'd bought something, which was now tucked into a large, maroon plastic bag with the name of the gallery in gold. "Forgive me for interrupting," he said. "I wanted to tell Ms. Dorn how much I admire her work. I just purchased the series of night views of Lincoln Road."

Lips compressed, Caitlin stared at the floor for a moment, then swung her hair off her face and looked directly at him. She didn't want Frank buying her photographs. Didn't want them hanging in his living room.

"Thank you," she said, forcing a smile. "Now excuse us? We're in a discussion here."

He touched her shoulder and she barely kept herself from recoiling. "May I have a moment to speak to Ms. Dorn privately?"

"Sure." The artist gave a confused smile and backed up a step.

She grabbed his arm, holding on to him. "No. People can't just come up and intrude like this."

"Really, it's okay, I don't mind—"

"You have to excuse Caitlin," said Frank with a wan smile. "We've been involved for eight years. Last week we had an argument—"

Caitlin spun toward Frank. "How could you come here?"

"You know why. I had to see you. You won't return my calls, you won't talk to me." Then he said to the other man, "I'm sorry. I'm going to pieces over this woman."

"Hey, it's okay."

Her voice hissed between her teeth. "Leave me the fuck alone. Okay? Can I possibly make that plainer?"

Frank pulled back as if she'd spit at him.

Confused, the artist said, "Caitlin, take it easy."

"You stay out of this. You have no *idea*."

He and Frank exchanged a glance. Sympathy, man to man. The artist blew a little puff of air through pursed lips and walked away.

Frank grasped her arm above the elbow. "What do you want from me? Tell me what to do, I'll do it. Words may mean nothing to you, but right now they're all I have. To the depths of my soul I love you. Catie, I can't sleep. I can't eat. I try to work and the only thing on my mind is you. Please. The lesson has been learned. I haven't had a drink since you left. No drugs, nothing. I'm clean, I swear. Don't you believe in redemption? People change. Now that we've learned so much, why throw it all away?"

"Bullshit. You're such a manipulator." She laughed. "Clients. Witnesses. The jury. Me. Not anymore. Now you talk and all I see is your mouth moving."

"Oh, look at you, baby. You sell a few photos, get your name in the paper, you forget what it was like on your own. You'll come back." His fingers tightened. "You always have."

His head swiveled to look at Tommy Chang, who had come up beside them, uncertain of what was going on.

"Caitlin, are you okay?"

"No."

Frank released her arm, making a production out of it, opening his hand wide, stepping back a little, smiling, lines in his face like slashes, deep and sharp. "I apologize once again." He buttoned his jacket as if for something to do. Then he smiled at Tommy. "I'll give you some advice, young man. Be careful with Caitlin. The last one your age didn't make it out alive."

Turning abruptly, Frank left the gallery, clutching the bag of photographs under one arm. He zigzagged through the dwindling crowd.

Tommy asked, "That thing he said. What was that supposed to mean?"

"Nothing. He's an asshole."

"I came over to see if you want to go out with Ali and
me. We've got a group together. Rafael's coming."
Tommy patted her back. "It's your night. Celebrate. And
forget him, okay?"

Tommy's face was guileless and open.

She smiled. "Sure. I'd like to come along."

On legs that still trembled, she went to thank the gallery
owner for the show. She knew now that beneath her rage
had yawned the queasy depths of panic. Maybe she was
wrong. It could be different betweeen them. She had
changed for the better, why couldn't he? But she'd just
sent him away. The man who had saved her from self-
destruction then put up with her for eight years. This
show had been a joke. A dozen photos sold, and six of
those to Frank.

Caitlin glanced toward the door. She could see his dim
figure through the glass, walking away on Lincoln Road.

Detective Eugene Ryabin, arm in arm with his wife,
slowed as they passed the DeMarco Gallery on the other
side of the street.

Anna asked, "Is this where they're showing Miss
Dorn's photographs?"

He moved to see around a street vendor selling African
jewelry. "I believe so. Yes."

"We'll go in if you want," Anna said.

"No. Let's keep walking." Ryabin's stomach was full
from a dinner at an Italian restaurant three blocks west,
and his head pleasantly fuzzy from the excellent chianti
he and his wife had shared. He put his hand over hers,
which rested lightly on his arm. "A perfect evening for
walking, Anna. Another two or three blocks. But we'll go
back if you're tired."

"Not at all." She patted his arm. "Don't fuss so,
Zhenya."

Anna was fifty-three, with not such a perfect heart, and
he feared that he would outlive her.

Melodies curled and ebbed on the faint breeze. Musi-
cians were spaced along the mall. He and Anna were now

passing a Spanish guitarist on a stool outside a natural foods restaurant, and at the end of the block a woman violinist in black concert attire played Beethoven. Still farther along, steel drums serenaded diners at candlelit outdoor tables.

Ryabin breathed deeply the humid, salt-scented air. What a wonderful place. He had seen Miami Beach change from depressed and shabby to sparkling and alive in the span of time they'd lived here, eons from Odessa. This was a shallow, emotional place, to be sure, but it was young, and one had to forgive much in the young.

One had also to be prepared against criminals and opportunists, who lurked everywhere, even on this pleasant street. Ryabin wore his pistol under his jacket. He would no more leave it at home than go without his trousers. This pistol, a 17-shot Glock, lightweight and deadly, had been a birthday present from Anna several years ago. *So you can have many more of them,* she had said, and kissed him. There was only a husband to dote on now. Their two sons had moved away—one to Israel, the other to California. Grandchildren were far away. Her own mother and sister were dead. After her mother's murder, Anna had asked no questions of the police. Having been a Jew in the Soviet Union, she had expected nothing. When the killer was found dead, she had only nodded. The death of her sister, Rivka, still weighed on her mind, but she assumed that this, too, would someday be made right. Ryabin wasn't certain anymore. He had wanted to bring in the drunks and vagrants who could have set the fire, but his lieutenant warned him about due process.

It had always mystified Ryabin, the reluctance of the Americans to take decisive action against criminals. Such a naive and optimistic people, believing that human nature was basically good. Consequently, they were always surprised when one of their number exhibited cruelty. *What is this world coming to?* they would ask, bewildered at the news of another bombing, multiple murder, or looting. As if the world had ever been otherwise. That reasonable, intelligent people could so allow themselves to be tied in knots by rules and procedure staggered him. Trials that went on for months. The law turned inside out by sophistry and guile. The guilty set free by confused and divided juries. He and Sam Hagen had argued about this many times. They had never come to an agreement. Sam was much too quick to believe in institutions, as if they had an intelligence beyond that of the fallible men and women who ran them. Ryabin had countered with an appeal to common sense. Are we more civilized for all the rules of law? No. Less so. With each new rule we become weaker.

"Ah." Ryabin stopped walking.

"What is it, Zhenya?"

He led Anna toward a storefront under a black canvas awning. "We've never been in this one, have we? Let's take a look."

Puzzled, she read the name written in jagged gold letters on the glass. "Otero? I don't think it's my style." Anna had a neat, plump figure, like a dove. In the window, stick-thin mannequins in leather glared arrogantly back at her. She began to laugh. "Oh, definitely not my style."

He said, "Anna, I have to speak with the manager. She's usually here on Friday evenings."

"Zhenya, are you on duty?"

With a guilty smile, he said, "For a few minutes. You don't mind, do you?"

Anna rolled her eyes. He held the door and they went inside.

It was nearly two in the morning when Tommy Chang dropped Caitlin outside her building. She got out of the Jeep, then leaned back through the open window to grasp both his and Ali's hands. She was clumsy from too much wine and the lateness of the hour.

"You babies be careful," she said. But they weren't going far. Tommy knew a friend with enough room in his apartment for two extra people.

Tommy said for her to go inside; they'd wait till she had unlocked the downstairs entry door. The engine throbbed softly on the quiet street, and the headlights pressed into the darkness. It had rained earlier, and the humidity was so thick any exertion would raise a sweat. Caitlin stumbled into one of the aluminum porch chairs, righted it, then unlocked the door. She waved good-bye as she opened it, and the Jeep turned the corner.

A row of overhead lights, each in a frosted tulip shade, extended down the hallway, which was painted pale yellow and floored in terrazzo. There was a staircase at each end, and through the jalousie windows on the landings, left open for the cross breeze, came the faint rush of traffic on Washington Avenue, two blocks away.

She closed the front door quietly. It would automatically lock. Harold Perlstein slept at odd hours. If he were awake he would open his apartment door a crack to see who was coming in at this time of the night. In the momentary silence she heard a noise from upstairs. A shifting, a footfall. But not in one of the apartments. Caitlin looked up at the ceiling. There was a staircase to her right.

Nothing had ever happened in this building, she reminded herself. A few thefts, but only among people who knew each other or had a key. There had been no muggings, rapes, or murders. But her nerves were as tense as electric wires, her ears alert to the slightest sounds.

She slipped out of her shoes and moved noiselessly along the hall to the back door, intending to go out that way. Before she could reach it, she heard footsteps on the front stairs. She hurried up the rear staircase and stopped on the landing. Pressing close to the wall, she peered along the upper hall at floor level. Frank Tolin was rounding the landing on the other stairs, going down. She pulled her head back, her heart jumping wildly in her chest. She went up two more steps to stay out of his line of vision. He knew she was here. He must have seen Tommy dropping her off. He had a key to the building, but not to her apartment; she had changed it.

She forced her breathing to slow down. There were people here. If she screamed someone would come out to see what was the matter.

Bending to look into the lower hallway, she saw a pair of cowboy boots coming down the stairs on the other side. She went farther up the back stairs. The upper hall was empty. If he came back up, he would see her clearly, exposed in the line of upstairs lights. She heard footsteps, then the front door opening. Closing. Then nothing. She waited for several minutes. Finally she fled toward her apartment at the front of the building, fumbling in her purse for her keys.

The key was turning in the deadbolt before she noticed what lay on her door mat. A pile of paper, tiny bits. It took her a few seconds to see what it was. Her photographs. Over four hundred dollars' worth of paper, ripped into confetti.

When she opened the door her tabby cat poked his face through. She scooted him back inside and locked the door. "Hello, you sweet old thing. Are you glad to see me?" Suddenly in tears, Caitlin dropped her purse and shoes, picked up the cat, and hugged him till he squirmed out of her arms.

The phone rang on her desk. The voice mail would pick up after the second ring, but Caitlin grabbed the receiver. "You think it's funny, what you did?"

"Are you alone?" Frank was probably sitting in his car, watching her windows.

"No. I have four Miami Beach cops with me. Listen to me, Frank. Stop calling. I'm not going to talk to you. It's over. For God's sake, let it go with a little dignity. You're being ridiculous."

"I saw you come home with that Chinese boy. You left the gallery at eight forty-five. What have you been doing for over five hours?"

"None of your goddamn business. Okay? Don't call me again. Don't come by, don't write, don't—"

"Did you fuck the Chinese boy tonight, Catie?"

"Don't speak to me again. If I get phone calls or see your face or see any evidence that you were near my apartment, I'm going to the police for a restraining order. I'll mail a copy to your partners, the Florida Bar, every business in your building and every client of yours whose name I can possibly remember!"

For a second or two the phone was silent, then came Frank's soft voice. "Be advised, Ms. Dorn. Find other accommodations. Monday at eight A.M., a crew will arrive to clean and paint that apartment. Anything left on the premises will be disposed of."

"Oh, go to hell. That's not even legal!"

"Sue me." He laughed. "You're hot shit now. Sell a few

photos to some faggots on South Beach, you don't need Sugar Daddy anymore do you, bitch?"

She slammed down the receiver.

Shaking, she unhooked the telephone, then went into the kitchen and did the same with the extension even as it started to ring.

It was dawn before she fell asleep, fully dressed and curled up on the sofa with the cat. Heavy boxes were stacked in front of the locked door, with a pan of silverware balanced to fall crashing, at the slightest jostle.

chapter
twenty-five

The arraignment of Klaus Ruffini and Marquis Lamont was set for Tuesday at 8:30 A.M. in courtroom 4-3, half an hour before Sam Hagen was due to begin jury selection in a murder trial in another division. Sam had told his co-counsel to stall till he could get there. The owner of a small auto repair shop in Hialeah had been killed and a worker critically wounded by a gunman who had already taken the cash. Shot as an afterthought, like turning off the lights when he left the room.

The media, however, were more interested in a celebrity rape case. The unsolved murders of a drug-dealing defendant and a male-model witness had fueled the hype. A TV camera was set up on the front row to feed three local and two network stations, and reporters clogged the spectator seats, waiting for the judge to enter the courtroom.

Sam could have come through the back, but he took the main corridor. As he'd expected, he was immediately surrounded by reporters. He made a statement, something about the state not being intimidated by defense references to selective prosecution. *It's ludicrous to imply an anti-immigrant, anti-minority plot. These men committed a crime, and they'll be tried like anyone else.* There was a question about the murders: Was either of the remaining defendants a suspect? *We're not ruling anybody out.* Was it true that Fonseca had requested immunity to testify for the state? *I'm not going to comment on that.*

Now Sam stood waiting for court to begin, talking to Juan Casares, deputy chief of the felony division. Casares was Cuban, but no fan of Eddie Mora. Sam had invited him to be present, get his face on the national news. The members of the prosecution team were already at the state's counsel table: Lydia Hernandez and Joe McGee. A female presence was wanted to stand in for the victim, and McGee would counterbalance the African-American defendant.

Directly across the courtroom, Norman Singletary and Gerald Fine were conferring with their respective clients. Marquis Lamont and Klaus Ruffini were here for show, not because their presence was required. Lamont stared down at his clasped hands or exchanged looks with his wife, seated in the first row. Klaus Ruffini leaned back in the wooden armchair with one foot propped on his knee, whispering into Fine's ear. Someone had persuaded Ruffini to wear a conservative blue suit. Both lawyers had co-counsel, who sat behind them. As there were no more seats at the table, the assistant public defenders had taken chairs near the court clerk's table. The dozen private lawyers whose cases were also scheduled for the 8:30 arraignment calendar stood along the walls. The jury box was filled with defendants who hadn't made bond, an assembly of mostly young, mostly black or Hispanic men, some wearing shapeless blue shirts supplied by the county jail. One man kept waving at the camera, which as yet had not been turned on.

The bailiff was telling the spectators to leave if they didn't have a seat. An argument broke out in the last row. Sam pulled back his cuff: 8:40. The judge was late. Generally the arraignment calendar was called in numerical order, but *State* vs. *Ruffini and Lamont* would be called first.

Juan Casares turned his back on the reporters to speak to Sam in a low voice. "Did you read the local section this morning?"

Sam nodded.

"What are you going to do?"

"Not a damn thing. What can I do?"

Victoria Duran, deputy chief of administration, had been asked for a reaction to news that Eddie Mora would

resign to run for national office. After the usual brown-
nosing reference to his accomplishments as Dade state attorney, she had expressed hope that Mora's successor,
whoever it might be, would put more importance on fighting street crime than turning trials into media events. The
allusion to the head of Major Crimes was obvious. Speaking to Juan Casares, Sam had kept his reaction neutral. An
hour ago, reading the article in his office, Sam had hurled
the paper into his trash can. He would return Beekie's dig,
but in his own time.

"All rise." Everyone stood while the judge entered. The
videocamera panned across the courtroom.

The judge read the charges. Ruffini, then Lamont, entered a plea of not guilty. Their lawyers asked for a reduc-
tion in bond, which was denied. Gerald Fine made a pitch
for getting Klaus Ruffini's passport back, which was also
denied. Singletary complained that the state was refusing
access to evidence held at the Metro-Dade police lab. The
judge granted the state's motion to supervise defense
examination of evidence taken at the scene. The clerk announced the trial date: Monday, August 6, at 9:00 A.M.

The arraignment was over, ten minutes after it had
begun.

As the clerk called the next case, Ruffini and Lamont,
surrounded by lawyers and reporters, pushed toward the
exit. Sam talked to the other prosecutors for a moment,
then went out the back way. He had already said what he
wanted to say. He was expected upstairs for a murder
trial.

The case upstairs pled out. As soon as Sam came into the
courtroom, the public defender asked for a conference.
The prospective jurors were sent back downstairs. The
judge took care of other business while the defendant
slouched sullenly in his chair and the jailer sat by the door
reading a newspaper. This courtroom was a small one,
with a low ceiling and two short rows of spectators' seats.
Sam and the P.D. went outside to talk. He was in his early
thirties, a frazzled man, a month overdue for a haircut.

The defendant would take life, he said. Minimum
twenty-five years.

Arms crossed, Sam leaned a shoulder against the wall.

"Not enough. I want two consecutive life sentences, no parole."

"He's nineteen fucking years old! You read the psychological report on this kid. Sexual abuse. Beatings. He's got an IQ of eighty."

"This kid, your scumball client, also has a rap sheet six pages long. He shot a sixteen-year-old in the back last year and got sixty days on a piss-ass weapons violation because the victim wouldn't testify. Now we've got one man dead and one who barely survived. Like I said. Two life sentences. No parole."

"You'd never get the death penalty in this case."

"Then let's go to trial."

Neither of them moved. Finally the P.D. said, "I know why you're bustin' his chops, man. You're running for state attorney. It's politics. All politics."

Sam gave him a long look. "Have we got a deal or don't we? I'm ready to pick a jury."

The P.D. nodded wearily.

If Sam Hagen had been introducing himself to a panel of prospective jurors in the small courtroom on the fifth floor of the justice building, he would not have seen Dale Finley, the state attorney's investigator, following Idelfonso García into an elevator. Sam had gone back across the street toward his office. Walking through the metal detectors, then around the corner to the elevators in the lobby, Sam first noticed Finley's white crew cut, then García, with his sunburned, *campesino* face. Finley hesitated a split second, registering Sam's presence just as the doors slid shut.

"What in hell?" Sam looked at the numbers. The elevator stopped at two, three, four, then finally five. People getting on and off. Or Dale Finley not wanting Sam to know where he was taking Adela Ramos's brother. Sam waited a minute to see who might come down, then took another elevator to the fourth floor.

The deputy chief of administration had an office not far from Edward Mora's. The state attorney himself had flown to Michigan for a meeting with Senator Kirkland's people. Sam had seen the picture in the *Miami Herald* this morning. Eddie and his wife, Amalia, smiling at the presidential hopeful on the porch of his country house.

Sam stood at the desk belonging to Beekie's secretary. The young woman's hands paused on her keyboard. A second later, she looked up.

He said, "Would you like to tell Ms. Duran I'm out here, or should I just go in?"

She paled a little, which told him he'd found Dale Finley.

Not precisely. Finley had escorted García to Vicky Duran's office, then had left him in a chair facing her desk.

"How are you, Mr. García?" Sam beckoned. "Ms. Duran. May I see you outside?"

She was just hanging up the telephone. Her secretary must have made the call. Idelfonso García, whose thick hands rested on his knees, nodded at Sam. No guilt on that face. It hadn't been his idea.

Beekie said, "Oh. Mr. Hagen. I was told you were unavailable in trial."

"Ms. Duran? Outside, please."

She apparently thought better of arguing in her office. In a conference room two doors down, she let go. "This is outrageous! What do you think you are doing?" Her heavy auburn hair seemed to bristle.

Sam closed in on her. "The uncle of a murder victim on one of my cases is in your office, and I want to know why."

"He came to see you, and you were in court, so I agreed to speak to him."

"That's a lie. You had Dale Finley bring him here."

Beekie pivoted away, spreading her hands in a shrug. "I was concerned about the relatives of the Ramos boy. The man who killed him was acquitted, and if this office was responsible in some way for that outcome, then I wanted to make sure—"

She flinched when Sam slammed his fist on the conference table. "What did you tell him? That you're personally going to retry Luis Balmaseda? Make sure you get him this time, Beekie, fuck double jeopardy."

"I didn't brush them off, Sam, as you did. I didn't embarrass Mr. García by using him as an object lesson for two new lawyers." Her brown eyes had dilated to black.

"You know that Luis Balmaseda has been threatening Adela Ramos."

"What the hell can we do about it that we haven't done? Have him arrested? I told them to go to the police. Have they?"

"Yes. And nothing has happened."

"Then let's get some rope and string him up!"

"I won't take your shit." She spun toward the door.

"Jesus Christ." Sam leaned on his hands. "Vicky, let me say this. You are out of line. So far out of line it staggers comprehension. And I thought when you shot off your mouth to the *Miami Herald* it was bad."

Pushing himself from the table, Sam said, "We're going back to your office. We will speak to Idelfonso García together. I don't care what words you choose, but you will be sympathetic. Tell him to make a police report. Tell him we'll prosecute."

"I *have* told him! I know the law!" Her body stiffened. "You don't give me orders."

Sam put a hand flat on the door when she went toward it. "You're afraid Eddie won't take you with him if he makes it to Washington, aren't you? His wife would raise a stink about it. So you want his job. And you want to make sure I look bad before the governor names an interim state attorney."

"Get out of my way." Her voice was a low growl. He was so close he could see the pockmarks under the makeup and smell her heavy perfume.

"We've got a quandary here, Beekie. I don't want to pick up the paper and read your opinions about Luis Balmaseda's acquittal. It would be embarrassing for Eddie, allowing the chief of administration to get into areas that are none of her business, and he'd have to fire your ass. Or send you to prosecute traffic cases in Liberty City. But I don't plan to bring this up with Eddie unless I have to."

Her mouth twitched. "What bothers you the most, Sam? That I'm telling the truth about Balmaseda? It was mishandled. You fucked up. Now the sexual battery case is falling apart. The main witness is dead, and the others are getting scared." She smiled. "Will you sacrifice yourself to put Miss Dorn on the stand? I doubt that your precious integrity would go that far. You're going to lose, and I think you know this already."

With great effort Sam kept himself from shoving Beekie Duran into the wall. He took a slow breath. His shirt collar was cutting into his neck.

She gestured toward the door. "Open it. Mr. García is waiting."

Her appointments with Frank Tolin had become as necessary to Dina as breath, or prayer. His office was so peaceful: the faraway buzz of a telephone, voices fading in the corridor, muffled traffic on the street ten floors below. Sunlight poured in like a benediction on the clean white walls. It gleamed on polished wood and rows of law books with their titles in gold. Sometimes Dina sat on one end of the sofa, Frank on the other, their cups of coffee in their hands. More often they took their traditional places across his desk: attorney and client. Dina would sit in an English club chair with wings, a buttoned back, ball-and-claw feet, and bright lines of upholsterer's tacks, not a hairsbreadth between any of them; she had looked. The leather itself was slightly mottled, its imperfection a reminder that once it had been alive.

The windows in the office faced east, toward the Atlantic. Listening while Dina talked, Frank would watch out the windows as if from a train moving steadily, steadily north. His chair was black leather. He would lean on one elbow, stroking his thin face with his fingers. Or he would lean farther back with his feet crossed on a corner of the desk. She had pointed out the mark his heels made on the wood, but he had said she shouldn't worry. Polishing would take it out. He had many pairs of boots. She had counted seven.

Dina always called before coming. Sometimes she stayed ten minutes; sometimes hours. They had established a protocol. Upon entering the office, she would inquire about progress in the wrongful death action. *Samuel J. Hagen and Constandina P. Hagen* vs. *Uncle Andy's, Inc., et al.* Her question: How is the lawsuit coming along? Frank's response: We're still in the process of investigation. Then he would invite her to sit down; he would buzz his secretary to bring tea or coffee. Dina had worried about fees, the original retainer long gone. Frank said it didn't matter. When they recovered in the lawsuit, they would settle up.

Thus freed, she had talked and he had listened. As if a plug had been stuck in her throat for months, the words came tentatively at first, then in a rush, a frothing swirl, a flood. She was swept in the current, sucked under, then thrown clear, then racing on a thundering tide of words.

She had talked about Matthew. His life. His wrongful death. Matthew. A long drop, a cataract! Her tongue and lips moving, words filling the room till she thought the windows might crack from the pressure. Everything she had wanted to say to Sam, who hadn't wanted to listen. Scenes thought of, dreamed and raged about and wept for. Sickening spins of anger, betrayal, and despair.

Frank listened to her talk about loss and death, love and betrayal, matters philosophical and mundane. They discussed justice, violence, decay, and the soullessness of cities. They had talked about their own lives. Dina's work, which meant nothing to her now. Frank understood; he could hardly bring himself to the office anymore. Somehow, yes, she had let go of the words about Sam's affair, but Frank said he already knew, not to worry. It doesn't matter anymore to me either, she had said. They talked about the burden of knowledge and the pain of truth.

Sam had been discussed in those many hours of conversation. His ambition, which had consumed him from inside. He was disintegrating. She could see cracks, as if he were a block a granite on unstable ground. They had talked about Melanie, about Frank's two boys, about the sweet ignorance of children. Dina had told Frank how Matthew rescued the cross on Epiphany Day, and how Sevasti Pondakos had killed a Turkish soldier with an ax when she was only sixteen. How she herself, Constandina Pondakos, would go back to Tarpon Springs before she died. And if she died tomorrow, she wouldn't be afraid. She would be with Matthew again, who was at peace. She told Frank, what matters is not how or when we die but what we do in those final hours, when our lives are brought to account. How dimly we see, when we are young. The closer to ultimate darkness, the brighter the light.

Such talks we have had, Frank.

The joy of it, the pleasure of moving lips and tongue and hands. An unburdening, a letting go, a nakedness, a primitive unawareness. Eden. If such a word as *happy* had a meaning anymore, she knew what it was.

Then she saw Frank staring at her.

She touched her hair. Asked why he was looking at her that way.

He took so long to answer that she thought he'd been struck dumb, paralyzed, or even had died with his eyes still open. Finally he said, "Sorry. I'm just now beginning to understand you, Dina."

Then she noticed the windows. How dark they were. The sky had turned a strange, sickly green. Dina walked over to see. From the west a huge mass of black, a summer storm, was moving quickly across the sky, pulling with it a dark curtain of rain. Lightning flashed inside towering clouds, making them glow and flicker. Her father had told her this meant quarrels among the gods and goddesses, who were hurling thunderbolts at each other. Dina wondered what it would be like inside the dark clouds, being carried up in a long spiral, arms outstretched, her cloak swirling behind her.

Turning back to the room she told Frank she'd taken too much of his time. There was no reason, was there, for continuing the lawsuit? Or even for these visits? She should go home before it started to rain.

"Is it going to rain?" He came to the window, frowning. "The sky's clear, Dina."

She pressed her fingers to the glass, felt the trembling of thunder, and told him of course it was going to rain, couldn't he see the lightning?

He looked at her for a long time, then took both her hands and brought them to his lips. His mustache prickled against her skin. She tugged, but he held her fast.

"Don't leave, Dina. I need to talk to someone I trust. I need that so much. Can't you stay a little longer?"

Finally she said she would. He led her to the wing chair and had his secretary bring them tea.

They talked while the storm rolled over the city. The lights flickered and went out, then came back on, and rain poured down the windows.

chapter
twenty-six

On Wednesday morning, Sam drove to Miami Beach police headquarters to see Gene Ryabin. He found him at his desk, talking on the telephone to someone who'd had her chain ripped off her neck while she dozed by the hotel pool. As Ryabin talked, he poked at a slice of chocolate cake with a plastic fork.

When Sam rolled a chair over, Ryabin slid some papers toward him—initial forensics reports on George Fonseca. Sam sat down and put on his glasses. The ballistics report was on top.

Fragments of two .45-caliber hollow-point bullets had been removed from Fonseca's abdomen and thigh, and other fragments had been found in the driver's side door and on the floor of his car. A third bullet, nearly intact, had been recovered from the seat. They matched the fragments taken from Charlie Sullivan's chest and head. No cartridge casings had been found at either scene, but the bullets were identified as 185-grain Remington hollow-points. As they'd been designed to do, these heavy, lumbering bullets had mushroomed, then had broken up as they tumbled through the victims' bodies.

Sam flipped to a narrative written by the crime-scene technicians. After hauling the Mustang to the police garage, they had sifted through the trash, bottles, and beer cans, finding scraps of polyester fluff and heavy, woven vinyl of the type used for luggage and gym bags. Some of the vinyl bits were partially melted.

Last Friday Sam had spoken to Dr. David Corso at the medical examiner's office. Corso said he had pulled a few fragments of black plastic and polyester fluff from the hole in Fonseca's thigh. It seemed likely to Sam that the shooter had fired through a bag. The blow-out had carried the melted vinyl into the wound, along with scraps of whatever the shooter had used to muffle the noise, probably a small pillow stuffed with polyester fill. Wrapping the barrel tightly in a loose fabric, such as a towel, might have jammed the slide. The bag also explained the absence of cartridge casings at the scene. Normally the casings would have been ejected from the chamber as the slide moved back.

The autopsy had been inconclusive on the subject of the shooter's height. The trajectory of the first shot had been slightly upward, but Sullivan had been six feet tall.

Now Ryabin was telling the robbery victim on the other end of the line to come in, make a police report, look at some photos. He'd take care of it personally. Then he grinned into the phone, saying thank you, he'd been told that many times about his accent. No, not France. Ukraine. On the Black Sea. Yes, very romantic.

His cork bulletin board was thick with notices, schedules, cop cartoons, Polaroids of suspects, snapshots of grandchildren, and postcards from Odessa. A drawing of an electric chair bore the caption: "Justice Done Well Is Justice Well Done." Across the room a detective was tapping a report into the computer, and Ryabin's partner, Nestor Lopez, was on the phone speaking Spanish.

Beyond the open door a uniformed sergeant sat on the desk near the holding cells. His feet swung slowly. Sam couldn't see who he was talking to. "You can't keep doin' this shit. You won't be sixteen forever. Wait'll you get to Raiford. They got guys up there that would love to get hold of you. You goin' up the state, Mario? . . . You sure about that?"

Ryabin finally hung up. He looked down at the little plate of chocolate cake. "It's getting stale. Someone left it in the refrigerator last week. At home I'm eating only grapefruit and toast for breakfast." His smile lifted the hound-dog pouches under his eyes. "Anna has put both of us on diets. This is what happens when you take your wife browsing in expensive boutiques."

Sam said, "Pretty cheap of you, Gene, not to buy her a dress."

Ryabin nodded, swallowing another bite. "If this were better, I wouldn't feel so guilty about eating it." He stuck the fork in the remaining cake and tossed it into his trash can. He flicked a brown crumb off the front of his immaculate shirt.

Sam gestured toward the police reports. "Looks like whoever killed Fonseca used a pillow as a silencer."

"Probably. The lab will do an analysis. Maybe they can tell us what kind of pillow. An airline pillow stolen off an Alitalia flight from Milan! Maybe we'll get lucky."

Nestor Lopez came over and leaned on the desk. "You can use anything for a silencer. Newspaper, oil filter. Grapefruit. I seen grapefruits on the floor next to a body. Said, man, what'd they do to this fruit? It's all squashed, juice all over. Then I observed the gunpowder."

Ryabin patted his pocket for his cigarettes—a habit; smoking was banned in the building.

Sam asked, "What about the beach where Sullivan was shot? I know that Corso found those bits of green cloth around the back of his head. Did you find any vinyl on the sand?"

Lopez shook his head. "We weren't looking for that, and now, Christ, people have been walking all over the sand for two weeks. The shooter might have shot through a bag, but we don't know."

Standing up, Ryabin said, "Sam, go with me outside. I need a smoke."

It wasn't a cigarette he wanted, but privacy. They climbed the stairs to the third floor and found a vacant office.

Last Friday night, Ryabin began, he had taken Anna out to dinner on Lincoln Road. Her birthday, of course, but also to visit the boutique owned by Claudia Otero. Anna, bewildered that her husband would take her to such an expensive store, went inside when he explained the purpose. They spoke Russian and pretended to admire the fashions while the manager, a young woman with short-cropped hair, snorted cocaine in the back with her friends. When Ryabin politely called her aside and asked if she would answer a few questions, she not-so-politely refused, because wasn't it obvious that these dumpy, middle-aged people were only looking, taking up her time? Then Ryabin smiled, pulled out his badge, and told her she was under arrest for possession of a controlled substance. She became more cooperative at the station.

Ryabin said, "I don't speak Spanish well, but Lopez does. You might not believe me, Sam, but Lopez is a talented man. At six o'clock Monday morning we're calling Spain. Then France. I'm running all over the building, finding officers to speak French and German. The telephone bills are going to be outrageous. In any event, Otero, the company, has the main offices in Madrid. I'm making a report in writing, which later you can read. Now I'll give you the gist. Claudia Otero's family left Cuba in 1961 and went to Spain. In 1968 they relocated to New York and became American citizens, but Claudia stayed in Europe. She studied art. She was a fashion model briefly, then married one rich man, then another, and became involved in designing. Ten years ago in Paris she opened a clothing store, then another in Madrid, then one in Nice, and so on. Now she has forty-six of them. Europe, North and South America, most of them resort areas. In Japan she has three. And a new one—but the opening has been postponed—in Cuba."

"Cuba." Sam locked his fingers on top of his head and leaned back in his chair. "Why was it postponed?"

"They say red tape with the Cuban government." Ryabin made a wry smile.

"Lots of tourists in Havana? With money?"

"Oh, yes. Many Europeans, many from Eastern European countries. Many English and Canadians. But not Americans, of course, because our State Department won't allow us to travel to Cuba. Some get in, family members, journalists, and so on, but Anna and I had to go through Jamaica."

"What were you and Anna doing in Cuba?"

"Enjoying the beach and the nightclubs. We went because the State Department forbids it." His face was round, smiling. "I'm an American now, Sam, but if I wanted restrictions on my travel, I would never have left the Soviet Union."

"You didn't see Amalia Mora dancing at the Tropicana?"

Ryabin laughed. "No. But she met Claudia Otero last October at a nearby resort town that caters to rich Spaniards and where, by coincidence, Claudia's store will be located—when it opens."

"The Cuban exile community wouldn't be pleased with Amalia Mora, if they knew."

"The American government wouldn't like Amalia Mora helping her sister open a business in Cuba." He added regretfully, "I believe this, but I don't have proof."

Sam had to get out of his chair and walk around the office awhile. He thought of what Caitlin Dorn had told him about the fashion industry. How insular and self-referential. He said, "Klaus Ruffini may have known about Claudia and Amalia, being in the same business. His wife, Tereza, is a designer."

Ryabin nodded. "That occurred to me, too."

"But why hasn't this made the news? Ruffini was arraigned this morning. He would have said something already."

"Maybe it's too late. You decided to prosecute. Eddie couldn't stop you. It was out of his control. If Ruffini talks now, Eddie might make it worse for him, if not in the criminal courts, then with his political friends. Ruffini could be deported. So. A standoff."

"Only until there isn't a case anymore," Sam said, "then Ruffini walks. Sullivan is dead. George is dead. My witnesses are scared, and I don't blame them."

Ryabin sat with his fingers knitted over his belly. He looked at Sam. "When the state attorney comes back, I think you should talk to him. Tell him that the Miami Beach police want to question him in connection with the deaths of Charlie Sullivan and George Fonseca, both of whom were prepared to testify on a case that he didn't want to prosecute. Ask about Dale Finley, his chief investigator, who once was a spy for the CIA in Cuba and who attempted to persuade Ali Duncan not to talk to you. And ask him about his wife's visits to Cuba and about her financial interests in Otero. Ask him if Amalia persuaded her sister, Claudia, not to open the boutique near Havana because she knew that it could ruin Eddie Mora's political future."

Sam laughed. "You looking for an early retirement, Gene?"

"No. I have two unsolved murders."

"Just doing your job. Does Chief Mazik know about this?"

"Not yet. No one knows except you and me. When you say to talk to Mazik, then I'll talk to him."

As he continued to look at Ryabin, Sam could see what he was doing. He was letting Sam decide if Chief Mazik should be told at all. He was handing over this information about Eddie Mora's wife to use or not, in whatever way Sam chose to do it. Push the state attorney up against a wall, or let him go.

When Eddie Mora had been put in charge, Sam's career—his *life*—had been stolen. He'd played the good soldier, getting right into line. And on the Duncan case, he'd been used. When Eddie Mora had needed someone to keep the shit off him, he'd come to Sam Hagen. Sam, snared by his own ambition.

On the porch of the Englander Apartments, the old man sat in a chair in the shade. Perlstein. He of the inky hand. The scribe. Not feeding the birds today, just watching the street. He watched Sam come through the iron gate and walk toward the building.

"Hello. It's my used-to-be-Jewish friend. Caitlin isn't here. She moved out."

Sam stopped, looking up at her window. The tangle of green plants was gone. The panes were empty, reflecting only trees and sky. "Where did she go?"

"She left. She went to New York."

"Already?"

"Saturday morning she's packing. Sunday there's a pickup truck and her friends to take her things away. My wife and I might have to move, too. This building is going to be turned into condominiums. They're going to raise our rent. Jordanians bought it, what do you think of that? Arabs. On Miami Beach, Arabs."

"Did she give you her forwarding address? A phone number."

Perlstein shook his head.

"She must have told you where she was going," Sam said. "It's important that I locate her." He came up the steps.

A woman's face appeared at the window behind Perlstein, peering through the glass slats. Her eyes were fixed on Sam. She said, "Harry. Your lunch is ready. Come eat." She leaned over a plump armchair. A cat lay across the back of it washing a paw.

Perlstein picked up his cane. "I have to go in. Excuse me."

Sam moved closer to the window. "That's Caitlin's cat."

"No," Mrs. Perlstein said, "it's ours." She shoved the cat off the armchair.

He took a step toward Perlstein. "You know where she is."

"Harry!" The wife's voice quavered. "Come in. Your lunch will get cold."

Sam saw he was frightening the woman; he was a maniac, a jackbooted thug here to break down doors and threaten the helpless. He took a card out of his wallet and held it to the screen. "Mrs. Perlstein, it's all right. My name is Sam Hagen. I'm a prosecutor with the state attorney's office. Caitlin Dorn is a witness on a case of mine, and I need to speak to her about that."

"Another man from your office came by yesterday, and we told him the same thing. We don't know where she is."

"What man?"

"I don't know. Not so young. He wasn't dressed in a suit, like you."

"White hair? A limp? What was his name?"

"I don't know his name, but the limp I remember. We told him, we don't know where she is. Harry, come inside!"

"A minute! Dvorah, in a minute." He waved a hand at the screen. "Go on. I'm talking to Mr. Hagen." He pushed himself unsteadily out of his chair and went to the other end of the porch. A mockingbird fluttered away to perch on a red hibiscus bush.

The hand that wrapped around Sam's wrist was surprisingly strong. Perlstein said in a low voice, "I think she left because of the boyfriend. He came around, making trouble for her."

"What do you mean?"

"Trouble. He bothered her. Phone calls, letters. Coming around, watching. I saw him parked up the block there. Last week he comes. He asks me where she goes, who she is with. Don't worry, I didn't tell him you were here. I never liked that man. I told her, This guy is no good for you, but—women! I hope she doesn't go back with him."

Sam felt his jaw clenching. He looked down into Perlstein's face. "Where did she go?"

"I'm sorry." He patted Sam's shoulder. "Caitlin made us promise not to say. This is what I'll do. I'll call her, and she can contact you. All right?"

"She's still in town, isn't she?"

He shrugged.

"I'm a friend, Mr. Perlstein."

From the window his wife shouted, "Harry!"

Rafael Soto lived on the third floor of a building on Pine Tree Drive. He opened the door far enough to talk. Behind him Sam could see cheap furniture and colorful pillows and lamps. Music was playing: a swing band from the forties.

He held out his card. "I'm Sam Hagen."

Soto didn't take it. "I know who you are."

The smell of pork and garlic came out into the hall. A Hispanic guy about Soto's age stuck his head around the corner from the kitchen. *"Rafael! ¿Quién es?"*

"Nada. Un abogado del fiscal."

"I'm here to see Caitlin Dorn."

"Caitlin isn't here."

"Where is she, Mr. Soto?"

"En route to New York. She'll call when she arrives to give me her address. I assume she'll contact your office as well."

"Look. I know she's in town. I have to speak to her about Ali Duncan's case. It's urgent."

"Well, if she's still around, it's news to me."

"You talk to me or to the police," Sam said. "Your choice."

"Pardon me, but we're in the middle of lunch."

The door began to close. Sam shoved a shoulder into it. Soto nearly fell, bumped backward into the living room. Sam raised his palms, moving away a step. He outweighed either of these guys by fifty pounds. "I'm not going to hurt anybody, but I have to know where she is."

Rafael Soto took off his glasses and tossed them onto the sofa. His eyes glittered darkly. He wouldn't be pushed around this time. His friend came back out of the kitchen with a long cooking fork, still greasy from the pan. Soto said, *"Julio, llama a la policía."*

"She ran from Frank Tolin, didn't she?" Sam watched Julio, who held the cooking fork out like a pitchfork to a wild animal as he sidled across the room and picked up the telephone. "Soto, if anything happens to that woman, you want to take responsibility?"

After a second, Soto spoke over his shoulder. *"¡Cuelga!"* Julio hung up the phone. Soto said, "He beat her up."

"Jesus. When?"

"A couple of weeks ago. So she broke up with him, and now she's worried what he'll do. He called her so much she had to disconnect her phone, and he's sent the most *obscene* letters. Unsigned, but is there any doubt? He told her to get out of the apartment and he slashed the tires on her car." Rafael Soto went over to the sofa for his glasses. He put them on, then looked directly at Sam. "Maybe as Frank Tolin's friend, maybe you can persuade him to leave her alone. I'm really afraid he might do something."

"Rafael, tell me where she is."

"Not here," Soto said. "She was, but she thought he'd figure it out. Till we go to New York, she's staying with Paula DeMarco, who has a house on Flamingo Drive. She owns the gallery where Caitlin had her show. There's a vicious Doberman, so she's quite safe. Oh, God." He pressed a hand to his forehead. "She's going to kill me. I swore on my mother's grave."

Sam opened the door. "Thanks."

"Wait! If you're going over there, you won't find her. She has a shoot outside Nick's at the marina. She's taking photos of jet skis."

"Jet skis?"

He made a rueful smile. "Yeah, I know. But it pays."

Sam left his jacket in the car and sat on a concrete bench near the docks at the Miami Beach Marina, which was located toward the southern tip of the island. Nick's, a high-priced restaurant Sam had never been to, took up the top floor, with shops on the bottom, everything under a turquoise roof, lush landscaping all around. Down the docks a bit, a store made to resemble a palm-thatched chickee hut rented catamarans, sixteen-foot outboards, and jet skis. They'd lined up three of the vile-colored machines outside in the grass. Each was at present being straddled by a model in a bikini. The girls were standing up, leaning over the handlebars. Cheesy. A couple of old guys on the docks getting the rearview, grinning. Sam would bet Caitlin hadn't posed this one.

Shifting on the concrete bench, Sam took out his hand-kerchief and wiped the sweat off his neck. Even in the shade of some palm trees he was too warm, wearing his suit pants and dress shirt and brown leather shoes. Out of place, everybody else in loose, light-colored clothing, and not much of it.

Sam had sat where he could keep an eye on her, waiting till she finished. He felt like a damned bodyguard, hulking and edgy. She knew he was there. Thirty yards away, he'd seen the bill of her khaki hat turn in his direction. Sunglasses hid her eyes. Sam went to the snack bar, bought a beer, and came back out to drink it.

Caitlin's arms showed in her yellow tank top. He didn't see any bruises. He hadn't seen any last week at her apartment. But she'd been wearing a long-sleeved blouse, he recalled. And heavy makeup. Sam thought about why she hadn't told him and decided it meant she was afraid he'd go have a few words with Frank about it. Get all three of them into a situation there was no easy way out of.

Finally Caitlin slung her camera bag over her shoulder. She spoke to a man with a beer logo on his T-shirt. He had his car keys out. She held up a hand, telling him to wait. Her hat turned toward Sam. She came to see what he wanted. He stood up.

Her nose was pink from the sun. Shoulders brown, a sheen of perspiration on her chest above the neckline of her bright yellow shirt. "How'd you know I was here?"

"I was just passing by and saw you."

"Sure."

"Don't blame Rafael. I held a gun to his head."

"And here you are." She shifted her weight to her other foot. The guy was still waiting for her, twirling his car keys.

Sam hadn't decided in advance what to say. Then suddenly, from nowhere, he knew what he wanted. He said, "Did you keep those photos of Matthew?"

She looked at him awhile, then said, "They're in storage."

"I've changed my mind. I'd like to have them."

They got in his car and drove north on Alton Road after Caitlin told the owner of the jet ski concession that she didn't need a ride. She pulled a bottle of Evian out of her bag and a cellophane pack of Cuban crackers, thick round wafers, curved from the baking.

"Bread and water," he noticed. "Can I buy you some lunch?"

"I'm not hungry." She nibbled on a cracker. "This is enough."

"What's going on with you and Frank?"

She looked at him through her dark glasses. "Nothing. We split up." Then she laughed. Her mouth was wide and full, and she wore no lipstick. "You lawyers ask such loaded questions. What do you really want to know? Caitlin, are you seeing Frank again? Caitlin, have you slid back into your old ways—again?" She unscrewed the cap on her bottle. "No, Mr. Hagen. I have not."

Sam braked at a traffic light. "Rafael said Frank beat you up."

"I knew it. Soon as you said you talked to Rafael. He gets so dramatic." She took a long drink of water.

"Caitlin, if I promise not to go over to Frank's office and kick the living shit out of him, would you please answer the question?"

She exhaled. "He didn't hit me. Satisfied?" She bit into another cracker.

"Didn't slash your tires?" Sam could hear his voice rising. "Send you filthy letters? Didn't force you out of your apartment?"

"Not really." She concentrated on the cracker. "We had a fight when I left him. He pushed me. I pushed him. We screamed at each other. We've done it before, but I finally got fed up and walked out. And he wants me back. He's persistent, what can I tell you?"

"So he cuts your tires and sends you obscene letters."

"I don't know who did the tires. I park on the street, all right?" She pulled off her sunglasses and shook back her hair. "Do I look beat up to you? Do I?"

Her skin was smooth and unbroken. He said, "I was worried."

"Well, thank you." She put her glasses back on. "The letters weren't obscene, they're pathetic. I was going to move out anyway. I didn't feel safe living alone after Sullivan died, and then George. You just never know. Oh, lord. I've got crumbs all over." She brushed the crumbs dotting her bare thighs into her palm, then wet her forefinger and dabbed at the tiny pieces. Her legs were shaved smooth, with fine, golden hairs closer to the hem of her shorts. "Your car's so clean, I'm afraid to ride in it." She pressed the automatic window button and dusted her hands off.

Sam let out a breath and rubbed his forehead. His elbow leaned on the door.

She looked at him. "You sound exhausted."

"I'm fine." He slowed at Sixteenth to cut behind Lincoln Road, which was closed to auto traffic. Caitlin had told him to go to the DeMarco Gallery. Her friend Paula had let her store some things in a back room.

Caitlin's face was turned toward the window now.

"Sam, I'm sorry about last week. I shouldn't have kicked you out."

"Forget it." He saw a parking place along the curb, then put an arm over the seat to back up. "Ruffini and Lamont were arraigned this morning."

"Yes, I know. Ali told me."

"Their attorneys want to take your statement as soon as possible. You going to be around? I can accept a subpoena for deposition on your behalf." The engine was still on. Cold air blew through the vents.

Caitlin smiled archly. "What do you want? The pictures? Or are you making sure you still have a witness left on Ali's case?"

"Do I?" He took the keys out of the ignition.

Her lips were set into a thin line. She said, "Ali went through hell that night. I won't run away to New York and forget it ever happened."

"You didn't tell me you'd moved out of your apartment. What was I supposed to think?"

"I would have called you." She got out and slammed the door.

They walked along the narrow street, then onto Lincoln Road to the DeMarco Gallery, which was deserted except for a clerk reading a magazine. Caitlin told him she had to get something out of the back room.

She led Sam past the office then opened a paint-spattered door and turned on a light, an overhead bulb that contributed little to illumination. The left side of the narrow room was taken up with metal cabinets and vertical wooden slots for paintings and prints. Not much was left; the season was over. Caitlin's things were stacked to the right, a disorderly pile of cardboard boxes in varying sizes and shapes, picked up at a supermarket. They had once held cans, bottles, cereal, paper goods. Now the contents were noted in black marker. *Kitchen stuff. Sheets and towels. Clothes. Film and paper.*

When Caitlin closed the door a tremor danced through Sam's muscles and settled in his gut. Dust floated in beams of light coming through a small, barred window near the ceiling. No sound intruded. He looked at the stack of boxes, the deep shadows they made. There was no oxygen in the room. He pulled in a breath. "I won't ask you to search through all this. When you get to New York and unpack, just put the photos in the mail."

Caitlin set her camera bag on the floor, then laid her hat and sunglasses on a cabinet. "No, it's all right. I remember where they are. Help me move some of these, will you? They're heavy. You never think you have that much, till you try to pack it all into boxes."

"Where's the furniture?"

"I gave some away. Most of it I left behind. It was secondhand, anyway. Let Frank worry about it."

Sam shifted boxes of books as Caitlin directed. She picked up a former pasta box marked *winter clothes,* leaning back to balance the weight.

"Do you ever wish you could reduce your life to the barest possible? Maybe to fit inside one suitcase. Or a bag to throw over your shoulder. Then you could go wherever you wanted, whenever. Just float away as the mood strikes." Laughing a little, she dropped the box beside *audio-video.* Then she studied the pile still left. She pointed. "There. That one."

The box was thick cardboard, about one foot by two. Zephyrhills Natural Spring Water. 6 gal. Now marked in heavy black, *Prints and Portraits.* It was against the wall, but away from the window and off the floor, protected. Sam looked around as if someone had come through the door. He gripped his right wrist and flexed his fingers.

Caitlin said, "Sam? Can you get that?"

"Sure." He braced a foot and reached over the boxes spread out on the floor. Unlike most of the others, this one was sealed with packing tape. Caitlin sat on her heels and worked a thumbnail under a corner.

Sam leaned against the cabinet.

The tape came off and she folded back the flaps. Inside, under a layer of newspaper, were dozens of folders and envelopes. Her fingers moved quickly along the top edges, then stopped and tugged on a white envelope. *Matthew Stavros Hagen.*

Caitlin stood up and turned around. She said Sam's name and it took him a second to hear her.

He raised his eyes.

She said, "You don't have to take them."

"Why not?"

"You might not like them. They aren't glamorous."

He smiled, held out his hand. "I'm sure they're very nice. Dina will be pleased. I said we had photos, and we do, mostly from when he was a kid. We took loads of snapshots on vacation, both the kids, actually, but I don't think we have any portraits. Dina's got his book from his modeling days, you know, and she complains the pictures in there don't look like him."

Caitlin stared at him. She still held the envelope against her chest. "Maybe you should see these before you take them home."

"All right." He felt his pocket, pulled out his glasses. Caitlin gave him the envelope, and Sam moved closer to the light coming in through the window.

There were a dozen photographs, big enlargements, all black-and-white, eleven by fifteen.

Interesting lighting. High contrast. Good balance, use of negative space. Caitlin had told him about photography. What to look for. They were all taken the same day, apparently. In her studio, a drape of white in the background. But no attempt to hide what was behind that: the concrete walls of the studio, the lights, the bare floor.

Matthew in a pair of worn-out jeans hanging off his hips. His hair needing a wash, coming just to his shoulders. A young man's stomach, every muscle defined. Some hair on his chest, which Sam recalled he had waxed off for a swimsuit ad. The vanity of these kids.

The pant legs were too long, hems frayed. Big, high-arched feet. Standing there with his thumbs hooked in his pockets.

Next photo. Matthew off the ground, legs tucked under, hair flying, covering his face, blurred by the movement. Arms stretched out, hands wide open, reaching. A tattoo just above his left nipple. Sam peered closer. A half moon. When the hell had he gotten that? It must have been covered with makeup for his bookings.

Then Matthew standing still, arms crossed over his chest. Heavy biceps. He'd put on some muscle that summer. He was staring into the lens. Angular face, sharp nose. Not the pretty boy in the ads. Age already tracing faint lines into his wide forehead.

What was he thinking of? So serious. Not a kid you could scare easily. But he wasn't a kid anymore. A man. But not that, either. He was somewhere between. But where?

Sam took a breath. The floor seemed to tilt.

More photos. Matthew laughing, God only knew at what. Smile gone, then back again, a soft expression in his eyes. Gentle. Then a profile, hair thick and wavy on a pale cheek. Then again looking into the lens. Sam touched Matthew's face and was surprised to feel only smooth paper under his fingertips.

Lights making bright dots in Matthew's eyes. White space around him getting less and less. Sam falling into the photograph.

The camera had focused so closely. Each hair in his dark, straight eyebrows, each eyelash. A chip in one tooth, a blemish on his cheek. Full lips, a glint of saliva. Stubble on his chin. Not a heavy beard, not yet.

Sam realized, after a time, that he was sitting on one of Caitlin's boxes. He felt her lightly bump his shoulder, reaching to take the portraits. They vanished upward. He heard the paper whispering against the envelope.

Then her hand was on his hair. He turned and reached for her, pressed his face into her stomach and cried. She wrapped her arms around his head.

"I loved him." Sam took a heavy breath, then another. "Whatever Matthew did or was or would have become, I loved him. And I never told him."

"He knew," she whispered.

Sam shook his head.

"Yes. Believe me, Sam. Please." She lay her cheek on his head. "Matthew told me. He said that's how you are. He even laughed about it, said one day you'd get off his case. But he respected you so much, as a father. As a man."

Sam felt something shift and crumble in his chest. He ached from the pain of it. Caitlin knelt to take his face in her hands and say his name. She put her arms around him and kissed his eyes, his mouth. He groaned aloud, tasting salt and heat.

He shifted on the box to pull her between his thighs, and she pressed into him. He let her go long enough to look behind them, to find the box of towels, brace himself, and stretch out an arm. He flipped the box over and the folded towels inside spilled out, disarrayed.

He couldn't hold her closely enough, get into her far enough. She cried out, muffling the noise against his shoulder. Blood roared in his ears, shutting out everything but the feel, the sound, the smell of her. The tightness giving way. Sparks behind his eyelids, then a long, sweet, breathless fall.

When Sam finally opened his eyes, his left leg was under a box that had tumbled down. Caitlin looked as if she'd been knocked unconscious, her hair in her face. He was still inside her. Everything wet. He thrust slowly, felt her tighten in echoes of the spasms that he'd felt before.

Her breath was raspy. She still had her yellow shirt on, pushed up now above one breast. He kissed its peak, then straightened her shirt and pushed her hair off her face.

She locked her arms around his waist. "No. Don't get up yet."

"Caitlin. My pants are around my knees. What if that guy walks in here?"

She made a low chuckle. "I think that would be as funny as hell."

"For who?"

"Give me a towel," she said, opening one eye.

They dressed. Then Sam lifted the boxes into place again while Caitlin brushed her hair.

She'd had them arranged in no discernible order before, but now he worked at getting the heavier ones on the bottom and the entire stack closer to the wall, out of the way. He watched her as he worked.

"I should never have left you, Caitlin."

She paused, arms raised, hairbrush behind her head. She pulled it through her hair.

He said, "I thought it was the right thing to do."

"It was," she said. "You had a family. We wouldn't have been happy."

"Neither of us is happy now. Nobody is. What if I'd had the guts to take what I wanted? Matthew called me a hypocrite. He was right. Maybe he wouldn't have been so angry. Maybe he wouldn't have self-destructed."

"Don't, Sam. You'll make yourself crazy, talking like that."

When she turned to put the brush away, he kissed her neck. "I want to start over with you."

She smiled, shaking her head. "As if nothing had ever happened?"

"We have to talk about it."

"All right. But not now."

"I know. When?"

"In a day or two. Call me. I'll give you the number." She glanced at the white envelope on the cabinet. "What about the pictures of Matthew?"

Sam looked at the envelope, frowning.

Caitlin laughed. "I guess it would be hard to explain to your wife where you got them." She bit her lips. "Oh, God. I didn't mean that." She picked up her camera bag, then put it down again. "I don't know what to do, Sam."

"It's more my problem than yours." He grabbed her wrist. "I don't want you to worry. I love you."

She stared at him. "Don't say that."

"I love you, Caitlin. You want to hear it again?"

Her face was pale. "What's going to happen?"

He said, "I don't know yet, but it's going to work out." He pulled her close. "When can I see you?"

"Not right away. We both need some time to think."

He tightened his grip on her arms. "Don't go back to Frank Tolin. I'll kill him before I let him touch you again."

"Sam!" She was horrified and pleased.

"If he comes near you, I want to know about it. You hear me? Caitlin?"

She nodded.

Sam went over to pick up the portraits of Matthew. He held the envelope, turned it one way, then the other.

Finally he said, "You're right. I don't know what to tell Dina. I'll have to think about that, do it the best way for everybody." He extended the envelope to Caitlin. "Keep them for me awhile. I promise you, it won't be for long."

c h a p t e r
twenty-seven

Running at dawn, Sam pressed his forehead into his upper arm to wipe the sweat out of his eyes. The humidity was so thick he could chew it. His clothes were soaked and clinging to his skin.

It had been a day and a half since he'd made love to Caitlin Dorn, forty hours, and there hadn't been one of them when he hadn't thought of her. Asleep, he had dreamed of her. He couldn't look at a telephone without wanting to pick it up and hear her voice. He had called her close to eleven o'clock last night from a convenience store, keeping it brief. *Hello, how's it going?* This was so fresh he didn't want to jinx it. Before he made love to her again—and it wouldn't be on the floor in a storage room—he'd have to straighten things out with Dina. Things would be done the right way. Or as close to right as he could get. Tuesday afternoon he'd come home just before Dina arrived, his emotions slamming between exhilaration and dread. He'd thrown his underwear and shirt into the washer, showered and dressed, then took his slacks out to the car to drop off at the cleaners. Neither Dina nor Caitlin deserved to be lied to; he wouldn't do it anymore. There had to be some honesty. Some consideration.

The lawns of the houses he passed were dewy, and the cars dripped as if it had rained last night. Silvery drops of condensation hung suspended at the point of every leaf and pine needle. Closer to his own house, Sam could see how overgrown the yard was getting. The grass was mowed, because the yardman came every week, but he hadn't trimmed the flowers and hedges. Dina reserved that job for herself. Lately, though, she hadn't shown much interest. Her obsession with gardening was gone, and she'd been putting in more hours at the office, the way she used to. Sam considered this an indicator. He had spent a considerable amount of time trying to predict how Dina would react when he told her he wanted out. She would be angry, but she wouldn't dive into another depression. Since their raging argument about Caitlin Dorn three weeks ago, Dina had turned her back on him in bed. He hadn't touched her, and she hadn't seemed to care.

The wrongful death lawsuit hadn't come to anything, and wouldn't, but it had at least given Dina a way to get over her grief. Now Sam could insist on ending their relationship with Frank Tolin. He didn't know exactly what he would say to Frank, but he had promised Caitlin not to mention her name. *Frank, it looks like this case is at a dead end*—you come near Caitlin again, I'll kill you—*so let's just call it off.*

Aware of his own calculations, Sam had thought about elections in November. Not smart, leaving a wife of twenty-two years for a former model, a prime witness in a highly visible prosecution. Better to wait—but till when? Till he was divorced? Till he was sworn in as state attorney? To wait would be a gross hypocrisy, but he didn't want to rush into a decision without thinking it through. At forty-six, a man had to be a little more careful.

As he jogged slowly up the driveway, cooling off, a minivan stopped in front of the house. He waved. The carpool mother inside, whose name he didn't know, waved back. Melanie hurried out the front door with her book bag, pretending he wasn't there. She finally gave him a grudging smile as she got inside the minivan, embarrassed that her father was out in the front yard dripping sweat into his socks.

He didn't know what to do about Melanie. Maybe she was at the age when kids had to be angry at the parents; he'd heard that somewhere recently. She didn't get along too well with her mother, and if she wanted to live with him, that would be fine.

There would be some adjustments to make, and maybe Melanie and Caitlin wouldn't like each other at first, but with some reason on all sides, it would work out. Caitlin couldn't have children herself, so she might become fond of his child. As for marriage—Sam couldn't think that far ahead, but sooner or later the subject would have to come up. He couldn't live with her unmarried. Not with Melanie to consider. Or his career. It couldn't be done.

It worried him that Dina would be vindictive. She had a tendency that way. He had thought of divorce lawyers, property agreements, alimony. He would give the house to Dina, along with money to run it. Before Matthew died, she had been earning good money as a CPA. He'd have to pay alimony, but it wouldn't last forever, once she was back on track. Sam would find an apartment with a good-sized room for Melanie, near here so she wouldn't have to change schools. He would damn well have to be elected state attorney to afford it all.

In the last day and a half, Sam had tried to apply some logic to the process, difficult because his own emotions were so shifting and tangled. But there had to be a solution, a way to balance duty, love, and common sense. If not a perfect solution, then at least an honorable one.

Sam trotted upstairs with an old towel around his neck. In the bedroom, Dina glanced at him from where she stood by her dresser, naked except for her panty hose. She picked a bra out of a drawer. At forty-four, her hips and breasts had softened, and a C-section scar marked the pale skin of her belly. Sam had seen his wife's body thousands of times, but now he felt embarrassed.

"I'm going to take a shower," he said, and mopped his face with the towel. Walking past the bed he noticed her suitcase on the end of it.

She said, "I'm going to drive to Tarpon Springs right after work. You don't mind, do you? I've already told Melanie. I'll be back Sunday."

Three days unexpectedly free. But three more days in limbo. He said, "Why do you have to go this weekend? I was hoping we could talk."

She looked at him a moment more, then took a white silk blouse off a hanger and put it on. "Tell me now, Sam." She buttoned the blouse and waited for him to speak. Somehow she knew. She had guessed. *I know what's in your heart,* she had once said. She had known before he had. "Is it the same woman or someone else this time?"

Letting out his breath, Sam hung on to the towel around his neck. "Dina, I didn't expect this. I never wanted—"

"Let's skip the part about how much you regret hurting me." She went into her closet and came back out with a deep green suit.

He said, "All right. Above anything, I want us to be honest with each other. We haven't been happy. It started before we lost Matthew. Before I got involved the first time. You told me he knew about it. Maybe if I'd said something three years ago, if we'd worked it out then, things would have been different. So now what? Do we die along with him? Grow old with our backs to each other? Dina, we've got a daughter, and she has to know that love means more than that."

A smile was playing at the corners of her mouth. "Only a lawyer could invent such a creative excuse for adultery."

He felt a prickling of anger. "What do you want me to do?"

"Do? I think that's your decision."

"No, it's ours. Do you want me to move out?"

"I want you to die of a heart attack." She zipped her skirt.

"Great." He raised his hands and moved toward the bathroom. "You think about it over the weekend. We'll talk when you get back."

"I have thought about it," she said. Her voice was trembling. "That's why I'm going to Tarpon Springs, to see if we could live there again. Is there work for me? A good school for Melanie? We have to get out of here. Sam, come with me."

"I can't do that."

"Does being the next state attorney mean more to you than your family?"

He said, "Dina, going to another place won't fix what's wrong with us."

She looked at him for a moment longer, then turned her back to fasten her earrings and necklace at the mirror.

Gold glittered against her skin. "Do what you like. I despise this city. Human beings weren't meant to live here. It's only rock dredged up out of the swamps, with a thin layer of sod so we'll forget what's underneath. There's going to be another hurricane sooner or later. It's all going to go."

She turned away and her hands fell to rest on the edge of the dresser. "No loss. Let it go. We could have had a good life together. But we wanted too much. Such pride. We've been undone."

"I am sorry," he said.

"Yes, I suppose you are." Dina put her feet into her high heels, standing regally now. She picked up her jacket. "I honestly don't know what to tell Melanie." Dina's eyes met his again, burning with dark intensity. "What you've done is sinful. Nobody uses that word anymore, do they? Sin. Wickedness. There's no eternity anymore and no punishment, and therefore everything is permitted."

"That isn't how I feel," Sam said. "I've got responsibilities and I won't walk out on you or Melanie. Hire a lawyer if you want to. I won't argue."

"Oh, yes." She laughed. "You'd better hire one of your own, because I'm going to make you pay for this."

The anger was building, but Sam held it back. "There's one thing I insist on. We need to let Frank Tolin go. The lawsuit isn't getting anywhere."

"Is that the reason? Call him, then. I'd love to hear what you say." She took the suitcase off the bed. "You're such a romantic. It's your power she's attracted to, darling. Women like that always are. Why, Sam Hagen is the deputy chief of Major Crimes. And soon to be state attorney. But do you really think you'll be elected, with her around your neck? And then what will you have?" Dina's smile faded. "I'm sorry, too, Sam. Sorry for us all."

The girl in the pink plaid dress looked lovely in the viewfinder, Caitlin thought. The light filtering through the pine trees gave her smooth skin a lustrous glow and put some nice highlights in her brown hair. She pressed the shutter, advanced the film, then took a few more shots. The telephoto and tripod were borrowed. The old

Nikon was the only camera Caitlin had left, but it was still good enough to take photos of a beginning model.

She was about twenty years old, tall and big-framed. She'd be doing the plus sizes, if she could get some bookings. She would pay Caitlin a hundred dollars and costs for some color pictures to show the agencies.

In a small park near the bay side of Miami Beach, Caitlin had found the perfect spot for some candid photos. There was a rundown mansion across the street, which would look good out of focus in the background. They weren't so far from Paula DeMarco's house. Caitlin felt safe. So far, Frank Tolin hadn't found where she was living, or else he had grown tired of harassing her.

"What a mooooo," Ali Duncan said under her breath.

"Shhhh," said Caitlin, looking through the viewfinder again. Ali had asked if she could come watch the shoot. Caitlin had said yes, but only if Ali helped out. Caitlin was short one assistant, with Tommy Chang taking final exams, and no money to pay him anyway.

She stepped away from the camera and called out, "Jennifer! Your bra strap is showing, honey." Jennifer's mother, who had come along to do hair and makeup, rushed forward with some pins.

"Caitlin?" Ali was winding a pine needle around her forefinger. Her hair was stuffed inside a ball cap, and she had her sunglasses on, still incognito.

"What?"

"I think I'm going to France."

Caitlin was aware of her mouth falling open.

"I mean, I want to go to France, but I have to explain it to Mr. Hagen?" The statement curled up into a question. "And I don't know what to tell him and everything. How about like if my dad in California got sick. Or I died. Could you talk to him? You're friends and everything."

"Wait. What are you saying? France?"

"Well, I sort of . . . got a job. It's for *Marie Claire* magazine. For August, I think."

"That's wonderful! Of course you have to go. Just give Sam a way to contact you for trial."

"No, I don't think I can come back, not for like a year or something, because I'll be totally busy."

Caitlin stared at her. "Who arranged this, Ali?"

Ali kicked at a rock. Her shoes were neon-green plastic. She said, "Tereza Ruffini."

"Oh, no."

"I have to, Caitlin. It's my chance."

"My God! You believe them? They'll take you over there and dump you. You're being used. Don't you see that?" Her anger was out of proportion, and not only for Ali.

"I can handle it! You couldn't when you were young, but I *can*! What have I got here? Nothing. Nobody will hire me on South Beach, I can't stand living with my mom, I don't have any money—" She made a little scream of exasperation, then said, "Caitlin, please. Can you talk to him? Tell him I had to leave."

A voice came from under the trees. "Yoo-hoo! I fixed her bra." Jennifer's mother was waving. "I think we ought to take some pictures sitting down. What do you think?"

Caitlin muttered, then called back, "Sure. Give her the chair." While Jennifer arranged herself on a folding chair, Caitlin stared at the rocky ground, carpeted thickly with pine needles. "I can't lie for you, Ali."

"It's not like it *matters*. I'm the one this happened to, and it ought to be *my* choice what to do about it, okay?"

"Okay. Then you explain it to Sam Hagen."

"He said he'd have me arrested for perjury if I changed my mind!"

"He ought to, after what you've put everyone through. Ali, would you please *think*? Tereza Ruffini does *not* want to help you. Two people are *dead*. Does that register at all?"

"They didn't kill Sullivan, or George either! Caitlin, she was really nice to me. She apologized for Klaus and everything. She said he was drunk and he didn't mean to, and they're so sorry—"

"What the hell else is she going to say?"

"*God!*" Ali spun around, then came back again, speaking quietly. "Are you going to tell Mr. Hagen about this?"

Jennifer's mother called, "Yoo-hoo! Miss Dorn?"

Caitlin tiredly shook her head. "No. It's your decision." She framed the next shot through the viewfinder, motioning with one hand which way the girl should move. "Here's some advice. Ask for more than you'll settle for, get it up front, get it in cash, and don't blow it. If I'd done that, I wouldn't be thirty-five years old living on the charity of my friends." She glanced at Ali.

Ali nodded. "Okay."

Looking through the lens, Caitlin said, "Be careful, baby."

When the session was over, Ali hugged her, then rode away on a borrowed bicycle.

Jennifer's mother took out her checkbook. Caitlin reminded her they'd agreed on cash, and the woman gave her fifty dollars as a deposit. Caitlin said the pictures would be ready by tomorrow. They would meet at the lab and choose the ones they wanted. And please bring the rest of her fee, plus ten dollars for each enlargement.

Caitlin tucked the money into a pocket and began to pack her things away. When had it happened, she wondered, that she had become so distrustful? She couldn't remember any particular event. More likely she had formed her cynicism as an oyster forms a pearl, one layer at a time.

It was almost funny now, the agony she'd gone through, finding the guts to stand up for Ali Duncan as a witness to a rape. Sticking around to testify, even though her first instinct had been to forget she'd ever been at the Apocalypse that night. In the end, it hadn't mattered. Ali would be flying off to Paris while Caitlin Dorn headed for a third-floor walkup in Greenwich Village.

Ali hadn't mentioned Tommy Chang in her plans. Poor Tommy, who was nuts about her. Meaning every word, Ali would probably tell him she'd write, she'd call. That she'd be back. But she wouldn't. Tommy would mourn for a while; then he'd find another girl. One truer than Ali, if he was lucky. But he didn't need luck. He was young.

Maybe Ali Duncan had planned this from the start, waiting till Klaus Ruffini was arraigned on felony charges before she said yes to a deal. Or maybe it had occurred to her somewhere along the way. Caitlin had learned that people lived from moment to moment and that the most sincerely spoken promises would be put aside when something more pressing came along.

Maybe people like Ali Duncan were the ones who survived. Caitlin had never quite learned how.

Walking across the park with her bag and tripod, Caitlin thought that her grumpy mood might be an aftershock from Tuesday. Making love with Sam. Thinking about it now, she felt her insides clench. She didn't want to think about it. She was trying not to be stupid about this.

She'd left her Toyota in the small lot near a children's play area. Coming closer, she noticed the paper under the windshield wiper. An envelope. No name on it.

Tensing, she looked around. There were only children and their mothers in view, the nearest boy riding a horse on a spring. A lithe male jogger ran along the bike path. A car went by. Farther along the street were a traffic light and shops on the other side.

Caitlin sat in the front seat with the doors locked and read the note, which was written with black ink on heavy white paper.

My darling, darling love, sweetest Catie. I would give up everything I own to have you back in my arms. Please give me one more chance to show you—

As if it were toxic she thrust the paper away from her.

"Damn it, leave me *alone!*" Her fists hit the steering wheel.

She grabbed the note and envelope off the passenger's seat, got out of her car, and ran to the children's play yard.

There was a trash can chained to a pine tree. Caitlin held the note over the trash, ripped it into pieces, and threw the envelope after. She looked down the street. She couldn't see him, but she knew he was there.

chapter
twenty-eight

By three o'clock on Fridays, the courts and the offices around them would begin to clear out, anticipating the weekend. The phones would stop ringing, and the horrible crush of work would become at least bearable.

Sam Hagen was finishing an extradition request that had to be taken to the federal courthouse by four-thirty today, without exception, when Joe McGee dropped by to talk about *State* vs. *Ruffini and Lamont*. Joe had been sweet-talking Norman Singletary, Marquis Lamont's lawyer, offering probation for Lamont in exchange for his testimony, but so far, no deal.

Juan Casares, the felony division chief, saw McGee standing in the doorway and came just inside to sit on the arm of the battered sofa, which was stacked with files. Sam listened with one ear while he dictated directions to his secretary for the extradition.

Sam's telephone buzzed, and he reached to answer it.

His secretary said, "Caitlin Dorn's calling. I know you're busy, but she says she has information on the Ruffini case."

He let his chair come back up. "Sure. Put her on." He swiveled toward the windows, wanting to throw his visitors out and close the door.

She had called to say hello. "Sorry for the little fib."

"No, it's all right. What's up?"

"Nothing. Just thinking about you."

"Really." He smiled. "I've been doing that all day."

"Liar, liar, pants on fire. You were supposed to call me."

"It's been beyond belief around here. Listen, I've got some people with me at the moment. Can I call back, say in half an hour?"

"Promise?"

"Sure."

"No, promise. And tell me what you want to do to me."

"Hey. You're a troublemaker, you know that? Talk to you later, okay?"

She told him to wait. There was a silence, then she said, "I love you, Sam."

"You sure about that?"

She laughed softly. "I think so."

"Okay. Good. I'll call you in a little while. Take care."

He hung up thinking that he'd royally fucked up that conversation. He stared out the window for a minute, then swiveled back around to finish dictating notes to Gloria, his secretary.

Over by the door, Lydia Hernandez had come in. Joe McGee was explaining the significance of George Fonseca's cellular phone.

"It was right there on the seat beside him, but he never called 911. Dr. Corso said the wounds weren't instantly fatal, so he had some time. Fonseca's hands were covered in blood. So why wasn't there blood on the phone?"

The Miami Beach police had checked phone company records. There had been no phone calls from Fonseca's telephone after four in the afternoon. The last had been to a video store to argue about an overdue rental. The police were interviewing everyone else Fonseca had called that day, but they had come up with nothing.

Juan Casares shrugged. "I'd say he was grabbing his thigh. Maybe the killer held the gun on Fonseca and waited for him to bleed out."

"No way. You going to wait around in broad daylight after you fire three rounds from a forty-five? Not even if the gun was silenced. All that blood on the windshield? No, Fonseca was unconscious. Or poisoned."

Lydia Hernandez laughed. "Poisoned *and* shot?"

"Corso said it looked like he was having a toxic reaction. Say the killer gives him adulterated coke or smack. Okay? Then Fonseca feels nauseated. He starts vomiting. He has to get medical attention, so he tries to drive away. Or he tries to get to the phone to call 911. What does the killer do then?"

"Shoots him," Casares concluded.

The telephone buzzed again. Exhaling tiredly, Sam swung around in his chair to answer it.

"Gloria, I have work to do."

"I know, but you won't believe who's calling," she said. "Klaus Ruffini."

"I can't talk to a defendant."

"I told him that. This is his third call in five minutes."

"Christ." He exhaled, then said, "All right, I'll tell him myself." He told Gloria to put Ruffini on hold. "Heads up, everybody, you're going to be my witnesses on this."

The three other lawyers stopped talking.

Sam punched a button on the desk set and replaced the receiver. "This is Sam Hagen."

The voice boomed through the speaker. "Hello. This is Klaus. I'm speaking to you in my car. I want to meet with you in person as soon as possible."

"Not going to happen," Sam said. "Where's your attorney?"

"In the restaurant finishing his drink. You know my car? The Cadillac? I decide I won't sue you for the damage. I told Jerry to do it, but now I change my mind."

Joe McGee was grinning, shaking his head. Juan Casares quietly closed the door.

Sam said, "I want you to listen carefully. I'm turning on a tape recorder, so I advise you to hang up." He hit another button. "This is Samuel Hagen. It is three-seventeen P.M., June tenth. Mr. Ruffini, your call is being taped. If you wish to communicate with the prosecution, tell your attorney—"

"No! I need my passport, for a small trip only, for business. Tereza went to Paris, and Miami is no good in the summer. I can't believe you would make such a big deal from this. I know why. You think I killed George Fonseca and the other guy, the model, because George wanted money. Did he call you? He said he called you. He said to me, 'Pay me or I'll testify against you.' Blackmail. You think I hired somebody to kill him, don't you?"

"Whatever you say can be used against you in court," Sam said.

"I didn't do anything!" Ruffini was screaming into the telephone. "Two men are murdered and now I have Franco with me, my bodyguard, to go even to the bathroom. Am I the next? They tell me before I came to Miami this is a dangerous place, like the Wild West cowboy days, but I said no, forget it, but it's true. You're going to make me stay in Miami, for what? To get killed?"

"Mr. Ruffini, I'm hanging up now." Sam reached toward the desk set.

"Wait! This is a mistake. You aren't supposed to do this! Talk to Edward Mora. Does he know what you're doing behind his back?"

Sam froze.

"He's going to Washington, I hear on television, and now you want to take over his job. My attorney tells me this."

Sam said quietly, "The tape is running, Mr. Ruffini."

"I don't care. Tape what I say, I don't care. You are all liars, all of you. I want my passport. I want to get out of here. This is a terrible city, no culture, the worst. You don't appreciate anything. Maybe I change my mind, I sue you for the car and when the jury sees that I'm innocent, I sue you for false arrest—"

Then Sam heard a man's agitated voice in the background asking Klaus who he was talking to. Klaus saying never mind, go have another drink. The man yelling now. *Franco, who the hell is he talking to? . . . For the love of God, hang up the fucking phone.*

The line went dead.

Juan Casares stared at the telephone, then said softly, "Christ Almighty."

"He's digging his grave with his mouth," Lydia said.

"Hey, I heard something really outrageous about Klaus Ruffini," McGee said. "He made Marty Cass kiss his behind. I'm not lying. He pulled down his pants and Marty Cass kissed his butt."

"Why?" Lydia laughed.

"Cass wanted him to buy some property, is what I heard."

"I didn't know the market was that bad."

Sam pulled the tape out of the recorder on his credenza. He looked at McGee. "Where'd you hear about it?"

"Reporter from the *New Times* told me." Hands in his pockets, Joe McGee leaned against the door frame. "They're working on an investigation of the politicos in Miami Beach, Hal Delucca in particular. Ruffini's name came up. They wanted to ask us some questions."

Sam shook his head. "Not yet." He unlocked a drawer in his desk and dropped the tape inside.

"That's what I told him. Delucca's saying he hardly knows Ruffini."

"Oh, really? Two months ago he would've puckered up for him."

Also locked in Sam's desk were prints of the photographs Caitlin Dorn had taken four years ago at the opening of Claudia Otero's boutique. Hal Delucca had been present, smiling into the camera alongside Marty Cass. Cass, the man who knew—or claimed to know— everything happening on South Beach. Detective Gene Ryabin wanted to question him, see what he could shake loose about the state attorney and Klaus Ruffini.

And then Sam would decide what, if anything, to say to Eddie Mora.

He had just picked up his papers again when the phone buzzed. Gloria Potter's voice came on the line. "Sam? I'm so sorry to break in again, but we've got a situation in the hall. Idelfonso García is asking to see you."

"What in hell?" The others looked at him. Sam put a hand over the phone and said, "Adela Ramos's brother is outside."

"Who's that?" Lydia asked.

Joe McGee started to explain it. The Luis Balmaseda case, the little boy thrown from the window.

"The receptionist is about to call security." Gloria was agitated.

"Look. Tell García to go up to the fourth floor and ask for Victoria Duran. She seems to have taken a personal interest."

"Sam, no! He says he's done something terrible, and he wants to talk to you before they take him to jail."

* * *

They did take him to jail. Two uniformed Metro-Dade officers arrived to place Idelfonso García under arrest for first-degree murder. They took him away in handcuffs, and Sam walked with them across the street.

García had nodded deferentially when Sam came to the small waiting area outside Major Crimes. He rose from the chrome-legged chair and said, "Now you can make another trial, Mr. Hagen, with me. I just killed Luis Balmaseda."

After the meaning of this hit him, Sam glanced over his shoulder and told someone to call security. People had gathered, staring, "Mr. García, come with me." He beckoned to Juan Casares. "Keep us company, Juan."

They went into the conference room to wait. Sam told García to extend his arms. He patted him down for weapons, found nothing, then told him to have a seat at the table. García sat. He was trembling slightly, and kept clearing his throat. He said, " *'Ojo por ojo, diente por diente.'* Do you know what that is?"

The lawyers stood on either side of him. Casares said, "It means 'an eye for an eye, a tooth for a tooth.' "

"Mr. Hagen, I want to tell you what I did."

"No. I'm not your attorney," Sam said. "I can't help you."

"But I came to talk to you, to explain."

Casares said quietly, "Advise him of his rights, Sam."

"Mr. García, listen to me. You will be taken into custody. You don't have to talk to us, you don't have to talk to the police, and if you—"

"I have to explain." García turned in his chair.

Sam held up a hand. "If you do say anything, whatever you say could be used against you as evidence. If you want an attorney, one will be provided. These are your rights. Do you understand them?"

"Yes." He laughed. "I have a lot of rights. That's good."

Sam exchanged a look with Juan Casares. The man could be out of his mind. He could be telling the truth. Or Balmaseda might be injured but still alive.

Casares asked, "What happened, Mr. García?"

He had thrown Luis Balmaseda out an eighth-floor window. Two floors higher than Carlito Ramos had dropped, but García said it was the only place he could find for his purposes. He had tied Balmaseda's hands and forced him up the stairs at knifepoint. Didn't want to kill him. Didn't want to knock him out. Wanted him to know what was coming for him, and why.

"It's not your fault, Mr. Hagen, that the jury let him go. I was so angry because nothing, nothing happened to Luis, but it wasn't your fault. They couldn't hear the confession, I understand this. And I understand the rule about only one trial. You told me about the law, but I said to myself, where's the law for Adela? For Carlito?"

Idelfonso García held up his hands, the skin leathery and dark. He had held Balmaseda over the window edge and told him, just before he let him go, to pray to God for mercy.

Looking down on the twisted body in the alley, García thought for a while about throwing himself over, too, but that was cowardly. Besides, he didn't want his blood mixed with the blood of a murderer. He knew that sooner or later the police would come for him. And so here he was, to give himself up. To explain. And to absolve Samuel Hagen, for truly, Luis Balmaseda had brought this on himself.

It was past six o'clock when Sam remembered Caitlin. Cursing under his breath, he pulled into his driveway and hit the button for the garage door. As it rolled up, he dialed her number on his car phone. No answer.

He fixed himself a drink and went upstairs to change clothes. Passing Melanie's door he heard the thud of music. He knocked.

When her face appeared at the crack, he said, "You want some dinner? How about we order some pizza?"

"I already ate." Her hair was uncombed, falling into her eyes, and her body was lost in a pair of overalls and a baggy shirt.

He said, "Can I come in for a minute?"

After a second or two, she nodded. He had to step over a pile of clothes to get to the chair. A small room, made more so by things strewn, dropped, stacked, or pinned to walls. One wall was painted pungent green. He didn't know when that had happened. A month ago, or less, her room had been reasonably neat.

"You mind turning the music down?"

Melanie lowered the volume, then stood in the middle of her room with her arms crossed. Sam felt like he was about to be interrogated. He moved some magazines and set his drink on a corner of her desk. "This was your last week of school. How'd the exams go?"

She shrugged. "I passed everything."

"That's good." Leaning his forearms on his thighs, he looked around the room. "What are your plans for this summer?" he asked.

"Hang out. I don't know."

"Maybe you'd like to go somewhere. A vacation. The two of us."

"Where?"

"Well . . . we could go fishing."

She stared at him.

"How about Disney World?"

"You're kidding, right?"

"No." He took a sip of his drink. "What would you like to do?"

"I don't know." Tossing her hair back, she sat on the edge of her waterbed and bobbed up and down before settling. They looked at each other a minute.

Sam said, "We haven't seen much of each other lately. I'm sorry about that." He put his glass on the desk. He turned back to her and said, "Melanie, I love you. If I haven't told you that in a while, I should have."

She looked at him steadily. "Are you and mom getting a divorce?"

He took a while to answer. "Probably."

Her expression told him this news came as no surprise. "Because you had an affair?"

"Did she tell you that?"

"No. I heard you and her fighting about it."

After a moment, he said, "I don't know what's going to happen. Your mother and I will figure it out. I don't want you to worry, okay? You won't have to leave your school, anything like that."

"She talked about moving to Tarpon Springs. I don't want to."

"You don't have to," he said. "Whatever you want, I promise."

Melanie started to cry.

Sam got up and stood beside her and awkwardly patted her back, then bent to kiss her cheek. She leaned against him and sobbed. He kissed her again, then said, "Come on, now. Where's my big girl?"

"Why is Mom the only one who gets to cry?" she wailed.

"Oh, honey. You can, too." He sat down on the edge of the waterbed and hugged her tightly.

She wiped her eyes on a corner of the sheet and said she was okay. Music was still playing on the stereo, something else now. Sam asked, "Since when do you like Led Zeppelin?"

Her voice was thick. "It's the Rolling Stones."

"Uh-uh. That's definitely Led Zeppelin. 'You Shook Me.' I used to know every cut on this album."

She got up to check. "You're right. This was Matthew's CD. I borrow them when Mom's not here. She doesn't like me to touch his stuff."

"Want me to talk to her?"

"She'll just say no."

"Buy your own, then," he said.

"I don't have any money."

"What do they cost?"

Melanie gave him a disbelieving look. "You don't even know? About fifteen dollars."

He leaned back a little to reach his wallet. He found three twenties in it. "Here. If you go to the mall this weekend you can buy four of them."

Melanie put her arm over his shoulder. "Dad. It's okay."

He nodded, then put the money back. "All right. So. No pizza, huh?"

"I'm on a diet," she said.

"Well, maybe I won't have any, either," he said.

She sat beside him again. "We could get a movie."

He looked at her. "You want a movie?"

"Sure."

"All right. We could do that."

Sam tried to call Caitlin again about ten-thirty, but her friend, the gallery owner, said she was out. He had to stop himself from asking where. He might have gone to find her.

Downstairs in the silent kitchen he fixed another drink, took a couple of aspirins, then topped off his glass with more bourbon. If he went to bed now, he wouldn't sleep. In the family room he watched the last of a police drama on television. Music was coming faintly from upstairs. Melanie working her way through her brother's CD collection.

A wrong thing to do, giving a kid money out of the blue. Sam didn't know what Melanie needed. If his ability as a lawyer were measured by his parenting skills, he would have been disbarred a long time ago. But he loved her. She had to know that. He'd just told her, and he'd tell her every damned day if that's what it took to keep her safe. To make her care if she lived or died.

Sipping his drink on the sofa, where he lay prone, Sam didn't know what he'd tell her if she asked him. *What's the point? Would somebody please just tell me what the fucking point is?* Matthew's question. He'd asked it as if he'd just figured out the entire world was crazy. Sam remembered giving him some inane response. Well, when you grow up, you'll find out the fucking point is not to ride around with your friends till three in the morning—

Sam wondered what he would do if someone murdered Melanie, and then a jackass prosecutor made a bad call and the guy was out walking the street. He might use his own hands to even up the score, as Idelfonso García had done. If García didn't wind up in the state hospital, he might get twenty years, be out in ten to twelve. Maybe he had saved Adela's life. Listening to García talk, Sam had wanted to pat the man on the back, not send him up to Raiford. What García *should* have done was push Balmaseda over the edge, but keep his mouth shut. Better still, choose some other method. Giving Balmaseda what he'd given Carlito was too obvious. Shoot the son of a bitch with a silenced .45. That had done the job with Charlie Sullivan.

In fact, Sullivan's death had been as fitting as Luis Balmaseda's. One bullet in his heart, another to take his pretty face off. Payback for what he'd done to Matthew. For putting his hands on him. For using him.

Sam was holding his drink on his stomach. He relaxed his grip on the glass, then took another sip.

Fitting that George Fonseca had thrown up blood and shit his pants before he died. Maybe he'd been the one to show Matthew how to cook smack in a spoon before injecting it. No big deal. Just a fad, all the models are into it.

Laughing a little, Sam lifted his glass. "Here's to you, Detective. You were right, by God. Everything balances. George earned what he got. So did Charlie Sullivan. The accounts are always balanced in the end."

Sam finished his drink, then suddenly clutched at the sofa as the room began to swing around. "Oh, Jesus." He sat up, staring blankly ahead of him.

Then he groaned aloud and thrust his glass toward the end table. It hit the edge and overturned. Taking several deep breaths, Sam walked into the kitchen and picked up the telephone, dialed a number. Hit the wrong button. Tried again.

Nicholas Pondakos answered on the sixth ring.

"Nick, it's Sam. I thought you might still be up."

"I am now. What do you want?"

From the icy tone, Sam knew that Dina had already told her family what he had done. He said, "I assume Dina's staying at her father's house?"

"Yeah. She always stays over there."

Sam closed his eyes and straight-armed the wall by the telephone. "Nick, I want to ask you something."

"No, don't get me involved between the two of you. I'm going to hang up before I say something rude."

"Wait. She's your sister, but I've got no quarrel with you, Nick. All right?" He could imagine Nick Pondakos, big arms and beer gut, trying to decide whether to slam the phone down or tell Sam Hagen to go screw himself.

"All right, but make it fast. I have to get up in the morning."

"Last time Dina flew up there—you remember? The third weekend of May. She caught a flight back from Tampa to Miami. What day was that?" For a minute Sam thought the connection had been broken. "Nick?"

"What day? Sunday. Right?"

Sam nodded, breathing again. "Did you take her to the airport on Sunday?"

"Yeah. After church we had lunch someplace, then I drove her to Tampa. What are you asking me this for?"

"It's—just something I was wondering about."

"You checking up on her? Let me tell you something, pal. She's not the one that needs checking up on."

"Okay. Good night, Nick."

"You guys have been married a long time. I can understand a little . . . you know, now and then, but that doesn't mean it's over. I like you a lot, Sam, but if you walk out on my sister, you can rot in hell, as far as I'm concerned."

There was a sharp click in his ear. Sam hung up the telephone, then let himself down carefully onto a stool at the kitchen counter, sucking in breath till his heart went back to a normal speed.

He felt as if he himself had been acquitted. But not innocent. And not falsely accused.

c h a p t e r
twenty-nine

It was the smell that tenants of the Delancy Apartments first noticed, the vaguely sweet, heavy smell that by Sunday morning, when they went into the hall to pick up their newspapers, could not be dismissed as someone's garbage or a dead mouse in the fuse box.

Detective Gene Ryabin, roused from a pleasant sleep with his wife, had gone to bed expecting French toast and freshly ground Jamaican coffee. Instead, he drank from a Dunkin' Donuts carryout cup while Miami Beach officers roped off the crime scene with yellow tape, and the technicians began the gruesome task of collecting evidence and photographing Martin Cass's bloated body. The air conditioning was on, which had slowed decomposition a little; Ryabin's partner, arriving first, had turned the fan to exhaust.

Now, Lopez had his fingers clamped on his nose. "Forget about replacing the carpet. They're gonna have to replace the fuckin' floor. He's soakin' into the wood."

While officers searched the three-room apartment, Gene Ryabin walked around, then stood quietly looking at the body. The medical examiner had been called; he would arrive shortly.

The paramedics, who had known when they entered the building that it was much too late, had found the door unlocked. Martin Cass lay sprawled fully dressed on his back beside the dining table.

The table apparently doubled as a desk, and there were

two glasses on it, one containing a dark liquid, lighter and more diluted at the top. Ryabin guessed Coca-Cola, as there was an opened half-empty liter in the refrigerator. The other glass had tipped over, wetting papers and splashing onto the typewriter. Cass had probably sipped it as he referred to a list of apartment buildings on a computer printout, which now lay askew on the table. A calculator was upside down on the carpet near Cass's left leg, and the chair was overturned.

Looking at all this, Ryabin thought that perhaps the visitor had been a potential buyer or seller of real estate, or an existing client of Cass's. He remembered the business card taped to the front door: *Martin Cass, Tropic Realty and Investments.* He and his visitor had sat at the table discussing investments and drinking a Coke, but the visitor hadn't touched his glass. Then Marty Cass had died.

Across the room talk radio played at low volume—a preacher talking about secular humanism, which leads inevitably to crime, abortions, and homosexuality. Ryabin went over to the cheap, wood-finish wall unit to look at the channel. This wasn't a religious station, except for Sunday, eleven to noon. But then, Marty Cass never struck Ryabin as a religious man. With the cap of his pen, Ryabin pushed the button to turn off the stereo.

He returned to the body. With a slight tremor of disgust, Ryabin took a deep breath before squatting down for a closer look. The flesh of Cass's right hand was split and oozing. The hand lay palm up, and there appeared to be a cut on the thumb and another wound dead center, though it was difficult to tell, with the hand so grotesquely swollen. Some blood, not much, had flowed out onto the beige carpet. The hand and arm had turned dark, putrefaction having set in. Cass's blue silk shirt was already soaked, mostly toward the back, which pressed against the floor. His neck, cheeks, and facial features had also turned dark.

Nestor Lopez stood by the table. "That looks like a stab wound to me."

A uniformed officer said, "You ask me, it's a bullet hole."

"No, it's not round enough. It's a cut. A defensive wound. I say he was stabbed to death."

"Where?"

"The back. It has to be in his back."

"Well, if that's a defensive wound, where's the wounds on his left hand? You don't defend yourself with just one hand."

"What it shows is, the assailant was left-handed, attacking from Cass's right side."

Four other officers had gathered around. Ryabin took his pen from his shirt pocket. Technically, the body wasn't supposed to be touched until the medical examiner arrived, but Ryabin pressed the pen into the carpet, then eased it under the back of Cass's right hand. He raised it an inch, then another. Rigor mortis had abated, and the limb was flaccid. Finally Ryabin made a murmur of discovery. As he had thought, the hole went completely through. The thumb dangled. It had been almost completely severed. Ryabin carefully lowered the hand.

Lopez said, "I told you so."

"Give me a paper towel," Ryabin said. Someone did so, and he wrapped the pen to throw away. A cheap pen; he would not have sacrificed his Waterman.

One of the officers wondered if Cass had bled to death. Another said, "From his hand? No way. There's not that much blood under there."

"I'm telling you, he was stabbed in the back. Look. He's got blood coming out."

"No, he had to be shot. Look at the carpet. There's blood spatter. You don't get spatter from a knife."

"You can."

"I still say he was shot."

"The neighbors I talked to didn't hear a gun."

"Maybe he got shot, then stabbed."

"That don't make sense. Who carries a knife *and* a gun around?"

"A lot of people. I arrested a guy yesterday had two butterfly knives, a Bowie strapped to his leg, and a twenty-two in his pocket."

Leaving them to speculate, Ryabin went into Cass's bedroom and put on a pair of cotton gloves. He planned to go through Cass's personal papers until the medical examiner arrived. He had considered calling Sam Hagen, but another man, the assistant state attorney on duty for homicides today, whoever that might be, had already been notified. And so far, despite the intriguing connection between Marty Cass and Klaus Ruffini, this death seemed to have no connection to any of Sam Hagen's current prosecutions.

Ten minutes later, as the assistant M.E. was taking his initial photographs of the scene, Gene Ryabin was working his way through four legal-size file drawers and a brown accordion folder in Cass's bedroom. He had opened the window and turned on the ceiling fan to reduce the odor, although the bedroom had its own aroma of stale sheets and unwashed clothing. The accordion folder, which had been kept on a nightstand, held a collection of full-color erotic photographs, alphabetized and cross-indexed by subject matter: *Anal Sex; Autoeroticism; Bears; Bondage; Breasts*—Ryabin lingered a bit over the folder, then turned his attention to the file cabinet in the corner. The contents, largely financial, confirmed what he already suspected about Martin Cass: a man whose net worth existed at some receding point in the future. Recent letters to creditors, neatly typed, alternately pleading and indignant, made assurances of payment. Soon. Within the month. *I am in anticipation of a sum of money within the month that will liquidate this debt.*

Returning the letters to their folders, Ryabin ventured deeper into Marty Cass's files. The second drawer contained other personal matters: medical, dental, a pending divorce from Uta Ernst. Ryabin recalled that Cass's wife had been one of Charlie Sullivan's toys. It was indeed odd, he thought, that the contents of the folders were in such disarray, when the erotica in the accordion file had been a model of organization. Some of the folders were even in the wrong order: *Car Insurance* followed a folder marked *Education*.

The third drawer was labeled *Grand Caribe*, and inside were brochures, floor plans, correspondence and assorted papers. Ryabin closed the drawer after taking a cursory mental inventory. The bottom drawer, titled *Real Estate, Personal* contained copies of legal documents related to property in which Cass had held an interest. Ryabin noted that Cass's residence was not a rental apartment, but a unit in a condominium. There were deeds to property which Cass had purchased, then sold, all listed alphabetically. Misfiled between *Morton Towers* and *Oceanside* was a familiar name, *the Englander Apartments*. Ryabin pulled out the folder. His own sister-in-law, Rivka Levitsky, had once owned that building, the first property she had purchased as a new American citizen. At her death in the fire, it had gone to Anna, who hadn't wanted to keep it—a sad memory. She had listed the property with Marty Cass, and Frank Tolin had eventually bought it.

Puzzled, Ryabin wondered why this folder had been filed with properties Cass had owned, if Cass had been involved in the Englander only as the real estate agent.

He was sitting on the end of the double bed reading the documents when Nestor Lopez opened the door. "Come on out, Gene, you're gonna love this."

Dave Corso, the M.E., had turned over the corpse. A few of the police officers had dispersed, wandering into the hall, or to the grassy backyard, which had a pleasant fountain to gaze at and flowers to smell.

Ryabin took a moment to recover, then asked Corso, "What did you find?"

Corso was sitting on his heels by the body. He looked up at Ryabin through his rimless glasses. "He was shot, Detective. It wasn't easy to see at first, with the decomposition, but a very big bullet chewed a hole right between his seventh and eighth vertebrae."

"It didn't go through him," Ryabin noted.

Nestor Lopez, who had his fingers pressed to his nostrils, said, "Take a look at what's stuck to his shirt."

As he moved closer, Ryabin saw the bits of shredded fabric, now dark with blood and putrefaction, which surrounded the hole between Cass's shoulder blades.

Stretching luxuriantly, arching her back, Caitlin kept an eye on Sam. He'd gone into the bathroom to comb his hair. Her head hung over the edge of the bed, and she could see him upside down. Nice, strong profile. Graying above the ears. The bank-executive type, if she had to put him in a magazine ad. But not in that sport shirt, with the tails still hanging out of his pants. As he combed his hair, she could see the muscles moving in his forearms and wished he hadn't put his clothes back on, so she could see the rest of him.

He glanced into the bedroom. "What are you smiling about, woman?"

"What do you think?" Caitlin said huskily.

He turned off the bathroom light, but the sunlight was coming around the edges of the heavy curtains. Votive candles still burned on the dresser. The ceiling fan rotated slowly overhead. He kissed her, and his mouth was velvety.

She reached up to hold his face. "Do you feel bad, coming to a hotel?"

"No. Not at all."

"It isn't tawdry and cheap, is it, Sam? I'd hate it if you felt that way."

"Caitlin, no. I'm glad you did this." He sat beside her to put on his socks and shoes. "I just wish we'd had more time."

"Next Sunday, too." She laughed. "Our Sunday services. And Wednesday prayer meeting. But it's going to cost a fortune. Oh, darling, we've got to stop meeting like this."

This had been her idea. She had called him to say, *I can't stand not seeing you. I've done something silly. I have a room at the Ritz.* The hotel was on the beach, flamboyantly art deco, but big enough to be anonymous. She'd spent the night here by herself, waiting for him to arrive in the morning. He couldn't leave his daughter alone at night; Caitlin understood.

She had decorated the room with flowers and candles and brought champagne and orange juice to make mimosas. At 7:00 A.M. she woke up and bathed in a scented tub. After room service left, she dressed in a negligee and sat with a cup of coffee, waiting, leaving the bed turned down and candles glowing in their holders.

Finished tying his shoes, Sam leaned over and kissed her. "It was wonderful."

"But you can't do it again," she said.

"Not right away. But soon."

"Do you think so, Sam?"

"Count on it." He glanced down, then took his beeper out of his pants pocket.

"I was hoping you hadn't brought that," she said. "Is there a problem with Melanie?"

"No, it's Detective Ryabin's portable phone."

"He calls you on Sundays?"

"Not usually."

On her knees in bed, Caitlin nuzzled his ear. "Don't call him back."

Sam dropped the beeper on the nightstand, turned around, and dragged her across the mattress so he could stretch out on top of her. The delicious, solid weight of him. She parted her legs and pulled the tail of his shirt out of his waistband and moved her hands on his back. She wanted him to lose control, to take her, to say poetic things, romantic things, about never loving anyone else, ever. *Oh, my sweet love. I would die for you.*

He kissed her, then propped himself on his elbows. "Caitlin?"

"I know. You have to go."

"I'll call you tomorrow," he said.

His wife would be back tonight. Caitlin said, "You'd better call. And don't forget, like you did on Friday." She quickly kissed his lips.

"I didn't forget," he said, his face growing serious. "I told you what happened."

"Uh-huh. So busy saving Miami from crime you can't take time out for one little phone call." She let him go.

He went over to the dresser for his car keys. He seemed to be thinking of what to say. "I'm going to talk to Frank sometime this week."

Caitlin sat up. "Just call him. You don't have to go to his office to fire him off a case, do you?"

"No, but I prefer to do it in person."

"You won't mention me, will you?"

"Of course not."

Standing now, Caitlin wrapped the sheet around herself. "Is this some kind of male territorial thing?"

"What?" He laughed. "No. Don't worry about it. Your name won't come up."

"But I don't understand why you have to talk to him at all. Mail him a letter. 'Frank, you're fired.' "

Sam looked at her. "Why are you reacting like this?"

She'd nearly forgotten. Samuel J. Hagen hadn't gotten

where he was by being thickheaded. She climbed off the bed, sheet dragging across the carpet. "Because, sweetheart, Frank isn't happy with me at the moment. If he thinks you and I are together, he'll be vile. He'll tell all kinds of lies. He could make it difficult for us."

"Don't worry about him. I told you that already."

"I know. I know." She let out a breath.

"It's going to work out this time. Just be patient."

"I will."

"Caitlin." He held her face. "You have to believe in me a little. In all this time, and all that's happened to both of us, I never stopped loving you."

"Oh, Sam. I could cry."

He kissed her forehead. "I should see what Gene Ryabin wants." He sat on the bed to make the call.

Listening to his side of the conversation, Caitlin couldn't make out what had happened, but his expression was grim. He hung up. "Somebody shot Marty Cass in the back."

"Oh, my God."

"In his apartment. It happened three or four days ago. Nobody saw anything. One of the neighbors called the police when the body started to smell."

Caitlin closed her eyes. She knew who had a reason to kill him. Knees going weak, she sat down on the bed. Sam was still talking, pacing now, the knuckles of one hand tapping across the surface of the dresser.

He said, "Marty Cass was killed by the same person who murdered Charlie Sullivan and George Fonseca. That's only a guess, but the evidence points that way."

Blinking, Caitlin looked at Sam. She could think of no reason, none, why Frank Tolin would have wanted to kill Sullivan or George. Clearly, then, he hadn't done this. No, it hadn't been Frank. She let out a breath. She'd come close to telling Sam about the arson, the blackmail. And then having to explain why she hadn't told him before. *Dear God. Leave it alone. He would never understand.*

Sam came over to her, and she reached up and hugged him around the waist. "Call me?" she said.

"I promise." He bent to kiss her. "I'll see you as soon as I can. Okay?"

"Okay."

At the door he looked back at her. "I love you," he said.

"And this is so you won't forget it." Standing up, Caitlin dropped the sheet. Naked, she did a model's walk across the bedroom, then looked over her shoulder.

Sam glanced into the hall, then whispered, "Don't ever stop doing that." Smiling, he closed the door.

The telephone rang five minutes later.

Caitlin clambered across the bed to pick it up. She hugged the receiver, laughing. "That was fast."

There was a second of silence, before a voice said, "My, my. Fucking the future state attorney in the middle of the day."

Every muscle in her body froze, an instant of reeling incomprehension.

She heard Frank Tolin's low laughter. "What do you think he's going to do, Catie, if he finds out what you did to his son? I'm still willing to take you back, but my patience is about to run dry."

Shaking violently, Caitlin slammed down the phone.

c h a p t e r
thirty

During the week following Dina's return from Tarpon Springs, she barely spoke to Sam. Her anger had lifted, so far as he could tell, replaced with cool indifference. Sam had been sleeping in his study, on a cot that had been stored in the garage. He had thought, before she came back, that he would find an apartment, but Dina told him not to bother. She herself intended to leave Miami as soon as possible. She had already given notice at her accounting firm. The speed and finality of this decision surprised Sam. Maybe she should think about it a little more? No, she had made up her mind.

Sam suggested they put the house up for sale; Dina could take the proceeds. He asked how much she needed in alimony. Did she want him to pay off her car? She listened politely for a minute, then said it didn't matter, to do what he wanted. Her plans for the future seemed hazy. No, she hadn't found a job in Tarpon Springs. She might stay with her father. Perhaps with Nick, it didn't matter. On the subject of Melanie, she simply said, *I can't force her to go.*

She didn't appear depressed. She seemed simply not to care, as if she had resigned herself to what had to come. This was a relief to Sam, who was supervising two major jury trials this week, and therefore less time than usual for his own concerns. He averaged five hours of sleep a night and on Tuesday stayed over at the office. At first he expected Dina to sink into weeping and lethargy, as she had after Matthew's death, but she continued in her unruffled mood. He asked friends for the names of divorce attorneys, but had no time to call any of them.

He hadn't seen Caitlin since Sunday morning, but her face or touch, or the smell or sound of her, had come into his mind, most often when he lay on the narrow cot in his study. They had spoken twice; she said she understood how busy he was, not to worry. She would be driving up to New York in two weeks with her friend Rafael, where she would spend the summer. Sam promised that somehow, before she left, they would have at least one day together.

The lunch crowd in the cafeteria on the ground floor of the Justice Building tended to empty out by two o'clock. Coming down during a break in a trial on Wednesday, Sam had no trouble spotting Dale Finley in the back corner behind a copy of *El Nuevo Herald*. The state attorney's chief investigator had stretched his legs out under the table, and one ankle had a holster wrapped around it. Brown socks, tan polyester pants.

Finley's eyes shifted when Sam sat in the chair across from him, and his white eyebrows lifted, making deep ridges in his forehead.

Sam said, "Got a question for you."

"What's that?"

"One of my witnesses on *Ruffini and Lamont* says you were looking for her at her apartment last week. Caitlin Dorn. Why?"

Finley folded the paper. "Just keeping track of everybody. I am under the assumption, correct me if I'm wrong, that the state likes to know where its witnesses are."

"You're not assigned to this case. So who told you to go looking for Caitlin Dorn?"

Leaning across the table, Finley smiled, and the scar on his chin whitened. "I'll be candid with you, counselor. I think it's highly probable that the witnesses, along with the victim, are going to flip on us. We're going to be left with our thumb up our ass. Now, the aforesaid Ms. Dorn, being the remaining prime witness, is of particular interest."

Sam laughed. "You wanted this case dropped, Finley. You tried to scare Ali Duncan off."

"Well, we don't always get what we want, in the parlance of the old song. My major concern at this juncture is to see that when *State* vs. *Ruffini* crashes, it doesn't fall the wrong way."

"On Eddie Mora."

"Being candid? Yes."

Leaning back in his chair, Sam watched a couple of private defense lawyers kid around with one of the county judges, down to grab some coffee before the afternoon session started. The judge had started out as a public defender, and one of the defense lawyers had been a prosecutor in the felony division. Sam had often wondered what it was like, jumping across the fence like that.

Finley said, "I told Eddie it would be wise to ask the governor to appoint you as the interim state attorney. They have to make a decision by next week, in case you were curious."

Sam looked back at him.

"My motives toward you aren't necessarily hostile," Finley said.

"You don't want a political enemy running for the office that Eddie left vacant," Sam suggested. "It would embarrass the people who want Eddie on Senator Kirkland's ticket. And you want out of Miami, don't you, Dale?"

"Pragmatism is my byword, I guess you'd say."

"What did Eddie have to say about your suggestion?" Sam asked.

"He was noncommittal. That's Eddie."

A cafeteria worker in a brown and orange uniform came by to clear the adjacent table. She put the trays on a cart and wheeled it away.

Sam asked, "What do you know about Marty Cass?"

"Marty Cass got himself shot," Finley said. "Too bad. Looks like somebody's cleaning house over on South Beach."

"Who do you think did it?"

"Don't ask me." Finley picked up his *café con leche*. He took a sip, then said, "Miami Beach police are looking for a reason to tie him to the other two, the model and Fonseca, but I don't see the connection."

"The connection is, they were all shot with the same gun," Sam said. Late yesterday Gene Ryabin had called him with the ballistics report on Marty Cass.

Finley smiled. "True, but the model and Fonseca were involved in that rape case. As for Marty Cass, well, he was just an annoying little shit."

Sam said, "He asked the city manager of Miami Beach to persuade the state attorney not to file the sexual battery case. Did you find that annoying, Dale?"

A laugh scraped out of Finley's throat. "Indeed. But I didn't shoot him. No, a man like Marty Cass, he annoyed a lot of people."

"Klaus Ruffini?"

"In spades, but Klaus wouldn't swat him down for that reason. The first two, maybe. But not Cass, unless Cass threatened him in some way. I can't figure out what it was."

"I heard Klaus Ruffini forced Marty Cass to literally kiss his butt before he made a real estate purchase," Sam said. "You don't happen to know the story on that."

"Ruffini didn't take the deal," Finley said. "And Marty Cass didn't actually have to press his lips to Ruffini's derriere. But the property. I do know about that. Marty Cass owned a small share, your ex-partner Frank Tolin the majority. The Englander Apartments. From which, in fact, a certain Ms. Dorn recently departed. I have an idea you might know where she went to."

When Sam only looked back at him across the table, Finley sighed and finished his coffee. "Well, on that note of mutual cooperation—" He took his folded newspaper and stood up, his weight on his good leg. He spoke softly. "As I said, counselor, my intentions are not hostile—at this point in time. Here's a suggestion. You should start worrying about Vicky Duran."

"Meaning what?"

"She had lunch Monday with Klaus Ruffini's lawyer, Gerald Fine. Not at the Oak Room downtown, you understand. I think it was a couple of burgers in the front seat of Mr. Fine's BMW, parked in a lot by the Orange Bowl. Much as I respect Ms. Duran as a person and an administrator, I don't think she's right for the job of state attorney. You might want to point that out to Eddie before she persuades him otherwise."

"What does she have on him?"

"About what you do," Finley said. "Guesses. Inferences. But she doesn't have photos of herself and Mr. Fine in conference."

Sam turned the salt shaker around and around, then pushed it aside. "What do you want?"

Finley said, "It crossed my mind that Eddie might not make it to Washington. Politics is unpredictable. Senator Kirkland could change his mind. The party might nominate somebody else. Who knows? I hope you'll remember me if you get into office. I might be out of a job someday. A little future consideration of that nature seems like a fair exchange. What do you think, counselor?"

"No deal."

"Well, the offer stays open for a while." Finley tapped Sam's arm with his newspaper. "Don't wait too long."

Riding the escalator upstairs, Sam braced his hands on the black rubber rails, thinking. He didn't need a photograph or even a transcript of the conversation between Victoria Duran, deputy chief of administration of the Dade County state attorney's office, and Gerald D. Fine, Esquire, to see what it was. Beekie knew about the city manager's call to Eddie, Hal Delucca's request that the state attorney ignore a sexual battery to save Miami Beach the embarrassment. She knew that Eddie would have told Hal Delucca to go screw himself, but there had been something there. Eddie had pretended to Sam to be concerned about image: How would it look if the state attorney's office failed to file a sexual battery case against a movie star? That had been bullshit, and Beekie must have known it. One of the defendants had Eddie by the shorts. Ruffini was the obvious choice. Marquis Lamont was in town for a movie; he had no other connection to Miami. The state attorney would have been insane to do any favors for George Fonseca. In any event, Fonseca was now dead. It had to be Ruffini.

Apparently what Beekie wanted from Jerry Fine was information. She wanted to know how his client, Klaus Ruffini, had pushed Eddie Mora, in exchange for which she would do the pushing. As payback, Beekie would dismiss the case against Ruffini when she had Eddie's job. The governor would be likely to go along with whomever Eddie named, and then with positive public exposure in the job for five months, she could be elected on her own.

The woman was delusional. Jerry Fine may have had his own people taking photos; he may have taped the conversation. He'd be a fool not to. A little something for a rainy day, in case the voters of Dade County ever put Victoria Duran in office.

Sam wasn't about to take surveillance photos from Dale Finley. The price was way too high. But the conversation had told him that he had to decide quickly whether to make his own move on Eddie Mora. Ask him how he'd like to have the local TV stations broadcast a story about his wife's trips to Havana, and Eddie's attempt to dump a criminal case against the man who knew about it.

The long, tiled corridor on the fifth floor echoed with voices. People surrounded the entrance to courtroom 5-3, waiting to go back inside to hear Sam finish dissecting a defense witness. Sam spoke to a crime reporter from the *Miami Herald* for a minute, then went over to talk to a couple of the city of Hialeah detectives on the case. Standing in the corridor, which had no windows and seemed to vanish into darkness at either end, and feeling his heart race in irregular patterns, Sam thought suddenly of Caitlin Dorn. Of lying in bed with her on a rainy afternoon, watching the curtains bell softly inward.

Frank Tolin was over by his bookcase pouring himself a scotch, neat. The sun was nearly down, slanting across the buildings, turning the clouds pink over the Atlantic.

Sam had called a while ago, told him he'd be coming around to pick up what was left of the cost deposit on the wrongful death case, if there was anything left. Frank had seemed edgy over the phone. He'd told Sam he would mail the check. Sam said no, he'd come on around.

"Sit down, Sam. My goodness, you look like you're just about to fly out of here. Have a drink. Scotch. Bourbon. Name something." The bones in Frank's face protruded. He'd always been thin, but now he looked gaunt. This is what losing Caitlin had done to him, Sam thought.

"I can't stay," he said. "Mind if I ask what you think I'm going to do? You left the door open, and a minute ago I saw one of your partners looking at me as if I was going to pull out a gun and shoot somebody."

With a soft clank, the stopper went back into the scotch decanter. Frank said, "You've been seeing Caitlin."

"Where'd you hear that?"

"She told me."

Sam sat down in the red leather club chair and put his ankle on the opposite knee. He said, "Dina and I are getting a divorce."

"No. I don't know what to say. You and Dina? She didn't tell me you had problems." Frank sat behind his desk.

"And I'm in love with Caitlin. I don't know if you're aware of that, but that's how it is."

Frank took a sip of his scotch and laughed. "I'll be damned."

"I'd appreciate it if you didn't contact her again."

"What's she told you?"

"That you sent her some letters. You called her till she had to take her phone out. You evicted her from her apartment." Sam spoke in an even voice, keeping it under control.

Frank looked at him awhile. "Well, when you're with a woman that long—eight years, Sam—and she walks out, it hurts. Deeply."

"Did you hit her, Frank?"

He laughed. "Yes. I hit her. My God, she was coming after me with a lamp. In my own living room. What would you have done?"

Sam could feel the pressure building in his neck. He smiled slightly. "I came to pick up a check, then I'll be on my way." It wasn't about the check, he knew now. Caitlin had been right: He wanted to look in Frank Tolin's eyes when he told him he had Caitlin Dorn.

Frank said, "Sure. I made it out after you called." He opened a drawer. "Two thousand dollars. Payable to Mr. and Mrs. Samuel J. Hagen." He extended it across the desk. "There you go."

"I didn't want all of it back. You must have spent something."

"My pleasure to help. By the way, I'll miss seeing Dina. How is she taking this?"

Sam folded the check and put it in his shirt pocket.

"Ironic, isn't it?" Frank said. "We've been talking to each other's women."

Halfway to the door, Sam said, "Don't push it, Frank."

"Wait a second. You need to hear this. We aren't friends—according to you—but still, I owe you something for saving my neck when we were kids." Frank had one of his fancy cowboy boots on the edge of the desk. "I know Caitlin Dorn better than you do, and there's something you need to hear."

Sam laughed. "She said you'd do this."

"Maybe she told you herself, but I doubt it. She lies. She lies constantly. I knew she was having an affair with you three years ago. She denied it. I know about her drug use, and an arrest in New York for grand theft, but she'll deny that, too. You ask her, but she'll deny it."

"Frank, shut the fuck up." Sam headed toward the door.

"Ask her about Matthew."

He looked back.

"Ask her."

Sam kept looking at him. Frank's eyes were sharp and hard as knife points.

"Ask her if she slept with Matthew. Ask her if she didn't take nude photographs of him in her bedroom. I've seen them. Ask her if she wasn't fucking your son up to the day he crashed his motorcycle. You ask her. Don't take my word for it."

In two seconds Sam was around the desk, hauling Frank Tolin out of his big leather chair, Frank kicking, everything hitting the floor. Sam dragged him into the room and rammed a fist into his stomach. When Frank doubled over, Sam jerked him back up and hit him twice in the face. Frank spun into the red leather chair. It crashed over, Frank with it. Sam went after him.

He heard men yelling, then felt himself being pulled backward. Two of Frank's partners had come in. Sam wrenched himself away, stumbled into a table by the sofa, and ended up on the floor.

The two men stood over him. Everybody was breathing

hard. The table leaned crazily on a broken leg. Frank was wiping blood off his mouth.

Sam sat up, holding his right hand.

One of the men said, "I'm going to call the cops."

Frank staggered across the room. "You want her? Take her." He laughed. His lips were swollen, and one eye was closing. "Find out what hell is like."

chapter
thirty-one

Waiting for Caitlin Dorn to arrive at the station, Detective Ryabin stood outside with a cigarette and watched the late afternoon traffic on Washington Avenue. He had obtained Ms. Dorn's address and phone number this morning from Sam Hagen, who had apologized for his bad mood: *not enough goddamn hours in the day.*

Ryabin didn't worry about the time it took to solve an unwitnessed murder. It was more often a matter of pure luck. A friend or lover of the killer would have a fight with him, then come to the police. Or the killer would confess. Freely. People wanted to talk, to explain, to justify. People liked to clear their consciences. More often than not, the killer was sorry. His temper had flared at a bad moment. A weapon had been available: a gun or knife, an iron, a skillet, a baseball bat, his fists.

Many killers were simply careless. They left fingerprints. They left their wallet on the nightstand in their dead lover's bedroom. They left a message on the answering machine announcing their purpose before arriving with a shotgun. The man who had beaten and robbed Anna's mother, for example. He had been stupid. He had traded her watch for crack cocaine. The police failed to catch him because they had not looked in the right crack house in the derelict apartments south of Fifth Street. If the man had been intelligent, he would have gotten away with it. But then, if he had been intelligent, he would have been in some other line of work, not committing robberies to support a drug habit.

The murders of Sullivan, Fonseca, and Cass, on the other hand, were not so easy. The killer was smart and without remorse. He—or perhaps she, not to leave anyone out—had planned well, picking the right time and leaving few clues. No fingerprints, no footprints, no witnesses. No advance warning or public threats. No blood except that of the victim. The crime scene technicians had vacuumed Fonseca's car and Cass's living room for hairs, but there were many different lengths and colors and no way to tell when they had been shed.

Ryabin took a final pull on his cigarette and flicked it into the bushes. In the afternoon, the entrance to the Miami Beach Police Department was in the shade, but the heat was still intense, over ninety and humid. He went inside the lobby, watching through the high, turquoise-tinted windows for Miss Dorn to arrive.

The toxicologist in the medical examiner's lab, as part of his routine blood work on George Fonseca, had done a cholinesterase determination. He had found traces of an organophosphate toxin, probably Parathion, a readily available insecticide. It would have worked even faster if mixed with Malathion. The poison had broken down the acetylcholine in Fonseca's blood.

Ryabin had inquired what that might mean. *Well, you need acetylcholine for your muscles to function.* As the toxicologist explained the symptoms of cholinergic poisoning, Ryabin had imagined Fonseca's death. He had begun to sweat heavily and to salivate. His muscles twitched. He felt nauseated. Severe abdominal cramping followed. His pupils contracted to pinpoints. The blood vessels in his nose ruptured, causing heavy nosebleed. His bladder and bowels let go and he went into convulsions. This may have occurred within five minutes. Shortly thereafter he was paralyzed. His breathing stopped. His heart stopped. The bleeding from the gunshot wounds had speeded the process.

The same poison had been found inside one of the beer bottles on the floor of the car. The bottle had spilled perhaps half its contents. The stuff had an odor, but such a small amount was required, a teaspoon, or so, it would hardly be noticeable in strong beer. Death could occur within minutes, or could take an hour, depending on the quantity ingested. Fonseca had died relatively quickly.

The killer had probably introduced the toxin into the beer in advance and had given Fonseca the appropriate bottle. Perhaps Fonseca had tasted it, refused to drink any more, and the shot into the thigh had been a way of encouraging him to finish. There was no way to tell.

Cass's murder had probably occurred during the day, as most of the neighbors came in or out in the morning or late in the afternoon and had seen nothing. The medical examiner had not been too helpful on this point. Cass had died sometime between noon on Thursday and midnight on Friday.

During that time, then, and probably during daylight hours, Cass had let the killer in. They had discussed real estate, perhaps one of the properties on the computer printout. Unfortunately, no one at Tropic Realty had been able to tell the police when the list had been printed, or for whom.

Being a good host, Cass had poured soft drinks. At some point, the killer got up with the bag which contained the gun. He stood behind Marty Cass, who sat at the table. He fired once. Cass's body slammed forward—the M.E. had found a horizontal bruise—then back, knocking over the chair. As Cass lay on the floor, the killer stabbed his right hand. One blow nicked the second and third fingers near the palm. One nearly severed the thumb. A third pierced the palm, and the last sliced completely through the hand, the carpet, and the padding, and had grazed the wood floor underneath. A post-mortem wound: the blood had oozed out, not pumped. The heart had already stopped.

Because of decomposition, Dr. Corso could not be certain of the width or thickness of the knife. However, it had been very sharp, or the killer had been very powerful. Why had he committed this final act of violence? It had been as gratuitous as the coup de grâce given to Charlie Sullivan as he lay facedown on the beach.

Ryabin had not discussed any of this with reporters from the *Miami Herald* and the TV stations. They had come around asking for details of the three latest homicides in a season plagued by them, but Ryabin had only shrugged and said the cases were still under investigation, and so far, there was no proof that they were linked.

Since Marty Cass's death, Ryabin had interviewed more than twenty people; Nestor Lopez, his partner, a like number. Many were the same ones they had spoken to regarding the deaths of Charlie Sullivan and George Fonseca.

Lopez had gone back to the condominium at different times of day. There were twelve units in the two-story Delancy, six up, six down. He talked to all the neighbors who had been in town during the time in question. As the murder had occurred several days previously, their memories had faded. Contradictory statements were made, and a man even reported having seen Cass on Saturday. One woman said she had heard a fight on Friday morning, but her husband reminded her it had occurred in some other apartment. Many of the people in the building didn't know who Marty Cass was. The most useful piece of information came from an elderly woman across the street who had come out of her apartment to get the newspaper. She had seen a man with black hair going into the Delancy at about eight o'clock on Saturday morning. Not so young, but not old. She remembered because he had been wearing cowboy boots, and wasn't that stupid, this time of year?

Yesterday morning, Eugene Ryabin had driven downtown to visit Frank Tolin.

Tolin's spacious office was tastefully decorated with antiques. Ryabin had admired them for a moment, then sat in a red leather chair with a high back. He remarked that he and Tolin had last seen each other at Pier Park, the scene of Charlie Sullivan's death.

"Did you know him?" Ryabin asked.

Frank Tolin said, "No, I just came along with Caitlin. She was following her friend Rafael, who was a boyfriend of Sullivan's. Or ex-boyfriend." Tolin spoke slowly, perhaps because his lower lip was split. A large purpling bruise darkened the left side of his face, and a bandage angled upward at the corner of his eye.

"Sullivan was also sleeping with Marty Cass's wife, Uta Ernst," Ryabin commented.

"Yeah. Sullivan went both ways." The mustache over the injured mouth moved in what might have been a smile. "It's hard to keep up with that crowd. They all fuck each other, Detective. Pardon my French."

"Pardon the question, but are you including Miss Dorn?"

"I don't know what the hell Miss Dorn did. Or does. We're not together anymore."

Ryabin knew that, because Sam Hagen had told him. He said, "Is that so?"

Frank Tolin said, "I've got some clients coming at ten o'clock. You said you wanted to ask me about Marty Cass?"

In response to Ryabin's questions, Tolin explained that he had met Marty Cass through mutual friends, and that they had done some deals together, but there was only one property left, the Englander Apartments. There was a buyer for the place, some Middle Easterners, but now the sale might be delayed because Cass's share, ten percent, would have to go through probate. Too bad about Marty, but it had been an inconvenient time for him to get himself killed.

As he talked Tolin played with a stainless steel letter opener, bouncing the point of it on the desk, making a musical dinging noise. He admitted having gone to see Cass on Saturday morning. He had knocked, but there hadn't been any answer, and he didn't go in.

"Why did you want to talk to him?" Ryabin asked.

"It was about the property. I hadn't heard anything in a few days, and I wanted to see how the sale was going." Tolin set the letter opener aside.

"Were you on good terms with him?"

"Sure. We had a pretty good working relationship. We didn't socialize, but we got along."

"Why did Cass have only ten percent of the Englander Apartments?"

"Where'd you hear about that?"

"I saw it in documents I took from his file cabinet," Ryabin explained.

"Well, he had ten because it was my money that went into it, but he managed the building. I didn't want to pay him a fee every month, so I said, here, take ten percent, you can have the headaches, not me." Tolin gestured toward his office. "I've got a law practice to run."

Ryabin asked, "Did you know that my wife sold you the building?"

"No kidding. I thought a woman named Rivka owned it. No, wait. She passed away. Then what? Your wife bought it from her?"

"No. Rivka was my sister-in-law."

"My condolences, Detective."

Ryabin leaned forward in the chair, frowning. "Excuse me, but what happened to your face?"

One of Frank Tolin's hands went automatically to his cheekbone. "A disagreement with a client. It's dangerous being a lawyer these days."

"Did you know Charlie Sullivan, the model?" Ryabin waited for an answer.

Tolin shook his head, frowning slightly at the change of direction. "Not personally. Why?"

"And George Fonseca? Someone mentioned that you knew him." This was pure conjecture, but Ryabin wanted to see what Tolin would say.

"Someone? The policeman's best friend. Someone is full of shit, Detective. I never met George Fonseca. Nor can I help you figure out why he and Charlie Sullivan were shot to death. And in case you planned to ask if I own a gun, the answer's yes. A thirty-eight revolver. Not what you're looking for. Sorry about that." His black eyebrows arched. " 'Someone' must have told me."

"Where do you live, Mr. Tolin? Not on Miami Beach."

"No. Coconut Grove. I've got a condo."

Ryabin nodded. "Do you know of anyone who might have wanted to harm Marty Cass?"

"Not really. You sure it wasn't a robbery?"

"We don't think so," Ryabin said. "Could you explain to me why Marty Cass's personal files were out of order? As if someone had been looking through them in a hurry?"

Tolin said, "No, I can't."

"You said you were at his apartment on Saturday morning."

"And I said I didn't go in."

"But we have a statement from a person across the street who says you did."

"Good try, Detective." Tolin made another of his painful smiles. Ryabin reminded himself that Frank Tolin was a trial attorney, skilled in tactics used on witnesses.

Ryabin said, "Eight o'clock on Saturday morning. On South Beach everyone is asleep. But you drove all the way from Coconut Grove to see him. If you didn't know Marty Cass so well, why did you think he would be up?"

"I took a chance."

"You didn't call him first?"

"No, I figured he'd be there. And he was, wasn't he? But in no shape to answer the door." Tolin stood up. "Sorry to cut this short, but I've got people coming in. Maybe we can get back together sometime next week."

From the chair Ryabin asked, "What was your schedule last Thursday and Friday?"

"Give me a break." Chuckling, Tolin walked around his desk. "I was in court."

A black leather desk diary occupied a spot next to the telephone. Ryabin went over and picked it up.

"What the hell are you doing?"

He flipped backward a week. Thursday afternoon, clients from two to four o'clock. Friday morning, a trial starting at nine. Friday afternoon—

Tolin snatched the book away and slammed it back on his desk. "Why don't you leave before I file a complaint with Chief Mazik, whom I happen to know personally." Tolin crossed the room. He tilted slightly to the left, as though protecting cracked ribs.

At the door to his office he said, "Good luck, Detective. I hope you find the guy. You can take this as gospel: It wasn't me."

Now, standing in the lobby at police headquarters, Gene Ryabin glanced at the big clock over the elevators. 6:20 P.M. Miss Dorn was nearly half an hour late.

Yesterday afternoon—for the fifth time—he had gone by Klaus Ruffini's house on the bay side of the island, and for the fifth time Ruffini wouldn't let him through the gate. This morning his lawyer, Gerald Fine, had complained to the chief about harassment.

At noon today Nestor Lopez had noticed the bodyguard, Franco, filling up Ruffini's red Cadillac convertible at a gas station on Fifth Street. He blocked the car with his unmarked sedan and threatened him with arrest for obstruction of justice if he refused to cooperate with a murder investigation. Where had Franco been at 10:00 A.M. on Friday, the precise time of Marty Cass's death? Having breakfast with Klaus and a few of his friends, including a producer for Miramax Films. Call him up and ask him. What about later in the day? Or the preceding afternoon? Franco had no answer for that.

Now Ryabin would ask questions of Caitlin Dorn. Often the girlfriend knew things. No longer a girlfriend. Ryabin assumed that Sam Hagen's reappearance had ended that relationship. And now Sam and his wife had separated. What a drama this had become.

Dina, who had lost both son and husband, would seek peace in her childhood home. And Sam and Caitlin . . . Ryabin worried about them. Such love affairs often turned into tragedies. No one could help them now. Ryabin could only watch with the detachment of a man in the autumn of his life, safely beyond reckless passion. His hand went to his shirt pocket, absently caressing his pack of cigarettes. There were five remaining. He decided to have one after his interview with Miss Dorn.

He paced for a while in the lobby, then looked again at the clock. 6:33. Caitlin Dorn wasn't going to show up.

c h a p t e r
thirty-two

When Sam let her in, Caitlin slid her hands up the lapels of his jacket and locked her arms around his neck. She stood on tiptoes to whisper in his ear. "You don't know how much I want you right now. Only four days and it seems like a month." She knew he could smell the perfume she had touched to her skin in the elevator. Her dress was pale green and gauzy, with a low neckline and a woven belt.

Sam's kiss was brief, but then he held her tightly. She could feel the strength in his arms, holding her as though it really had been a month since they'd seen each other. Or as though it would be a year till the next time. Over his shoulder she noticed the room: terribly anonymous, she thought. But he had said to come to the Holiday Inn downtown, so she hadn't expected a suite with a marble bathroom.

When he let her go, Caitlin walked to the dresser to put down her bag. She withdrew a box of crackers, some cheese, a bottle of red wine. "I thought this would be good. It's nearly dinnertime. And look. More candles." They filled her hands, six colored-glass holders.

He stood at the end of the double bed, the bed still tightly made up, and Sam in his dark suit. She put the candles back on the dresser. "What's wrong?"

"We need to talk, Caitlin. Sorry it has to be here." His tone was so neutral she couldn't read the emotion under-

neath. "Not much of a room, is it? I couldn't think of anything else. Neither one of us has our own place to go to."

"No, it's all right." Then she noticed his right hand.
He was wearing a wrist brace and a bandage over his
knuckles. "Sam! What have you done to yourself?" She
went to see.

He turned his hand over, looking at it, the thick palm
and fingers. "I got this at Frank Tolin's office. It hurts
like hell." He made a short laugh. "I'm too old to be
brawling."

"Why did you hit him?" She touched his injured hand.
"What did Frank say to you? Something horrible, no
doubt. I told you he would."

Sam took so long in answering that she knew what
he was going to say before the words came out of his
mouth. At the core of her body she felt a sudden cold-
ness. The light filtering through the curtains seemed to
fade.

"You said he would lie to me. I told myself that's what
it was. A lie. A bomb he threw at me to even up the score,
so why not just ignore it?" Sam exhaled. "I tried to,
Caitlin."

There were two chairs at the small table by the windows. He sat in one of them and motioned for her to have
a seat, but she remained standing. He casually crossed
his legs.

"Frank said you slept with Matthew."

When Caitlin didn't reply, Sam said, "I've been a
trial lawyer for almost twenty years. I thought I was better
at picking up on things. You told me he wasn't gay.
How were you so sure about that? You said you'd
taken nude pictures, and it went right over my head.
In those portraits you showed me, he was wearing nothing but a pair of jeans. I didn't pay any special attention
at the time. But the way he looked into the lens—at
you—"

Caitlin grabbed the votive candles off the dresser and
threw them back into her bag, heard the crack of breaking
glass. Pieces flew out onto the dresser. "I'm not a defendant in one of your damned trials. I'm not on the stand.
How could you do this? To ask me to come *here*. Not
telling me it was for *this*."

She was reaching for the doorknob when he caught up and swung her around. She gasped and raised an arm over her face.

"Caitlin, stop. I'm not going to hit you." His left hand tightened on her elbow. "You're going to tell me what happened."

"Oh, God, Sam. Could it possibly make a difference?"

He put her on the end of the double bed, standing over her. "I wish I'd done what you told me to. Stay the hell away from Frank. Remain blissfully ignorant. But I didn't. I'm trying to be fair, to understand."

"No. Frank has poisoned us." She looked up at Sam. "He knows you so well, and he knew what would hurt you most."

"And what were you thinking of, Caitlin, when you slept with my son? Did you realize that he knew about us? He did. His mother told him. Did you and Matthew talk about it?"

She shook her head. "He didn't tell me he knew about us."

"So what was it?" Sam leaned against the dresser. "He was good looking. Young. But you're still young, aren't you? A beautiful woman. When I was a kid, I had a thing going with a woman who lived down the road. I used to take care of the orange trees in her backyard. She started coming outside in her swimsuit, getting a suntan, and one day she asked if I'd like to come in for a cold drink." He laughed. "But she hadn't been sleeping with my father."

"For God's sake." Caitlin turned away.

"When you were with Matthew, was it me you wanted? Or maybe you were still so angry at me for ending our affair that you wanted to get even."

"How simple. Yes, maybe that's it."

"Tell me what it was, Caitlin." A piece of blue glass from one of the broken votive candles lay on the dresser. Sam picked it up. "Was it Matthew's idea? At his age, I was a spec five in the army. I'd worked in my groves since I was twelve years old. I had to earn every dollar I spent. Matthew had everything he wanted, and he couldn't care less about it. The fact that you and I had been together wouldn't have meant a damn thing."

Sam tossed the glass into her canvas bag. "No. Maybe it did. What better way to make a point than to screw the woman I used to sleep with."

"Stop it!" She stood up from the end of the bed and pushed past him. "What did you tell me, Sam? 'I love you, Caitlin. Be patient. It will all work out this time, Caitlin. I *promise*.' "

"I didn't know about this!" he said. "You deliberately withheld the truth."

She laughed. "And you would have been so understanding, wouldn't you?"

He closed on her, furious. "My son—the only son I will ever have—is dead. He drank. He took drugs. He got on his motorcycle—after he'd had six or eight shooters at a bar—and he might as well have blown his brains out. So when I ask you—you, Caitlin, who were sleeping with him and presumably knew his state of mind—when I ask you what the hell he was doing, then I expect to get an answer."

Sam gripped the back of a chair, then winced and pulled his right hand away. He held it gingerly with the left and cursed under his breath.

The room fell silent, only the air conditioner buzzing under the window. Caitlin said, "You think he wanted to die."

"I don't know what he wanted," Sam said.

"It was an accident."

"That's what I used to tell his mother. Nothing caused it, Dina. Just accept it and buck up, honey. Nothing you can do. It's not your fault."

Caitlin sat down in the other chair, still trembling a little. "You know something? You're not what I thought, either. Well. I guess we all see what we want to see."

"I guess we do."

Sam sat on the corner of the bed with his forearms on his knees. His suit coat pulled on his shoulders. His shoes were heavy wing tips with worn-down heels. She smiled slightly and looked away. She had mended her bra strap with the wrong color thread in the rush to get here. They might as well be sitting naked with the curtains pulled open all the way. Candlelight had been prettier.

She looked back at Sam. "I met Matthew about a year and a half ago. I don't remember the first time we met because he probably didn't impress me as being different from any other young male model. He was handsome, but so many of them are. He called himself Stavros. Just that. Stavros. I didn't know who he was. Then he asked me to do his composite. He said he'd heard about my work, and that his real name was Matthew Hagen. He said he was from Miami, and his father was a big deal at the state attorney's office. I almost told him I was too busy, find somebody else to take his pictures. And besides that, he was as arrogant as hell. But I needed the money, so I did it. And I guess I was curious about him, too. Sam Hagen's son.

"We saw each other in the business. He was on a few shoots I did. Or I'd see him by accident on the street. That sort of thing. We got to know each other. I didn't think of him sexually. I'd seen so many beautiful young men, after a while they all run together. Anyway, he was too young. And he was your son. That put him off limits.

"What surprised me at the time—but now I understand it—he was interested in me. Nothing heavy, just flirtation. He'd kid around, and that was it. We'd talk about whatever would come up. I'd been in the fashion industry for a long time, and I gave him some advice. I lent him money. He usually paid me back. I knew he was into cocaine, but I wouldn't let him have it around my place. Later on I found out how bad it was and that he was shooting up, too. He said he didn't do it a lot. He could control it.

"What I always sensed about Matthew was his anger. Sometimes I'd feel it was directed at me. Now I can see that it probably was. One night he came to my apartment, drunk, and so angry he was shaking. He wouldn't say much. Then he kissed me. I pushed him away. He was very strong, and he held me down on the sofa and it wasn't gentle, but I didn't want to scream and have everyone come running. And for a minute I was thinking about you, and it was so awful. I said, 'Matthew, please.

Please don't.' He stopped. Just like that. He got up and
left. A couple of days later he came back to apologize.
Now I understand. He'd known about you and me all
along. He hated me. Hated and desired me. And, yes, it
was crazy. It was all tied up with you and his mother and
me and what he thought was the wrong I had done to all
of you.

"Even with that, we became friends. It wasn't sex. Or
maybe it was, in some way, and maybe we both knew it,
but there was a line there, and we didn't cross it.

"Matthew had a hard time making it as a model. He was
undisciplined and impatient. I tried to help. I made him a
new composite for free, and he looked terrific. He got
some work, but it was so hard, finding his way in a business where, really, nobody looks beyond the surface. He
was on and off drugs, he was drinking. He got a few good
jobs. That was when he bought his motorcycle. He was
beginning to be known. People were starting to ask for
Stavros. Then I didn't see him for a while. Someone told
me he was involved with Sullivan. I was surprised, and
yet I wasn't. You might want to blame Sullivan for what
happened to Matthew, but you can't, not completely. We
all share complicity in what happens to us. Oh, yes, Sullivan had his despicable moments, but he did care
for Matthew, as much as Sullivan could have cared for
anyone.

"I don't know how it happened. I never asked. As I
told you, it was brief. I heard through someone else
that they'd argued. Then Matthew came to my apartment to pick up some prints I'd made for him. He
was having trouble again. He had no money left. I
fixed him a sandwich because he hadn't eaten all day
and he was hungry. We had some wine and we talked.
He said he wanted to give up. He didn't know what to
do. Sullivan had told him he'd never make it. 'Stavros,
you're a pathetic little faggot, an irresponsible child.'
That's what he said. Matthew couldn't shrug it off because there was enough truth to cut deeply. He was so
ashamed. He started to cry. My God, like everything in
him had been smashed and it would never be put right
again.

"Yes, I slept with him. I did it because he needed

me, and he was yours, and I loved him because he was part of you, and because of who he was, himself. Matthew. I told him to stay with me awhile. He did, for nearly two weeks. That's when I took the photographs. Just before he died.

"I've never met a man who was so sweet, so innocent, even with everything that had happened to him. He said he'd marry me when he grew up. Isn't that funny? We both laughed. Then he said no, maybe he'd just be my devoted friend forever. We talked about you. He wanted so much to please you. To have your respect, and for you to know how much he loved you. But he never mentioned you and me, Sam. That would have been cruel, and he wasn't that way.

"You want me to tell you he was a slacker and a failure, that he would have died no matter what. That you didn't lose much. Is that what you want? You said he was lost years ago. No. He was right there all the time. You're the one who was lost.

"He didn't choose to die. He didn't die because of me or Sullivan or you or his mother or because he had failed you or himself. He died because he was going too fast on his motorcycle. He was happy, Sam. He would have been all right. That's what you saw in the portraits. That's what I wanted you to know, and why I showed them to you. He was happy."

Caitlin sat for a while, pulling at the strings tied in a decorative knot at the end of her belt. She listened to traffic noises on the street.

Sam had gotten up as she spoke, and now he was leaning against the wall with his arms crossed.

Finally he looked at her. His eyes seemed hollow, as though he might fall through them and disappear.

She said, "I'll be leaving in a week or so. Rafael's going to help me drive."

"What will you do?" Sam asked.

"Something will turn up." Caitlin crossed the room for her bag. "You know, it's odd. I have nothing left except one old camera and a car with a hundred thousand miles on it, but for the first time in years, I know I'm going to be okay."

"That's good." He nodded.

"What about you, Sam?"

He hadn't moved from where he leaned against the wall.

"Me?" He smiled. "I'll be okay, too."

c h a p t e r
thirty-three

Eddie Mora wasn't looking at the photos anymore. He was gazing the length of his office and tapping his tented fingers on his chin. His hands jerked as though brain and muscles had disconnected.

There was a line of fifteen photographs on Eddie's desk, clearly showing the state attorney's deputy chief of administration parked outside the Orange Bowl in the middle of the day with a criminal lawyer who was currently representing a defendant in a highly public sexual battery prosecution. Each picture had the date and time in the lower right-hand corner.

Sam had explained the situation.

Eddie finally spoke. "Well. That's it then." He glanced down as if a dog had chosen his desk for a place to squat. "Are these duplicates?"

"Keep them," Sam said. "I have my own set." Dale Finley had given him doubles but had kept the negatives. Eddie had asked where the hell the photos had come from, but Sam had declined to say. One day there would be a reckoning for this. One day, when Sam was sitting behind the state attorney's sleek walnut desk, he would pick up the phone and it would be Dale Finley.

Eddie scooped the photos into a pile, opened a drawer, and dropped them inside.

Sam said, "I resent being used, Eddie. So call it even, if it makes you feel better."

An artery beat in Eddie's temple. "Nobody expected

the girl to go through with it. This case was going to wash out."

"But it didn't," Sam said. "You sent Dale Finley to scare her off."

He made a short laugh. "No, that was his idea."

"An investigator doing his own thing can be a liability," Sam said. "Are you going to take him to Washington? Assuming you make it to Washington."

"No, he's all yours now. You tell yourself you won't use him, but you will. Finley can be a useful guy to have around. Just don't turn your back on him."

"What about Vicky Duran?"

Eddie's hands moved outward in an expansive shrug. "Yes, what about Vicky? You decide, Sam. Soon as I talk to the governor, this will be your job, and Vicky will be your problem."

Sam said, "She just wrote her own resignation letter, getting into bed with Jerry Fine."

"Here's some advice. Try to arrange a job for her first. Something with the county, say. A decent salary." Eddie suddenly grabbed a heavy coffee mug, the closest object, and hurled it across his office. The handle broke on the edge of a bookcase and the mug bounced to the carpet and rolled unevenly to a stop.

Sam looked back at Eddie, who was straightening his cuffs.

Eddie's smile was more of a twitch. "You know, I didn't mind coming down here to live, but Amalia never liked Miami. The muggy weather, the lack of culture, the insane political landscape. You might not believe this, but what I did was for her. She begged me to find a job somewhere else."

"No, Eddie. I don't believe it, but it sounds very noble of you." Sam added, "I'm curious about something. Ruffini never told the press about Amalia's trips to Cuba, even after you allowed the case to proceed against him. Why?"

Eddie weighed whether to answer, then said, "Because it was too late. I didn't file the case—you did. I couldn't very well dismiss it. So what would he gain by opening his mouth about my wife? He's here on a damn tourist visa. He knew that once I got to Washington, I could have his ass on a plate. So the prosecution had to roll on—unless he could help Victoria Duran take over as state attorney. She would have repaid him by scuttling the case somehow. He and his lawyer were counting on that."

Sam said, "If the police link Ruffini to any of these murders, I'll have to bring your name up. Don't even think about asking me to keep you out of it."

"Ruffini wouldn't have had them killed," Eddie said, looking miffed. "Granted, he's better off with Sullivan and Fonseca dead, but it's easier to deal with Miss Duncan. And I don't mean shoot her. I mean bribe her. Give her what she wants. Klaus Ruffini would rather pay her than go through a trial." Eddie made a sly smile. "He's afraid of you, Sam. He doesn't want to face you in court."

Suddenly eager to get out of there, Sam stood up. "You've got some balls, Eddie. How long did you think you could keep the media from finding out what Klaus Ruffini already knew?"

"Long enough for Senator Kirkland to decide whether it mattered," Eddie said. "We discussed it last week, when Amalia and I flew up to Michigan to see him. His advisors said not to worry. The average voter doesn't care about Cuba. He doesn't care that the vice presidential candidate's sister-in-law is investing in Cuba. Claudia's a citizen of Spain; she can do what she wants to. It's good politics, in fact, to stand up to the Miami exile community. The embargo should have been lifted years ago. Fidel Castro would have been gone as soon as the first McDonald's opened its doors in Havana."

Sam said, "Sorry to point this out, Eddie, but Amalia broke U.S. law going there."

"You prove she went. Then we'll talk."

At the door Sam turned around, laughing softly. "Jesus. A small thing. That's what you told me. Such a small thing. It hardly seemed worth the trouble to hide it."

"You'll see, Sam, how much you have to hide when you're in this office. People are absolutely irrational, what they think is important and what isn't."

"Doesn't it bother you?"

"Not really. You get used to it."

Sam took another look around the office. "I'd appreciate

your calling the governor as soon as possible. This afternoon. There are some changes I want to get started on."

Eddie's round face seemed to puff with rage. "Get the fuck out."

Almost a year had gone by since Sam Hagen had been inside the Club Deuce with Gene Ryabin, but it was just as dim, with a carefully maintained ambiance of dusty ceiling fans and neon beer signs. It had the same cracked linoleum squares on the floor and probably the same drink coasters under the short leg of the pool table. Still no locks on the bathroom doors. The staff wanted everybody to know they might look in and see who was doing what.

Gene Ryabin came in about six-thirty, and Sam motioned to him. The crowd was thin on Mondays.

Ryabin brought his beer to the wall-mounted varnished-plywood bar under the front window. He was grinning, showing the gap in his teeth. "For you, my friend, a token. What is a title? Pah. They respect more a visible sign of your power." He pulled from his coat pocket a miniature guillotine, which he set on the bar.

Sam smiled around the lip of the beer bottle at his mouth.

Ryabin stuck a cigarette in a hole under the blade, then neatly chopped off the filter. It rolled to the floor. "Now. Give me your finger."

"What good is a state attorney with a missing digit?"

"Trust me." Ryabin spread a hand on his chest. "A magic guillotine. Not one drop of blood if you are truly worthy."

"That's what I'm afraid of." Laughing, Sam extended his left hand as Ryabin raised the tiny blade in its tracks. "If this wasn't my third beer already, I'd never let you do this, Gene." The blade swept downward, clicked, and seemed to pass through Sam's index finger. "Not bad."

Ryabin was pleased. He showed Sam how the blade pivoted into the frame. "I like to show this in the men's room at the station." He slid the toy across the bar, then raised his beer bottle, a salute. *"Nastrovye."*

"Maybe I'll use it on Beekie Duran," Sam said. "But her dick might not fit through this little hole here."

Ryabin felt inside his coat. "I have also the initial toxicology report on George Fonseca, along with the latest narratives of our investigation." He handed the folded pages to Sam.

Sam turned directly to the report from the Metro-Dade toxicologist. Not a full report; that would take a few more weeks. Already, however, the lab had found a cholinesterase inhibitor in Fonseca's blood. Common name, Parathion. Traces of it had been found in a beer bottle on the floor of the Mustang. A nasty way to die, Sam thought, remembering the vomit and excrement on Fonseca's body.

"Nastrovye," he said and lifted his bottle of Heineken.

Ryabin grinned down at Sam's right hand. "A strange coincidence I'm seeing here. Wednesday I went to interview Frank Tolin at his office, and his lip is split and his face is bruised."

"Too bad," Sam said.

Ryabin asked, "What was it about?"

Sam took another swallow of beer before answering. "Caitlin Dorn. I went to close the wrongful death case; then we had a discussion about Caitlin."

When Sam didn't elaborate, Ryabin nodded toward the papers on the bar. "My notes from the interview are in there, too. Tolin says he was friendly with Marty Cass, but I don't think so. When you were working with Tolin, what was your impression?"

"I didn't see a problem," Sam said, "but that was four years ago." He sat and read the police reports while Ryabin went to get another beer and watch a white-haired woman shoot pool with a leather boy, beating him handily.

Ryabin pulled out his stool and sat back down. He was short and had to step on the bottom rung to do it gracefully. "What would Miss Dorn have to say about Frank Tolin and Marty Cass, if I asked her?"

"I have no idea."

"She was supposed to come to the station last week, but she didn't show up. I left messages, but she doesn't call."

At the pool table, the balls rolled and clicked and dropped neatly into the correct pockets. The white-haired woman's next opponent was a tourist from Scotland who couldn't stop laughing. Probably high on something, Sam thought.

He looked back at Ryabin, "I haven't seen Caitlin since last Thursday."

"She doesn't return your calls, either?"

"I haven't called."

Ryabin was playing with a cigarette, but he didn't light it. "Does this mean that I can't ask you to find out from her about Frank Tolin and Marty Cass?"

"I'll let you do it." Sam finished his beer. "When you talk to her, Gene, ask where Ali Duncan is. I think we may have a problem. Her mother says she doesn't know where Ali went, but I have my doubts. I don't know if she's dead or in hiding, or if Klaus came up with the right numbers."

"Did you tell Eddie Mora?" Ryabin asked.

"Not till after the announcement hits the paper tomorrow about my appointment. Maybe I can bring her back, maybe not. Eddie was right, Gene. The case is a loser. The son of a bitch was right."

c h a p t e r
thirty-four

'm sorry for not getting back in touch with you." Caitlin
Dorn escorted Ryabin into the foyer. "I've been so busy
getting ready to leave."

He followed her long strides and swirling cotton skirt
down a narrow, tiled hallway, through a living room remi-
niscent of an Italian country villa, then to a patio overlooking the intracoastal. Across the narrow stretch of
water, luxury hotels lined the northern end of Miami
Beach.

The house, she explained, belonged to a friend of hers,
Paula DeMarco, who owned a gallery on Lincoln Road.
Ms. DeMarco had already gone back to New York, but
her relatives resided here year-round, none of them home
at present.

There was a conversation area in the shade. A fountain
gurgled into a fern-draped swimming pool, and marble
sculptures of headless torsos guarded the access to the
dock, where a mildewed sailboat was tied. While Caitlin
Dorn poured them glasses of peach-flavored iced tea,
Ryabin looked around for a place to hang his jacket, finally folding it over the arm of his chair, a monstrous
painted wood thing resembling a child's crayon drawing
of a chair. The entire house, he had noticed on the way
through it, was jammed with such oddities. Beside the
steps, tiled in pieces of broken dishes, a black Doberman
lifted its lip at Ryabin and a low growl rumbled in its
throat. Caitlin told the dog to be quiet.

"When do you go to New York?" Ryabin asked. He smiled at her over his glass.

"This weekend, I hope." She sat in a matching chair and crossed her legs. Such long, slender legs. "I have some jobs to finish."

"Taking more pictures of beautiful young people. Such bother."

She laughed. "No, tonight I'm shooting a birthday party. A twenty-year-old boy. It's not what I like to do, but— well, Mom and Dad are loaded. She told me they've hired a live rock band."

"For my son's birthday I sent a card." Ryabin noticed that between the chairs was a red metal ashtray that looked like an open mouth. He reached for his pack of cigarettes, then returned them to his pocket. He had promised to smoke ten a day, no more, then the next month, eight. Already he was regretting this, but he had never broken a promise to Anna.

"Miss Dorn, do you know where Ali Duncan is? Sam Hagen says he can't find her."

Caitlin Dorn's mouth fell open a little. "My God. I haven't heard from her either. So that's it. She's gone. About a week ago she told me that Tereza Ruffini had offered her a job modeling for a French magazine. I think she must have taken it."

Ryabin put his glass of tea on the flat yellow arm of the chair. "I am guessing from what you tell me that Ali Duncan won't be back to testify against Tereza's husband."

"Oh, Ali." Caitlin Dorn pulled up a knee and rested her elbow on it. Then she laughed. "She made them pay her. I wonder how much? No, she won't be back, not till her money runs out, and if she's smart, that won't be for a long time. Poor Sam. All that effort for nothing." She reached for her glass, took a sip, then said, "I heard on the news last night that he's been appointed interim state attorney. So I guess he isn't 'poor Sam' after all. Next time you see him, say I sent my congratulations."

For a few seconds her green eyes seemed to gaze vacantly at the patio, then she fixed them on Ryabin. "You said you had some questions about Marty Cass."

He inquired what she knew about him, and she repeated essentially the same facts he himself had already uncovered in his investigation several weeks ago for Sam Hagen. Then he asked her if she knew Klaus Ruffini.

"Not well. I've met him a few times."

"People say that he and Marty Cass had recently a disagreement, a falling out."

"Over the Grand Caribe Resort," she said. "Marty wanted more control, and Klaus thought he was incompetent, which, well, he was. The Grand Caribe was in financial trouble after Klaus was arrested. The city didn't grant the zoning permits. Marty threatened to go to the backers and persuade them to pull out entirely unless Klaus paid him off. Everyone thinks the Grand Caribe was Klaus's, but it wasn't. He used his name, and he has a lot of rich friends. He pulled them together. That's his talent. The Ruffini money is really his wife's, Tereza's. She has the say-so."

"How do you know this?"

"Well, I pick up a lot, just being around." She combed her hair back from her face with her fingers. A beautiful woman, such shiny blond hair.

Ryabin took a cigarette out of the pack. "Miss Dorn—may I call you Caitlin?"

"Of course."

"Forgive such a personal question, but, did you ever have a sexual relationship with Charlie Sullivan?"

She laughed. "Are you serious?"

"He slept with women, too. He never suggested . . . ?"

"All right, he suggested. I told him no."

"Your boyfriend at the time—Frank Tolin?—he didn't mind?"

"Yes, but he got over it." She shook her head, smiling as if the man beside her could be shocked by such things. "Look, Detective. I was a model. I'm used to men coming on to me. It doesn't mean anything. Why on earth did you ask me about Sullivan?"

Ryabin made a noncommittal noise and drew his cigarette back and forth between his fingers.

"Are you going to smoke that?"

"I promised my wife I would cut down."

"I'll help you," she said. She took the cigarette then let him light it for her. "I've quit, too." She inhaled deeply.

Ryabin took another and lit it for himself. "Now I won't be able to have one after lunch."

"Yes, you will. Smoke the one you've scheduled for after dinner. That's what I used to do," she said. "But then I'd advance the one from after breakfast the next day. I think I got something like a thousand cigarettes ahead of myself."

She tapped her cigarette into the red-lipped ashtray.

"Caitlin, you're not with Frank Tolin anymore. Correct?" Her expression said she knew that he already had the answer to that. Ryabin said, "Does he have a cocaine habit? Was that a problem between you?"

She exhaled smoke. "You're awfully interested in my relationships."

"It's a professional interest." Ryabin smiled. He had been told that women found the space between his front teeth endearing. "I heard from I don't remember who that George Fonseca sold him drugs."

"Sometimes," she said slowly, perhaps wondering if this police detective was going to accuse her of a narcotics violation. Then she made a short laugh. "More than sometimes."

"Maybe you can help me." Ryabin sat forward in the bizarre wooden chair. "Last week I talked to Frank Tolin. I asked him to tell me about Marty Cass. What kind of man was he, and so on. Tolin said Cass couldn't be trusted. They'd had problems. I asked him what he meant, but then, suddenly, he didn't want to talk about it."

Her eyes told him he had hit a vein of truth.

Ryabin furrowed his brow. "He mentioned some property they owned together."

"You don't think Frank shot Marty Cass."

"Why not?" She stared at him, and Ryabin decided to embroider the truth. "What if I told you that Frank has no alibi for the time of Martin Cass's death?" He paused, then added, "And that we have a witness who saw a man in cowboy boots go into his apartment." Ryabin watched for a reaction. "What would you say?"

She seemed frozen into the chair. Then she took a breath. "Marty was trying to extort money from Frank. You're right, it was about the apartment building I used to live in, the Englander. Four years ago Frank wanted to buy it. The owner didn't want to sell at the right price, so Marty arranged for a fire. It was supposed to be a small one, but something went wrong, and the owner died. I understand she was your wife's sister."

"Rivka Levitsky."

"Yes. I didn't know till Frank told me. I'm so sorry."

"And Frank's part in it?"

"Nothing, except being involved with Marty. After the sale went through, Marty told him what had happened. Then about three weeks ago Marty came to Frank's condo and demanded money. He said he'd tell everyone that Frank had planned it, unless Frank gave him a hundred thousand dollars."

"Did Frank ever pay him?"

"I doubt that he would, but I can't say. That was the only time we talked about it."

Ryabin watched a plastic penguin rotate across the pool, driven by a gust of air. "Frank told you all of this?"

"Yes, after Marty left." She sat silently for a while. "No, I didn't hear the conversation. So Frank could have lied to me. With Frank, I believed what I wanted to believe. I spent eight years making excuses for him. And for myself, for not having the guts to leave him."

"What do you think, Caitlin? You know him better than anybody. Is he capable of pulling a trigger? Shooting someone in the back?"

She took a long time to answer. "I think he's basically a coward. He used to hit me. Well, I hit him too. We had some pretty bad moments. When I left him he became hostile. The awful letters, the phone calls. He made threats. I was afraid, but he didn't come after me. I haven't heard from him in over a week. Some men love too much. They become so jealous and angry they kill what they supposedly love. But Frank? No, he's too much in love with his money to go to jail, not for me or for Marty Cass." She shrugged. "Anyway, that's my opinion."

Sitting in the bright red-and-yellow chair on the patio of this mansion, Gene Ryabin thought fleetingly, sorrowfully, of Adela Ramos and her son Carlito, the boy who had been murdered because someone had loved too much.

* * *

Sam finally told his secretary to hold his calls. There had been so many calls of congratulations on Monday, and people dropping by to chat, that today Sam had fled to the third floor to talk to Juan Casares, head of the felony division. The two men talked about changes to be made when Sam officially took charge next week. Sam had already noticed that people had begun to speak to him differently. More deferentially. He thought he could get used to it.

Joe McGee knocked on the door, then stuck his head in. "Sam? News flash. Ali Duncan's on her way to Paris, courtesy of Moda Ruffini."

"What?" Sam stared at him across the room.

McGee said, "Detective Ryabin called. I thought you'd like to know."

Before the door closed again, Sam said, "Joe?" McGee came back in. "Find out what happened. Track down Ali Duncan if you have to and get a statement. Tell her she won't be prosecuted when she comes back to Dade County. I want that son of a bitch Ruffini charged with witness tampering. Then we'll bring in Immigration and tell them to deport his ass."

"You got it."

Sam looked across the office at Casares, who seemed amused. Sam shrugged. "Yes, Juan, I know Immigration has better things to do."

Casares said, "Is Ruffini trying to help you get elected in November?"

"If I run into him again," Sam said, "I'll have to say thanks."

Dina Hagen sat on the deep leather sofa in Frank Tolin's office with her coffee on her lap. The coffee cup was French porcelain, with little feet and gold leaf around the rim. The handle was of the precise thickness and angle to accommodate a woman's thumb and first two fingers. Yellow roses decorated the cup itself, and more of them formed a wreath on the saucer, which had also been touched with gold. Ordinarily a male lawyer would not have provided such a thing for his clients but now that Dina had come to know Frank Tolin better, she understood how it revealed his nature.

Frank was sitting on the other end of the sofa, weeping softly. His elbow was on the arm of the sofa and his hand was over his eyes.

The first time he had wept, she had been embarrassed, but he'd said he needed for her to listen, and so she had. Now he expressed his emotions as freely as a woman, and had told her many times that if not for her, he would have killed himself. He wanted to die like Matthew had died, *Oh, forgive me, Dina, but I would buy a motorcycle, run it off the causeway, and drown myself. Not linger in pain, but end it quickly.*

Dina took another sip of coffee. There was no rush to get back to work because she had no work to go to. The managing partner at Jacobs Ross & Rendell had called her to his office over a week ago and asked if she needed more time off. She had told him she would be leaving soon, please send her final check. But she still got up early, as usual, and dressed and drove into Miami. She walked. She sat in the library. She hired a service to do her résumé, which she mailed to accounting firms around Tarpon Springs. She went to the Cathedral of St. Sophia's every afternoon on the way home. And she had been at Frank's office every day.

A long sigh came from the other end of the sofa. He cleared his throat. "Dina? Could you hand me another Kleenex? I'm sorry to get like this."

"Well, of course, it must have been so awful for you." His cheekbone was still bruised, and she touched it lightly.

"Dina, please. Don't patronize me. I feel bad enough already. I've never been struck by a woman before, not one I loved so much." Frank fell back against the sofa and closed his eyes. "It's like she took a knife to my privates. I apologize for being graphic, and I know, I know I ought to forget the whole thing, but I can't. I thought the stars were in that woman's eyes," he said. "She's so beautiful."

"A spider." Dina sipped her coffee. "Don't blame yourself."

"No, I don't. But I worry what else she'll do." Frank moved closer on the sofa. "I could tell you—" He stopped speaking.

She put the cup into its saucer. "What, Frank?"

"Tommy Chang. I've seen them together. Do you know who I mean?" Frank took her hand. "He's a young man, about Matthew's age."

"Yes, I know who you mean," Dina said.

"She was kissing him on the mouth. I saw them, Dina. She took him into her house."

"Are you going to get upset again?"

"No." He fixed his eyes on hers for a long, long moment. Brown eyes, almost as dark as Matthew's had been. "I worship you, Dina."

"Oh, Frank. Don't be dramatic."

"You're an angel. A goddess." He slid down to the carpeted floor beside her.

"Stop that." She laughed.

He put his forehead on her knees. After a minute she stroked his head. He had such thick, dark hair.

c h a p t e r
thirty-five

Sam found Melanie watching MTV in the family room. She was stretched out on the floor with her head on a small sofa pillow. He leaned over and ruffled her hair. "Hey, honey. Where's your mother?"

"She went to the grocery store." Melanie had a plastic bag of carrots and offered him one. He declined. "I saw you on the news," she said. "You're going to make a great state attorney, Dad."

He smiled at her and sat down on the sofa. There was a staff meeting in the morning to prepare for, but Sam had no energy. He knew he ought to be either working or celebrating, but he couldn't bring himself to do either.

"Are you all right, Dad?"

"I'm feeling old and gray."

"You're not old and gray." She twisted her neck around to see him. "I thought you looked really nice on TV."

"Thanks, but you're supposed to think that."

There had been a few moments in the last week or so when he wondered just how in the hell he was going to do this, raise a daughter. It would be just the two of them. Melanie was still a kid, really. There were still plenty of chances to commit a major screwup.

On the television, a barechested man with a guitar was playing in the desert without benefit of electricity, and a young woman wound herself around his legs like a snake.

"You doing okay, Mel?"

She glanced at him. Must have caught something in his

voice. "Sure, Dad." She smiled. She rolled over and hugged the small pillow under her chest. "You want to hear something weird? I was thinking that one day I'll be older than Matthew."

"How's that, honey?"

"This is his birthday, but he's still nineteen and I'm getting older. I'm almost fifteen now. And one day I'll be older than he was when he died."

Sam had to think. "This is his birthday?"

"Yes. June twenty-first."

"Jesus," he said softly, then looked back at her. "He was a good kid, Melanie. Don't ever forget that. He loved you a lot."

She smiled at him. "I know, Dad."

Sam went into the kitchen to make some coffee and drank it looking out into the backyard, which was turning into a jungle. Somebody had forgotten to pay the yardman, so the yardman had forgotten to come by and mow the yard.

They would have to sell this house. Soon as Dina came back from the store they'd have to talk about it. Nearly a week had gone by since he and Dina had engaged in any sort of conversation about their future. It was time. The subject hung over them like a toxic fog.

"Jesus," Sam repeated. "Twenty years old." It made him feel strange. He wouldn't have been the father of a teenage boy anymore. Ever since last week, when he'd spoken to Caitlin, he'd felt strange. Dislocated. She'd given him a word: lost.

A dull ache twisted in his chest. He had almost wanted Caitlin to lie to him, and to do it so expertly that each word would fit to the next as tightly as the pages in a bible on the judge's bench. But she hadn't lied. She could have, but she hadn't.

He finished the coffee in his study. He set the mug on his desk and picked up the telephone. He looked up her number, which he'd written on a card in his wallet, and punched the buttons. A woman answered and he told her who he was, and asked to speak to Caitlin Dorn. He sat on the edge of the cot to wait. The blankets and sheets were disarrayed. He tossed the pillow to the proper end of the bed.

There was some delay. Then the sounds of voices, then heels on a tile floor.

"Sam? I can't talk, I was just on my way out." Then she said, "What is it?"

"A huge apology. I'd like to start there."

He heard the silence. Then a sigh. "You don't need to do that."

He said, "When can I see you?"

"I'm leaving in a few days, and I'm just swamped with work to finish."

"Tomorrow. Give me an hour." He rested his elbows on his knees. "I have so much to tell you, Caitlin. I'm not sure right now if this sounds coherent, but I've thought so much about everything you said."

"Sam, please. I'm really happy for you, making state attorney, and I'm sure you'll be the best—"

"It doesn't matter, Caitlin, what happened between you and Matthew."

"I'm not going to talk about this any more."

"That's what I'm trying to say." He stood up. "It's over. Let's go from here."

She laughed a little. "No. Things like that are never *over*. They will always haunt you. Always. I know you, Sam."

"No, you don't," he said. "But I want you to."

He listened, the receiver pressed to his ear, and there was the sound of a breath.

"Caitlin, go to New York. I know it's important. Go wherever you have to go. But listen to me, please, when I say this. I love you. I know that as clearly as I've known anything in my life. Maybe I destroyed what you felt for me. I hope not, but it doesn't change what's in my heart for you. Will you remember that?"

After a while, she said, "I'll remember."

"Okay," he said. "That's all I wanted. Go on, I don't want to make you late."

He heard nothing, then a click. He replaced the phone.

Through the window of his study, which looked into the backyard, he could see shadows stretching across the lawn. Thick grass had sprouted between the herringbone bricks in the walkway. The hedge leading to the gazebo was heavy with red blossoms. Vines wrapped themselves around the fence, and pods on the tamarind tree were bursting open. Everything in the yard was growing wild, pushing out roots and tendrils and leaves.

Laughing a little, Sam let the curtain fall back into place. Caitlin wouldn't be gone forever. Gene Ryabin had come by the state attorney's office at noon today. If Ryabin's theory was correct, Sam could wind up prosecuting Frank Tolin for the murder of Martin Cass. And he would have to call Caitlin Dorn as a witness. Fly her to Miami from wherever she was. Bring her back.

She would testify to motive. The elderly woman across the street would say Frank had entered the building a day or so after Cass's death. Forensics had already found his prints on the files in the bedroom. He'd been rifling through them, looking for notes, anything, proving Frank's role in the arson. The police didn't have enough yet for an arrest. They hadn't tied him to the other homicides—yet—but he was clearly tied to this one.

Sam flexed the fingers in his right hand. It still hurt, but not as much. It had been worth every bruised knuckle and cracked bone. Funny that Frank hadn't made a police report. And even odder, why had he hacked at Marty Cass's hand?

Frank could have been out of his mind, completely unhinged. After he had shot Marty Cass in the back he had stretched Cass's arm out on the floor, had turned his right hand palm up, and had savagely stabbed it four times, one blow going all the way through flesh and muscle, between the bones, and through the carpet. As if he were making a statement.

Idelfonso García had made a statement by throwing Luis Balmaseda out a window, as Balmaseda had done with his sister's boy, Carlito Ramos. *This is what he deserved.* Cass had tried to reach out and take Frank Tolin's money. A hundred thousand dollars of it. He deserved to have his hand slashed.

If, as Ryabin suspected, Frank Tolin had been jealous of Charlie Sullivan, what better statement than to shoot him in the heart, then take off his pretty face? It all fit. It fit with George Fonseca, who had supplied drugs to Frank. But why would Frank poison his drug dealer with Parathion? Had Fonseca threatened to turn him in?

For a moment, then another, and another, as if he were dreaming and at the same time *knowing* he was dreaming, Sam saw himself standing by the window, a man holding his broken right hand. A tall, broad-shouldered man in suit pants and shirt and loosened tie, home from the office. Now looking out the window again, into the deepening shadows, at the shed in a corner of the backyard.

Unlatching the patio door, going along the walkway, then across the thick grass. Sundown, nearly dark. A few birds making a racket in the neighbor's tree. A woman's voice over the fence. Calling the kids to dinner.

The shed was small, about six by ten, made of heavy-gauge aluminum. The door opened smoothly on strap hinges, and the rich, warm smell of fertilizer rolled out. Sam ducked his head to avoid a pot hanging from the gently sloped roof. They had never run current out here, but light came through the door and a single window, and Sam could see well enough. Dina kept it well-organized. An old electric mower and some yard furniture were stored to one side. Pots were stacked according to size under the workbench, and over it hung a neat row of small gardening tools on metal hooks. Shelves took up the wall to the right.

It was still hot and stifling in here, and sweat broke out on Sam's neck. He peered closely at the boxes, cans, bags, and bottles on the shelves. Miracle-Gro. Fire-ant spray. Raid. Black Flag. Rose dust. He cursed for not having his glasses. Toxadust. Aphid pellets. Brown glass bottles with ingredients in print so small he couldn't make the words out. He took three bottles to the door of the shed, balanced along his left arm, holding them carefully with his right forearm, unable to use the hand. Malathion spray. Parathion.

One bottle crashed on the concrete step. Sam slowly put the others on the workbench and took a breath. The acrid, greasy stench of poison filled his nose. He told himself to wait, wait. Wait.

They had all been killed by the same person. Good. Because Dina didn't even know George Fonseca. And when Charlie Sullivan died, she was out of town. And Marty Cass? She didn't know him either. Every backyard

gardening shed in Miami, every one, had insecticides.
And Sam wasn't going to make another insane telephone
call to Tarpon Springs.

In a neat silvery row over the workbench hung her gardening tools. Green wood handles, worn from use. A
small rake with clawlike tines. A narrow, pointed trowel.
A tiny shovel with a razor edge. And the clippers Dina
had been using when she accidentally slashed her hand.
Blood had dripped onto the red bricks of the walkway.
Sam ran a thumb over their points.

He closed the door of the shed carefully and walked
across the yard. As he went through the kitchen Melanie
asked what was that awful smell? Was he all right? Dad?
He told her he had to make some phone calls, never mind
dinner.

Upstairs in the bedroom with the door shut he dialed
the number.

"Nick? It's me. Sam. Listen . . . No, goddammit, listen,
it's about Dina . . . No, she isn't all right. . . . Nick,
please. You've got to tell me. When did she leave Tarpon
Springs that weekend in May? Saturday or Sunday . . . I
know you told me. Tell me again. . . . I am not, I promise
you, going crazy. . . . She might be in trouble. If you love
your sister, for God's sake—"

"She thought you were cheating on her, Sam. She flew
back a day early to find out."

"Oh, Jesus."

"She made us all swear, that if you called—"

"All right." He took a breath.

"What the hell's going on?"

"Nick, it's okay. Can I call you tomorrow? I'll take care
of it. Don't worry." He hung up.

When she came back from the grocery store—
she should have been back already, but when she got
back—they would talk. He would find out. He would
ask her.

Shaking, Sam went into the bathroom and turned the
water on and splashed his face with his left hand. He
would have to be calm about this. Sit her down in the chair
in their bedroom. Dina, tell me. It's going to be all right. I
promise. I'll take care of you.

He would hire the best attorney. They would enter a plea. Not guilty. Not guilty by reason of insanity.

Sam lowered his head to his arm, which lay across the sink.

Nothing would happen to her. He wouldn't let anything happen to her. He would find a place. The best doctors. He had always taken care of her.

Slowly he stood up. In the mirror a madman looked back at him. Maybe he was going crazy. This was his own delusion, a product of rage and desire. He hated the men who had destroyed Matthew, hated them enough to want them dead. *I would have shot the bastard myself, for what he did to Matthew.* His desire for Caitlin Dorn had led him to suspect his own wife of murder. He wanted to be free of her. He would place on Dina the burden of his own guilt. *Yes, Nick, I did commit adultery with a blond model eleven years younger than myself, so your sister had every right to see what was going on behind her back.*

He dried his face on a hand towel. But Dina hadn't known Fonseca. She didn't know that George Fonseca had given Matthew heroin. Ruffini had a better reason to kill Fonseca. He had tried to blackmail Ruffini. And Ruffini hated Charlie Sullivan in the long feud over Claudia Otero. And Ruffini had known Marty Cass. Sam laughed. Shit, maybe Eddie Mora had sent Dale Finley to pull the damn trigger. Or Beekie Duran. Now there was a theory and a half.

He looked at his pants. They stank of insecticide. He changed quickly into sneakers and old slacks and a T-shirt, and went downstairs. He dumped his ruined pants into a plastic bag.

Melanie was taking a dinner out of the microwave. One of her low-calorie entrées.

"Did your mother say when she'd be back?"

"No, she just had to go to the store for something."

"All right. When she comes home, tell her I'm in my study." Sam threw the plastic bag into the trash.

Caitlin Dorn had been waiting in the parking lot behind the performing arts center for ten minutes or so. The woman she'd spoken to about the party tonight lived on one of the private islands. She had said that directions to her house were simply impossible at night, so just wait there for her.

The party would be outdoors, she explained, so wear something cool. But, please, try to look like one of the guests, not like a photographer. So Caitlin had worn her gauzy green dress, the one she'd worn to meet Sam Hagen at the hotel. That had turned into a total disaster.

While she waited she'd been thinking about his telephone call. Trying to decide how she felt about it. Burdened. In a few days she would be driving to New York, she and Rafael Soto. She hadn't wanted to take anything along, not even Sam's wish that she go because it was important to her. Sam had problems of his own. Right now she wanted to be quiet. Mend. Take care of herself for a change.

She looked at her watch. It would be nice if Mrs. Costas would show up. It would be hard for them to spot each other now, anyway, with cars beginning to fill the lot. There was something going on at the theater tonight, a concert of some kind. If she hadn't already been paid an exorbitant deposit of $500, Caitlin would have left. Then she saw the headlights. The car parked next to her, a Volvo a few years old, which surprised Caitlin a little. She had been expecting something more expensive.

A woman in black slacks and a red knit top got out. A handsome woman in her mid-forties, with dark curly hair.

"Hi, I'm Sevasti." She had a firm handshake and a nice smile. "I am so sorry for running late, but the caterers had half the food wrong, and the band was stepping all over my flowers—" She laughed. "Well, you don't want to hear all that."

Caitlin was almost sure she had seen her somewhere, and said so.

Mrs. Costas smiled. "Well, probably you have. I've lived on the Beach for years." She walked back to her car and put her keys under the seat. "Listen, my daughter is playing violin in the orchestra tonight, and I told her I'd leave my car for her. I'll just ride with you, all right?" She put her bag over her shoulder, then went around the Toyota and smiled through the window while Caitlin unlocked the passenger's door from inside.

c h a p t e r
thirty-six

Sam fixed himself a drink, sat in the kitchen with it till he could breathe again, then walked to the door of the family room.

"Mel?" His daughter, still on the floor, was aiming the remote control at the television. The big screen popped and flashed through the channels. "Melanie."

"Oh. Sorry." She turned off the volume, then craned her head around on the little sofa pillow.

"I'm in my study," he said. "I've got some work to finish."

"And when Mom gets home, tell her to go see you."

"No. It's all right. It's getting late." The clock on the VCR said 8:10. "What time did she get home from work?"

"She didn't go today." Melanie sighed. "I wasn't supposed to tell you. She took the day off."

"Never mind." He said, "Hey, is that one of your mother's good sofa pillows from the living room?"

"I can't find the one I like to use." Melanie sat up and smoothed the wrinkles out. "It's gone. I think she threw it out. She said it was dirty."

Sam had closed the door to his study and was unsnapping his briefcase before he heard what she had said. Gone. The little green pillow that Melanie liked to use was gone.

He went back to the family room. She was on the sofa. "Mel? When was the last time you saw your pillow?"

She shrugged. "A couple of weeks ago, I guess. Why?"

"No reason."

He returned to his study. As soon as his vision cleared, he reached on top of the bookcase and found the key to his gun cabinet. He unlocked the door. His Colt pistol and one clip full of hollow-points were gone.

He stared at the empty box.

The pistol wasn't there. He grabbed at an explanation. Somebody had broken into their house. Dina couldn't have committed murder. Not Dina. She didn't know the victims. Didn't know they'd been involved with Matthew. Sam wondered if he had mumbled their names in his sleep.

Then he thought of Frank Tolin. Frank had known Marty Cass. He had known Sullivan and Fonseca through Caitlin. Or from hearing things said in conversation. Gossip. Then Frank had inadvertently passed this knowledge to Dina? Incredible.

But the facts themselves thudded into Sam's consciousness like perfectly hewn blocks to form a logical, irrefutable structure. The pistol was gone. And so was the pillow. Dina had taken the pillow. She had used it to muffle the noise when she had shot Charlie Sullivan in the chest. One in the chest, then one through the back of the head. The blow-out had imbedded bits of green cloth and pillow stuffing in his scalp. She'd carried the gun in a bag. Natural for a woman to carry a bag. Why had he gone with her? What reason had she given?

There would have been another reason for George Fonseca. A party to plan? Drugs to buy? Then the poison in his beer. Appropriate. He must have felt it working, and she had to kill him to get away. And Marty Cass. But why? Why Marty Cass?

Sam remembered Dina at the dining room table, balancing accounts. Looking for the money, twenty thousand dollars, that Matthew had spent. Money stolen, she had said. And Marty Cass had taken it?

His head reeled, and Sam's laugh came out as a groan. Matthew had blown every last dime, had wasted it all, but Dina couldn't believe that. Dina believed that Marty Cass had stolen it, sending her son a little farther toward the rocky shallows of Biscayne Bay. So Dina had shot him in the back, then had tried to hack off his thieving hand. Maybe she had used her clippers. Or the trowel. Or whatever gleamed most brightly across the dim shed when she opened the door.

Dina had killed them all, each one guilty of destroying her son. Then she had come home and cleaned the pistol. She knew how. Sam had showed her at the gun range how to clean it. How to fire it. As if the gun might reappear, Sam stared once more into the empty box.

She had his pistol. She was somewhere on Miami Beach with a Colt pistol fully loaded with .45-caliber hollow-points.

Sam staggered to his feet. "Caitlin!"

Mrs. Costas said to keep going straight on Alton Road.

"I thought you lived on one of the islands," Caitlin said.

"We're picking up my son's girlfriend first. I told you. No, I guess I didn't. Sorry, it's been so hectic today." Her voice was melodious and self-assured. "Take the next left."

Caitlin drove into a quiet residential area north of Forty-first Street. The street led past some two-story houses, then onto a narrow road marked No Outlet. Through the trees Caitlin could see the Miami skyline a mile or so west, broken by the outlines of the small, uninhabited islands in Biscayne Bay. Slightly south, the lights of the causeway extended across the dark water.

"Park there." Mrs. Costas pointed to the turnaround at the end of the street.

The headlamps picked up the mottled trunks of the pine trees, a tangle of underbrush, and a glint of broken glass. In the rearview mirror the nearest house was at the other end of the block. Caitlin put on the brakes. "Wait a minute. Nobody lives down here."

Her hands still on the wheel and the motor idling, Caitlin turned to look at Mrs. Costas. Pale face, framed by heavy waves of hair. Full lips, hollow cheeks. And her hand around the grip of a gun whose barrel, like a single eye, looked directly back at Caitlin.

The woman's mouth moved. She said something. Caitlin's hands would not loosen from the steering wheel. She stared into the barrel of the gun. It was a heavy, squarish gun with a silvery sight rising up from the half-inch circle of black pointed at her face. The raised barrel sloped down and down to the curve of a hammer. The gun gleamed dully in the light from the dash.

A thumb moved onto the hammer and pulled it back, a hideously smooth clicking of metal.

"Caitlin. I said, take the keys out of the ignition and give them to me." When Caitlin didn't move, Mrs. Costas's hand turned the keys, then withdrew them, jingling softly in the now-quiet car. She dropped them into her bag.

Caitlin began to tremble.

"I'm going to get out now. You come across the seat this way. We're going to take a walk, not far. We'll talk for a while; then you can go home."

The tires on Sam's Honda slid, then grabbed, screaming, around the corner to the Palmetto Expressway, and a car behind him blew its horn. He shot up the entrance ramp and scattered gravel swerving around a truck. Taillights seemed to hurtle toward him, then flash past to the left or right.

He would go east across town, then over the MacArthur Causeway to Miami Beach. And then—and then where?

Hitting a clearer stretch of road, Sam grabbed the car phone with his injured hand and nearly dropped it. Wedging it between his knees, he punched in Gene Ryabin's number. He would be home having dinner with his wife. Had to be.

No answer. Sam hit the numbers for a call-back.

He dialed the number at the DeMarco house, where Caitlin had been staying. He had called her an hour ago, or less, and he still remembered it.

A young voice answered. A girl.

Sam forced himself to speak slowly. Where was Caitlin Dorn? This was an emergency.

She didn't know. A birthday party. Taking pictures. Yes, for a woman. No, I don't know her name. No, no, she didn't say where she was going.

The girl was on the point of hysteria when Sam hung up.

Over the high-pitched noise of the Honda's four-cylinder engine, he could hear himself shouting aloud, unwilling to accept this, even now. Dina had gone out to the firing range. Or she had thrown the gun away, fearful of having it in the house.

Impossible that he could live with her and not know. Who would believe that? When she went to trial—if she was declared competent to stand trial—he would also be judged. His career was over. He would have to resign. It would take everything they had to keep her out of the electric chair. Better to have her declared insane. Save her life.

Sam slammed his right fist onto the console between the seats, wanting the pain, but barely feeling it. Where was she?

If he found them in time—*please, God, let me find her*—he could save Caitlin. He could see himself holding out his hands. *Dina. Give me the gun.* He would plead with her, tell her to think of Melanie. Everything would be all right. Caitlin would go to New York. Forget this happened. Then he would take care of Dina. They would move to Tarpon Springs together. No one would know.

He laughed out loud. It would never happen that way. He didn't know where in hell she was. It would be a deserted place. Dina would take Caitlin there, reach into her bag as if for a cigarette, slide her hand around the pistol, and pull the trigger. Then she would drive home. She would ask Melanie, *Where's your father?* And Sam would arrive soon afterward. And then what? Whatever his decision, their lives would be over. But Caitlin might survive. Again and again he muttered a prayer: *Please, don't let her die*.

The toll plaza on the Dolphin Expressway was directly ahead when his car phone rang. Toll booths stretched across the highway, a row of green and red lights. Sam aimed his car for an unmanned lane in the middle and took out the wooden arm as he went through. The spotlighted buildings of downtown Miami moved toward him in the windshield.

He picked up the phone. It was Gene Ryabin.

The shore on the west side of Miami Beach, unlike the gentle, sandy incline on the east, was a rocky shelf of shallow water, warm as a bath this time of year. It smelled of salt and algae and seaweed. Except in rare patches, there was no beach, only dark and pitted coral rock and crushed shells. It was these that Caitlin walked on now in her canvas sandals, a few yards out from the shore, in water to her knees. The hem of her green dress dragged behind her. Mrs. Costas walked just along the edge of the land. She had her bag over her shoulder and the gun at her side.

She motioned with it toward the south. "Keep going."

Ahead of them a hundred yards, the land took a sharp turn to the right. A seawall held back a grassy slope planted with trees—royal palms among flowering oleanders with their long, pointed leaves. Lights blinked in and out among the foliage.

Keeping her eyes on the gun, Caitlin stumbled when a rock shifted under her foot. She caught herself on her hands, feeling the sting of salt. "What do you *want*?"

"Listen to me carefully. Before we reach the road, I want you to understand why you're here."

"I've never seen you before in my life," Caitlin said. "Why are you doing this?"

The woman glanced at the ground, stepped over a piece of rotted, barnacled lumber, then said, "You really don't know who I am, do you?" Amusement played through the rich voice.

In the shadow of the trees the woman's face was indistinct, but even so, the knowledge flared in Caitlin's mind. She stood still for a few moments, looking at her. "You're Sam's wife."

"Yes. Dina Hagen. We met a few times. Where? Do you remember?"

Caitlin's mouth was dry and her voice shook. "I saw you—at Frank's office. It's been a long time."

The barrel of the gun motioned Caitlin on. "But you do recall. I wonder. When you shook my hand, had you already touched my husband?"

Her left shoe, which had come untied, now slipped off entirely. Rocks scraped at the sole of her foot. "We're not having an affair! I swear to you. I'm leaving Miami." Her legs swirled through the water. "If you're getting a divorce, it isn't my fault."

"He told you we're getting a divorce?"

"I swear to Christ, I'll never see him again."

"Be quiet, Caitlin. I want to tell you something."

"Look. If you do anything to me, you'll go to prison. Sam will probably lose his job. Is that what you want? What about your daughter?"

Dina Hagen raised the gun and cocked it. Caitlin gasped and backed up.

"Stop there! I'm ready to pull this trigger. Do what I tell you. Keep walking. We will have our talk. Then you can flag down a car. Do whatever you like. But for now, listen to me." The barrel of the gun, with its staring eye, gestured toward the road.

Caitlin walked, limping.

Dina Hagen pushed a branch aside, then looked back at Caitlin. "We're not here because of Sam. It's someone else. Let's see how smart you are. Can you guess who it might be?"

"No! Who? Frank?"

"Not even close. Someone considerably younger."

Her legs buckling under her, Caitlin fell on her knee, grinding the skin against crushed shell and rock.

"You know who I mean, don't you? Get up."

"No. I can't." She sat in the water, leaning on her hands, weeping now.

"I told you. We're walking to the causeway. Then you can go. I'm sorry about the gun, but you wouldn't have come with me otherwise. Now. Stand up. And when we get there—before I let you go—I want your apology for what you did to him. So think about how you're going to phrase it. I want to hear you tell me—the mother of this young man, this *boy*, whom you ruined—how sorry you are."

Ryabin begged Sam to slow down; he could hear the engine roaring over the car phone. Did he want to kill himself? Sam hit the brakes coming off the MacArthur Causeway Bridge, keeping just ahead of the flow of traffic.

"Gene, can you call in a bulletin for her car? It's a Toyota, a blue one. Damn, I don't know the model. Dina's, then. It's a 1992 white Volvo sedan. Four-door."

He was quickly approaching South Beach. The line of bright streetlights would lead past the private islands on the left, then past the Coast Guard station and the marina. The road would dead end on Ocean Drive. He would have to turn before that to avoid the traffic outside the restaurants and clubs. Dina could be anywhere from the park at South Pointe to the big hotels five miles north.

Ryabin's voice was low and measured. "Are you certain this is all correct? I was so sure about Frank Tolin."

"No, I'm not certain. I may be going crazy." With the phone pressed to his ear, Sam said, "What did Caitlin tell you this morning? Where was she supposed to go?"

"Wait. Let me remember." There was a pause. Then some words muttered in Russian. "A birthday party, which you know about. A live rock band. His twentieth birthday. I'm sorry, that's all she said."

The narrow, curving flyover to Alton Road was approaching on the left. From the far right lane, Sam hit his brakes and cut across the street. Two other cars swerved and nearly collided.

Coming down off the ramp, heading north, he said into the phone, "Gene, I think I know where they are."

Dina Hagen was walking directly behind Caitlin now, both of them splashing at the water's edge. Dina wore thick-soled black sneakers. Caitlin was limping. Her hope that anyone would see them vanished as they came closer to the causeway. To her left were trees; ahead she could hear the traffic but couldn't see it past the thickly planted oleander. To her right was the bay, its surface moving, glinting with lights.

"Stop here. Don't move."

Caitlin stopped. There came rustling noises from behind her. Then Dina's fingers were winding through her hair, holding tightly. Something firm pressed into her back.

"Please. Don't. Don't do this." The muscles in her neck strained.

"My son died here," Dina said. "He wanted to die. He drank until he could hardly stand up. Then he got on his motorcycle and he killed himself. Maybe it was better that he did die. After you and the others were finished with him, he had nothing left, not even his dignity."

"Please. I didn't do anything. I tried to help—" Caitlin cried out from pain when the hand pulled backward on her hair and the thing that Dina held against her spine dug in deeper.

"Matthew was traveling over sixty miles an hour on that road, trying to go around a truck. He lost control and went into the water. It was very shallow, and they could reach him easily. He was still alive, just a little. He was so badly hurt. He asked for me. Then he died. Right there."

Caitlin's words were a ceaseless babble. "No. No, please don't. I didn't mean it, I swear. Dina, please."

She could feel Dina's warm breath on her cheek. "Have you heard of the Furies?"

Caitlin was sobbing.

"It's an old Greek myth. The Furies are the goddesses of vengeance. They bring punishment. They act purely, freely, without regard to mercy. I suppose that sounds overly dramatic to you, but I think it fits." Dina jerked downward, and Caitlin tried to pry back the fingers that wound through her hair. The hand tightened. "Now. Kneel down. I'll make this very fast."

Shoving a shoulder into Dina's chest, spinning around, Caitlin heard the gun go off, a loud pop. Dina's right hand was hidden inside her black shoulder bag. Flames glowed from a hole in it for an instant, and bits of fire hissed, then vanished on the wobbling surface of the water. Dina pulled her hand free, and the long barrel of the pistol rose out of the bag. The gun fixed on Caitlin's face.

Then wavered. Dina had glanced toward shore, puzzled, her brows knitting together.

Putting all her strength into a single movement, Caitlin lunged to one side. The fingers closed around her hair again, but not soon enough. She felt her hair tearing from the roots. Then there was a tremendous explosion of noise, a blaze of light, and a great weight that spun her around. She fell, dragged herself to her feet, then ran limping through the shallow water toward shore. Warmth gushed from her waist, and she knew it was her own blood.

Stumbling toward the shadows under a dense sea grape

tree, she collided with something in the darkness. Someone had caught her. She began to collapse, but Frank Tolin held her up.

"Frank! Oh, God. You're here!" Caitlin clutched at him. "It's Sam's wife. She's trying to kill me!"

His fingers bit into her upper arms, and the faint light from the causeway deepened the hollows in his sharply boned face. A bandage shone white at the corner of one eye. He shook her. "I never wanted this, Catie, believe me. I loved you."

"Frank, help me, please!"

Whipping her around by one arm, Frank pulled her toward the water. He was yelling, "Dina! I've got her."

Dina Hagen's face was pale, the eyes enormous. Water to her knees, she stood motionless, the gun by her side. "Frank?"

He half-dragged, half-carried Caitlin. "I followed you, Dina. I had to make sure she didn't hurt you. Look what she did to me. She did worse to Matthew. She told me about it, Dina. She admitted what she did, sleeping with your boy. Doing dirty things to him. She laughed about it."

"Dina, no!" Caitlin struck out at Frank and gasped from the pain. She touched her side and felt bone coming through the fabric of her dress. "He's lying! I never slept with Matthew. He wants to kill me because he hates me! I wouldn't go back to him. He lied! Dina, he lied to you. Matthew was a boy. I'd never have touched him!"

Frank slapped her and she staggered. "Dina, please! Matthew never mentioned Marty Cass, did he? They never knew each other. Frank lied to you. He wanted Marty dead, because Marty was blackmailing him. He used you like he uses everyone! He made you believe—"

His fist slammed into her face. Caitlin fell, and the water covered her head. When she came up, coughing and gagging, Dina was staring at Frank.

"You told me. You said Marty Cass stole everything from Matthew. You *told* me that."

Ryabin could see it happening as he swerved and dodged through the oleanders. He could hear them. Caitlin and Tolin yelling. Dina closing on them, the pistol in her hand.

Then Dina's long scream, her face tilted to the sky.

Sam hurtled past Ryabin, leaping over the retaining wall, his T-shirt a moving spot in the darkness. Ryabin reached into his holster for his pistol and slipped on the damp grass planted on the slope of the causeway.

He saw the heavy gun fall to Dina's side. A half second later Caitlin twisted away from Tolin. Sam was shouting, closing the distance fast. Tolin saw him and leaped toward Dina for the gun. But Caitlin got there first.

Sam yelled for her to drop it, don't shoot.

Caitlin lifted the gun with both hands and swung it toward Tolin. Inches from his face, the barrel flamed. Tolin's head jerked backward and bits of it kept going. Water splashed around his body when he fell.

Nearly there now, Ryabin saw Sam take the pistol out of Caitlin's hands. A dark stain was covering her dress. She collapsed near Tolin's feet.

Gasping for air, hand on his chest, Ryabin reached them, gun drawn.

For a minute they all seemed frozen into position, except for Dina, who was rocking back and forth, keening. Her eyes were closed.

Ryabin reholstered his pistol. Frank Tolin's body floated in a foot of water. The toes of his cowboy boots pointed upward. The bullet had entered just under his right eye and had taken the back of his head off. Caitlin was bleeding but alive, moaning, supporting herself on one arm. Sam stared at his wife.

Sloshing through ankle-deep water, Ryabin went over and looked down at the pistol Sam was holding on his lap. "This is yours?"

As if waking up, Sam nodded, then looked around, blinking.

Ryabin said, "Is it licensed in your name?"

"What?"

"Licensed! Do you have a license for this pistol?"

"No. I brought it back from Vietnam."

Ryabin thought for a moment, then said, "I think Tolin brought it back." Wiping off the gun with his handkerchief, he walked over to the body shifting and bobbing in the water. He picked up the right hand, pressed it around the pistol, then let hand and pistol drop.

"What are you doing?" Sam struggled to his feet.

"I think that Frank Tolin just used this gun to commit suicide," Ryabin said. He was still breathing hard, but not so much from physical exertion anymore. Now his mind was running, madly racing to fit a hundred details together before it was too late.

He gripped the fabric of Sam's T-shirt in his fist. "Tolin shot Caitlin, then himself. She was going to reveal that he had murdered Sullivan, Fonseca, and Marty Cass. He had to kill her. But he missed. Believing she was dead, he shot himself."

Sam stared at him. "Are you out of your mind?"

"Do you prefer to see your wife arrested for three murders?"

"I'll tell them I did it."

"Don't be stupid. They won't believe you. But if you go, right now, Sam— No one is looking for her. They won't look for you."

"We can't run away, Gene. For God's sake—"

"Who's guiltier here? Dina killed Charlie Sullivan and George Fonseca out of madness and grief. Tolin realized this. She went to him to file a lawsuit, and maybe she told him what she had done or maybe he guessed. Tolin worked on her mind. He convinced her that Cass defrauded your son and took his money. And what about Caitlin? She left him, and Frank made Dina believe—forgive me, Sam—that Caitlin slept with your son. I heard them arguing about it as I approached. Frank Tolin pointed Dina like a gun at Marty Cass, then at Caitlin Dorn. Dina pulled the trigger, but it was his hand that guided her. Can you prove it? Never. In the eyes of the law, Frank Tolin was an innocent man."

Ryabin put a hand on Sam Hagen's chest and shoved. "Take Dina and get out of here! Let them see a murderer obsessed by Caitlin Dorn. He brought her to this place. He shot her. Then he turned the gun on himself. This man who has killed already three people."

"I'm supposed to be sworn in as the state attorney next week!" Sam spun toward Caitlin Dorn. He dropped down and put an arm around her. He touched her side and his hand came away bloody. "My God. Oh, my God."

Ryabin said, "I'm sorry. Of course, this is your decision." He crouched beside him. "My friend. Listen to me. Whatever you decide, I'll back you up. But you must decide quickly. Someone must have heard the gunshots."

"This won't work, Gene." Sam shook his head. "We'd go to jail for the rest of our lives."

"You think so?" Ryabin smiled. "Who would want to believe that the wife of our new state attorney should be arrested for murder. Trust me."

Stumbling slightly, Sam slowly stood up. "All right. I pray to God you can tell a good story." He held out his hand. "Give me Dina's bag." Ryabin threw it to him. "I'll call 911 from my car. I'll say I was passing here ten minutes ago. I saw a man taking a woman to the water. She was struggling."

"Don't give your name," Ryabin said.

Sam leaned over to take Caitlin's face in his palm. "Oh, God. Look at you."

"Go on!" Ryabin pulled on his arm. "I'll take care of her. Get out of here, you and Dina. I'll call an ambulance on my radio."

For a moment Sam's eyes fixed wildly on Ryabin, unwilling to believe this, even now. Then he went back to Dina. She was a statue with staring eyes. He lifted her across his arms and carried her quickly out of the water and up the slope toward the road.

Ryabin bent to look at Caitlin's wound. Another inch farther in, and it would have torn her to pieces. He put a hand on her shoulder. "Do you understand what's going on?"

"No!" She was sobbing, trying not to collapse into the water.

"Come with me. I'll explain. You can lie on the grass and listen." He put an arm around her and helped her stand. She moaned. He said, "Can you hear me? Pay attention. If you don't follow my instructions exactly, you'll be arrested for murder."

He spoke quickly as they walked across the rocky shore. On the grass he rolled his coat to cushion her head, then lit a cigarette, his last allotted for the day. His nerves more settled, he made the call from his unmarked car.

She would do what she was told, being a sensible woman. She had herself to protect, of course, but Ryabin was certain that she would protect Sam Hagen as well. He sat down beside her and smoked his cigarette. His hands trembled a little but gradually grew steady. He thought of what he would say to his lieutenant.

Frank Tolin tried to kill her. Then he shot himself. Luckily, she had spoken to me earlier today, saying she was afraid of him. She can show you his letters. She said she had a job tonight, so I drove by to make sure she was all right. Through some miracle of fate, I saw his car, and she was in it with him. I followed. I arrived here just in time.

Tolin held the gun to her head. I had my own pistol aimed at him. He confessed everything. How his love for this woman overwhelmed him. He was insanely jealous. He found out she had slept with Charlie Sullivan, the model—she will admit this to you. So Tolin murdered Sullivan in a fit of passion.

He also killed George Fonseca, his supplier of drugs. Fonseca wanted to avoid jail for sexual battery on Ali Duncan, so he called Sam Hagen, the prosecutor—surely Hagen has a record of the call. Fonseca offered to turn against Frank Tolin, a prominent lawyer who had become one of his best customers. And Marty Cass? Cass was blackmailing him. Ask Caitlin Dorn. She was present at Tolin's apartment and heard their conversation. We already have his fingerprints on Cass's files, and it was he, Frank Tolin, whom the old woman saw returning to the apartment two days after the murder. How did he get in? Well, presumably he left the door unlocked after the murder in his hurry to get away. He must have thought of the files later. And why did he stab the right hand of Marty Cass? Well . . . I neglected to ask. He told me all this in the presence of Caitlin Dorn, who will attest to it. He shot her, then himself. Luckily her wound was not fatal.

Look at the crime-scene photographs of Frank Tolin. You can see the gunpowder and stippling on his face. The water washed the gunpowder from his hand, but his fingerprints were on the gun.

Ryabin knew he would be believed. This explanation made more sense than the truth. He knew also that Sam Hagen would suffer, whatever the outcome. If Sam wavered, Ryabin would remind him that he had a duty not only to his conscience but to the reputation of the state attorney's office as well. And a duty to his wife, his daughter, and even to his son. And also to Caitlin Dorn, who had said—as she lay bleeding on the ground—

He paused to light another cigarette. He inhaled deeply, then blew smoke toward the stars, considering what Sam Hagen would like to have heard her say. Caitlin had murmured, *If I die, please tell Sam that I loved him. Tell him never to forget me.* Yes, perfect.

The wail of a siren grew closer.

Standing up, Ryabin could see the lights. He took a puff of his cigarette, then snatched it from his mouth and stared at it. It was nearly half gone. His eleventh. Anna would ask him when he got home. How could he explain?

He flicked the cigarette toward the dark water. It made a brief orange arc, then disappeared.

chapter
thirty-seven

Tarpon Springs
August 17

Dear Sam,

How's everything in Tampa? We're all fine here. I
got your check, as usual, though it's more than we
need for now, so I put the rest in the savings account.

Dad got out of the hospital for his kidney trouble
yesterday, and he's better, but we don't think he will
be with us much longer. We haven't told Dina, but she
senses it. She and Costas sit on the back porch together in the evenings. He rocks in his chair and she
watches the river. It's a comfort to him, having her
home again.

Her new thing on Saturday is cleaning the sanctuary at the cathedral. It's hard for me to see my sister
scrubbing the floor, knowing what she used to be, but
she says it makes her feel closer to God, the more
she's down there on her knees. Aunt Betty says if she
wants to do it, let her. Dina still has no memory of
certain things, and that is a blessing. I won't say she's
happy, but she's not unhappy.

I hope you're liking your new job. I guess it's a
change, but we know you'll do fine, like you always
have. (Now, ole buddy, the next thing is to turn you
into a fan of the Tampa Bay Buccaneers. Ha.)

The girls send their love to Melanie, and did she get the pictures they sent? Dottie just told me to tell you hello and take care of yourself. Maybe we can all get together over the Labor Day weekend.

Best regards,
Nick

822 W. 11th St.
New York, NY
September 22

Dear Sam,

Thank you so much for the lovely letter, which I just this minute read. After a week in Canada, it was nice to be welcomed home by that familiar scrawl.

To answer your question: Yes, of course! I'd love to see you for Christmas. (Only you, Sam, would plan things so far in advance.) And yes, I'll send you subway maps and bus schedules and lists of touristy things to do, or (my humble suggestion) you could just forget about all that for once and let me show you around. I'm a terrific tour guide.

Naturally you'll want to have a long visit with your cousins in Brooklyn (how did you find them after thirty-five years?!), but why not let Melanie spend a day or two with me? I wasn't much older than fifteen when I first saw Greenwich Village. My new place is a shoebox, but there's room for two girls in it. I should know: Ali Duncan came through town after a shoot in London, and she stayed with me for nearly a week. (Here's some gossip: Moda Ruffini U.S.A. filed for bankruptcy, and the store in Miami has closed. Even better: Tereza Ruffini kicked Klaus out of their villa in Milan when she caught him with her fitting model. Ali couldn't stop laughing when she told me about it.)

I'll be in Miami at the end of the month. It's just a weekend, to take some shots of the new trade center. I know Tampa isn't across the street, but if you could pull yourself away from your clients for only a day . . .

I realized, Sam—dearest Sam—as I read your letter,

that next week is the first anniversary of Matthew's
death. I hope you don't mind my mentioning it, but I
have thought of him lately—and not with sadness. He
just comes into my mind; then he goes out, like paying
me a visit. It's good to think of him without dwelling
on all the other stuff. If there is a heaven, I'm sure
he's up there. That's all. I just wanted you to know.

Since our last phone call, I've been doing some
thinking, as you asked me to. Really, I can't tell what I
want to do in the long term. It's much too soon to say.
I know you don't want to put any pressure on me, and
I feel the same. However . . . it's good to know that af-
ter all the hell they've been through, two people can
still care about each other. I mean really care, not just
say the right words. But your words are right. *No*
pretty phrases, just the facts. Oh, well. I don't try to
figure anything out these days. I just look in the lens
and click the shutter.

Write soon,

Love,
Caitlin

The noises of South Beach faded and the late summer
glare dimmed when Harold Perlstein closed the heavy
door. Sam looked around, his eyes adjusting. The place
belonged to another country. Another century. Dark
wood. The curtains, the candles, the carved pews. Then he
noticed the deep turquoise carpet. Not so far from Miami
Beach after all.

He put on the yarmulke that Perlstein handed him, pat-
ting it down onto his hair.

"You'll have to excuse me for not remembering much. I
haven't been in a synagogue since I was a kid. I'm just in
Miami for the day, anyway."

"I know. You told me. You're not religious. That's all
right." Perlstein led him through a side door. "Come on,
I'll show you around." They went down a short hallway
tiled in cracked squares of green and tan linoleum, then
through another door. "This is where I work."

The room was brightly lit, painted white, with sunlight
streaming in along one side. An air conditioner dripped

into a bucket. Perlstein's desk was heavy oak, scratched from years of use. The veneer was peeling up.

Perlstein wore a blue knit shirt with a horizontal white stripe, and pale yellow pants. "How did he die, your son? You didn't say." He dropped a bib apron over his head, then tied it in the back.

"In a motorcycle accident," Sam said.

"Ohhh. Too bad. Kids. They go so fast on those things." He handed Sam some folded pages. A pamphlet. "This I got for you from the rabbi. Look. This part here. *Yiz-kor Elohim nish-mas b'nee haw-ahoov—*"

"What does it mean?"

Perlstein took it back, read it over, then said, " 'O heavenly Father, remember . . . the soul of my beloved son, who I recall with love in this . . . solemn hour. His memory is in my heart. May his soul . . . live in eternal life.' Something like that. 'Amen.' Nice, right?"

"Very nice," Sam said.

"Yes." Perlstein patted his arm. "Okay, sit here."

He clicked on a metal lamp that held a long fluorescent bulb. On a wooden shelf above the desk there was a mug from Cypress Gardens with several big feathers in it. Perlstein pulled one out, a heavy brownish-gray with white flecks. "This is a goose-quill pen. I make them myself. The parchment is calfskin, but I don't know how they do it. And the ink is made special. The rabbi blesses it, and so on."

From the table to his right he lifted a sheet of brown wrapping paper and pulled from under it a page of parchment. The sheet was pearly white and already bore several sections of squarish black letters.

"This Torah, when I finish, will last for hundreds of years, longer than you or I. When we're dust, this will still be here. What do you think about that?"

Sam nodded and put on his glasses. Harold Perlstein settled down with his quill and ink. His hand was big, with knobby knuckles, but it moved quickly, leaving a trail of tiny, precise letters. Ink had worked under his cuticles and into the ridges and crevices of his skin.

"There's a prayer for each letter," Perlstein said, dipping the quill into the ink, shaking off a drop. "I think that's so we keep it slow and don't make mistakes. But

I'm pretty fast." He scratched more letters, writing right to left, lifting his hand to make sure he didn't smear the ink, blowing on it from time to time. As he worked, Sam could hear the minor-key notes and see his lips move. From time to time the old man would glance up at a printed page stuck to a corkboard with a thumbtack, but generally he kept his face bent to the parchment.

Finally Perlstein straightened up and leaned back in the chair. "Okay. You see how it goes. I've stopped so the next letter is *mem*. Like an *M*. For Matthew, your son. Now, you put your hand on mine. Not so heavy. Lighter. Yes, like that. We'll put him here, on this line."

Perlstein's skin was like parchment itself, sinking between the tendons. He sang the chant for *M*; then his hand moved, and Sam's moved with it, and the black ink flowed onto the page.

BARBARA PARKER,

the new master of the legal thriller

Barbara Parker's first legal thriller, *Suspicion of Innocence*, was a finalist for the prestigious Edgar Allan Poe Award for Best First Novel by an American Author. Her second, *Suspicion of Guilt*, gained even wider critical acclaim and legions of new readers. The triumphant *Blood Relations* confirmed Barbara Parker's place among the very best lawyer–writers. Now she's back with *Criminal Justice*, the explosive story of a burned-out prosecutor who gets a nasty surprise when his girlfriend is found murdered . . . and he is the prime suspect. A female lawyer on the case believes he is innocent, but she walks a dangerous line when she begins a passionate affair with him. *Criminal Justice* sizzles with its hot Miami setting, a tangled web of crime and justice, and the gripping drama of human beings trying to hold on to their battered ideals.

Turn the page for an exciting preview of *Criminal Justice* by Barbara Parker.

A Dutton Hardcover on sale in January 1997

As soon as the bubbles cleared, Dan Galindo looked up through his dive mask. The boat's pointed shape bobbed on the surface, and a line of yellow polyester rope angled toward the bottom, ending at a grapnel hook sixty feet down, caught on a pitted white ridge in the reef.

He inverted, kicking slowly with his fins. A school of chub eyed him, then shot away, their sides glinting silver as they turned in unison. Dan moved along at a shallow depth, ten feet or so, till he ran out of air. At the surface, he blew seawater out of his snorkel, took a few deep breaths, then went under again, deeper. A few seconds with his ears above water had been enough. The girl he'd come with had turned the radio to a rock station. Dan had glimpsed only dark hair under a baseball cap, and her shoulders huddled in a sweatshirt. She was probably wishing she had stayed in bed.

Two hours before dawn he had come fully awake, a bitch of a hangover finally catching up like an icepick through his eye sockets. The moon was a ghostly white globe in a corner of the window. He had carefully lifted Kathy's arm off his chest, but she woke up and asked where he was going. He told her the truth before he could stop himself—out on the boat to see the sun come up.

His apartment was only a block from the marina near the causeway at Seventy-ninth Street and the bay. Dan carried the bag with his dive gear. Kathy followed, stumbling sleepily, holding a mug of coffee. She wore a swim-

suit under jeans and a sweatshirt, but she didn't want to
go in. She didn't like the water, which Dan thought
bizarre for someone who had moved to Miami from Ohio
or Iowa—he couldn't remember which.

It was still dark when he turned his twenty-five foot
outboard south on Biscayne Bay. In moonlight, Dan
passed under the causeways connecting the mainland to
Miami Beach, then picked up speed once beyond the
bridge to Key Biscayne. Streetlights began to wink off as
the sky turned from gray to pale blue. Not many boats
were in the water at this hour on a Monday morning—an
old shrimp boat coming in and some million-dollar sport-
fishers churning at high speed for deep water. A stain of
pink appeared on the horizon. A few miles farther along,
with the mainland reduced to a line of misty green in the
west, he guided the boat through the narrow channel at
Sands Cut, just north of Elliot Key, then headed for Tri-
umph Reef. The sun had risen ahead of them, a fiery ball
of orange.

The depth finder held steady at thirty then went to
forty, fifty. Dan slowed. At sixty he cut the engine. Their
wake caught up to them and the boat rose and fell. Another quarter mile out, the bottom would drop quickly to a
depth of hundreds of feet.

For a while they drifted, hearing only the gurgle of water on the hull. Then Kathy started telling him about the
gig coming up next weekend, and the demo record her
band was going to do, and the no-talent little bitch who
was trying to take over the vocals, and can you fucking
believe we are up this early? It was when she started fid-
dling with the dial on the radio that Dan tossed the anchor
overboard. He cleated off the bow line, clipped the dive
flag to a pole, then suited up.

He told Kathy he'd be back in a while, don't go away.
He lowered his mask, bit down on the snorkel, and
jumped in. The sea closed in over his head in a froth of
bubbles, and he sank into perfect silence.

Dan kicked slowly, moving along, watching a queen
parrot fish with its beaklike mouth dart and turn below
him. The fish was bright turquoise now, but bring it to the
surface, the color would fade as life ebbed away. Visibil-
ity was good all the way down, where patches of sand

appeared bone white among the grayish rocks of the reef.
The uneven terrain dropped into rocky holes between out-
croppings of coral, where purple fan grass waved in the
slight current. The reef was alive with fish. Dan spotted a
longnose butterfly, blue tang, and a gray angel. Rolling
over, he took the snorkel out of his mouth and blew out
air. The bubbles floated upward, rocking side to side, then
were lost against the bright surface of the water. He
wanted to follow them, to climb back into the boat, sit in
the sun till his headache went away. But Kathy was up
there waiting for him. Coming along to be a good sport,
but wanting to go in now, let's get breakfast. Or worse,
she would take off her clothes and expect him to finish
what he hadn't been able to do last night. It was enough
to make him consider sucking in a double lungful of
seawater.

A curse bubbled from between his lips. His watch
showed eight-fifteen. There was a client coming at ten
o'clock. A competent secretary, if he had one, might help
him out. Why, Mr. Galindo just called from court. His
appointment with the judge (or trial or emergency bond
hearing) is running longer than expected. . . . But Alva,
who belonged to the old lawyer Dan rented space from,
might look up from slamming the keys on her ancient
electric typewriter long enough to take her cigarette out of
her mouth and say, No, he's not here. I don't know where
the hell he is.

Coming up again, Dan pushed his mask to his forehead
and looked toward the boat. Kathy was asleep on the bow
with the radio blaring. Her forearm was over her eyes, and
one foot moved to the beat of drums and a screeching guitar.
Her swimsuit top was off, and the rosy nipples pointed sky-
ward. There was a dagger tattooed on the underside of her
breast.

Dan spit into his mask and sloshed it with seawater. He
began to breathe deeply. In, out. Slower. Pulling air into
expanded lungs, then pushing it all out, purging the car-
bon dioxide. He was going to the bottom. He counted fifteen long breaths, took a look at his watch, then did a
one-eighty.

His weight belt, eleven pounds of lead, would allow
buoyancy to fifteen feet. Any deeper, he would sink.

When he felt the subtle shift, he stopped kicking. He glided down, eyes closed, ears popping. It would take about twenty seconds to reach bottom. He felt water flowing past, colder now. The mask pressed into his face and a few bubbles squeaked out of his wet suit. He tongued the snorkel out and pressed his lips together.

His father had told him to close his eyes—the brain consumes less oxygen that way. Dan didn't know how it worked, but it did. On land Raul Galindo had been as ungainly as a wading bird. Underwater, his body achieved a sort of grace, his long fins curling, uncurling, flowing behind him like the tail of a fish.

The light through Dan's eyelids dimmed, and he sensed the bottom. He flicked his eyes open once, then again. His watch showed twenty-five seconds elapsed. With thirty to get back up, being careful, he would have thirty-five more to lie here. He settled on his stomach in a patch of sand, gloved fingers hooked on a rock to keep from drifting. The only sound was a slight buzzing in his ears. The headache was gone.

It had been a month since he had been in the water, and not since last summer had he dived with any regularity. To stay under a minute and a half would be difficult, but possible. As a kid, he had nearly grown gills, catching tropicals for spending money in high school, or going spearfishing on long weekends in the Keys. There were more good fish then. Big, meaty snapper, grouper, and yellowtail. Gradually, though, overfishing and fertilizer runoff had reduced their numbers. Dan remembered, or thought he did, that the waters from Miami to Key West had been full of marine life when he was a kid, but his dad had complained how it had diminished. And now the new residents were saying what a paradise they had found.

Dan clamped his teeth together and tightened his throat. Already he needed air. He opened one eye. The second hand on his watch gave him twenty-two seconds. Twenty-one, twenty.

The thought of not going back up drifted morbidly through his mind. In two weeks he would turn thirty-five. The number was somehow portentous. The halfway point of a man's allotted three-score-and-ten.

Between hangovers and periods of generalized funk,

when he had dared to reflect on the tattered state of his psyche, Dan slammed up against the horrifying vision that he would never get beyond the ratty office where he worked now, with its cheap, cigarette-burned carpet and wheezing air conditioners. That one day he would be popping Prozacs and swilling bourbon like the lawyer who owned the place. If he drowned, who would give a shit? His ex-wife had insurance on him. His son, Josh, would get a college education out of it, and the mortgage would be paid. Lisa had the house, a red-tiled, cutesy piece of stucco in one of the gated areas of a snotty subdivision called Westlake Village. Dan and Lisa had bought it when he was making eighty grand a year at the U.S. attorney's office. Things had been pretty rosy then. Before he got fired. More accurately, before he was transferred to handle VA claims and civil forfeitures, which amounted to the same thing. So he quit. The career went, then the marriage. Dan moved back to Miami to find a job. A woman he'd worked with at the U.S. attorney's office got in touch to say she knew a lawyer who needed someone with expertise in criminal cases. Dear Elaine. The charity of friends.

Dan's chest involuntarily heaved, and his lungs were burning. He had heard that drowning was a pleasant sensation. What if he hooked himself to the anchor with his dive belt? Kathy would haul on the rope, and there he would be, limp as a gaffed squid. Dan checked his watch. He tried to focus, to remember where on the dial it would reach thirty seconds. He decided to count down from fifteen. A black grouper came closer, checking him out. Its undershot jaw opened and shut, and when Dan made a slight motion, the fish turned abruptly and vanished into the coral.

Thirteen seconds left. Twelve. Eleven.

Dan and his father had been spearfishing off Marathon when a bull shark saw them, an eight-footer. Sharks usually swam on by. This one didn't. Raul Galindo extended his speargun at arm's length, pivoting, motioning for Dan to stay behind him. The shark glided closer and he nudged it in the head—easy, not wanting to make it mad. With a flip of its tail, it scooted away. And then came back. Fast. His father fired, hitting it just above the eye. The shark was a thrashing, twisting piece of meat, leaking red. Back in the boat, Raul started the engines and said they should leave the area because of the blood, but as soon as they anchored somewhere else, they would go back in. At twelve years old, Dan screamed "No, Dad, no," but his father threw him in anyway. Don't be afraid, I'm here. Raul Galindo died driving home from Key Largo when a drunk crossed the center line.

Dan could see little sparkly lights behind his eyelids. He was sixty feet underwater. The height of a six-story building. If he passed out, he would stay down here, weighted down by his belt, until his body bloated and the currents lifted him away.

Six. Seven.

At the marina this morning he had seen a notice about a tournament in Cat Cay. Spearfishing. Six weeks away. He had the equipment. Not a boat good enough to make it to the Bahamas, however. Not nearly.

His watch had stopped. Dan looked closer. No, another second ticked by. Eight. Why not go to the Bahamas? Rent a damn boat. Take Josh with him. Lisa couldn't say no. Father-son bonding and all that. He could see Josh now, in fact. Josh was seven, a quiet boy with brown hair and eyes. Like mine, Dan thought. Why not join up with some other boats, make a flotilla? Feel the sun and wind on their faces. The boat skimming over the water like a pelican with outstretched wings.

His vision dimmed. He opened his eyes, panicked. Heart slamming in his chest, he pushed off and began kicking frantically. The surface seemed dark now, impossibly far away, the boat tiny as a matchstick. He rose, feeling the pressure subside. No. He wasn't going to make it. It was too far. How sad. Unutterably sad. He was too heavy, too tired. He would black out before he reached the surface and fall back to the bottom.

Dan thought of Joshua and his chest lurched, almost a sob. Air burst from his lungs and he gagged on water. Too late, too late. His hands, clumsy in the gloves, fumbled for his weight belt. With his teeth he tore one off. He grabbed for the plastic clip. Then the thing dropped away and Dan kicked, no strength left now, but the light getting nearer.

There was a splash as he broke through. He dragged in a breath. The rush of oxygen made him drunk, almost euphoric. He rolled over, wheezing, barely keeping his face above the surface. The sun blasted his eyes. He kicked steadily for the boat, reached for it, then a wave lifted it away. When the boat fell back, Dan curled his extended fingers over the gunwale and hung on.

"Kath—!" He tried to yell her name over the music and went into a spasm of coughing. "Kathy, for God's sake, would you wake the hell up!" He pounded the hull.

She sat up squinting, looking around, not seeing him. "Dan?"

"How stupid can you be?" he screamed. "I was diving, goddammit! You have to pay attention when someone's diving!"

"What happened?" She looked over the side and finally saw him bobbing in the water near the rear of the boat. "Oh my God, did a fish bite you? Are you hurt?"

"I almost fucking drowned!"

"I'm sorry! Dan, I didn't know!" wearing only her bikini bottoms, she clambered through the gap in the windscreen. "You didn't tell me."

Dan spit saltwater. His aching sinuses were full of it. When he was fairly sure he had enough strength, he told her to move, he was coming in. He handed her his flippers and mask, then took hold of the dive ladder and shakily hauled himself up past the outboard engine and over the transom, scraping his shin. He flopped to the bottom of the boat like a heavy fish, his sides heaving.

She crouched beside him, pushing her hair behind her ear. "Dan? I'm sorry, okay? What can I do?"

He retched. After a while, he sat up, leaning against the rear bench seat. In over twenty-five years of diving, he had never dropped a weight belt. He had never come that close. He took off his remaining glove and his booties.

"Get me a towel, would you? And turn off the damn radio."

He dried his face and hair, and when he had stopped shaking, peeled off his wet suit and put his windbreaker back on. Dressed now, Kathy hustled around repacking everything in his dive bag, not saying much. Dan took her hand. "I'm sorry for screaming at you. I was scared."

"It's all right." She hugged him around the waist.

"Come on, let's go get some breakfast."

Engine roaring, Dan turned the boat north. He stood up behind the wheel and let the wind rush into his lungs. The sky was incredibly, intensely blue, the water a sheet of silver. The boat danced over it. A gull dipped, then swung away. He laughed out loud. He was thinking of Cat Cay again.